# THE BEIRUT
# CONFESSION

# THE BEIRUT CONFESSION

# DAVID CULLEN

Culpro Books

The Beirut Confession
First published 2014

A catalogue record of this book is available from the British Library.

This is a work of fiction. Deceased historical characters have been used with respect. Fictional characters have been used with abandon.

ISBN: 978-0-9559911-6-5

www.lulu.com/davidcullen
Facebook: DavidCullenBooks

Published by Culpro Books
an imprint of Cullen Productions

*Where no counsel is, the people fall; but in the multitude of counselors there is safety*
- King James Bible, Proverbs XI:I4
also the motto of Israel's Institute for Intelligence and Special Operations (Mossad)

For Pauline
alpha to omega


and for
Barry Howard, Maureen Williams and Mick Day
with thanks

**Confessionalism** - a system of governing based on the distribution of political and institutional power proportionately among communities, usually (but not solely) based on religion. For example, in Lebanon the Doha Agreement of 2008 specifies that there should be 54 Christian parliamentary deputies and 54 Muslim parliamentary deputies. Within these two groups, seats should be allocated according to the demographic weight of each community (eg Sunni Muslim, Shi'a Muslim, Druze, Maronite Christians).

In this context, a **Confession** is one of the groups (eg the Maronite Confession). It can also be used as a collective noun for any group of people sharing similar beliefs or causes, even clandestinely.

**Confession** is also, of course, an admission of something.

And it is good for the soul.

A Glossary of Arabic and Hebrew Words and Phrases used in the book is on pages 317 to 319

Lebanon

# Cast in order of appearance

Ghazi Kanaan [Abu Yo'roub] – *head of Syrian security in Lebanon 1982-2002, Syrian Interior Minister 2004-2005.*

The Damascene [Marwan Mebarak] – *a mercenary, an assassin.*

Mahmoud Abdel Rauf al-Mabhouh – *co-founder and senior commander of the military wing of Hamas.*

An Israeli assassination team.

Brigadier Wissam al-Hassan – *Head of Intelligence Division, Lebanese Internal Security Force.*

Captain Jihad Merhi [Abu Samer] – *Lebanese Internal Security Force.*

Gisele Merhi – *wife of Jihad, a trainer for the Lebanese Department of General Security.*

Sergeant Deeb el-Gharib – *Lebanese Internal Security Force.*

Captain Fadi Lattouf – *chief of the Civil Police of the Palestinian Security Force in the Beirut refugee camps.*

A policeman in the Sanayeh police station, Beirut.

Major Pierre Ghanem – *Lebanese Internal Security Force.*

Violette Ghorra – *secretary to Major Ghanem.*

Larry – *doorman of an apartment building on East 39th Street, New York City, USA.*

Benjamin David – *a* sayan *in New York City, USA.*

Carla Chedid [The Djinn] – *Lebanese Department of General Security.*

Sergeant Nabil Haddad – *a spycatcher of the Lebanese Internal Security Force.*

Sergeant Claude Gerges - *a spycatcher of the Lebanese Internal Security Force.*

Sergeant Tamer Khalef - *a spycatcher of the Lebanese Internal Security Force.*

Love – *a* houri *and a mercenary.*

Paradise – *a* houri *and a mercenary.*

An old man in the Bourj el-Shimali refugee camp.

Captain Manar al-Jayouchi - *chief of the Civil Police of the Palestinian Security Force in the Bourj el-Shimali refugee camp.*

Abdul Abdulrahman – *a Palestinian Israeli spy.*

A Corporal on reception duties at the State Security Building, Jonblat, Beirut.

A mechanic on a tow truck on the Beirut River bed.

Sergeant Kanj – *Bourj Hammoud police, Beirut.*

Corporal Skaff – *Bourj Hammoud police, Beirut.*

Dr Mohammed Patel – *Medical Examiner at the* Hôtel Dieu de France *Hospital, Beirut.*

Lana Lattouf – *daughter of Fadi and Nada Lattouf.*

Sergeant Alarab - *Civil Police of the Palestinian Security Force in the Bourj el-Barajneh refugee camp.*

The owner of a boys' toys shop in Snoubra, Beirut.

A Corporal on security duties at the State Security Building, Jonblat, Beirut.

Corporal Jad Chadidi - *Lebanese Internal Security Force.*

Corporal Omar Mostafa - *Lebanese Internal Security Force.*

Corporal Michel Yammine - *Lebanese Internal Security Force.*

Corporal Peter Harrak - *Lebanese Internal Security Force.*

Corporal Emad Hmedeh - *Lebanese Internal Security Force.*

A Lieutenant of the Lebanese Internal Security Force.

A minion of the Facilities Unit, Security Services, Ras en Nabaa, Beirut.

Lieutenant Sebastien – *Lebanese General Security Unit.*

Sergeant Christof Howdra – *Lebanese General Security Unit.*

A Corporal of the Lebanese General Security Unit.

# PROLOGUE
## مقدمة اثنين

**12 October 2005**
**8 Ramadan 1426**

## Damascus, Syria

"I didn't think it would be you."

Ghazi Kanaan, the Minister of the Interior of Syria, did not turn around from the window. He could see a translucent reflection of his visitor in the glass, standing by the closed office door, still, like a wraith. Like Nemesis. Like Death…

Kanaan had always liked this view out over the Barada River and across the northern suburbs, that was why he had commandeered this office on his appointment a year ago, rather than take on the ministerial suite of his predecessor Ali Hammoud. The formal offices were too low down. Kanaan liked it here in his eyrie.

Staring out over Damascus helped him reflect. Reflect on everything that had happened in the last year, how Syria had been thrown out of its thirty year presence in Lebanon after the murder of Rafic Hariri, how the United Nations were now investigating Hariri's death, how the UN had imposed travel restrictions and an assets freeze on all individuals suspected of involvement in the assassination. How he, Kanaan, was one of those individuals…

The irony was not lost on him. He had tried to protect Hariri, to save him from what, in hindsight, was inevitable. He had liked Hariri. Not only that, during Kanaan's twenty years as head of Syrian intelligence in Lebanon when he had effectively ruled the country, he had come to *respect* Hariri. And this was the thanks he got.

There was one other thing to reflect. The cracks in the eggshell façade of Syria's ruling al-Assad dynasty were beginning to widen, not least due to his own subtle and clandestine destabilising efforts. With a former Vice President of Syria, he was developing a challenging powerbase against President Bashar al-Assad within the Syrian Regional Branch of the Arab Socialist Ba'ath Party.

A powerbase that had been discovered. And he knew the punishment for discovery.

He turned to face Death.

Death was a tall, dark, powerful man holding a .38 Smith and Wesson. He wore jeans and a loose, collarless white shirt. His long black hair was tied back into a simple ponytail, falling down either side of his face, concealing the burns and lack of left ear. He was known as The Damascene and he was Kanaan's creation.

"Of all people," continued Kanaan, "I didn't think it would be you."

The Damascene's eyes pierced into the very soul of the man whom he hated above all others. The man who had captured Lebanese Army Captain Marwan Mebarak, who had tortured him to within a centimetre of his life and shot him in the head and, when he realised the angle of the gun had not been acute enough for the bullet to pierce the skull and instead had just shot off his left ear and severely burnt his face – and mindful of the fact that this broken husk of a man had just killed five armed Syrian *mukhabarat* with his bare hands – had taken him, brainwashed him and turned him into his own trained killer.

That had been six years ago. A lifetime.

"Life can be strange," said The Damascene. "Have you phoned the radio station?"

Kanaan nodded. "As instructed. I told them that could be the last statement I would ever make."

"How right you were."

"Do you have my body?"

"Yes."

"Where is it?"

"It is standing outside."

"Oh. Fresh then."

"Fresher than you will be."

Kanaan, the 'King of Lebanon', the butcher, the man ultimately responsible for thousands of deaths, gave a sad smile. "It is my time then. There is no other way?"

"No."

He nodded. "Better get on with it."

The Damascene walked across the room and grabbed Kanaan by the hair, pulling him down onto the chair behind his desk. Kanaan did not struggle, resigned to his fate. What had to be done, had to be done.

The Damascene yanked harder on the hair and Kanaan gasped, his mouth opening. The Damascene pushed the gun between Kanaan's teeth, deep into his mouth, the knuckle of his trigger finger pressing onto the older man's lips.

With a small movement, he tilted the gun so it was pointing up into Ghazi Kanaan's brain...

*[Just after 10:00 on 12 October 2005, Major General Ghazi Kanaan was found dead in his office in the Interior Ministry in Damascus. He had been shot through the mouth by a .38 Smith and Wesson. The official verdict was suicide. On 9 November 2006 his brother Ali Kanaan also 'committed suicide', his dismembered body being found on railway lines near his farm in the Syrian coastal city of Jalba.]*

**19 January 2010**
**3 Safar 1431**

## Dubai, United Arab Emirates

Emirates flight EK912 from Damascus landed on time at 14:35 that afternoon. By 15:20, the passenger travelling under the name of Mahmoud Abdul Raouf Mohammed had passed through immigration controls in Terminal 3 and had picked up his baggage, a single small suitcase. He did not even warrant a glance from the Customs Officer on selection duties.

He was dressed in slacks, open-necked shirt and jacket. Immediately he stepped outside the air-conditioned terminal, the desert heat wrapped itself around him like a high-tog duvet, even in January. His portly body began to sweat and he quickly removed his jacket as he waited in line for a taxi.

"Al Bustan Rotana," he said as he settled in to the back of the cab. The uniformed Indian driver nodded and they pulled out.

Mahmoud knew that it would only be a short drive, that was why he had picked this hotel, to be near the airport. Tomorrow he was leaving for Bangkok.

He was not too tired after the flight, it had only been three and a half hours, but he would need to adjust his body to the two-hours-ahead time difference here in the UAE. Perhaps a little retail therapy would help, something nice for his wife...

The cab used the overpass to turn left off of D89 Airport Road and onto the D70 Casablanca Road. Then it U-turned and bore right into the driveway of the hotel, passing the fountain on the left and pulling up as close as possible to the hotel's entrance.

Mahmoud handed over a note but did not thank the driver. Likewise he dismissed the Philippino porter who was opening the trunk, removed his case himself and walked into the hotel.

Check-in was smooth and soon he was taking a lift to the second floor, carrying his own case, no porter needed. He was in room 230.

The first thing he did on entering was to check that the room was as requested: no balcony, sealed windows. So the only way in and out of the room was through the door. That was good. Less danger.

He rarely travelled without his bodyguards, and the reason they were not with him now was mundane: there was no room for them on the flight from Damascus. Mahmoud had booked his ticket online just a few days ago and he assumed his bodyguards would also get tickets when they went online immediately after him. But he had reckoned without the annual Dubai Shopping Festival! He had bagged the last seat on today's EK912, and his bodyguards had only just managed to squeeze onto the flight tomorrow.

He would be on his own for a day in Dubai, so what? He had no business here (other than shopping and possibly a massage) and nobody knew him. He had a sealed room. He would relax. He was safe. Or so he thought.

But Mahmoud had made a mistake. Usually any bookings for any tickets he required were made by others on his behalf, using a wide selection of aliases. This time, because his trip was so secret and was made at such short notice, he had booked his air ticket and hotel reservation online himself.

Which was silly. Mahmoud had been monitored for years. Any electronic activity, any phone call, any text message, any stroke on any keypad he had ever made, had been noted, reported and stored.

For he was not Mahmoud Abdul Raouf Mohammed. He was Mahmoud Abdel Rauf al-Mabhouh, a senior Hamas military commander, one of the founders of the Izz ad-Din al-Qassam Brigade, the military wing of Hamas. He had been involved in many armed actions against Israel, including the abduction and killing of two Israeli soldiers, Avi Sasportas and Ilan Sa'adon, in

1989. He was suspected by Israel of smuggling weapons and explosives into Gaza, and recently he was known to be forging secret connections between the Hamas government in Gaza and the Al-Quds Force of the Revolutionary Guards in Iran. He was wanted by Israel, Jordan and Egypt.

And that day he was going to die.


Mahmoud had spent nearly three hours shopping in Deira City Center, and returned to his room at 20:24 (with something from *Al Masroor* jewellers for his wife and a little electronic boy toy from *Sharaf DG* for himself). His killers were waiting for him inside his room *[the VingCard Locklink electronic doorlock system used by the hotel at that time could be reprogrammed directly at the door; they had cloned Mahmoud's keycard earlier].*

Two of the assassins were in the bathroom, the third was lying on the floor by the side of the bed, against the bathroom wall and out of sight of the door.

As far as Mahmoud was concerned, his room was empty. The only thing that registered as strange, too far down in his deep subconscious even to have a thought formulated about it, was that his bed sheets had been turned all the way down to the end of the bed. Only as he put his carrier bags down on the chair was he aware of a small shape on the floor and then a sharp scratch on his left leg. *In the name of Allah, what was that - ?*

The heat roared through his body as he instinctively backed away from the shape on the floor.

Suxamethonium (colloquially referred to in medical circles as 'sux') is an almost-immediate-acting muscle relaxant. It causes instant loss of motor skills but does not induce unconsciousness. As Mahmoud swayed, awareness of his legs seeming to vanish beneath him, two men walked quickly from the bathroom and simply pushed him onto the bed. Mahmoud tried to struggle as they began to rip off his clothes, but his muscles were not working, his limbs were no longer his.

The assailants were rough but not brutal. As they threw off

his clothes, the third person – the shape from the floor – picked them up and put them neatly on the chair on top of the shopping bags.

Soon Mahmoud was stripped down to his black shorts and he was laid on his back on the bed, fully conscious but now with no control over his body. It was all he could do to focus his eyes on the pillow that came down onto his face...

Murder is never clean. Humans are not a clean species. The human body is tenacious. The heart usually beats on after trauma, death only occurring after the victim has bled out or has suffered massive internal injury and shock. Pure, physical death can take a while.

The pillow was pressed onto the face of Mahmoud Abdel Rauf al-Mabhouh for ten minutes after his heart had stopped, to ensure physical death and brain death. The body had pissed itself and had expelled methane (causing one of the attackers to mutter "*Harah*, what has this *benzona* had to eat!"), but the piss was covered as the sheets were pulled up across the body and tucked cosily under his chin. His eyes were closed and he looked like he was sleeping. It would be over twelve hours before he was found by a chambermaid the next day.

By that time, his assassins were out of the country. Subsequent reports vary as to the number of the hit team, estimates ranging from nine to twenty-six. Certainly later investigations showed that eighteen people had entered the UAE on false passports in the twenty-four hours prior to the murder. Generally it is accepted that the hit team probably consisted of eleven people: lookouts, point men, distractors, transporters, technicians, killers.

CCTV from the hotel would show that just after 21:00 that evening, three people casually walked along the second floor corridor, waited in the lift lobby (smiling, chatting, not a care in the world), got into the lift, exited on the ground floor and left the hotel. Two men and one woman.

The woman, it was later determined, was travelling on an Irish passport under the name Gail Foliard – but she was neither Irish nor Gail Foliard. She was a woman of eastern Mediterranean origin, petite verging on the delicate, long black hair held at the back in a bun.

She had been the one on the floor of the bedroom, the one who had injected the sux. The shape that had been one of the last things Mahmoud Abdel Rauf al-Mabhouh ever saw…

## 19 October 2012
## 3 Dhu al-Hijja 1433

## Beirut, Lebanon

Brigadier Wissam al-Hassan was the head of the Information Branch (the Intelligence Division) of the Lebanese Internal Security Force. He was also one of Lebanon's most secretive figures. Outside of the ISF, most Lebanese did not know what he looked like – which was how he liked it. He was forty-seven years of age and had been made head of the Information Branch nearly seven years previously on 19 January 2006 (19 Dhu al-Hijja 1426), tasked with leading the investigation into the 2005 assassination of former Prime Minister Rafic Hariri.

Which was ironic. Because al-Hassan used to work for Hariri as his Chief of Protocol, and as such he should have been with Hariri in that fatal motorcade on 14 February 2005 (5 Muharram 1426) – but he had taken the day off to study for a university exam [*a fact which the UN Special Tribunal for Lebanon found to be a 'weak and inconsistent' alibi. Although the Tribunal recommended that al-Hassan warranted further investigation regarding Hariri's assassination, he was not amongst those indicted in January 2011*].

al-Hassan was an enigmatic contradiction. He had ties with *Al Mukhabarat Al A'amah* (Saudi intelligence). He had close and private liaisons with Syrian President Bashar al-Assad and yet was strongly linked to the anti-Assad confessions in Lebanon (some believe he may have been a double agent). It is said he facilitated the passage through Lebanon of money and arms from the Gulf States to the Syrian opposition.

On home soil, despite some insiders claiming that he had ties to Mossad, he had uncovered and overseen the dismantling of a network of Israeli spies, leading to the arrest of over one hundred individuals suspected of collaborating with the Jews.

His division was involved in the al-Mahdi incident in 2010.

Just two months ago, in August 2012, he had led an investigation that culminated in the arrest of former Lebanese Information Minister Michel Samaha who was charged, together with Syrian National Security Bureau chief Ali Mamlouk (in absentia), with transporting explosives into Lebanon in an attempt to destabilise the country.

Every true Lebanese agreed that al-Hassan's tenure at Lebanese Intelligence had been a great success.

But there are those that do not like success…

al-Hassan had been in Paris with his wife Anna and sons Majd and Mazen three days previously when he had received the encrypted phone call. He had intended to stay in Paris over Eid al-Adha, returning next week, but the message he received was clear: he was needed back, now. An important item the Internal Security Force had been looking for for over two years had been located and apprehended. But the item would talk only to Hassan (despite the ISF's best persuasive efforts).

al-Hassan left his family in Paris and returned to Beirut on 18 October. As always, he travelled using an alternative (not fake) passport, using an alternative (not fake) name. At Beirut's Rafic Hariri International Airport he picked up a hire car. Those unused to the subtleties of Lebanese security might think this strange – surely the country's intelligence chief would travel at least in an armoured car if not in an armoured convoy? But that would be expected – and an armoured car and armoured convoy, with state-of-the-art surveillance and frequency jamming equipment, had not stopped Rafic Hariri being blown to *al-janna*. A hire car was good camouflage.

It was late and he went home, driving from the airport through the Hizbullah heartland of South Beirut without incident.

The next morning, he was in his office early. He had much to deal with, even only having been away a few days. The 'item' was being held at one of the ISF's secret offices not too far away near Sassine Square, and al-Hassan arranged an afternoon appointment.

At 14:30, al-Hassan and his driver Ahmad Suhyuni left the ISF headquarters in the Hotel Dieu area in the hired car. The drive up the narrow, winding back streets of Ashrafieh was predictably slow (where *did* Beirut's traffic come from? Where was it going?).

At 14:49 they crawled along Ibrahim Monzer Street, the secret office in sight. Nearby were the offices of the Kataeb political party. Just up the street were the headquarters of the March 14 political alliance, currently the opposition in the Lebanese parliament.

At 14:50, as al-Hassan prepared to get out of the vehicle, a nearby parked car exploded with the savage force of thirty kilograms of TNT, the blast contained and assisted by the narrow street. al-Hassan knew nothing about it. His life simply ended. He was killed instantly along with driver Ahmad Suhyuni. Two other people died and one hundred and ten people were injured, the explosion leaving a large crater in the road, tearing off the balconies of nearby buildings and blowing in windows, knocking down shelves in the ABC shopping mall two hundred and fifty metres to the north.

Ironically, Wissam al-Hassan died in an identical manner to Rafic Hariri. And, also in a manner identical to the Hariri assassination, a figure on a motorbike – no helmet, long black hair tied back in a ponytail - was seen leaving the area shortly after the explosion...

# PART ONE
# الجزء الأول

# THE GARDENER
# البستاني

# 21 October 2012
# 5 Dhu al-Hijja 1433

## Jounieh, Lebanon 07:00

"Well, that's it," said Captain Jihad Merhi of the Internal Security Force. He was leaning against the worktop next to the sink in the kitchen of his spacious mountainside apartment sixteen kilometres north of Beirut. In his hands he held his breakfast: a triple espresso and his second Camel King Size cigarette of the day. At fifty-three he was still slim, reasonably fit for his age, and greying gracefully. He was also tired. So damn tired. "War has returned to Lebanon."

"Is it not an overreaction?" asked his wife Gisele, seated at the small breakfast table against the wall, a more fulfilling (and marginally more healthy) half-eaten *za'atar* croissant next to her orange juice and coffee. "Not you, dear husband," she hastened to clarify, "but..." She waved her right hand to encompass 'out there'.

Jihad shrugged with his mouth. Yesterday had been declared a national day of mourning following Friday's assassination of Brigadier Wissam al-Hassan, Jihad's ultimate boss (although twice-removed up the chain of command). Anger had erupted across the country, in Sidon in the south, in Tripoli in the north, but especially in Beirut. Opposition supporters had set up road blocks and burnt tyres, denouncing Syrian President Bashar al-Assad and his allies in the Lebanese government. There had been gunfire.

"An overreaction to the Brigadier's murder?" mused Jihad. "*Bien sûr.* But it is just another excuse, another catalyst of many catalysts - "

"Another excuse for a fight?"

"To put it succinctly, yes."

Gisele broke off a piece of croissant and put it into her mouth, her tongue coming out to receive it. Even though they had been married many years, Jihad was just a teensie bit jealous. If there was such a thing as reincarnation, he was coming back as a *za'atar* croissant.

"Did the events ever really finish?" A flake of pastry bounced on Gisele's lower lip. [*'The events' is how many Lebanese refer to the 1975-1990 civil war.*]

"We both know the answer to that." Jihad stubbed out his cigarette. "And now today we have the Brigadier's funeral. The army is out in force, but God knows what is going to happen."

Gisele stood up. "I worry about you." She came across, entwining her arms around her husband's waist. She could smell the smoke and coffee off him.

Jihad bent his head and licked the crumb off of his wife's mouth. "No need," he said softly. "And since I no longer *have* to wear a uniform, things are easier on days of civil unrest."

"And you have your friend." Gisele patted the bulge on his waistband. His official-issue Browning 9mm High Power (recently changed from the Herstal 9mm because the Lebanese Finance Ministry had 'got a good deal').

One of only two friends that never let me down, thought Jihad. He said, "When are you next due in?"

"I have a class next Thursday."

"Things will have calmed down by then. *Insh'allah.*"

For many years Gisele had been a member of the GSD, the Lebanese security service, firstly in the field and then latterly as a trainer. She had been involved in the Princess Diana incident in Paris in 1997, she still had the raised scar on the left side of her neck as a souvenir. Forty-something and now officially retired from field work, the slim, dark-haired 'Libanette' (as her husband sometimes referred to her) had recently been persuaded back to help train the influx of recruits into the Lebanese internal and external security services, a patriotic recruitment surge fuelled by the threat of the Syrian civil war overspill into Lebanon.

"Got your building ID?"

"Oh shit," Jihad tap-danced his hands around his jacket. He found it in his left hip pocket, the plasticised ID card with his photo; the blue lanyard with the pattern of twee little Lebanese flags was wrapped around it. It was a new thing in the State Security Building, everyone had to wear an ID around their neck. Also a metal detection system had been installed at the entrance – ironic, and more than a tad inconvenient, because each member of the Security Service carried a gun. But Management had deemed it necessary - now that the Syrian war was spilling over into Liban it was difficult to tell friend from foe.

Jihad pecked his wife on the lips. "Right, I'm off." With a lingering movement of his hand against her small breasts, he moved Gisele to one side and went out to the hallway, collecting his jacket. "I'll see you tonight."

*"Prends soin"* she said as he walked down the stairs. "Take care."

As she closed the door she said softly, "My husband."

## Jonblat, Beirut 21:00

It had been worse than expected, reflected Jihad Merhi as he led his team back into their offices in the old Annexe to the State Security offices in northern Beirut, just west of downtown. Worse. Which, perversely, was exactly as expected!

Wissam al-Hassan had been laid to rest alongside the tomb of Rafic Hariri near the Mohammad Amin Mosque in Martyrs' Square. It had been a state funeral attended by thousands including significant political figures from all the confessions. During the ceremony, President Michel Suleiman had awarded al-Hassan the National Order of the Cedar in Grade of Grand Officer, one of Lebanon's highest honours (and I'm sure al-Hassan was grateful for it, mused Merhi).

Then the trouble had started. A large crowd had headed the three hundred metres down Emir Bechir Street to the Prime Minister's offices, the Grand Serail, demanding the resignation of Prime Minister Najib Mikati, calling him and the government 'Syrian puppets'. They had been pushed back by troops firing live bullets into the air and tear gas directly at the protestors. There was fighting.

Thankfully, Merhi and his much-reduced team of six (economic staff cuts) of Sergeant Deeb el-Gharib and five Corporals were not responsible for street security, that was the police and the army. It was Merhi's responsibility to assist in the discreet security of the 'significant political figures', alongside their own security teams. That had gone well.

But even now, hours after the funeral, the fighting continued in the streets. In some areas, gunmen had set up checkpoints, scrutinising the sectarian identity of passers-by. Shots had been fired. Sunni upon Shi'a, Shi'a upon Sunni. Hundreds of arrests had been made.

The occasional sound of gunfire and the constant rumble of rioting could still be heard from not too far away as Merhi entered the General Office with his team. He headed directly to the small table on which sat a kettle and a newly-acquired but before-the-ark filter coffee machine. He picked up the coffee pot, grimacing. This morning's brew of sludge had burnt and solidified. Handing the pot to a Corporal (who took it out to the gents' WC to empty it as best he could), he took out his fortieth Camel King Size of the day.

Merhi stared at the *seejaere* in one hand and the empty packet in the other, shaking his head. Why did he do this? His doctor was always on at him to quit. More importantly, so was Gisele. Carefully he aimed the cigarette at a nearby waste bin – then he changed his mind and lobbed the empty packet in instead.

Lighting up, he said to el-Gharib "I'll be in my office for a few minutes and then I'm going home."

"Right, boss. You want any sludge?"

"If I'm still here."

His office was just metres down the corridor. He went in, closing the door behind him, the door with the cracked pane of opaque glass (the crack had been there for seven years, Facilities should be getting around to it soon). On his desk was a new pile of folders – which could stay there, until tomorrow or when he took a shit, whichever came first (might as well put the contents to some good use).

He stretched, yawning – and felt a tingling down his right leg. Quickly he put his arms down, fearful that the heart attack he had always feared was starting. But wasn't that supposed to be in your arms and neck?

The tingling stopped. Then started again. Then stopped. Then started again. What the…? Looking heavenward, he put his hand into his pocket and pulled out his iPhone which he had left on silent-vibrate.

He looked at the Caller ID. A local number which he did not recognise and which was not one of his Contacts.

His finger hovered between the green and red icons. It had been a long day, he should just decline the call. His finger pressed down on the red icon – and somehow brushed the green icon first.

Shit.

Tentatively he raised the phone to his ear. There was a lot of noise, background shouting, raised male voices. "Hello?" said a voice.

"Hello?"

"Abu Samer?"

It couldn't be. Not today. Not now. Lord, was there no mercy?

"Mm."

"Evening of joy, my dear, dear friend. It is Lattouf!"

Oh Christ. "Fadi, how are you?" Merhi didn't mean it, he didn't want to know, it was just how all Lebanese started their phone calls.

"I am well, my friend, well. And you and the charming Gisele?"

"As ever, Fadi."

"And your boys? Are they coming home at the new year?"

"Probably. Fadi, I can't really talk right now - "

"My friend, I am sorry for calling you at this hour. But I am in – how do you say? – a little spot of bother, and I wondered if you could help me?"

Merhi sucked a full centimetre off of his cigarette. As he swallowed the smoke, he sighed deeper than he had ever sighed before. "What is it, Fadi?"

There was a pause on the other end. Then, "Jihad, I am at Sanayeh police station."

"And what are you doing there?"

Another pause. "I have been arrested."

## Sanayeh, Beirut 21:30

The Sanayeh police station was within walking distance of the State Security Building. Just across the René Moawad Public Garden and a dogleg along Mary Eddeh Street. But Merhi took his car, the official-issue decuma grey Toyota Land Cruiser V8. He wanted to go home after he had sorted out this little matter. It would not take him long to get Lattouf out, he had the clout. Lattouf would be a free man in a matter of minutes, unless he had committed murder (and even then...).

Merhi smoked as he drove down Sanayeh Street (for medicinal purposes only, to counteract his tiredness and the stress of the day), and thought of his friend.

Fadi Lattouf. Or more precisely Captain Fadi Lattouf of the Civil Police of the Palestinian Security Force in the Bourj el-Barajneh refugee camp in southern Beirut. A giant of a man in all ways: his appetites, his oral and bodily volume, his presence, his physique. He was nearly two metres tall and measured the same around his stomach. Bearded and bald, save for the few strands of greying black hair that swept over his head from just above his left ear.

Because of his size, his rolling gait, his manner of speaking (often traditional, sometimes quite formal) and his perceived (though not necessarily actual) clumsiness, people often dismissed Fadi Lattouf as an idiot. It was a mistake they made only once. Idiots did not spend many years policing the Gaza Strip. Idiots did not become the senior police officer in charge of the Palestinian refugee camps in the Beirut area, enforcing as much discipline as was possible in the overcrowded slums while maintaining the eggshell bridge of contact with the groups that really ruled the camps: Fatah and Hamas.

Merhi and Lattouf had met many years ago. Part of Merhi's duties was to be the liaison link between the Lebanese Internal Security Force and the Palestinian Police controlling the Beirut refugee camps. Captain Fadi Lattouf was his opposite number.

Outside of the formal liaison, fate had thrown them together on other occasions, most notably during the Hariri assassination in 2005 and the al-Mahdi incident in 2010. And they had socialised with their families, despite Merhi's initial (and sometimes continuing) reluctance.

Destiny moves in mysterious and inexplicable ways, and Merhi had now accepted that his lot was to be a friend of Fadi Lattouf.

The holding cell in Sanayeh police station was compact at the best of times. With Lattouf in it it looked like a doll's house cupboard with a grizzly bear trapped inside. It was possible Lattouf's body touched all four walls at the same time.

Lattouf was at the bars, and his reaction when he saw Merhi coming down the corridor accompanied by the duty police officer was like a dog on seeing his owner.

"Jihad! Abu Samer! Evening of joy, my dear friend. Thank you, thank you."

"Evening of get out of jail free, Fadi." Merhi nodded at the policeman. "Let him out."

The policeman unlocked the door and Lattouf stepped out, giving him a disdainful look. "I told you he was my friend."

The policeman shrugged.

Lattouf was dressed in rough blue denim jeans, for which he was about thirty years too old and fifty kilos too heavy, and a loose pink and blue checked shirt – the outfit he always wore when he wanted to be casual. Merhi had known the outfit for as long as he'd known Lattouf: nine years.

"What happened?" asked Merhi as they walked back down the corridor.

"He pushed me, I pushed back." Lattouf sounded like a child called to explain himself.

"What were you doing there anyway?"

"I had come to pay my respects to your Chief. To say the *Salat al-Janazah*. It was dreadful what happened to him. Dreadful."

Merhi was touched. "Thank you, Fadi. So what happened today?"

"The crowd, it became unruly. I was swept along."

"*You* were swept along?"

"Nada has me on this diet, as you can see." (Merhi couldn't.) "I am wasting away. It's a wonder you recognised me."

Merhi raised his eyebrows. Lattouf continued. "One of the mourners pushed into me. I pushed him back…"

"Let me guess. You didn't know your own strength."

Lattouf shrugged. "It was just a gentle shove. He will be all right. If he wakes up."

They had reached Merhi's car out in Omayads Street. "Get in," said Merhi. "I'll give you a lift home."

"No, no, that is fine." Lattouf opened the passenger door. "I am parked over near Debbas Square. If you could take me there please." The Toyota dipped markedly to the right as he got in.

"Might not be a good idea," Merhi's weight made not one degree of counterbalance as he climbed in the driver's side. "They are still rioting. If they see a blue Palestinian Police van in the street - "

"What? Oh, I don't use that any more, except when I am on official business. No, it's my Bluebird."

Merhi remembered. The garish orange Datsun Bluebird rust bucket that Lattouf had inherited from his cousin Chadi. He said, "Same thing applies though. It might be dangerous downtown tonight. I'll give you a lift home. You can come back and get it tomorrow – or whenever this dies down."

Lattouf nodded. "Your advice is always good, my friend. I will take it."

Merhi offered his newly-opened packet of Camel King Size. Lattouf raised his hand. "I have given up. Nada's orders." Merhi went to pull the packet away. "But," Lattouf reached out, "I cannot refuse a man's hospitality in his own vehicle. Thank you." Merhi lit both cigarettes.

They drove off, turning left into René Moawad Street. This straight road would become Rachidine Street and then the wider Subah es Salem es Subah Avenue, leading down eventually to the area of the Bourj el-Barajneh camp.

Savouring the cigarette, Lattouf looked at his left wrist although there was no watch on it. "It is getting late but you must let me thank you."

"No, no, it is not necessary." Merhi knew what was coming and he dragged in desperation on his Camel.

"Nada would have kept my supper for me. There will be plenty."

Oh hell. "You are too kind."

"To feed you is the least I can do. And I will wake the children up. It has been a long time since they have seen their Uncle Jihad."

Oh Christ.

For something to say, Merhi asked "How old is Little Wissam now?"

Lattouf smiled, thinking of his youngest son. "He is five. He looks more like me each day. Little Fadi!" He laughed.

Merhi's mind was boggling. Distractedly, he said "I'm surprised you stopped at six. I thought Number Seven would be well on his or her way by now."

Lattouf looked out of the side window, seeing the myriad posters and pictures hanging from buildings and across the road. Some of local martyrs, some of the green arm and fist holding the Kalshnikov AK47 assault rifle on a yellow background, but most of Sayyed Hassan Nasrallah, the leader of Hizbullah. In the darkness of the night it was disconcerting.

"We all get old, my friend," he said quietly. He turned back towards Merhi. "My winkie, it is not how it used to be. For sure, it is still interested. It comes up to have a look around. But then it goes down again, too soon."

The cigarette nearly fell from Merhi's mouth and he started coughing. After a while, he said "Thank you, Fadi. That is too much information."

"You are welcome, my friend."

They drove on into south Beirut.

# 22 October 2012
# 6 Dhu al-Hijja 1433

## Jounieh, Lebanon 07:00

"I am surprised you are hungry this morning, after such a late meal," said Gisele.

Her husband spoke through a mouthful of custard doughnut. "I'm not, it just counteracts the goat and rice. Lies heavy." He patted his stomach. "I had already eaten last night as well, anticipating the late evening."

"But not anticipating Lattouf."

"How can anybody anticipate that? He always turns up when you least expect him, at the most inauspicious times."

Gisele came over and, with light flicks of a finger, brushed sugar from Jihad's mouth. "How was Nada and the children?"

"The children were sleepy, but well-behaved like they always are. I gave them some money. Nada was her usual self, as big as ever and yet she has put *him* on a diet."

"Yet another one?"

"He was allowed only two plates of goat and rice instead of three."

Gisele nodded. "The weight will be falling off of him then. He will be like a catwalk model in no time."

Jihad laughed, kissing his wife and leaving her with sugary lips. He knocked back his triple espresso. "Right. let's see what horrors await me today." He pushed away from the kitchen worktop and headed out into the hallway.

"Will you be late again?"

Jihad shrugged as he shrugged into his jacket. "Who knows?"

"Ring me. Let me know."

"Sure. You going anywhere today?"

"I might go out shopping."

Jihad turned in the doorway, adjusting his jacket, making sure it covered his gun. "Well, spend wisely, and be careful if you go into town. There will still be uncertainty on the streets after the al-Hassan protests. For me the good thing is, I've had my Lattouf fix. He wanted to meet today for lunch when he goes in to pick up his car but I said no. Said I would be too busy. Wasn't a lie, we've got a section heads meeting this morning. So the next time we'll see him will probably be New Year. You take care now." He pecked her one more time on the lips and then started down the stairs.

In the world of security, 'probably' is an unacceptable adverb. 'Probably' denotes uncertainty. It is a seed of doubt.

And there was no doubt that, that day, Jihad Merhi was going to be wrong.

## Jonblat, Beirut 11:30

"Abu Samer, may I have a word?"

The use of the *kunya* always grated on the Maronite Jihad Merhi, but it was one of the foibles of his boss, Major Ghanem.

"Major?"

"My office."

The section heads meeting was over and the men were dispersing. During the meeting, Major Ghanem had informed them that Colonel Imad Othman was taking over as the Head of the Intelligence Bureau. Colonel Othman had not been present, and it seemed to Merhi that he was going to be as anonymous as his predecessor, the assassinated Wissam al-Hassan (in the nearly eight years al-Hassan had been Head of the Intelligence Bureau, Merhi had not met him once).

Up on the fifth floor, Merhi nodded at Ghanem's secretary Violette Ghorra as he followed 'The Old Man' into his offices.

He was rewarded with a smile.

Ghanem did not invite Merhi to sit down. From his trouser pocket he took out some keys, attached to his belt by a chain, and unlocked a drawer in his desk. "As you know, the late Brigadier had many great successes during his tenure."

"*En effet.*"

Ghanem sniffed. "Some more successful than others. One he is noted for."

"Samaha?"

"Before that."

Merhi nodded. "Ah." He knew better than to say it out loud. The Listeners were everywhere.

"Our new Colonel wants to shake things up a bit." (As they all do when they take over, thought Merhi.) "He is a great believer in delegation. He has delegated this matter. We will be in charge of it. That means you will be in charge of it." Ghanem's hand came out of his drawer holding what looked like an ATM card. It had no writing or markings on it whatsoever, just a single embedded chip towards one end. It was deep red in colour, almost maroon.

Ghanem held it out but Merhi held up his hands. "That," said Merhi, recognising the colour for Above Top Secret, "is above my pay grade."

Ghanem was quiet for a moment, still holding out the card. Then he said, "No longer, *Ra'id* Merhi."

Merhi's eyebrows rose. *Major* Merhi?

"Also as of today I am *Muqaddam*," said Ghanem. Lieutenant-Colonel. He gestured with the card. "Well?"

Merhi was at a loss of what to say. Had that just happened? Had he been promoted? He desperately needed a Camel but Ghanem was probably the only man in Lebanon who did not smoke. "Con...gratulations."

"It does not affect our jobs or location," said Ghanem, brushing away the niceties. "At least at this time. You will still report to me. You will still have your team, only now because of your rank it can be augmented as you see fit and as necessary. You are autonomous in such matters. Come on, take it." He thrust the card again.

Merhi reached out and took the card, turning it over in his hand.

"Sole systems access at ATS level," said Ghanem. "You do not need me to tell you what will happen to you if you ever lose it. You can access all the Brigadier's files and reports. Give me a report on what, if any, current action we need to take by next week. Also report on any changes you will be making to your team."

Merhi shook his head. "This… this will not fit my computer. I have no card reader ports."

"Facilities are replacing the equipment in your office as we speak. You will be required to provide scans for biometric access also. Any questions?"

Merhi thought for a moment, still looking at the card. The card that had just changed his life. Then he nodded and asked, "If Facilities are in my office, do you think that they can replace that cracked glass in my door?"

"You are a Major now," said Lieutenant-Colonel Ghanem. "Fucking arrange it yourself."

Major Merhi did not register the other staff who were using the echoing back staircase as he walked down the three flights from Ghanem's office, although he nodded to a few of them. He had his iPhone in his hand and he was trying to call Gisele. Twice the connection failed, the third time he got her voicemail.

"Hi Gigi… er, just to let you know - " He stood back, holding the landing door open for one of the female PAs. As he hovered a little too long, watching her bottom go up the stairs, he realised that his new rank now qualified him for one of those – a PA, that is. Also he realised that he shouldn't say what he was about to say on a hackable voicemail.

He went through the door and walked down the corridor. "I

might be home early tonight. I've got some news. Definitely I'll be there for dinner."

"Boss!" Sergeant Deeb el-Gharib shouted from the General Office.

"Take care." Merhi took the phone from his ear, squinting at the icons, his thumb finding the red one.

He was past the General Office and from behind him el-Gharib called again, "Boss!"

"Not now, Deeb," he said over his shoulder. "I'll be in in a minute."

"Boss..."

Merhi entered his office and stopped. There were two things there that hadn't been there earlier.

First was a small, quite discreet and yet almost sinister-looking black rectangle on his desk where his old PC used to be.

The second, standing over by the window, was Fadi Lattouf.

Lattouf was dressed in his uniform trousers and light blue shirt, his police jacket draped over the back of the wooden chair in front of Merhi's desk. He turned as he heard Merhi enter, a wide grin splitting his face. Around his thick neck, the standard-length ID lanyard looked like a choker.

"Morning of happy coincidence, my dear Captain!"

For a moment Merhi said nothing. Then he frowned. "Fadi, I said I couldn't do lunch today. Even more so now."

"I understand, my friend. But I am not here for *ghadae*. It is the way these things happen. *Yadreb asfoorayn behajar.* I am killing the two stones with one bird."

Merhi raised an eyebrow.

"I had to pick up my car," continued Lattouf, "and I need to see you – officially. Something very important has happened. I received a phone call - "

"Don't!" snapped Merhi.

Lattouf was taken aback.

From the doorway, Merhi mimed an expansive room-embracing gesture with his hand and then pointed to his ear.

Lattouf continued frowning and then the metaphorical light bulb went on above his head. "Ah," he nodded.

"Was your car all right?" asked Merhi.

"What? Oh yes, yes."

"How are the streets?"

"Here it is fine, your army has done a good job, but coming up through Tariq el Jedideh things were still very tense. I think there will be trouble there later."

"How *did* you get in to town?"

"My sergeant drove me in the van. Dropped me off."

Merhi nodded, realising that he had yet to move from the doorway. He walked in and shook his friend's hand, becoming aware of a louder-than-usual commotion of bipping horns and shouting out in Bank of Lebanon Street. He looked beyond Lattouf, out of the window, knowing, just knowing, what he was going to see.

Sure enough, down below a garish orange Datsun Bluebird rust bucket had been parked at such an angle that it was blocking one lane of the street. Vehicles were jousting to get around it.

Merhi turned back. "You know, Fadi," he said, "lunch *would* be a good idea, if you're hungry."

"I could squeeze something in."

"Let's go down to Hamra."

"Shall we walk?"

"No. We'll take your car."

As he walked back past his desk, Merhi glanced at the sinister black rectangle: a laptop. Then he looked at Lattouf. He wondered which of the two was going to cause him trouble.

As it happened, it would be both.

## Hamra, Beirut 12:45

Hamra Square was busy but they had managed to secure a table, Lattouf moving with surprising speed when he saw one becoming free, cutting off an elderly couple who were also heading for it. The Bluebird was parked in a side road off Makdissi Street, and Merhi was off buying falafel, coffee and something sweet.

Lattouf loved it here. In times past Hamra was *the* shopping district of Beirut. Many of the famous names had now moved to other locations, such as the malls and back into the rebuilt city centre, but the area still buzzed. The retail shops and the sidewalk stalls were as popular as ever, the shouts from the street-hawkers vying with the noise from the traffic to see who could be the loudest. And there was a stall on the square here that did the finest *mekhallel* this side of Gaza! He had his car, he could stock up on the pickles.

He saw Merhi doing a little belly dance past the tables, carrying a large, oblong tray. This looked like more than falafel!

And indeed it was. The tray was piled with falafel, stuffed vine leaves, bread, hummus, *tabouleh*, and chicken and lamb kabobs.

Lattouf looked like he had died and gone to *janna*. "Bless your hands, my friend! Your generosity is overwhelming."

Like your stomach, thought Merhi. Out loud he said, "I've got another tray - "

"I'll get it!"

"No, no. You sort these out. And remember I'm eating too."

He was back momentarily with a tray containing a box of *baklava*, a bag with ten *ma'amoul*, a packet of four cupcakes, two king size Americano coffees and one triple espresso. "There, that should see you all right until Nada feeds you tonight."

"I might just make it," conceded Lattouf without a trace of satire. He had tucked a small paper napkin down the open neck of his shirt. It looked like, and was as effective as, a postage stamp on the outside of a tent.

Merhi noted that a lamb kabob had already disappeared. He sat down, ensuring his jacket covered the gun on his waistband. Time was he could have left the weapon in his office when he was not in uniform, but those days had gone. Beirut, indeed the whole of Lebanon, was now a jungle of refugees, radicals, extremists, fanatics, terrorists, spies, moles, agents, kidnappers, assassins, not to mention opportunist criminals. The Syrian uprising had seen to that. And in a jungle you took whatever precautions were necessary.

He chose one of each kabob, one stuffed vine leaf and two falafel.

Lattouf frowned. "No bread, my friend? *Tabouleh?*"

"No, these will do. And the chocolate cupcake's mine." He moved his espresso into his own territory, just to be on the safe side.

"You are not hungry?" Lattouf was sweeping up hummus with folded-over flatbread.

"I have other things on my mind. I didn't supersize the meal because I know you are on a diet."

"I am grateful for your consideration. Nada will thank you."

"I'm sure," Merhi pulled some chicken off the skewer with his fingers. "Fadi, I've..." He stopped and watched as Lattouf tilted his head back, lowered an entire kabob into his mouth, closed his teeth and denuded the skewer as he took it back out. "...got something to tell you."

"Andivegotsomthtellyou."

"What?"

Lattouf swallowed. "And I've got something to tell you, my friend. That's why I came to see you."

"I've - "

"You first."

Merhi watched as another lamb kebob was executed. Then he said, "I've been promoted."

Lattouf stopped chewing, staring at Merhi, his face

expressionless. Then he frowned. Saying nothing, he picked up a stuffed vine leaf and popped it into his mouth whole, like posting a letter.

"Er," said Merhi, "it is usual to say congratulations?"

For a moment Lattouf was far away, then he shook his head. "Yes, yes, I am sorry, Abu Samer. *Mabruk.* Allah's blessings upon you. So you are now...?"

"Major Merhi."

"Major." Lattouf raised a greasy hand and gave a greasy salute. "Truly, my congratulations."

"*Merci mon ami.*"

"But where does it leave us?"

"Us?"

"I assume you will be moving on to other duties? Will you be replaced? Will I have to liaise with someone else?"

Ah, that explained his reaction. Merhi smiled. "It doesn't work like that, not nowadays. I take on a wider remit, in many additional matters I now become autonomous, running things myself. Everything is down to me."

"You will at last be given credit for your successes?"

"And will have to pay for my failures..."

Both men ate, each thinking back seven years to when they were within two minutes of preventing the assassination of Rafic Hariri.

But what was done, was done. Merhi shook off the thought. "I also retain all my present responsibilities. So, my dear Palestinian friend, you are still mine. And I am still yours."

Lattouf was now beaming. He picked up one of the king size cups of coffee, liquid sloshing out where he was gripping it too tight, and raised it in a toast. "To us! What a team! Lattouf and Merhi. Together forever!"

Merhi just maintained the shaky smile on his face while fighting the urge to pull out his gun and blow his own brains out. The eventual consequences of Lattouf's next remark made him subsequently wish he had followed through with it.

"Well, my dear Major, as my formal link with the Lebanese authorities, I have an official request. Last night I received a call from my counterpart at the Bourj al-Shimali camp. They have made a serious arrest down there. An Israeli spy. They wish to hand him over. As the senior officer of all the camps, they want me to come down and pick him up. But, as you know, outside of the camps I have no jurisdiction, no powers. So would you come with me, please? To Tyre."

## Jounieh, Lebanon 16:45

Gisele was not in when Jihad returned home, she was probably out shopping like she had threatened or meeting with her friends, doing what girls do. He had tried ringing her again from the car on the way up from Beirut but calls were still going to voicemail. So he decided the first thing he would do, while waiting for her, was to look at this black, unbranded laptop that was now his.

Actually, no. The first thing he would do was to pour himself a large Johnnie Walker and have a Camel, *then* he would look at the laptop.

Earlier, he had returned to the office with cakes, bottles of quality orange juice for the Muslims and champagne for the non-Muslims and had broken the news of his promotion to his team – hastily reassuring them that he was not moving anywhere except upwards in rank. Someone from IT had been waiting for him and had conducted digital and retinal biometric procedures and associated them with the laptop. Then he had been visited by someone else from IT who could have been no more than twelve years old and who gave him an introductory, very fast and very condescending run-through on the machine.

Now Merhi stood on his wide balcony in the early-evening sun, whisky in one hand, cigarette in the other, and looked out over the mountainside, across the main Coastal Highway far below and out over the Mediterranean Sea.

He had agreed to go to Tyre with Lattouf. What else could he do? He could delegate it, especially now he was a Major, but he would not foist Lattouf onto a junior (he stopped short of thinking that he would not wish Lattouf on anybody). And anyway, Fadi was a friend. Lattouf had wanted to go tomorrow but Jihad had explained that this was not possible. In his new role he had things to do, new staff to meet.

They had agreed on a trip south in three days time. The local Palestinian Civil Police Captain would look after the spy until then. They would be going in Merhi's Toyota – Merhi thought Lattouf's Bluebird was unlikely to make the 160 kilometre round-trip, despite Lattouf's protestations that he had recently given it a good service. And, reasoned Merhi, even if it did get down to Tyre its garish orange colour was too much of a target so close to the border with Occupied Palestine. Lattouf could not argue with that.

But it was bizarre. Was Lattouf a mind reader? A *sahir*, a wizard? The breaking of Israeli spy rings in Lebanon had been the other noted triumph of the late Brigadier Wissam al-Hassan. Hundreds of arrests had been made over the last two years, and overseeing the now-finishing project had been delegated to Merhi this morning. He had to report on it to Ghanem in a week, that was why he had brought the laptop home, to get up to speed.

That Lattouf had come to him with an arrested spy on the very day he had been assigned the project was, well, pure Lattouf. How he always managed to do it, Merhi did not know. Lattouf was always in the right place at the right time, bumbling about like a wayward pinball, trampling over evidence, intimidating suspects, but always getting it right in the end, even if most times he did not realise it.

Lattouf was a *marid*, a giant, powerful genie – a djinn.

Jihad took a final draw on his cigarette and flicked the butt out over the mountainside. He smiled as he finished his whisky, memories that had never gone away rolling to the forefront of his mind, exploding in Imax 3D and surround sound.

A djinn…

He had known a djinn. Twice their paths had crossed. The first time during the Hariri business, then throughout the al-Mahdi incident.

This djinn took the form of a woman, a woman who worked for the DGS, the external security service. A woman who, he had found out, was married to an unnamed Lebanese mercenary. A mercenary who had also been involved with al-Mahdi and had caught Gisele's attention as much as The Djinn had caught his.

The Djinn had even stayed with him and Gisele for a while. He remembered the small, olive-skinned body, the long dark hair, the black eyes. And the scent that followed her wherever she went and lingered wherever she had been: jasmine.

A beguiling, exotic, dangerous creature…

## Murray Hill, New York City, USA 11:15 (local time)

"Thanks, Larry."

"You have a good day, Miss Chedid." The doorman touched the peak of his hat with his index finger and admired the firm, athletic legs as the olive-skinned, deep-voiced no-longer-a-babe-not-yet-a-cougar from Apartment 3030 turned left, heading west on East 39th Street. The smell of jasmine made promises to his nose which would never be kept.

Her long, black hair was down, held in place by an ornate black and gold hair clip, swaying very gently from side to side as she walked. Today she was wearing a short, loose blue dress covered by an open, padded coat, her dark grey Barbour wax cotton messenger bag over one shoulder. Larry preferred it when she wore pants or jeans and a small jacket – although there was less skin on display, he could see her ass better. And imagine.

And imagine was all he could do. Because he knew two

things about her. She was a diplomat, Egyptian or Syrian or something, working over by the UN. Not an inhibitor in itself, but when combined with the fact that she was married to the tall, hard man with the long black hair and scarred face, the man who returned only occasionally, who rarely spoke and who emitted an aura of complete and utter menace, it meant that she was well off limits. She was Major League, Larry was not even Triple A – he was Saturday ball park.

Larry might have known those two things but what he did not – and never would – know was that Carla Chedid was a Gatherer, working for the Lebanese Department of General Security. Based at number 866 United Nations Plaza at The Permanent Mission of Lebanon to the United Nations, her diplomatic status was recorded officially as an Assistant Counsellor. But in reality she gathered information, facts, ideas, theories, thoughts, anything and everything that may or may not affect the security of Lebanon. She had been based in New York for seven years. Seven years since, under another name, she had been exiled from Lebanon after the Hariri assassination.

She ran a network of assets in other embassies here in Manhattan, and one or two in the UN itself. She was on her way to see one now.

She was, quite simply, a spy. A spy who would seduce when necessary. A spy who would pay when necessary. A spy who would blackmail when necessary. A spy who would kill when necessary, efficiently and without compunction.

She was also known as The Djinn.

## Midtown, New York City, USA 11:30 (local time)

By the Mid-Manhattan Library, Carla turned right into Fifth Avenue heading north. Then she doglegged into East 40th Street past the side of the New York Public Library and down into Bryant Park.

It was a sunny, blue sky, late October morning and the

temperatures were now dropping, so she headed for the Southwest Porch eatery and sat at a table under the pergola.

He would find her.


Fifteen minutes later, spot on time, she saw him coming in from 42nd Street. Tall, quite beefy, cropped reddish hair, rosy cheeks, dressed in a suit and tie, looking very much the all-American Manhattanite. He would have walked from the Consulate at 800 Second Avenue.

Of the four asset-control methods of seduction, payment, blackmail or threat, this one was seduction. Therefore he smiled when he saw her, her coat open, legs crossed, dress ridden far up her olive thighs. He thought of what was above them. He *remembered* what was above them…

She returned the smile and watched as he came in.

"*Shalom*," he leant forward and kissed her on both cheeks. "*Mah Ha'Inyanim?*"

"*B'seder*," she said. "I am fine. And you?"

"*Mamash Tov*. Really good. It always helps when I see you. You smell delicious as always."

She did not respond but her black eyes showed warmth – and promise.

"Can I get you anything?" he asked.

She nodded at the Americano in front of her. "This is fine, thank you."

He made gestures to an orange-shirted server that he would have the same. Carla inwardly smiled at his mirroring.

They made small-talk until his coffee was delivered. As the server left, Carla asked "You have something for me?"

He sipped his coffee, giving the impression of thinking. Putting his cup back down he said, "Do *you* have something for *me?*"

Softly she said, "You know what I have for you."

"And I get to have it again?"

"Yes."

"When?"

"If your information is good - "

"Oh it's good."

"Then soon. Boys must learn patience." She reached across with both hands, touching his arm. Not for the first time, he saw the one flaw in this otherwise perfect creature: she had no fingernails. None at all, on either hand, just corrugated skin. It looked like the nails had been there once but had been... removed?

But he did not recoil. Her fingers were nevertheless elegant – and he remembered what she could do with them. What she could hold with them, where she could put them... He felt himself reacting under the table. He wanted her. Quickly he drank some coffee.

"Well?" she prompted.

Had he ever heard her accented voice so deep? "When?" he asked again.

"Tell me first." Her eyes were like black pools in which he wanted to drown.

He felt his temperature rise, any control that he ever imagined he had slipping away.

She reached over again and squeezed his arm. "Are you all right, *habibi*?"

He pulled at his collar. "It's hot under here, have they turned the heaters on?"

"Well it is October. Finish your coffee and let's walk. It is cooler out there."

He left money for his drink and then stood up, not caring if she saw the evidence of his desire as he moved out from the table.

Out from under the pergola, she linked her arm in his. For a while they walked in silence, the noise of Manhattan a humming, beeping background musak. Then she said "Right now if you wish."

"Right now what?"

"Good boys should be rewarded. If they deserve to be. Come, sit. Tell me what you have and you will get your reward."

They sat on a bench, passers-by paying them no heed. She held his hand, waiting.

"It's preliminary," he said eventually. "But they do not like what has been happening. They are planning on fighting back."

She sighed. "They are *what*? I thought that was all in the past. Didn't they learn their lesson in 2006? And recently?"

"That's just the point. Hands up, we have been routed. We know it, you know it. Hizbullah will never be expecting a return so soon."

Carla shook her head. "No. They must not do it."

"But we have to," he continued. "Hizbullah are in it up to their necks in Syria and now they've started foreign operations as well. Last year's attack in Istanbul, the recent one in Bulgaria. And we have hardly any eyes or ears on the ground in Lebanon, just the few they did not discover. We must get back in. Here," from a pocket of his jacket he pulled out what looked like a cigarette lighter. Quickly he took off the cover to reveal a USB memory stick, then clicked the cover back on again. "Information. Plus a list of names." He pulled down his tie and opened his shirt collar. "Do you have any water?"

She took the lighter. "No. Was there anything else?"

"Not right now. But I'll monitor. I'm really thirsty." He looked back towards the eatery.

She reached up and touched his face, leaning closer. Gently her fingers moved his head back round towards her. He could smell jasmine. "You deserve your reward," she said softly.

He felt the fingers of a djinn move down to his groin. His heart was pounding as he leant against the back of the bench, his thirst forgotten. Was she going to do it here? In public? Her slightly open lips came towards his, her warmth breath on his chin an overture to the delights of her mouth. Their lips touched...

Carla stopped and smiled, then moved backwards.

He was asleep.

She had dropped enhanced gammahydroxybuterate into his coffee when she had reached out to caress him back in the eatery. Normal GHB caused memory loss. This stuff created heightened imagination. Whatever he had been thinking would appear as real to him. She had used it on him before and he was the ideal subject for it – because she had never, ever, had sex with him although he seemed to think she had. A flirt, a kiss, a glimpse, a heavy pet – and she had let his imagination and the drug do the rest.

Now she ran her index finger over her lips, checked to ensure there was nobody in the immediate vicinity, surreptitiously undid his fly, rummaged, pulled him out (circumcised but generous even in his relaxed state) and rubbed lipstick from her finger onto the helmet. She put him back in but left the fly undone, a gentle prompt to his imagination.

She stood up and walked away.

Benjamin David, a *sayan* working as civilian support at the Israeli Consulate, would be asleep for about an hour. When he woke up he would remember forever some of the greatest oral sex he had never, in fact, had.

## Jounieh, Lebanon 17:45

Jihad Merhi sat on one of the sofas in his lounge, whisky in his left hand, cigarette in his mouth, sinister black laptop open on the coffee table in front of him. He had never before officially seen an Above Top Secret report and he was impressed by its detail and thoroughness.

The Israeli spy network had covered all of Lebanon, overt and covert. The overt was down south in Occupied Palestine (which they called Israel). All along the border, from En Naqoura on the coast to the Sheeba Farms in the east, the Israelis had set up spying posts (equipped with radar stations, listening devices and other gadgets) from where they collected all types of data from Lebanon's wireless networks. Nicolas Sehnaoui, Lebanon's Minister of Telecommunications, had confirmed that the Israelis received "everything that passes through the air, from waves and vibrations to tapping of telephone cables that are above ground".

The covert was a network of spies across the entire country. Not Jews, not infiltrators, but local Lebanese recruited either by threats, blackmail or payment. They came from all backgrounds and faiths. They operated either singly or in small cells (or 'confessions' as Brigadier al-Hassan put it in his report).

But al-Hassan had routed them. Over an eighteen-month period, nearly one hundred arrests had been made across the country, all sorts from all confessions: three army colonels, a mayor, business people, school teachers, even a gas station owner who was accused of planting bugs in vehicles used by Hizbullah. Over twenty people had been indicted for the death penalty for treason.

The biggest arrest had been Adib al-Alam, a retired Brigadier General of the GSD, who was accused of running a twelve-member cell that included his wife and nephew, a GSD corporal. [*In June 2013, Brigadier General Adib al-Alam was sentenced to fifteen years hard labour and his wife, Hayat Saloumi, was sentenced to four years hard labour on charges of 'collaboration with the Israeli enemy'.*]

The most recent high-profile arrest had been a director of the Alfa telecommunications company that runs Lebanon's cellular phone network.

al-Hassan had seriously disrupted Mossad's operations inside Lebanon, much to the Israelis' embarrassment. He had poked out their eyes and cut off their ears. Not only had he discomfited Israel but Hizbullah too – the existence and national spread of the spy cells was an immense security failure by the Party of God.

Merhi drained his glass. Now this had been passed to Ghanem and himself. Their job was to oversee and monitor the project. He would introduce himself to the relevant members of al-Hassan's team tomorrow. Mossad had been routed in Lebanon but the arrest of the Palestinian down in the Bourj al-Shimali camp proved that they must never become complacent. The weeds of espionage were pernicious – pull one up and another popped up somewhere else.

He was refilling his glass when he heard the front door opening. Moments later a pile of bags from various outlets in Beirut's ABC shopping mall rustled their way into the lounge. Gisele was somewhere amongst them.

Jihad winced inwardly but smiled outwardly. *"Ciao belle habibi,"* he didn't even realise he had spoken three languages in one three-word sentence as he stood up, helping to extract her from the bags. The contents felt soft – clothes. Something harder bashed on his leg. Shoes. "I've been trying to call you all day." They kissed on the cheeks.

"Dead battery," she rummaged in her handbag and then waived her phone in the air. "It was over fifty per cent when I went out but I left my shopping list on."

"Drink?"

"In a minute. I just have to get out of these clothes – and let you see the new ones. Fancy a fashion show?" She noticed the object on the coffee table. "What's that?"

Jihad played it nonchalant. "My new work's laptop."

"Strange-looking," she bent over it.

"It's an ATS, issued only to Majors and above."

She didn't take in his nuance. As she straightened up she said, "You've borrowed it? With permission, I hope, I know what you're like."

"No, I haven't borrowed it. It's mine."

"Well I hope you know how to work it, I was never trained on something like that…" She frowned, looking into her husband's face. "But you just said they were for Majors and above only."

"Yes, I did."

"You mean?"

"Yes, I do."

Her hand went to her mouth.

He smiled. "I hope you are going to show Major Merhi the respect he deserves."

She ran into his arms. Jihad was not the tallest of men but he was a good head above his wife. He squeezed her tightly.

Gisele kissed his lips, forgiving him the whisky and tobacco flavoured breath. *"Mabruk, habibi. Mabruk, mabruk, mabruk."* She pulled away, frowning. "But I suppose that means I will see you even less now."

"Not necessarily. We have a new regime. A new way of working. We'll have to see."

She pecked his lips again. "Bravo. That is so good. *Habibi, you* deserve this, it's been a long time coming."

"I never thought it would. But this new chief had other ideas."

"Will there be..." she became faux-coy, pouting. "More money?"

"Considerably more."

"Excellent." She took his hand. "You can tell me all about it after. *Yalla.*"

"Where are we going?"

"Where do you think?" She pulled him out into the hallway, towards their bedroom. "Help me get out of these clothes. Come. Didn't you just ask me to show you the respect a major deserves? Let me kneel before you, my handsome hero..."

## Murray Hill, New York City, USA 22:00 (local time)

Apartment 3030 of the building on East 39th Street was in darkness. In the bedroom, the blinds were open and the occupants of the bed had an unrestricted view north over the lights of Midtown and the Upper East Side, if they chose to look. But they did not. They had seen it many times before and they were too engrossed with each other.

Carla rolled off of The Damascene and snuggled in under his left arm. Neither of them was out of breath but they were both completely satisfied. The sheets were wet.

She kissed his left nipple, lightly sucking.

With his right hand he stroked her luxuriant, but now tangled, black hair. "You can trust him?" he asked, continuing their conversation which had been interrupted for the last fifteen minutes. "He is not just a *bodel* trying to make a name for himself?"

She stopped her sucking and rested her head on his lightly-damp chest. "No, he is a *sayan*, a good Jewish boy from the Bronx. A *bodel* would have no access to any information. But - " she raised herself on one elbow, her left hand resting on his stomach, fingers caressing the line of one of his scars, "I do need to check what he has given me." In one movement she leant forward, licked the scar then rolled off of the bed.

In the diffused Manhattan light coming in from outside, The Damascene watched her naked silhouette as she walked into the en suite bathroom. The picture of her superb bottom lingered in his mind as he heard sounds of wiping, peeing, wiping, washing, and drying. Shortly she came back out, moving noiselessly, not even disturbing the air. Like a djinn.

Her shadow stopped over by a small table. "Mind your eyes." She switched on a low wattage lamp. Looking back at the bed, she asked "You are satisfied, my husband?"

He opened his eyes. "With you, always."

"It does not look like it."

He gave a small laugh. "*That* is your fault." He looked at her small, lithe body, naturally totally hairless. "It does not mean I am not satisfied. But being satisfied does not mean I don't want you again."

"I will be with you in a heartbeat." She turned and opened the MacBook Pro on the table.

As the computer was powering up, Carla floated across to the other side of the room, rummaged in her Barbour bag, and floated back again. This time a waft of jasmine and natural musk caressed The Damascene's nose.

She sat on a stool, removed the USB memory stick from its camouflage cigarette lighter cover and inserted it into the computer. Momentarily, two folder icons appeared on the screen. "Jpegs," she said over her shoulder. "Too much to ask for documents copies, I suppose. Still, I can zoom."

The first folder contained photographs of three typewritten pages, a report of some sort. She looked at it briefly, her eyes moving down each page like a scanner. Even though it was in Hebrew, she would be able to recall it without needing to look at the photographs again.

The second folder contained one photograph of a list of names. She looked at this one longer, nodding. Then, to herself, she said "Well, well."

"Worthwhile?" he asked from the bed.

She swivelled on the stool to face him. "Oh yes." She tapped her head. "I will read the report in detail later. After. But the list of names is very useful. I know some of them on there. So do you."

"And what does it mean?"

"It means..." She turned back round, rubbed her finger on the trackpad, clicked twice and pulled the memory stick out, putting it back into the cover. Closing the lid of the MacBook, she said "It means I need to go back." She stood up, the memory stick in her hand. "And it means you need to destroy this for me."

She turned off the lamp and glided over to the bed, the room again in silken semi-darkness. The Damascene took the stick and effortlessly snapped it in half. Then he applied crushing pressure. He opened his right palm, showing small pieces of mangled plastic. Stretching out, he put the pieces on a damp, used tissue on the bedside table and scrunched it up. He brushed slivers off his hands.

As he lay back on the bed, Carla admired his hard, muscular, equally hairless body. The many scars, almost too numerous to count, she found deliciously attractive. The long black hair, missing left ear and scarred face completed the picture of the man whom, at one time, she thought she would have to kill, even though she was in love with him. But that had not happened. Yet.

She touched his groin. "Now," she said. "Let us see what we can do about your hard drive…"

# 23 October 2012
# 7 Dhu al-Hijja 1433

## Jonblat, Beirut 09:00

Major Jihad Merhi was surprised. The small office up on the fifth floor into which he had been led by Lieutenant-Colonel Ghanem contained just three men.

"We are expecting more?" he asked Ghanem.

"More what?"

Merhi gestured at the men.

"No, this is it," said Ghanem.

This was it? The team that had broken the Israeli espionage presence in Lebanon consisted of just three men? Plus their murdered leader, of course.

Merhi had seen the men about the building before but he did not know them by name. They had stood up when he and Ghanem had entered, a respect that Merhi was not accustomed to. He'd best get used to it now he was a Major.

"Please, as you were," he half-smiled, wondering if it was in fact the senior ranking officer's privilege to say that, not his. Whatever. He could do with a Camel King Size.

"As you probably know, this is Major Merhi," Ghanem spoke to the men. "Your new OIC and Directorate head. You report to him, he reports to me." He turned to Merhi. "Let me introduce you."

In fact Ghanem did not introduce anybody, the men said their own names as Merhi shook their hands.

"Nabil Haddad." Tall, slim, clean shaven, balding.

"Claude Gerges." Still tall but stouter, lighter complexion, of obviously strong French stock.

"Tamer Khalef." Short, plump, bearded.

One Muslim, one Christian and Haddad who could be either. It would be in his file. All three were sergeants.

After the handshakes, Merhi squatted on the edge of what turned out to be Haddad's desk. "Sit, please."

"I'll leave you to it," said Ghanem.

Merhi nodded. "I'll report to you in a week, as agreed."

"Good." Ghanem closed the office door behind him.

Merhi turned back to what were now his men. "Firstly, my condolences on the loss of your Chief. If you agree, let us have a quiet moment." He lowered his head.

It was a gesture that was appreciated by the men. It was a sad fact that killing was commonplace in Lebanon. At times it waxed and waned, waning particularly during the Hariri years and then waxing with his assassination and the many murders thereafter. It was now rife with the sectarian strife of Syria also being played out on Lebanon's soil. Quite frankly in the current climate, nobody was safe, especially if they were in the government, the military or law enforcement. But that did not demean or lessen the fact that a death was a death; a life lost, a life taken by people who had no business, no right, to take it; a life never to be replaced.

Merhi looked up and waited for the men to do so. Then he said, "So, only three of you? What are you, superheroes?"

## Murray Hill, New York City, USA 13:00 (local time)

They kissed at the doorway to their apartment, their tongues thrusting, parrying and lunging like fencing masters. After a final flick, Carla pulled away, her height reducing by fifteen centimetres as she went back down on her heels. The Damascene bent back upwards.

Carla's cab was waiting downstairs. She was booked on the

17:00 American Airlines Flight 44 from JFK to Paris; from Paris she would travel onwards to Beirut on Middle East Airways Flight 206. The journey would take thirteen hours in all.

"*Khodi balik*," he said as he lifted her small suitcase. They walked over to the elevator.

"I will be careful, do not worry." She pressed the Call button. "Last time was... exceptional." She looked down at her nailless fingers and for the briefest of moments thoughts flashed into her mind of the retribution she would take against the monsters who had done this to her. She said, "This time *I* will be the aggressor. I will administer penance to the confession." She took the case from him.

"I will be there soon," he said. "If you need me - "

"I always need you. Will you bring my presents?"

"One should always make offerings to a djinn."

She smiled. As the elevator doors opened, she reached up and pulled his head down, her mouth open and soft.

There were two other people in the elevator so she did not linger.

The Damascene watched as the doors closed, his face showing no emotion.

Back in the apartment, he stripped off his shirt and jeans and shook out his ponytail, pulling the hair over the hole of his missing left ear even though he was alone. Naked, he walked over to the lounge window and looked out over Midtown. Sun glistened off the Chrysler Building to the north, some rays reflecting off of the art deco tower and back across the three blocks into the apartment, onto his body.

He was not pleased. He had failed in his last assignment. Carla had known it but she had been gracious enough not to mention it. He had been very well paid to advise on the security and protection of the head of the Information Branch of the Lebanese Internal Security Force, Brigadier Wissam al-Hassan. He had succeeded for two months, since the threats had first been issued after al-Hassan's arrest of former Lebanese

Information Minister Michel Samaha. It had even been The Damascene's idea that al-Hassan travel in non-descript rented vehicles. But no matter how good you were (and, without false modesty, The Damascene acknowledged that he was good), you could not legislate for the carefully placed roadside car bomb – especially in the traffic of Beirut! It was how Rafic Hariri had been murdered seven years before.

It irked him that he had failed, but 'protection' (and with it the implied *ad infinitum* – when does a threat end?) was always a tenuous undertaking, unlike the other side of the coin - assassination – which always had a definitive outcome.

But there was a third element of his business, linked to protection but of a more finite variety: transportation. That was his next assignment. Yesterday he had received a cryptic message on one of his three cell phones. His clients were ready. Ready to go public. Ready for transportation. Like Carla, he too would be returning to the Levant.

Raising his arms in the air, he joined his hands in a static shoulder stretch. Momentarily he would begin his daily thirty minute regime of stretching exercises, but first there was something he needed to do.

He walked into the bedroom and went over to the table. The MacBook Pro came on instantly when he raised the lid.

Over at the bed he put his hand down the back, underneath the headboard, pulling out the memory stick that Carla had been given by the *sayan* – less the cover which he had crushed last night.

Sitting down on the stool, he inserted the stick into the computer. The two folder icons appeared on the screen. He opened the first one and read the report. Then he opened the second one and very carefully read the list of names…

# Coastal Highway, Lebanon 18:00

The superhero had been Wissam al-Hassan - although, from what Merhi knew of him, the late Brigadier would never have even thought of himself as that. al-Hassan's task had been massive: how do you fight one of the most sophisticated intelligence services in the world with the limited, fractured, sectarian resources that make up Lebanon's security services? In terms of sheer ability, if not size, it was like David and Goliath.

It had been al-Hassan's idea to fight the Israelis using their own methodology: don't put your own people in, use locals who are already there. al-Hassan's team (now Merhi's team) had raised a country-wide network of true Lebanese, those who would put country before confession (there were still some left). They used their eyes, they used their ears, they used their mouths: watching, listening, reporting. And, over two years, the results had been startling. No one could have ever imagined the extent of the Israeli espionage penetration in Lebanon, most of it aimed in just one direction: Hizbullah.

In 2006, Hizbullah had taken on the might of Israel. And, much to the world's surprise, had won – or at least had held them to a stalemate. At the cost of much destruction and thousands of innocent (and not so innocent) lives, the Party of God had stood firm against the satan from the south.

But the Israelis did not like to be beaten. They never would be beaten. They were coming back into Lebanon. Under the shadow of the Syrian war they had planned to make a massive, pre-emptive strike from within against Hizbullah, to annihilate them, to clear the way for – who knows what?

And Wissam al-Hassan and his team had stopped them. But Merhi knew that the Jews were persistent: they might lose battles but they refused to lose wars. Their espionage network in Lebanon had been routed, but what was now Merhi's team could not sit back on their laurels. The Israelis must never again be allowed to saturate Lebanon with spies. Any re-emerging shoots had to be nipped in the bud…

The Toyota Land Cruiser V8 powered forward as Merhi accelerated, the Coastal Highway traffic thinning beyond Nahr el Kalb, Dog River. Cigarette between his lips, left elbow on the open side window, he smiled at his simile. *Nipped in the bud…*

He was a gardener. He had to keep the Elysian Field of Lebanon free from the weeds of Israel. The garden would require constant, daily attention. Thankfully he had the right team and network to do it. Even now they knew that they had not got everyone. There was some pernicious knotweed that they had not eradicated, probably in the Beirut area. They did not know where, they did not know who, they did not know how many. A small group, a confession.

And, as every gardener knew, the smaller the weed the more difficult it was to find. Perhaps the spy they had arrested down in Bourj el-Shimali might 'volunteer' information…

The Gardener turned the Toyota off of the Coastal Highway just after Kaslik, heading for his home in the mountains.

# PART TWO
# الجزء الثاني

# THE BOND OF SALT
# الملح سندات

# 24 October 2012
# 8 Dhu al-Hijja 1433

## Bahla, Oman, Arabia 15:00 – 17:30 (local time)

The small town of Bahla in the north-west of Ad Dakhiliyah province of Oman sits at the foot of Jabal Akhdar, the Green Mountain range. It is an old town, pre-Islamic, and is dominated by Bahla Fort, the largest of the estimated five hundred forts in Oman. The fort closed twenty-five years ago and visitors had long since given up coming to Bahla unless they had another reason, such as visiting the Aladawi Clay Pots Factory or any of the other pottery makers behind the souk. Nowadays the main Highway 21, linking Muscat (120 kilometres to the north-east) with the United Arab Emirates (200 kilometres to the north-west) ran nearby.

On the outskirts of Bahla, outside the ancient mudbrick town walls, well away from the fort and the highway, was a villa. Set in its own walled compound, it had a spacious inner courtyard shaded by trees, and a fountain supplied with water by the *falaj*, the underground irrigation system, of Bahla Fort. The villa had small, ornate arched windows, and large arched doors of thick studded wood - and something rarely seen in Oman: two *barjeel*, wind towers. *Barjeel* were the old Iranian form of air conditioning, capturing cool air to funnel down into the house whilst also allowing hot air to rise and escape. But here they also had another purpose: as watchtowers. Because the villa was a safe-house, purpose-built with money siphoned from Syria and the Levant by the man who had been based there for the last seven years.

A man who was dead.


The local people kept well away from the villa, and for good reason. In Omani folklore, Bahla is famous for its supernatural associations. The town is said to be the haunt of djinn, the mischievous type not the benevolent kind. Legend has it that djinn appear in the middle of the night, flying off with objects or taking possession of any human that has offended them, causing misery, pain and sometimes death. Most houses in the town contain a *nazar*, an eye-shaped amulet, or a *hamsa,* a palm-shaped amulet with an eye in the centre, to protect the house and its occupants from *ayn al hasud*, the Evil Eye and its associated demons. Many women (and some men) wear a *sumt*, a large round silver pendant said to contain an imprisoned djinn, so warning off any demon that considers attacking them.

Even the tree in the middle of Bahla souk is decorated with amulets and chains to prevent its removal by supernatural forces.

It is all pure superstition, of course, as the occupants of Bahla will tell you. Djinn have not been seen in the town for generations (although some will reason that this is because of all the precautions taken by the townsfolk). And anyway, everyone knew that there were no djinn in the villa on the edge of town.

The villa contained *houri*.


As the woman drove the black Jeep Wrangler Ultimate past the old town walls, she heard the *azan* for *asr salat*, the call to afternoon prayer, coming from the Bahla Mosque nearby.

Even though the desert temperatures were still in the thirties, the detachable top was off of the Jeep. The windrush as she drove along Highways 15 and 21 had kept her cool. She was dressed in a full, plain black *abbaya*, the voluminous overdress worn by local women in Arabia, and a plain black *shayla*, headscarf. The *abbaya* was open from the thighs down to allow her legs to move, and the *shayla* was over her head and drawn across her face as a veil. Only her eyes were visible. Rich, brown eyes. Almost an unnatural colour.

She had been shopping in Muscat. As well as buying provisions, which were now stacked in the back of the Jeep, she had been to the Mutrah Souk to buy *luban*, frankincense, both in tear form and as oil. She had bought *hojari*, silver frankincense, the best. They would use the tears in their burners and rub the oil into their bodies

She pressed the small remote control to open the outer gates of the villa and drove in, another press on the remote closing the gates behind her. She pulled up near the tinkling fountain. She was pleased to be back, even though she had been gone only since that morning. She did not like to be alone. She felt incomplete.

She took the carrier bags of *luban* off the passenger seat and then carefully lifted the smaller purple bag that had been next to them. She smiled. As well as the provisions and *luban*, she had bought something else.

Something for Paradise.


The woman called Paradise looked at her own reflection. At the pretty face with the full red lips and pert nose, at the long wavy naturally blonde hair newly-released from the *shayla*, at the pale porcelain skin and tall, statuesque bearing. And at the eyes now that the contact lenses had been removed, at the white eyeballs and black pupils which others found so frightening, so intimidating, hence the need for lenses on journeys outside.

She kissed herself on the cheeks five times, and ended with one on the lips. Her mouth was enticingly soft, her breath pure.

She hugged herself. "My darling, you have travelled safely," she said to her identical twin sister. "Your trip was fruitful?"

The woman called Love caressed her sister's face. "I found everything, darling. They even had some new *hojari* oil in, so we can rub some into each other later. Our skin is feeling good today."

Paradise licked Love's fingers as they passed her mouth. "That is wonderful."

"Everything all right here?"

"Yes, he has been upstairs on his computer all day. He received a call this morning but he hasn't said what it was about."

"If we need to know, he will tell us."

"Indeed. So, what did you buy? It is my turn to cook today."

"In a minute. Firstly, this is for you." Love held up the small purple bag.

Paradise gave a wide, wide smile. She knew what it was, of course, because they were identical not only physically but also mentally. Conjoined twins in everything but the physical join. The moment her sister had stopped at the Amouage Perfumery on the way back, near Muscat Airport, she had known. She looked inside the bag and brought out the 100ml bottle of Amouage's signature *Gold* perfume. "You are wonderful."

"*You* are wonderful." They kissed again, on the lips, lingering. "Now," said Love, as they pulled apart, "come help me unload the Jeep. I have fruit, rice, some exquisite dates, some fresh camel and even some wild oryx which a Bedu sold me."

"Oh, he will like that."

"After which," said Love, "I will need to bathe. The sand gets everywhere. Into our hair and all sorts of other places."

"Yes, I have felt it."

"Will you help me, sister?"

"Yes, we must be clean," said Paradise. "Let us unpack the bags. After which you can relax in the *hammam* while I prepare the food. Then I will come and wash us while the oryx is roasting..."

The *hammam* was at the back of the villa, compact, ornately-tiled with a plunge pool and a domed ceiling which connected to one of the watchtowers for ventilation.

Love lay face-up between Paradise's legs as her sister finished rinsing her hair, the water running down her face, warm, perfumed, cleansing. She felt her sister's naked flesh against hers, also warm and perfumed.

"There now," Paradise kissed Love's crown. "We are clean. Come, my darling, I must check on the oryx. " Love leant forward as Paradise stood up. "You stay here, relax, take your time. I will call you and Abu Yo'roub when the food is ready." She stepped up out of the bath, the water dropping from her body like a falling gossamer veil. Instantly she was dry but she picked up a towel anyway, gently rubbing those places from which the water could not, and did not want to, escape.

"Leave the towel," Love smiled as she watched. "I will use it, save wetting another one."

"As you wish, my sister." Paradise nodded to Love and a message went between them. She bent over from the waist, deliberately and provocatively, and placed the towel by the edge of the pool. Slowly she straightened up.

Then she turned and walked out of the room, knowing that there were two sets of eyes watching her...

Up above, through one of the supplementary air vents around the bottom of the domed ceiling, Abu Yo'roub watched.

He was naked, lying on his side, his breathing heavy, his face intense. He was old now but that did not mean he no longer appreciated the female form. And these women, these twins, these white-eyed *creatures* that had been with him for the last five months, were sublime. Bizarre but sublime.

It was eerie how similar they were, identical in every way – even down to the bullet scar they each had on their left shoulder. Abu Yo'roub could not tell them apart – except for when they were going out. Then they put in the contact lenses; one wore brown, the other wore green. But when the lenses were out it was as if it was one person occupying two bodies. One person in two places at once.

He finished what he was doing and lay on his back, his heart racing. As he waited for it to calm down, he thought about his situation. He thought about Syria.

Abu Yo'roub – Major General Ghazi Kanaan, latterly the Minister of the Interior of Syria, formerly the man who had ruled Lebanon on Syria's behalf for twenty years – had committed suicide in his offices in Damascus on 12 October 2005 (8 Ramadan 1426). At least, that was the official story. That's what it said if you Googled him.

As if he would do such a thing! What idiot would think that? But he had needed a way out. He had been developing a powerbase against President Bashar al-Assad within the Syrian Regional Branch of the Arab Socialist Ba'ath Party, a powerbase that had hoped to oust al-Assad and install a less dynasty-based leadership for the good of Syria.

But he had been found out. His arrest had been only a matter of time. He had needed to disappear. So he had called in an expert. They had set up the elaborate suicide ploy, using a 'volunteer' who had born a passing resemblance to Ghazi Kanaan (in the body, the head did not matter if the face had been blown off).

Kanaan had fled the country, to wait for the day he knew would come soon. The day the uprising came to Syria, the rebellion which some fools sweetly called The Arab Spring. It had come on 11 March 2011.

Now Syria was in turmoil, a proxy regional war being played out on its streets: the Shi'ites of Syria, Iran and Lebanon (including the ruling Alawites) against the Sunnis of Syria, Qatar, Saudi and Lebanon. The Alawites, the Ba'ath Party, were simply not giving up like the rulers of other countries had done. No matter how many of their own people they killed.

But soon they would need a new ruler. What had started out as an insurrection against the Ba'ath Party and the Alawites had turned into a singular rebellion against the rule of the al-Assads. Kanaan was an Alawite but he was not an al-Assad. He would be a good compromise, a good interim ruler.

'Interim' being a very subjective term, of course…

Naked, Kanaan walked carefully down the narrow spiral staircase from the wind tower, supporting himself with the hand rail. One floor below, there was a discreet, waist-high service door. He opened it, bent down and went through. Across a small space of two metres there was another door. Bending through this one also, he was in the wet room of his suite.

He showered, his third wash of the day, and then went out into his spacious bedroom. He had left fresh clothes on the bed earlier, and now he dressed: a white cotton *izaar* underneath a white ankle length *dishdasha*, and house shoes.

He checked himself in the full-length mirror. His iron-grey hair was now long, down to his shoulders, and his beard was full. Before he returned to Syria his hair would be cut and his beard shaved off, but for now they served as a good camouflage. A disguise for a dead man.

"Abu Yo'roub."

Kanaan jumped and nearly pulled a muscle as he twisted around. One of the women was standing there. He had not heard her come in, he had not seen her reflection in the mirror. She was dressed like a western whore in tight denim jeans and a white cotton vest, her feet bare.

"Our meal is ready," she announced. "We telephoned but you did not answer."

"I – I was washing," he said instinctively, immediately cursing himself. These women were employees, he did not have to explain himself to them.

"As is right," she held open the bedroom door. As Kanaan walked past her, she asked "You have had a… *satisfying* afternoon?"

He did not reply. Curse these women, these *creatures*, and their temptations. Until they had arrived, he had lived here in

Oman in seclusion, in peace, for six years. In this house which had been built with *his* money. Just him, his two trusted assistants and a maid. Then, five months ago as the situation in Syria escalated into the all-out war against al-Assad, things had changed. His assistants and the maid had gone (they were buried out in the desert somewhere) and his expert had installed these two. Professional protectors, professional transporters. He trusted his expert, after all he had gotten him this far when really he should have died in that office in Damascus seven years ago. But why did he have to install *women*?

Behind him on the stairs, Paradise glided silently on her bare feet, smiling, as if she could hear his thoughts...

In the dressing room of the twins' suite on the ground floor, Love pulled on her jeans. Paradise had not worn underwear so neither would she. Flipping her long blonde hair out of the back of the white vest, she bent down to check herself in the dressing table mirror.

Her white eyes stared back at her. Or were they Paradise's eyes? She always thought when she looked in a mirror that she was looking at her sister, not herself. Mirror, mirror on the wall...

In their first few weeks here, they had worn their contact lenses when they were interacting with Abu Yo'roub, so as not to frighten the old man. But his attitude had not been good, he had been disdainful, querying the decision to install them, moaning that he did not need *these women*, saying he wanted back his assistants and the maid. So they had taken out their lenses and had let him see them as their true selves. And Abu Yo'roub had known what they were.

They had also explained about the conversions that had been performed on the assistants and the maid. Conversions from sentient beings to dead rotting carrion. The staff would not be coming back.

Love was content with what she saw in the mirror and she straightened up. As she did so she glanced at the large round silver pendant, the *sumt*, which was draped over one edge of the mirror. Folklore had it that a djinn was imprisoned inside each *sumt*. But there was no djinn in this one – yet. But it did contain something else.

As she often did, Love reached over and gently shook the pendant. The objects inside clicked against their prison walls. Fingernails. Ten of them. Love remembered the day in Byblos when she and Paradise had ripped them off of their captive.

The *sumt* had waited two years for the rest of The Djinn and it would wait for as long as it needed to.

One day, Love and Paradise knew, they would find her. *Houri* never left business unfinished…

# 25 October 2012
# 9 Dhu al-Hijja 1433

## Bourj el-Barajneh, Beirut 08:00

Major Jihad Merhi could not believe his eyes. He was leaning against his Toyota Land Cruiser, dressed casually in trainers, jeans and grey shirt, having only his fourth Camel King Size of the day, when Fadi Lattouf stepped out of the battered front door of his small house into Annan Street.

Merhi straightened up, raised his dark glasses to confirm what he was seeing, and let them drop back down again onto his nose.

Lattouf had stopped, hand still on his doorknob, likewise staring at Merhi.

"Go and get changed," said Merhi.

"M-morning of joy, my dear friend."

"Morning of joy, Fadi. Now go and get changed."

Lattouf was dressed in his full uniform: blue trousers, blue shirt (my God, he was even wearing what passed as a tie), Captains' jacket over his arm, peaked Captain's hat balanced perilously on the back of his huge head, like a skull cap. "But we are on official business, no?"

"Yes. In the south. Near the border. You should not be wearing that. Just like your car," Merhi pointed to the glaring orange Datsun Bluebird parked nearby, one front wheel up on the kerb. "I doubt it could even get past the airport without breaking down, but if it did get to the south it would be a target for the Jews. So will your uniform. Didn't you think?"

Lattouf humphed. "We should not be intimidated in our own land."

Merhi was not even going there. You were a Palestinian, Fadi, your people were long-term guests enjoying the hospitality of Lebanon. This was not your land.

"But," nodded Lattouf, " I understand what you are saying. I will change." He pushed the front door back open, shouting "Nada! Open my wardrobe. I need clothes, quickly woman!" and disappeared back inside.

He was back fifteen minutes later, chewing on a little something he had picked up on his way out. He was now dressed in his usual casual outfit, probably the only one he had: the loose pink and blue checked shirt and rough blue denim jeans, above old trainers. His black and grey chest hair poked out of the open neck of his shirt like a 1970s porn star, and his stranded comb-over was freshly slicked down. And he was wearing sunglasses, like Merhi.

He pointed to his glasses as he came over. "Like them? Genuine Ray-Bans. I got them off a stall in Hamra the other day. Only thirty-six thousand pounds."

Merhi shook his head. "You were done, Fadi. You should have knocked them down." Thirty-six thousand Lebanese pounds. Twenty-four dollars. Nineteen euros. Fifteen pounds sterling. For genuine Ray-Bans. "*Yalla.*"

Lattouf got into the passenger side of the Land Cruiser while Merhi had to climb noticeably higher back into his side. As he stretched round to find his seatbelt, Lattouf let out an almighty burp which must have fluttered the banners across the road within a ten block radius. "Unstrained goat's yoghurt," he explained. "Excuse me."

Merhi both turned up the air conditioning and nudged the down button on his window as the sour air glided up his nostrils. Well, it was mild compared to some of the odours and noises Lattouf had emitted on previous occasions in this vehicle.

On perfect, pernicious cue, Lattouf leant to his left, raised his right butt cheek and let out a stentorian blast of gas. "Last night's giblets and rice."

Merhi just looked at him, keeping his finger on the window button so that it opened fully.

Lattouf settled down comfortably, his head almost touching the ceiling, even in this large, powerful car. He smiled. "I feel better now. Well, my friend, let us go. We have a spy to collect. *Yalla.*"

Praying to God that traffic on the southern Coastal Highway would be light, Merhi engaged Drive and pulled out.

Heading south.

## Southern Coastal Highway, Lebanon 09:00-11:00

Some say southern Lebanon is the most beautiful part of the country, unspoilt, less developed than cosmopolitan Beirut and places to the north. It has coastal beaches, the beautiful blue Mediterranean, groves of bananas, oranges and lemons, and pine-forested mountains culminating in the snow-capped Mount Lebanon range in the mid-distance to the east. Druze live in the Chouf Mountains, Sunni Muslims in Sidon and Shi'a Muslims around Nabatiye. But it is a part of the country where tourists and casual visitors rarely venture – because of its recent history. Only in May 2000 was the south liberated from its twenty-two year Israeli occupation. Twice, in 1996 and 2006, the Israelis 'mistakenly' massacred hundreds of civilians in the once-pretty town of Qana on the pretext of attacking Hizbullah to stop their Katyusha rocket bombardment of northern Israel. In 2012, the extreme south below Tyre was still patrolled by the Lebanese Army and UNIFIL (the United Nations Interim Force In Lebanon), a presence which did not stop sporadic attacks from Lebanon into Israel and Israel into Lebanon. And the border area still remained full of unexploded landmines and other ordnance.

Merhi and Lattouf drove south along the highway. The

further south they went, the more military and paramilitary roadblocks ('security checks') they encountered, but they passed through them unhindered, the bored guards giving them only cursory visual checks. They passed banana plantations and citrus groves, roadside traders holding up freshly-caught fish, stalls brimming with locally-grown vegetables and fruit. Eventually the temptations – and Lattouf's pleading – became too much. Just beyond el Jiye, Merhi pulled over and bought some bananas and oranges from a wizened old Druze who looked so ancient he must have been alive at the time of the Prophet (Peace Be Upon Him).

Back in the Toyota and back on the highway, orange and banana skins popped out of the passenger window at regular intervals, as if marking a trail for them to find their way back. Momentarily, a banana skin was caught on the edge of the roof, flapping like a dog's tongue in the wind before velocity whipped it off into the air.

They travelled onwards, through more security checks, through the eastern edge of the coastal town of Sidon, now the municipal capital of south Lebanon and once the northern border of Canaan. Three kilometres further, they passed a huge statue of the Virgin Mary on a hilltop to their left, marking the village of Maghdouche to where it is said Mary came after the crucifixion of Christ, to await his resurrection.

Then the road split at a roundabout dominated by statue of a hand holding a huge Soviet-style sickle, a memorial to a freedom-fighter killed in the war against Israel. The road to the left headed up into the hills to the town of Nabatiye, said to be the spiritual home of Hizbullah and the Shi'a faith. Merhi stayed to the right, continuing down the coast.

As the coastal flatland became more rugged, more desolate, so the highway petered out. 'Under Construction' signs appeared, although there was little sign of any construction going on. At Masrat el Ouastra they doglegged right onto the old, small coastal highway and drove the final ten kilometres along the edge of the Mediterranean down into Tyre.

## Bourj al-Shimali, Lebanon 11:20 – 14:30

Turning left just beyond the vast al-Bass archaeological site on the landward side of ancient Tyre, they drove for three kilometres, back across the proposed highway, to the Bourj al-Shimali refugee camp.

Lattouf wiped his beard, his mood darkening noticeably as they pulled up, the Toyota attracting some curious looks. "Another shit hole," he said quietly. "May Allah have mercy on them."

Merhi had to agree. Created in 1955, the camp housed an estimated nineteen thousand people, mostly refugees from the villages of Hula and Tiberias in Palestine. Being on the edge of the UNIFIL zone, it had attracted its share of bombardments from the occupied country to the south, although it was not the nearest camp to Palestine: that dubious honour was held by Rashidiyeh, five kilometres away.

It was similar to Lattouf's camp at Barajneh, but wider, more spread out. Still the basic brick constructions which pass as dwellings, not quite as tight together as Barajneh; some paths possibly enjoying the opulence of a full three-metres width with a sewage channel running down the middle. There were the usual broken water pipes, broken windows and hanging cables. A basic refugee camp, it could have been anywhere. A displaced people of dignity stripped of their dignity.

An old man using two makeshift crutches passed by, looking into the car, rheumy eyes in a weather-beaten face beneath a black and white *keffiyeh* worn turban-style.

Lattouf nodded at him, then shook his head after the old man had hobbled on. He sighed again. "This is wrong, so wrong, after all this time."

Merhi rarely saw the serious side of his friend, and he could only wonder what thoughts were going around his head.

Lattouf rarely spoke about what he had experienced as a corporal in the West Bank and then as a sergeant in Gaza, before his promotion to the relative 'luxury' of the Lebanese camps. In fact, Merhi knew very little about the backstory of his friend. He needed to rectify that.

But not now. "Do you know where the police office is?" he asked.

"Just in there, to the left. Our offices are always on the edge of the camp, for obvious reasons."

They got out, a noticeable wheeze of relief coming from the Toyota's suspension on the passenger side. Lattouf pulled his underwear out of his crevice. Merhi ensured his shirt was covering the gun in his waistband.

Before they had gone two paces, a deep subwoofer voice from behind them said, "Gentlemen welcome, *al-salaam 'aalaykum.*"

Lattouf turned. A man was walking down the road towards them. Tall, bald-headed, clean shaven, deeply tanned, dressed in a light blue shirt with dark blue cargo pants tucked into black boots. A gun bounced in a holster on his belt, next to other little pouches containing handcuffs and other law-enforcing nick-nacks. He exuded a strong presence.

"*'aalaykum al-salaam,*" Lattouf smiled and gave a small bow. "Abu Jad it is good to see you again. How are you? How is your family?"

"They are well, *alhamdulillah*. And your family, Abu Fadi?"

"*Alhamdulillah.*"

They shook hands and then embraced. Coming out of the hold, Lattouf said "May I introduce you to Cap – Major Merhi of the Internal Security Force. Major, this is Captain Manar al-Jayouchi."

"*Salaam,*" Merhi shook the proffered hand.

"*Salaam, Ra'id.* You have come for the spy," said al-Jayouchi. "He is waiting for you."

"Has he said anything?"

al-Jayouchi shrugged with his mouth, shoulders and forearms. "He is finding it difficult to talk."

Merhi could imagine. Swollen mouth, perhaps? Any of his teeth left?

"But let us not worry about the traitor for a moment," continued al-Jayouchi. "You have both come a long way. You must take refreshment." He began to lead them into the camp. "How are things in Beirut now?"

It was Merhi's turn to shrug. "Fragile."

"Indeed. These Syrians, what are they doing to themselves? How will it end, I wonder?"

"Badly," said Merhi.

They stopped outside a single-storey breezeblock building, possibly the only structure in the camp with unbroken windows. On the roof were various tall antennae and even a satellite dish; inside, electric lights were on. al-Jayouchi beckoned them in. "You must be hungry after your journey. I have coffee, dates and fish stew. We will eat together."

"You are too kind," said Merhi. "But we really - "

"Have to build up our energy for our long journey back," Lattouf patted al-Jayouchi on the shoulder. "Thank you, my friend. May Allah bless your hospitality." He went into the building, metaphorically already tucking a napkin into his neckline.

"And," al-Jayouchi turned to Merhi as Lattouf went ahead. "I have a particularly fine whisky. A malt from Scotland. From Egypt via Gaza. Excellent quality. Would you like a drink, Major? To celebrate *Eid*?"

The holding cells were not in the breezeblock building but out the back, across a rubble-strewn yard. In the one crumbling brick construction, there were two peeling solid wooden doors, with two small unglazed air slits just below the level of the combined wooden roof. Merhi thought it looked like an old outside toilet, literally the shit hole Fadi had been talking about;

it certainly smelt like it.

One of the doors was ajar, the other closed with a wooden batten across it. Captain al-Jayouchi raised the batten and pulled open the door. Hot, putrid air rolled out, making Merhi snap his head to the side involuntarily.

After the initial pungent eruption had levelled off into a general all-embracing stench, Merhi squinted into the dark interior. He had been right. Towards the back was a hole in the ground where countless souls had deposited their personal waste over the years. And next to the hole sat a male with a sack over his head, his hands in front of him, tied with rope, blood-stained where it had chafed his wrists. The head in the sack moved, turning towards the door.

"Your spy," said al-Jayouchi.

Merhi's voice was mellow and slightly hoarse after three thick coffees and three whiskies (not to mention the fish stew and dates). "Get him out."

Lattouf went in and grabbed the prisoner by his arm, dragging him outside into the sun. Roughly he pulled him upright, supporting him with one giant hand when it looked like his legs would give way. Merhi ripped off the sack.

It was a boy, a teenager, probably about eighteen. Dark hair, dark skin, bum-fluff beard. His face was bruised, lips cracked and bloodied – but it looked like his teeth were intact, at least those that were left. He scrunched his eyes against the sunlight.

For a moment, Merhi studied him, taking in the sandals, worn denim jeans and dirty, blood-spotted shirt. Then he asked, "*Ma shimkha?*"

There was no reaction, the prisoner kept his head down, but Lattouf and al-Jayouchi looked surprised at Merhi speaking Hebrew.

"*Chou esmak?*" Merhi tried again in local Arabic. "What is your name?"

The prisoner raised his head, a glimmer of understanding in his eyes, but he did not speak.

"The cat has his tongue," Lattouf shook him roughly. "Let me loosen it."

"Later, Fadi, later." Merhi looked at al-Jayouchi. "Do you know him?"

al-Jayouchi shook his head. "No. Says he's been living here for years - "

"And you don't know him?"

al-Jayouchi raised his eyebrows. Lattouf said, "We keep the peace, we are not census registrars. Especially with the amount of people in our camps."

Merhi nodded acceptance of the point. "Why do you think he is a spy?"

al-Jayouchi opened the flap of the right pocket in his cargo pants and pulled out a small Nokia cell phone, handing it to Merhi. "He was seen to leave this beneath some stones out by the highway. An old woman was passing, thought he had dropped it. When she tried to give it back to him, he said it was not his."

"It is not mine," mumbled the prisoner. His accent was Palestinian.

"Ah, so now he talks!" Lattouf shook him again.

al-Jayouchi continued, "So she brought the phone to me. She knew the traitor, had seen him about the camp. She pointed him out."

"But why do you think he is a spy?"

"Look at it. At the photos." He saw Merhi was fumbling. "Here, give it to me."

With a few finger-presses, al-Jayouchi opened the photo app. "Look," he passed the phone back.

Merhi pulled reading glasses out of his pocket, ignoring Lattouf's comment of "Hey, I have never seen those. You look good. I must get some next time I'm in Hamra."

Merhi shielded the small screen from the sunlight. The first pictures were of a village. Normal homesteads… then destroyed homesteads. Then something which could have been an unexploded rocket. Some mortar shells. At the sight of pictures of two memorials, he began to understand where it was. He looked up. "Qana?"

al-Jayouchi nodded. "It is a ten kilometre walk. He has no explanation of why he was there."

"It is not my phone - "

"Shut up!" Lattouf slapped the prisoner round the back of the head. "You speak only when the Major speaks to you."

Then there were pictures of UN troops and UN vehicles in convoy, then some amphibious craft on the shore. Finally there were pictures of hand-held missile launchers, carried by men with their faces covered by their *keffiyeh*. Undoubtedly Hizbullah.

"Surely the Israelis are not thinking of a third strike on Qana?" mused Merhi.

al-Jayouchi sniffed. "I would put nothing past those bastards."

"Maybe that is just what the Party of God is thinking too," said Lattouf. "Where better to hide your arsenal than a place the Jews would not dare attack again?"

Merhi looked at his friend. He never ceased to be amazed at the insightful pearls that, just occasionally, came from Fadi Lattouf. Lattouf was right, of course and as always.

"Do you have anything to say?" Merhi said to the prisoner.

Silence.

"By the way, what is his name?"

"Abdul Abdulrahman," said al-Jayouchi.

Merhi did not comment. Unimaginative parents.

"Well?" said Merhi.

Abdul Abdulrahman was silent.

"Who were you leaving this for, out on the highway? Who was going to collect it? When?"

Nothing.

"Ah, the cat she is back!" Lattouf nearly ripped the prisoner's arm off with his shaking. He was close to causing minor brain damage at the very least. "We will loosen it! I will make this bastard talk. Give me something to insert into him."

"He will talk, Fadi," said Merhi. "He will talk. But not here, back in Beirut. You will be the official Palestinian observer at his interrogation."

Lattouf smiled at the honour.

Merhi put the phone into his pocket and turned to al-Jayouchi. "I think we are done here. Thank you, Captain. Excellent work."

al-Jayouchi inclined his head in gracious acceptance.

Merhi nodded at Lattouf. "Fadi, bring him."

As they were walking back across the rubble to the main building, Merhi said "There is just one thing before we go, Manar, if you would be so kind."

"Of course, Major. What can I do?"

Both men looked as the prisoner stumbled and fell to the ground in front of them after a too-hard shove from Lattouf. He was immediately yanked back up again, dust covering his jeans, Lattouf berating him and telling him he would need to brush himself down, he was not getting into the Major's car in that state.

Merhi shook his head then continued, "For the road. Perhaps just one more shot of your Egyptian Scottish whisky...?"

## Southern Coastal Highway, Lebanon 14:30-16:30

Having had five whiskies, Merhi decided to let Lattouf drive the Toyota back, at least until they got to the Bourj el-Barajneh camp in southern Beirut where he would drop Lattouf off and then take the prisoner into the central lock-up in the Hotel Dieu district.

Lattouf was like a child at Eid as he familiarised himself with the controls before setting off. The weight of Merhi and Abdul Abdulrahman in the back seat provided an element of counterbalance but the fulcrum still erred in favour of the front.

Now they were on their way. They had curved into and back out of Tyre and were heading north along the old coastal road. Traffic was medium-light, most security checks were unmanned.

Abdul Abdulrahman sat on Merhi's right, so that he was not behind Lattouf. He was sullen, looking out of the window, hands still tied in front of him with the blood-stained rope. And, despite the car's air conditioning being on full blast, he stank.

Anticipating the prisoner's piquancy, Merhi had opened the back windows before they set off.

They all wore seatbelts, not only because Lattouf was driving (reason enough) but also because the car would start beeping at them if they did not.

The Toyota purred along. They could see the Mediterranean to their left and hear it breaking on the shore below the escarpment a few metres beyond the edge of the road. The warm windrush was pleasant and not too loud, a small price for the reduction in smell in the car.

"When will we start the interrogation?" asked Lattouf loudly so that he could be heard, left arm on the window edge, lightly controlling the steering wheel with his right hand.

"Tomorrow," said Merhi from behind him.

"Not today?"

"No."

"I could make him talk. The first thing I would do, Major, is to pluck out his eyes, like a sheep's head at a feast. Then I would cut off his sweetbreads one by one - "

"Yes, thank you Fadi. Enough. We have more... sophisticated techniques."

"But are they as effective?"

Merhi hmmphed. Lattouf had a point. He looked at the prisoner next to him. "You can make it easy on yourself, you know. Talk to me. Why did you take those pictures? Who were you leaving the phone for? Who was going to collect it?"

Abdul Abdulrahman continued to look out of the window,

saying nothing.

Merhi shook his head. Foolhardy bravery. And the chances were that this fool did not know the answers anyway. He wasn't a Jewish spy with his raincoat collar turned up, hat pulled down over his eyes, with the theme from *The Third Man* playing in the background. He was just a skinny runt of a Palestinian, probably being paid what to him would be a fortune (but which would not buy a cup of coffee in Beirut) to take some pictures and leave the phone somewhere.

They would get the information, or lack of information, out of him, but it might cost him his life. Or at least his sanity.

"Your choice," said Merhi.

"Major," said Lattouf. "We are coming to the turning for the highway, but can we stay on this coastal road, at least to Sidon? It is very pretty, no? I have never seen it before."

"Why not?" said Merhi, staring out to sea. "There'll be much less traffic, chances are we'll make better time this way anyway."

"*Shukran!*" Uncharacteristically mindful of other traffic, Lattouf flicked on the left indicator to show he was travelling straight on and not dog-legging to the right as most of the other cars would be doing. The vehicles behind him pulled more to the right, including a motorbike.

They passed the turning. The cars turned off, the motorbike stayed on the coast road.

"Hello, what is this?" frowned Lattouf, looking across into the right side mirror. "A stupid motorbike trying to overtake on the inside. We'll see about that." The Toyota jolted as he wrenched the wheel to the right, closing off the gap for the bike.

Above the gentle roar of the windrush, Merhi heard an angry bip-bip from the bike as it was forced back behind the Toyota and out to the left.

"*Ahbal!*" shouted Lattouf. "Idiot! Learn the rules of the road!" This from a Palestinian. In Lebanon.

The bike growled loudly as it accelerated. Merhi looked to his left. It was a big, powerful machine, probably a Ducati or similar. The rider was dressed completely in black: black boots, black leather trousers and blouson, black helmet with a black visor. One black glove -

And a black Herstal FN Five-SeveN in the other hand.

"Gun!" shouted Merhi.

As always in moments of mortal danger, everything happened at once but to the protagonists it seemed like it played out in slow motion.

A flame shot out of the barrel of the gun. Merhi dived to his right, making a grab for Abdul, hindered by his seatbelt, unclipping it, fumbling for his gun. He felt the heat as the bullet missed him by five centimetres.

Lattouf swung the car to the left, nudging the bike. It wobbled, the rider fighting to keep control.

Merhi pulled Abdul forward, ordering "Stay down!" Then he raised his gun, pointing it out the window.

The bike accelerated, speeding off down the road.

"I'll get him!" screamed Lattouf, stepping on the pedal. "You fucking *kakhbah!*"

"No, Fadi, no, no!" shouted Merhi. "Pull over, pull over." He tapped Lattouf rapidly on the shoulder. "Leave him, let him go, let him go."

They were on the left side of the road and Lattouf slowed down, pulling up onto the sandy verge.

"Are you all right?" Lattouf undid his seatbelt, turning.

"I'm fine. I'm fine. Fucking felt the bullet go past though."

"What about him?"

Merhi grabbed Abdul by the shirt and pulled him back up. The boy was alive. The bullet must have passed clean through the car, in one open window, out the other.

The boy was trembling, lips quivering, bound hands shaking. A look downwards showed that he had pissed himself.

"Oh, thank you so very much," sneered Merhi.

"What?" Lattouf looked over the seat.

"He's pissed himself. Get out before it goes on the seat." He leant over and undid Abdul's seatbelt. "Go on, out, out. We should have brought your car, Fadi."

"Talking of which," Lattouf stepped out of the car, the suspension bouncing. "Funny how a brush with Allah loosens your natural functions." He walked three paces away from the car, onto the top of the escarpment. Standing with his back to the road, legs apart, he undid his fly.

With his gun still in his hand, Merhi got out to meet Abdul coming round the back of the car. "You too," he instructed. "Come on. And take your trousers and underwear off, you're not sitting in my car in those."

Abdul went up and stood near Lattouf, who had begun to urinate like an elephant.

Abdul dropped his trousers and then his grubby underwear, stepping out of them and kicking them away.

"Not too close, *merci ktir*," said Lattouf staring straight ahead.

But then Abdul took off, over the top of the ridge.

"No!" shouted Merhi. "Fadi, grab hold of him!"

But all Lattouf had hold of was something the size and colour of a salami sausage which he was pissing out of.

"I can't - !"

"Shit!" Merhi slithered down the embankment. "Abdul! Come back, you idiot!"

The boy was running across the sand about five metres ahead, naked except for his shirt.

"Abdul! Abdulrahman!" Merhi tried to keep up, sand flying up in puffs around his feet and into his shoes, the effort pulling at his calves. "Stop now! Stop, or I *will* shoot!"

But Abdul kept on running. He was hampered by his hands tied in front of him, but he was moving further away, Merhi losing ground.

"Oh hell," said Merhi, his breath going. "Oh fuck." He stopped. "Abdul!" It was almost a plea.

The boy did not turn round.

Merhi raised his gun. "Abdul…"

He fired.

A mist of red and pink sprayed upwards from Abdul Abdulrahman. His back? His head?

He did not stop running but he veered to the left, towards the sea. Then his legs began to buckle, wobbling like a new-born foal. He staggered, wobbled, reached the water, and fell face-down into the waves.

He was still, not moving, not trying to raise his head for breath.

Merhi clenched his teeth, growling first and then shouting. "Ohhhhhh BOLLOCKS!"

There was a huffing and puffing as Lattouf wheezed up beside him, still fumbling with his flies. When his zip was up he said, "Amazing shooting, my friend. Allah has guided your hand." He saw Merhi's grim, ashen face. "He is not a martyr, he is a traitor."

"He was a boy."

"There was nothing else you could do. He was an escaping spy."

They watched as Abdul's body bobbed gently on top of a beach break wave, then a backwash took him and he was accepted by the sea.

"I should go get him," said Merhi.

"No," said Lattouf. "He will wash up. He doesn't care, Shaitan has him now."

Or Allah, thought Merhi, depending on which side you were on.

Both men heard a faint noise and they turned at the same time. Up over the escarpment, the Toyota's doors were open and it was ping-pinging a warning that somebody had taken their seatbelt off while the vehicle was still in motion.

*Ping-ping-ping, ping-ping-ping, ping-ping-ping…*

## Coastal Highway, Lebanon 17:00-19:00

It was a subdued journey back, Lattouf shutting up after his reassurances that there was nothing else Merhi could have done had fallen on deaf ears. As he drove, he ate the remaining fruit they had bought that morning, propping the bananas between his legs while they awaited their fate. Visually unfortunate.

After the adrenalin high of the shooting, Merhi had plunged back down into a vortex of gloom. He knew Lattouf was right, there was nothing else he could have done. The prisoner had been trying to escape, and both Lattouf and Merhi were too old for a successful chase and apprehension. It was not the first time he had taken a life but he never liked doing it, especially as the target had been a scared, unarmed boy.

He was angry. Not at Captain Fadi Lattouf, not at Captain Manar al-Jayouchi, not even at himself. At Abdul Abdulrahman he was annoyed (you stupid, stupid boy) but he was angry at the Israelis. They said all was fair in love and war, but using a boy, a Palestinian whose parents they themselves had thrown out of their homeland, was low, really low.

It was interesting though that they had tried to kill Abdul after he had been captured. Firstly, how did they know? Had they been watching? Or perhaps when the phone had not been under the rock, they had put two and two together? But why try to kill him? That seemed to indicate that the boy knew something, something the Israelis did not want getting out.

Merhi dragged on his Camel King Size and snorted at his thoughts. Well, whatever it was, Abdul would not be telling them now – because Merhi had done the Israelis job for them! *Ya khorg!*

## Bourj el-Barajneh, Beirut 19:10

Lattouf pulled up the Toyota with his trademark one front wheel on the kerb. Both men got out. Darkness had fallen.

"You will come in, my friend?"

"*Merci*, Fadi." Merhi shook his head.

"Nada is preparing *maqluba* tonight. She knew I would be hungry after a hard day's travelling."

"The temptation is great but no, thank you. You have my portion." Merhi slid slightly as he got into the driver's side, the leather seat had not yet adjusted back to normality after supporting Lattouf's enormous arse for four hours.

Lattouf pushed the car door closed. "You are going into the office?"

"No, it can all happen tomorrow. I thought of getting the local boys to look for the body, maybe the Coastguard. But you know what?"

"What would be the point?"

"Exactly. He is with his deity. Sorry there won't be any interrogation for you to attend."

"That is life, my friend. Or death."

Merhi lit up a cigarette, offering the packet to the Palestinian. Lattouf jumped back as if scolded, making negative hand gestures in front of his body, nodding backwards and shaking his head, eyes panicking, ending with his mouth stretched across and downwards. A human *Emoji*.

Merhi smiled, understanding. The power of wives. "Okay then." They shook hands through the car window. "New Year if not before, Fadi. And thanks for everything today."

"*Eid Mubarak*, my friend. Allah's blessing to Gisele and your family."

"And *Eid Mubarak* to you and yours. What a way to start a holiday! Give Nada a big kiss from me. *Khaetrak*." Bouncing the wheel off the kerb, Merhi drove off.

Lattouf watched the Toyota's lights disappear northwards. Then he waddled over to his doorway. He did not have a key, there was no outside lock only inside bolts, and the door was never bolted until Baba was home. As he went in he shouted, "Baba is home, children! You are safe for another night. *Eid*

*Mubarak!* Wife, come here! I have something to give you from my good friend Jihad…!"

## Jounieh, Lebanon 21:15 – 23:59

Traffic was manageable on the main Coastal Highway heading north out of Beirut (in other words, it was moving), which was just as well because Merhi's mind was not particularly on his driving. He was tired and he was grumpy. And his mood was not helped by the thoughts of the amount of paperwork he would now have to fill in because he had shot someone. Even an Israeli spy demanded reams.

He supposed he would have to get used to it now that the eradication of spies was within his remit. Thank God the late Brigadier and his team (which was now *his* team) had cleared most of them out. As far as he could tell from the meetings he had had already and the reports he had read, there was only a small caucus left, in the Beirut area. A small confession. A little group of hardy weeds which The Gardener had to eradicate.

Today had been an offshoot, a little sucker springing up way outside the main infestation. Minor, non-pernicious… But Abdul Abdulrahman was important enough for somebody to try to kill him. Who had it been? Merhi had no reason to doubt his earlier supposition that it was the person who had been sent to pick up the phone with the photographs. The border with Palestine was porous, a Jew on a motorbike could come across anywhere.

But there was something, just something, nagging at Merhi. Something about the attempted execution, something that had subliminally registered with him at the time but which he had then lost in the tumult of Abdul's forlorn escape. Something that had come and gone as quickly as his bullet had entered Abdul Abdulrahman and ended his life. What had it been?

He shrugged and threw the butt of his cigarette out of the window as he turned off the highway, reducing speed as the road narrowed and began its climb into the mountains...

It was a moonless night and the full beams of the Toyota sliced into the darkness like the heat-ray eyes of a gas-guzzling monster as it turned off the mountain road and bounced down the dirt track that led to the apartment block. The block was built into the mountain in such a way that you entered from the side in the middle, at the third floor level. The Merhis' apartment was on the fifth floor, the top.

He reversed into his usual place a little way past the main entrance in a gravelled area where the other eight residents of the building also parked, next to Gisele's older ex-official issue blue Toyota Land Cruiser LC5 (on which he had got a good deal). There were allotted parking spaces underneath the block, but as that was two stories further down the mountainside nobody ever bothered. Here was fine, by mutual tacit agreement.

Merhi switched off the AC, the headlights and the engine, and sat for a moment. He could see the lights were on in their apartment above. Gisele had been in the office giving a training course today and she would have picked up some food on the way back. He was hungry but he hoped it wasn't her speciality, *sayadieh*, fish with rice, not after the *delights* of the fish stew down in Tyre. Then again it might be good to counteract it.

He flipped the steering column wand as he stepped out of the car so that the headlights went back on to illuminate his way to the front door. They would stay on for thirty seconds after he had pressed the remote central locking button.

Halfway to the door, he held the key fob over his shoulder and pressed the button. The car did not beep but the indicator lights flashed as it locked.

"Hello Captain."

He froze, the shock of the voice from the darkness nearly making him expel the fish stew. Instinctively his right arm pressed against the gun on his waistband.

He did not move. Ahead, his own shadow from the car's lights grew and spread across the ground, losing itself in the cliff-edge bushes. Way out at sea he noticed lights on a boat. Carefully his hand unclipped the top of his holster.

He turned but his car's beams were blinding, he could see nothing. He heard the lightest of footsteps on the gravel.

Then the lights went out, plunging the area back into darkness. And still he could see nothing, just an impression of the beams seared onto his retina.

The footsteps moved closer, coming from behind the parking area. Up above, he could now see the stars sprinkled in the black night sky, his eyes adjusting.

A small shadow came towards him, between the two Toyotas. His hand remained on his holster but he had not drawn his gun – because he had recognised the voice. The deep, deep voice. A voice he thought about often.

The shadow stopped two metres in front of him.

"It – it's Major," said Merhi. "Not Captain, Major."

"Really? I'm impressed. Well, okay then *Major* Merhi. It has been a while, are you not pleased to see me?"

Carla Chedid took three paces forward, reached up and kissed Jihad Merhi full on the mouth.

Gisele Merhi had four emotions when her husband came through the door with a woman, with *this* woman. Jealousy - of course, goes without saying, she was a Lebanese wife after all. Surprise – an unexpected visitor, and this late in the evening, and after she'd had a hard day's work as well. Pleasure – she liked Carla, they had formed a close bond when they had met previously. Distress – at the fact that she was not dressed to receive a visitor, indeed she was hardly dressed at all. Okay, she and Carla had seen each other naked before when they had gone shopping and had tried on clothes and done other girlie things together, but it was hardly polite to greet a guest in just a thin red T-shirt and small yellow shorts, both of which showed that she was wearing nothing underneath. But then, Carla was hardly dressed formally either: loose white T-shirt over black leggings with black and white baseball shoes. And her T-shirt showed that she was wearing nothing underneath either.

After gasps of greeting, the women embraced with three cheek-kisses. Gisele smelt jasmine.

"I found her downstairs," explained Jihad who was only slowly recovering from the hint of tongue he had received. (Had it been deliberate, accidental, or just instinctive?)

"I found *him*," smiled Carla. "I was here first. I was halfway up the stairs when I realised I had left my phone, so I went back down to get it. And along comes your husband."

"Well come in, come in. You are always welcome to our home. Dinner is just about ready."

"Oh no, really - "

"Nonsense, there is plenty."

"You have had your haircut," said Carla. (Jihad raised his eyebrows. Girl-talk already and she was hardly through the door.) "I like it."

"I think it is too short. It does not hide my *wasm*." Gisele stroked the scar on her neck, the souvenir of Paris in 1997.

"It is beautiful." Carla reached out and lightly touched the back of Gisele's hand. "We all have our souvenirs of battle." She wiggled her fingers, drawing Gisele's attention to the lack of nails. The last time Gisele had seen Carla's fingers they had all been bandaged. "And my husband has many, many scars."

"He is not with you?"

"No, he is doing other things."

Their eyes held for a beat and then Gisele said, "Jihad, make our guest comfortable while I serve the food." She turned to her husband.

And, her look said, find out what the hell she is doing here.

"Gisele, *habibti*, that was wonderful. I have missed your cooking." Carla settled herself into one of the sofas in the lounge, placing her small, handleless cup of Turkish coffee on the side table.

"It was just *moghrabieh*," Gisele carried in the *rakwe*, the long-handled coffee pot, and put it on the table. She sat down on the same couch, at the other end.

"It is never *just* with your dishes, darling."

"You are too kind."

Jihad came in, coffee in one hand, cigarette and glass of whisky in the other. He paused when he saw the two women on the same sofa and then he sat down in the one opposite.

The room was warm, the lighting low to befit the hour.

Two subjects had dominated dinner: how things were in New York (interesting, there was never a dull moment at the UN, especially in the Security Council) and how things were in Lebanon (going to hell in a handcart and the speed was increasing). As a corollary, talk also turned to *Major* Merhi, with congratulations, respect and teasing dished out by the women in equal portions.

Now Jihad stubbed out his cigarette in a glass ashtray. "So - "

"Why am I here?" Carla had long ago taken off her shoes and she tucked her feet up under her, mirroring Gisele's naked olive legs. "Not only here in Liban, but why am I here with you?"

"There are still people who want to talk to you about the Hariri killing. The International Tribunal is due to report at any time."

"I bet it will be years yet. And when they do, it will be a fudge. Either that or civil war will return to Liban. Whenever a Sunni dies they blame the Shi'ites, and *wa'l-aks* whenever a Shi'ite dies. Sometimes there are other answers. And anyway, they want to talk to Zahia Zalloum not Carla Chedid. Zahia Zalloum disappeared on 14 February 2005... as you know."

"Hmm." Jihad drank whisky.

"Have the investigators spoken to *you*?"

Jihad paused with the glass on his lips.

"I thought not," continued Carla, "so we both have

something to be grateful for."

And something to hide, thought Jihad, finishing his drink.

"I am here because I have been given some information." She heard the question before Jihad had a chance to ask it. "It is too important to transmit electronically. I must speak with someone. Tell them face to face."

"Who?"

She shrugged her shoulders and took a sip of her coffee, stretching and topping up her cup as she put it back down on the table. She raised the *rakwe* in the air. Gisele held out her cup for refilling. Jihad shook his head.

"I do not know," said Carla. "Up until a week ago it would have been Brigadier Wissam al-Hassan."

For a moment, silence. Jihad's face was stone. Then he said, "What?" The temperature in the room had plummeted like a rock thrown down the mountainside.

Carla's black eyes stared into his. "Who has taken over from him? I need to speak to him."

"Why?"

"Jihad?" Gisele had picked up the abrupt change in her husband.

"Why, Carla? We all know that the Brigadier was my ultimate boss."

"Yes, that is why I came to you."

Jihad knew he could not outstare the black eyes, but he made a valiant effort, his face hard. In eye wrestling, a djinn would always triumph over a mere mortal. As he felt her winning, he broke the hold and stood up, going over to a cabinet. He slid open a door to reveal bottles of various whiskies and *arak*, the Lebanese male's alcohols of choice. He filled his tumbler with Johnnie Walker.

"I am sorry about his death," said Carla. "But it is imperative that I speak to his successor."

Jihad was shaking his head. He walked over to the patio window which led out onto the balcony. He could see nothing in the darkness except a muted reflection of the room behind him. He spoke to the glass. "Things have changed. Already. Things have been delegated, devolved."

Carla said nothing but in the reflection Jihad could see her looking at him. Looking into him.

"If you could tell me what it is about...?" he continued. "And don't say 'Sajida was right' because I will personally throw you off this balcony, djinn or no djinn."

Carla smiled at his reference to the al-Mahdi incident. She looked from Jihad to Gisele. They were all security cleared, she by the Department of General Security, the Major by the Internal Security Force, Gisele by both. She finished her coffee and said, "I have seen a report. From Tel Aviv. About the Israeli spy cell network in Lebanon, which your Brigadier demolished."

"Almost demolished."

"More than you think. Although spies are self-replenishing and it will be an ongoing battle, for the time being he got them all."

"I am pleased to hear that. We thought we had a few still to go."

"It seems not. You have got them all. Except one."

Jihad turned from the window. "Except one?"

Carla took her feet down and leant forward. "Major, there is one left. And it is internal. You have a spy in the ISF."

# 26 October 2012
# 10 Dhu al-Hijja 1433

## Jounieh, Lebanon 00:00

Spies in the security forces of Lebanon were nothing new. Retired Brigadier General Adib al-Alam and members of his family had been awaiting trial for over two years accused of spying for Israel. In the report Merhi had seen it was alleged that al-Alam had been recruited by the Jews as far back as 1992, twenty years ago. Twenty years of spying.

In a country run on confessional lines there would always be spies, each faction spying on the other even while they worked (or pretended to work) side by side. It was almost a game the confessions played, clandestinely striving to be the first to obtain intelligence on their rivals.

The confessions tolerated each other's spies. And Syrian spies were a given. But spies for Israel were not acceptable.

"You know who it is?" asked Jihad.

"No. But I have a list of names."

"Show it to me."

Carla shook her head. "It is not written down."

He took a large mouthful of whisky, rolling it between his teeth. "Tell me then."

"Tomorrow," said Gisele, leaning forward, hands on her knees. "It has been a long day, for you in particular my husband. Why don't you both continue this in the morning, with rested heads? The spy is not going anywhere."

Carla smiled, touching Gisele on the arm. "Always the good trainer." Her black eyes moved to Jihad. "You have had a hard day, Major?"

Jihad shrugged with his shoulders, down-turned mouth and raised eyebrows. He had driven to south Beirut, collected Lattouf, driven down to Tyre, eaten fish stew with Captain Manar al-Jayouchi in the Bourj al-Shimali refugee camp, picked up a prisoner, tried to interrogate him, been ambushed and shot at, had killed the prisoner - an unarmed Palestinian youth - had driven back, had deposited Lattouf, had been French kissed by a djinn, and had been informed there was an Israeli spy in the ISF. Just a normal day really.

Carla stood up. "I will go. You are right, *habibti*, fresh heads tomorrow. Shall I attend your office in the morning, Major?"

Gisele also stood up. "You have somewhere to stay?"

"I shall find an hotel. I just picked up my transport at the airport and came straight here."

"Then you will stay with us."

"Oh no no. Really I - "

"Nonsense, you cannot go back to Beirut at this hour. Tell her, Jihad."

"Well - "

"Things have changed in the last two years. It is not safe to go south in the dark. And even if it was, the hour is too late. You have eaten our food, it is our duty to look after you. And our pleasure. We have the bond of salt. Stay with us for as long as you need to."

Carla looked from one Merhi to the other, wondering how much protestation to make. She decided on very little. "You are too kind. Both of you. Thank you." She reached out and stroked Gisele's hair. "Truly you are my friends." Her fingers moved lightly over the scar on Gisele's neck, what Gisele called her *wasm*, her camel's brand. Then Carla leant forward and kissed Gisele on the lips.

Over by the window, Jihad drained his glass and felt just a little bit jealous.

But of whom...?

# Jounieh, Lebanon 02:30

Darkness. No noise except for the sound of whisky-induced heavy breathing coming from the master bedroom.

Carla glided into the lounge, not even disturbing the ambient air. She was dressed only in her white T-shirt, which ended halfway down her bottom. Her feet were bare, her bed-hair fuzzy.

Normally the patio door would complain, grumble and resist when someone tried to open it, but for her it slid across noiselessly.

Outside, myriad star pinpricks in the ceiling of the sky made up for the lack of moon. Down below there were a few lights on the Coastal Highway, even at this hour. Beyond the highway there was just blackness where the sea should be.

She waited, goose-bumps popping up on her exposed flesh as a cool breeze hit from the west. Two minutes later, her left hand glowed.

She raised the phone to her ear. *"Habibi."*

The smallest of communication pauses, then: "All is well?"

"All is good. I am in." She spoke softly, cupping her right hand over the phone.

*"Brava.* How are they?"

"They are well. He is a Major now."

"Does that help or hinder?"

"They have a new way of working, so it helps a great deal."

"Good. And the earlier matter?"

"Not as successful but it confirms the information received. *Kifak?"*

"I am fine. I'm about half an hour out."

"You will be careful?"

"Of course."

"And I will get my present?"

There was a longer pause, then: "Yes."

Carla shivered. She whispered, "The thought excites me."

"You are excited?"

"Always when I talk to you."

"Let me move your hand."

"What?"

"I am moving your right hand. Can you feel me?"

"Yes, I can feel you moving my hand. It is on my thigh..."
Her nail-less fingers caressed her goose-bumps.

"I am moving your hand again. To the left... upwards. You
are so smooth. Can you feel what I am doing to you now?"

"Yes..."

Out over the Persian Gulf, the Qatar Airways Airbus A321 from
Doha to Muscat banked to the south, heading inland, preparing
for the first stages of descent.

## Bahla, Oman, Arabia 06:30 (local time)

As always, Paradise and Love awoke at the same time. The
daily routine was that one would shower while the other went
down to prepare *ftoor*, breakfast. Then that one would come up
for her shower while the other one went down and prepared the
*qahwa*, coffee. They had an hour, Abu Yo'roub always got up
around seven-thirty.

Today it was Love's turn to prepare *ftoor*. As a naked
Paradise walked into the bathroom, Love slipped on a pair of
white cotton harem pants and a white cotton sleeveless vest and
tied her hair back in a ponytail. Barefooted, she went downstairs
and crossed the open-plan *majlis* into the kitchen.

An iPod Touch was sitting on a small dock near the
microwave. She turned on the unit and scrolled to what she
wanted. Immediately, Elissa's latest album *As'ad Wahda* began
playing. Love kept the volume low, but she knew Paradise
would hear it up in the shower, in her head.

She began to prepare today's *ftoor*: *labneh*, strained yoghurt,
with mint, olives and olive oil; pita bread with *za'atar*; dates and

bananas.

Fifteen minutes later, leaving Elissa entertaining the empty kitchen, she walked back out into the *majlis*. And stopped dead.

A man was sitting on one of the low cushioned couches.

They exchanged stares, Love's head inclining to the side. Most people would be disconcerted by the white snake eyes, the blinkless gaze, the almost-white blonde hair, the white vest and pants emphasizing the pale skin. But not the man in the denim jeans and loose white collarless shirt, long black hair falling down either side of his face, hiding the missing left ear.

Their eyes were locked, like a hunter and feral prey. But which was which? Flexing her fingers, Love slowly began to move into the room. The man stood up.

Love made no sound but she bared her teeth and flicked her fingers, like a cat showing it's claws, daring it's opponent. You really want some?

Carefully the man took a step towards her. Love moved to the left, away from the stairs, the man turning with her.

Love stopped when she had the man at the right angle. She raised her arms in the air, her hands bent forward like cobra heads. Her nostrils were flared. Her eyes did not leave his.

Then she grinned, like a victor about to administer a *coup de grâce*.

He had heard nothing. The first thing he was aware of was a displacement of air behind him. Then something was on his back, like a *ghouleh*. Strong naked legs wrapped around his hips, bare arms seized him around the neck. A thumb (or was it a claw?) found one of his eyes.

The man bent forward, rocking his body, trying to shake off the demon.

Love laughed. Her sister was too strong for this mortal, he stood no chance.

Paradise grabbed his face with her right hand, pulling up his hair with her left. Giving the lowest of growls she moved her head around, pushing her viper's tongue into the hole where his left ear had been.

The man stopped struggling. Love stood right in front of him. Still on his back, Paradise withdrew her tongue and began to lick the scars on his face, her tongue wet, barbed but sensual.

Love placed two cobra fingers between his lips, prising his mouth open, then she leant forward and put her tongue into his mouth, kissing him ferociously, biting the inside of his lip. Making him bleed.

Paradise's legs slid off his hips and she swung around to the front. She was completely naked. Something glistened on her thighs. Her eyes closed in pleasure as she experienced her sister's kissing.

Then Love pulled her head away, breathless. Paradise too was panting.

He could feel their hot breath on his face. One woman was on his right hip, one on his left hip. The closeness of cats. Four white eyes stared at him.

Then the eyes lowered, almost in deference. Together they said, "Master."

He did not react.

Paradise looked up. "We were wondering when you would come."

"We have missed you," said Love. She moved herself against the hardness in his groin, reaching up and rubbing the blood off his lip with her thumb.

"Abu Yo'roub is not up for half an hour," said Paradise.

"We want you," said Love.

"Take us."

"Take us now."

They said in unison: "And take us hard."

Elissa was still playing as the *houri* led The Damascene up the stairs to their bedroom.

## Jounieh, Lebanon 05:30

Carla, back in her white T-shirt, black leggings and baseball shoes, propped the note up against the upturned *rakwe* draining next to the sink, where the Merhis would be sure to find it.

> Gisele/Jihad,
> Thank you for receiving me, for your bond of salt.
> I have things to attend to. Jihad, I will be at your office at 9.30.
> Gigi, I need to go shopping, get some clothes. Are you free later today? I will ring you.
> C
> xxx xxx

Silently she left the apartment. Walking down the stairs, she smiled inwardly. The bond of salt. The old Arabic code where a visitor would receive shelter and food and the host's protection for the duration of their stay and for three days afterwards. Three days being the length of time it took for the host's food to pass through the visitor's body. If the visitor was thought to retain just one grain of salt from the host, protection would be given.

She passed through the building's lobby and went out through the main door. Outside it was a crisp late October morning, and she shivered in just her T-shirt. It would warm up later, and she genuinely looked forward to a girls-together shopping trip with Gisele. But first she had other things to do.

The vehicles outside were parked in a single line side by side. Interestingly Jihad had not queried why last night she had approached him from *behind* the cars. He had probably been too dazzled by the lights and too surprised to see her to wonder about such things. And he had had a long day.

She squeezed between one of the Merhi's Toyotas and another resident's Ford Explorer, going behind the cars to the two-metre wide area in front of the gorse bushes of the mountainside. Where she had left her motorbike...

## Bahla, Oman, Arabia 08:30 (local time)

*Ftoor* was finished. Because they had an unexpected guest, Love had also brought out the remains of yesterday's oryx and rice to supplement the other food, so the men were full as they sat down with their coffees in the *majlis*. The Damascene, in particular, had an appetite.

The twins also sat with their coffees, but behind the men. They were both dressed in the white sleeveless vests and white harem pants.

"I have had contact from Paris," said The Damascene. "Assad is weakening."

Ghazi Kanaan rubbed his beard. "That's not what I hear. On the radio, on television, online, they all say Assad is holding fast."

"The Ba'ath Party might be holding fast, the government is still solid. But Assad is losing favour."

"They are sure?"

"The dynasty is ending. His support is waning."

"And this means...?"

"It is time for a new leader, as planned. An open, progressive leader, but someone who is still a member of the party, an Alawite. The country is ready."

"The timing must be right. I have not waited seven years for it all to go wrong now."

"Your waiting has been necessary. Remember, you should be dead. I should have killed you, but you persuaded me otherwise."

"And paid you handsomely."

The Damascene poured himself another coffee. He did not offer a refill to Kanaan. "There is that."

"I do not want them to think that I am a replacement Assad in all but name."

"I have been told that you have the support of Hizbullah and the SSNP *[the Syrian Social Nationalist Party in Lebanon]*. On the other side, the FSA *[Free Syrian Army]* and the Salafists know of the plan and they are willing to listen."

"That is all? Listen?"

"What more do you expect? You will have to prove yourself."

"They know I am alive?"

"No. They know a new leader will be installed. A leader who will negotiate, a leader who will listen to *them*. A leader who is willing to have a peaceful transition. They have not been given a name."

Kanaan was nodding slowly. "So the time nears."

"No, the time is here."

For a minute Kanaan said nothing, finishing his coffee. Then he asked, "What happens?"

"First we get you to Beirut, where you will meet with them all. If all sides agree, you will be given safe passage to Damascus. There you will be installed and you will effectively open the gates of the city to all parties. A ceasefire will be called."

"And what of Assad?"

"What of him?"

Kanaan sat forward. "I see. And do I have written guarantees of my safety, from all sides?"

The Damascene also sat forward. "Abu Yo'roub you do not even have a guarantee of your safety from *me*. Never forget that. Once we take you from this place, there is no coming back. It is a one-way street. To power... or to death. And if either side decides you are no longer to their liking, it will be my pleasure to do what history records I did seven years ago."

Anger flared across Kanaan's face. The old anger that for twenty years had been the most feared emotion in Lebanon. "You are a callous, ungrateful bastard."

The Damascene gave no indication of disagreement.

Kanaan breathed deeply, aware the women were watching him. He composed himself. "So," he continued, calmer. "I have no choice?"

"Dead men never do."

Kanaan raised his right arm in the air, clicking his fingers and then pointing at his cup which was only half a metre in front of him. "*Qahwa!*"

Love stood up and came over, picking up the *rakwe* and pouring thick coffee into Kanaan's cup. Her eyes lingered on him as she went back to sit beside her sister.

"There is one thing I ask," said Kanaan. "One thing you can do for me."

"What is that?" asked The Damascene.

Kanaan looked behind him. "Get your pet bitches to put their contact lenses in. Those white eyes are so fucking disconcerting."

## Mount Lebanon 07:00

On the main Damascus road out of Beirut, before she reached Jamhour, Carla took a left off the road onto a rough cinder track. A few metres along she pulled up in front of a three-storey apartment block. She parked in the front, by the main door.

Taking off the black helmet, she shook out her hair, giving it a finger-comb, and looked up at the block. It had been new when she had first been here seven years ago, and it had not changed. The troubles of Beirut rarely reached up here to the slopes of Mount Lebanon (except when the Israelis decided to bomb the nearby electricity generating plant, which they did in 2006). The block had magnificent views out over Beirut and in her pocket she had the keys to one of the two apartments on the top floor. The keys her husband had kept when he had 'killed' the owner, Syria's Interior Minister Ghazi Kanaan. And everyone knew a dead man had no use for keys.

She wondered if the blonde Englishwoman and her Lebanese husband still lived next door with their three children, the boy and the twin girls. They were probably long gone by now.

She could have used this as her base while she was in Lebanon, she still had some clothes and other stuff up there. But she needed to keep a protective eye on the Merhis, so she would accept their bond of salt and let them think she had nowhere else to stay.

At least until she had figured out the meaning of the Israeli intelligence report she had pdf'd into her head…

## Coastal Highway, Lebanon 07:30

Major Jihad Merhi drove south along the Coastal Highway, cigarette between his lips, both hands on the wheel. As always, the morning traffic heading into Beirut was heavy. On his left, the sun was making promises about the day; on his right, the Mediterranean sparkled.

So, there was an Israeli spy in the Lebanese Internal Security Force. It was interesting that Carla had been so specific: the ISF, not the security forces in general *(Brigadier General Adib al-Alam had worked in the GSD, the General Security Directorate; the CIA to Merhi's FBI)* – it narrowed the field but that still left a suspects pool of thousands.

Even though he was now autonomous, he would need to report this to Lieutenant-Colonel Ghanem. And the new Head of the Intelligence Bureau, Colonel Othman, would need to know. But it would be down to him, Jihad Merhi, to locate and eradicate the weed.

Where to begin? Well, with that list of names Carla had in her head. He looked at his watch. She would be with him in two hours. Where had she gone to so early this morning? He had discussed it with Gisele but, wise trainer-head as always, Gisele had pointed out that he shouldn't worry about it, The Djinn always moved in mysterious ways – just remember everything that had happened two years ago during the al-Mahdi turbulence.

Merhi blasted the Toyota's horn at an old fruit lorry that was crawling along, and forced his way out into the second lane.

Something else had occurred to him. There was another entity who might need to know about the remaining spy: Hizbullah. All Israeli espionage activity in Lebanon was focused on the Party of God and, although it would never be admitted, Hizbullah owed the ISF big time for weeding out the incredible Israeli penetration of their activities.

*That* was something he did not look forward to, but at least he had his new team of superheroes. They must have liaised with Hizbullah before, they would know where to go, who to go to and, importantly, how to speak to them.

Thoughts of the murdered Brigadier Wissam al-Hassan flashed into his mind but were quickly forced out by other thoughts. Thoughts of Carla. Very special thoughts. Thoughts that a fifty-something married Major of the Internal Security Force should not be having…

## Bahla, Oman, Arabia 09:30 (local time)

Both men were dressed in white dishdashas and red *keffiyehs*, the headscarves worn straight and held in place by black rope *agals*. They were followed out of the villa by two women in plain black *abbayas*, heads covered by plain black *shaylas*, faces visible. One woman had green eyes, one had brown eyes.

Each person wheeled a small, cabin-baggage style suitcase.

The woman with green eyes locked the villa's solid, ornate front door. Turning, she held up the keys.

Without speaking, The Damascene held out his hand. She dropped the keys into it.

The men climbed into the back of the Jeep Wrangler Ultimate, leaving the cases to be stacked in the back by the women. Then the women climbed into the front of the Jeep, the one with brown eyes in the driver's seat.

As if in choreographed unison the women turned to look at the men. The men said nothing. The women turned back.

The outer gates of the villa opened and the car started. They passed the now-still fountain and drove out, the gates closing after they passed through. The tyres kicked up sand on the local track as they picked up speed.

Soon they had reached  Highway 21. They turned north-west, heading for Dubai.

## Jonblat, Beirut 09:00

The time was eerily accurate when the telephone on Merhi's desk shrilled with the internal ringtone.

"Reception, Major. A Madame Suzi Saad to see you."

"Who?"

"Madame Suzi Saad."

"Ah, yes, yes. I will be down. Sign her in, will you?"

Suzi Saad was wearing black Cuban-heeled ankle boots, denim jeans and a green shirt with black buttons that matched the size and colour of her eyes. A dark grey Barbour wax cotton messenger bag was on one shoulder. As always, her voluminous black hair cascaded over her upper body like a waterfall, an ornate black and gold hair clip holding a scrunch of it at the back. She wore little make-up; she didn't need to.

She had passed through the metal detector and was waiting for Merhi in the small seating area. Shortly she saw him coming down the stairs (all over Beirut people avoid lifts if they can help it because of the power cuts).

"Madame Saad," Merhi gave a half-bow in greeting, right hand on his heart. He shook hands only when she offered hers, as propriety dictated.

He nodded at the Corporal behind the desk and held open the door into the stairwell, letting Madame Saad go first. She knew the way.

"You've been shopping already?" he asked as he followed her up the stairs.

"Just something I quickly picked up down the road," said Carla. "Do I look all right?" Did she actually wiggle her bottom or was he imagining it? "I've phoned Gigi and she's meeting me this evening. Will you come shopping with us?"

"Er, maybe not."

She giggled. "Wise. But afterwards how would you like to take two beautiful women to dinner?"

Reaching the second floor, he stretched forward to open the door for her, replaying her last sentence without the words 'to dinner'. "How can I resist?"

Her boots echoed down the corridor. In the General Office, the veteran Sergeant Deeb el-Gharib was tapping away at a keyboard. He looked up when Carla passed by the door, looked back down and then did a double-take.

Merhi had paused by the General Office door. "Coffee?"

She turned back. "That would be nice, thank you Major." She followed Merhi into the General Office. "Ah, I see you have a coffee machine now."

"It's still sludge."

"Sludge will be fine. Hello Sergeant. *Al-salaam 'aalaykum.*"

Deeb el-Gharib was frowning, trying to place her. She looked familiar. He stood up, right hand on his heart. "'*aalaykum al-salaam...*"

She held out her hand. "Suzi Saad, GSU. We've met before."

His memory flashed back two years. A vague recollection. Did not recall the name though. "Oh yes. How are you?"

"I am well, thank you. And yourself?"

"Overworked, underpaid..."

"Yeh, yeh, yeh," said Merhi pouring sludge.

"It *is* quiet in here," said Carla.

"Just me and five Corporals nowadays," el-Gharib swept his arm around the empty office. "They are out. The Lieutenant and the other Sergeants, *poof* gone! Staff cuts."

"We are in a transition," Merhi came over holding two mugs which might last have been washed during the French mandate. "I have another team upstairs. We will be merging soon."

Carla took the drip-striped mug that might once have been white. The very same mug she had drunk from two years ago. The Visitors' Mug.

"Nice to see you again," said el-Gharib as he sat back down.

"Ms Saad might be around for a little while," said Merhi. "Popping in and out. Don't broadcast it. Need to know. If anyone asks, tell them... she's my new temp PA."

"Okay, sir."

In the four days he had been a Major, Merhi had noticed how 'boss' was being replaced by 'sir'. Now, as he followed Carla down the corridor, something was puzzling him. Just a little niggle, a little flag that had gone up in the last ten minutes. Something he couldn't put his finger on.

"The glass in your door, it is still cracked," said Carla as she entered Merhi's office.

"Facilities are on to it."

She draped her bag over the back of the wooden chair in front of the desk. "Do you still...?" She made twirling motions with her hands next to her ears, then pointed at her eyes.

Merhi made similar motions, saying "Yes" to the ears and "No" to the eyes. Carla nodded understanding.

Merhi unlocked a drawer and brought out the black laptop, clicking it into a multi-port on his desk. "So," he said, choosing his words carefully, giving The Listeners enough so that they did not become suspicious but not enough for any adverse interest to be taken. "I will need to report the situation to my Lieutenant-Colonel, so I'm glad you're here. He wasn't in half an hour ago, but I'll try him again shortly. Meantime - "

"Meantime," Carla pulled a face as she put the mug down on

the desk. "Let us go and get a proper coffee. Your sludge has not improved over the years. In fact it has got worse."

## Dubai, United Arab Emirates 13:00 (local time)

During the financial crash of 2008 many ex-pat workers fled Dubai, unable to meet their commitments when their surreal bubble burst, afraid equally of their creditors and of the punishment for financial default. They left in a hurry, literally thousands of them leaving their huge, expensive 4WDs in the airport car parks, sometimes with notes of explanation and apology on the windscreen, often without.

Although the rush to depart had slowed to a trickle of miscreants and unfortunates by 2012, sand-dust covered vehicles could still be found in the airport car parks waiting forlornly for their owners who would never return, for the finance companies who could not be bothered to reclaim them or for the thieves who would eventually take them for shipment to Africa.

Such would also be the fate of the black Jeep Wrangler Ultimate. It was the sisters' vehicle of choice but, unlike men, they did not become attached to mere machines - and anyway, when working for someone as generous as their current employer, they knew that another one was already ordered and waiting for them at their destination.

The two men in the white dishdashas and the two women in the black *abbayas* left the jeep on the lower floor of the car park at Terminal 3 and, each wheeling their small cabin-baggage suitcases, made their way up to Departures, the women walking behind the men.

Their Lebanese passports showed that they were a family. The older man was Mounir Ibrahim, the younger was Joseph Ibrahim and the twins were Jenna and Jaime Ibrahim. The sisters had checked-in online during the journey from Oman and, having no bags to drop off, they went straight to Passport

Control and soon were making the long walk to the world's most extensive Duty-Free Departures Lounge. Once there they went into their gender-respective washrooms, washed and made themselves comfortable, and changed from their local garments into western clothing.

Within minutes of each other they emerged from their washrooms. The bearded grey-haired older man had his long hair tied back in a simple ponytail, as did the tall black-haired younger man, only in his case the hair fell slightly over the left side of his face. Both were dressed in comfortable chinos, loafers and a shirt.

The two women, attracting the usual *oh-look-how-sweet-twins!* stares, also had their blonde hair in ponytails and were dressed in identical white blouses, slim-fit capri-style denim jeans and sandals. They both desperately wanted to remove their contact lenses which had gathered sand-dust during the journey, but they knew they could not.

Soon the Ibrahim family were sitting outside Gate 22 awaiting Emirates Flight EK953 to Beirut.

## Hamra, Beirut 09:30

It was nice, reflected Jihad Merhi, to sit at a table in Hamra with just two coffees and not have the residue of the district's entire stock of cupcakes, falafel and God knows what else strewn all over the place. Carla was the very antithesis of Fadi Lattouf: neat, precise, concise, small, beautiful. And very attractive.

They were at *café Hamra* at the end of Hamra Street, just beyond the Crowne Plaza hotel. The walk down Bank of Lebanon Street and Hamra Street had been taken up with social pleasantries and the usual grumbles about work. *How were things in the ISF? How were things in the GSU? Congratulations again on the promotion. How was Merhi going to organise things in this merged team?*

Now at the table with her coffee, Carla got straight down to business. "So, I was given a copy of an internal Mossad report on the state of their cell network in Liban. In fact, it was a post mortem. The mighty Mossad could not believe it. Brigadier al-Hassan really routed them."

"He was a good man."

"He was a hero."

"And what thanks did he get? His life taken from him." Merhi proffered his packet of Camel King Size. She shook her head. As he lit up, he said "I sometimes wonder whether it is worth it. Do any good in this country and you end up getting killed. A fine reward. In Lebanon, there are more dead good people than live good people. And every one of those dead good people have been murdered. And they will be quickly forgotten."

"Not everyone is forgotten. Rafic Hariri will be a hero forever."

Merhi blew smoke down his nose. "He is a dead hero. If asked now, do you think he would chose martyrdom over life? Do you think he chose it then? He had no choice, others decided he would die. And Hariri is the exception. What about all the others that have been murdered? Can anyone except their families and friends remember their names now? You are alive for just a very short time. You are dead forever."

Carla drank her coffee. "It has always been this way. The history of Lebanon is written on the bodies of dead good men."

"It needs to fucking change."

For a moment they were quiet, sipping coffee to the backdrop of the buzz of Hamra. Then Carla said "I have that list of names."

Merhi took out his phone. "Give them to me."

"Do not write them down, not even on your phone."

"You expect me to remember them?"

"Yes. You will remember them. I can, so can you."

"I am not..."

"A djinn?"

"If you like. I was going to say 'as retentive as you'."

Carla smiled. She steepled her fingers together and closed her eyes. When she spoke, her deep voice was flat, as if she was channelling, like they were having an outdoor seance. "Deeb el-Gharib, Jad Chadidi, Omar Mostafa, Michel Yammine, Peter Harrak, Emad Hmedeh, Nabil Haddad, Claude Gerges, Tamer Khalef."

Merhi stiffened. "What?"

"The names."

"Those are the names of my men. The old team and the new team."

"Really? I did not know. They are just the names I have been given."

"Are you kidding me, Carla? Are you messing with me?"

"Do you want me to mess with you?"

"Stop it. Are you... are you saying that one of those is the Israeli spy?"

"It is the list I have been given."

"Shit." Merhi sat back, taking a full two centimetres off his cigarette in one drag. "Haddad, Gerges, Khalef are al-Hassan's team, I don't know them well. The rest are my team, some I have known for a long time. I trust them."

"Of course you do."

"al-Hassan's team were the ones who eradicated the spy cells, so it can't be one of them. So, you are telling me that one of my own team is the spy?"

"I am telling you nothing. That is just the list of names I have."

"Shit." Merhi put his hands on his head, cigarette balanced in his mouth. He looked around. "I need another coffee." He asked her the question with his raised eyebrows.

"Yes, espresso."

Still mumbling "Shit" and reaching into his jacket for money, Merhi went back inside *café Hamra*.

Carla watched him. Like a she-wolf watches a tethered goat.

What was he going to do? Indeed, what was *she* going to do? For there were things that she had not told him. She had not told him it was a list of potential spies, he had just assumed that. And she had not told him the other three names on the list. Three names which took the total up to twelve.

Top of the list was Wissam al-Hassan, the assassinated Brigadier, the one her husband had been charged with protecting. Then there was Pierre Ghanem, Merhi's boss.

And then, of course, the final name, the obvious name: Jihad Merhi.

## Jonblat, Beirut 11:30

"That is absolute shit," scoffed Lieutenant-Colonel Ghanem."Where did this report come from?"

"A contact in the GSU."

"Who got it from where?"

"The horse's mouth."

"The Jew's arse, more like."

Mentally, Jihad Merhi looked to heaven.

"And how do we know it is not disinformation?" continued Ghanem. "A report. What sort of report? And a list of names with no direct cross-reference to the report, just a list of names. And on this you are willing to believe that one of your team is an Israeli spy?"

"I did not say that. We have a report that the Jews have a source somewhere within the security services - "

"Tell me something we don't know."

" - and a list which names every person in my division."

"They could have gotten that from an internal telephone directory."

Merhi sighed. "I just thought you should know."

Ghanem's stare was cold. "You are at a level now where you report results, not theories. Theories stop with you. Understand?"

"Yes, sir."

"If you think you have an Israeli spy in your ranks, find them and deal with them. Then report the result to me."

And to The Listeners, thought Merhi. Twat.

"I will do that."

"Otherwise, don't bother me."

*Ya khorg.*

"He's not interested," said Merhi as he walked back into his office.

"You are surprised?" Carla was sitting cross-legged on the windowsill, like an imp.

"Not really, he's never been the most supportive of bosses."

"Yet you were promoted."

"Probably not on his recommendation."

Carla undid her legs and let them dangle. "So what are you going to do?"

Merhi lit up a Camel then threw the packet down onto his desk. He nodded at the ATS laptop as smoke flowed down his nose. "I'll have a detailed look at the nine names, something I should be doing with the new three anyway as they're now under my command. See if there is anything, *anything*, in the background of any of them which would indicate a susceptibility."

"And if there is?"

"They will be dealt with, commensurate with the susceptibility. But if one of them *is* a spy, it will not be that easy. Their cover will be deep. They will be the one I will not be able to find."

He watched as Carla hopped off of the windowsill. Although she wore the ankle boots, her feet now made no sound on the wooden floor as she came across to his desk, unlike earlier when she had clip-clopped down the corridor. She flicked hair back over her shoulder with her nailless left hand. For the first time, he noticed she wore no rings.

She said, "So you do not need me right now, you have no use for me?"

He bit his tongue and pushed the thoughts he was having out of his mind. Thoughts of the use he could make of her...

Instead he said, "We are certain of the provenance of the report? And of the list? It is something Ghanem asked. Could it be disinformation? A distraction?"

Carla shrugged. "It is always possible. But I got it from an Israeli source, in New York. How would they know I would do anything with it, let alone come straight to you? They are not that clever. I run them. They do not run me. Nobody does."

*That* was true, thought Merhi. Like you could never tame a cat, you could never tame a djinn. Unlike lapdogs. He said, "Well, I'll have a look at these personnel files, security reports, appraisals and all the rest of the crap, and let you know tonight if I find anything. Then we can discuss our next step. You will be staying with us?"

"I have nowhere else to go. Unless you think I should go to an hotel?"

Their eyes locked. The grey eyes of a Major of the Internal Security Force and the jet black eyes of a djinn. For a moment the world did not exist. The spell had been cast many years ago and it was as strong as ever. He said, "Now why should you want to do that?"

She smiled. "Thank you. You are always kind to me."

"We have been through some adventures, you and I."

"And it looks like we shall go through some more. For the sake of Lebanon."

"For the sake of Lebanon."

For a full thirty seconds they looked at each other, then, with a giggle, she broke the gaze (but not the spell, that was unbreakable). She picked up her bag from the chair. "Then I shall go shopping. I need more clothes. Even now I have no underwear."

*Quoi?*"

"Underwear. A girl needs her pants, no? At least, some of the time." She smiled. "I phoned Gisele, we are meeting at five. And don't forget you are having us both tonight."

Merhi opened his mouth but the power of speech had suddenly deserted him.

"For dinner, Major, for dinner. Have you forgotten? You choose the location, we will meet you there."

"I... I will."

"There is one other thing," Carla was in the doorway. "Just something to think about. Probably just my suspicious djinni mind. You said you doubted Lieutenant-Colonel Ghanem recommended you for promotion. Well if he didn't, who did? Your other boss was murdered, the new Chief would not know you. So it must have been Ghanem. I grant you have a new structure, but would he really promote you if he did not want to?"

"What are you saying?"

"I am saying *why*? In hierarchical structures there comes a level where a person is no longer directly responsible. In the civilian world they call it higher management, where someone underneath you always - how do they say? - carries the can, and the shit never sticks to *you*. Ghanem has now reached that level and you are the person underneath him."

"So you think I'm being set up?"

"I think nothing, Jihad. It is you who must think. Have you been left holding the injured baboon as the lion approaches? Are you a patsy?"

She left, closing the door behind her, once again her boots clip-clopping down the corridor.

Immediately the office felt empty. The strong presence, the strong soul, had gone, leaving behind just a memory - and a waft of jasmine.

## Jonblat, Beirut 13:00

Merhi knew he should not be doing it but, under the circumstances, who could blame him? It was just lunch with an old friend. God knows they had much to discuss.

The killing yesterday – was it only yesterday? – of the Palestinian boy spying for the Jews. Using the killer on the motorbike was a professional attempt at silencing, and how ironic that he had done the assassin's job for him.

Now he is told there is an Israeli spy in the ISF. Was it one of his new team? Was it one of his old team? Was he going to approach Hizbullah and tell them that, despite previous assurances, the security forces had *not* eradicated the complete Jewish spy network? Or should he keep quiet?

And what about Carla Chedid? Or Suzi Saad as she was now calling herself? Coming back into his life *again* and telling him a lot without telling him anything. And planting the seeds of doubt about the intentions of his senior officer. What was she up to? And, worst of all, was she right? And why was she so damned attractive, so hypnotic?

And what was it that was bugging him about her sudden reappearance in his life. His subconscious had picked up on something earlier but for the life of him he could not remember what it was. Like with the assassin on the motorbike yesterday: he saw something, registered it – and then forgot it.

He was getting old.

He needed to discuss things with someone he could trust, someone who had never let him down, or deceived him or kept things from him. If anybody could help him find the answers, it would be his old friend Johnnie.

Johnnie Walker.

He took out the square bottle from the lower drawer of his desk and poured the whisky into his mug until it was two-thirds full. Normally he would fill it all the way, but he had a long afternoon and evening ahead of him – and anyway he would be driving later.

He took a huge swig of whisky and looked at the ATS laptop waiting patiently on his desk. It showed the wallpaper of the ISF symbol: white shield on a light blue background, two dark blue hands on the shield, the one of the left holding a sword, the one on the right holding an upright sprig of laurel. On top of the shield was a dark blue ISF cap with a grey cedar tree above the words *Internal Security Forces* in Arabic.

And bouncing around over it was a screensaver of a Lebanese flag: sideways stripes of red, white and red, with a green cedar tree in the middle. Bounce, bounce, bounce...

Merhi ran his finger over the trackpad and the flag disappeared. One second it was there, the next it was gone. An allegory for Lebanon itself, thought Merhi, if this Syrian civil war got any worse.

Cursing the fact that he could not delegate the work, Merhi clicked onto the Human Resource system.

Right, Johnnie, where should we begin...?

## Somewhere in Beirut 13:00 – 15:30

The cursor moved across the screen of the MacBook, in time with the keystrokes being made by Major Jihad Merhi on the laptop in his office in Jonblat. The Confession smiled as 'personnel files, security reports, appraisals and all the rest of the crap', as Merhi had called them earlier, popped up on the screen.

The Confession liked the Lebanese, but they could be so innocent, so naïve. Fancy even thinking that their wonderful ATS laptops were secure and impregnable. *No* computer was impregnable, even more so when you were up against the cream of Israel's cyber security black hats. Years ago they had been the first to invent the system which became known colloquially as Barking Dog, the universal hacking programme which could access any, *any*, computer system in the world.

Barking Dog was effective for its age but it had needed vast amounts of equipment, memory, storage space and *time*.

Nowadays all that was needed was a portal of opportunity, either physically with a computer or online, and the black hats could not only see everything that was happening on a presumed ultra secure computer but, if they so desired, take it over completely. The Confession had taken the opportunity when it arose.

Now whatever Merhi did on his ATS was watched and replicated. Merhi was doing exactly what they wanted him to do.

Now The Confession could begin...

# PART THREE
## الجزء الثالث

# THE RETRIBUTION
## القصاص

# Jonblat, Beirut 15:30

After two and a half hours of looking through personnel files, security reports, appraisals and all the rest of the crap, Merhi was punch-drunk. And frustrated. All his staff checked out. All had good histories. All were subject to annual security vetting. All had a clean bill of health.

He had known this would be a fruitless exercise, he had said so himself – a spy's cover would be deep and it would be good. What had he expected to find, a little note against somebody's name with *'This man is a spy'*? That man would have been removed from the ISF long ago, probably removed from life as well.

And this was a spy for Israel he was looking for. The Jews' clever way of using locals rather than infiltrating their own men meant that any back histories would be true not fabricated.

He was getting nowhere. This was pointless. He need another way…

There were two men in the small room on the fifth floor when Merhi entered: Nabil Haddad and Tamer Khalef, two-thirds of Brigadier al-Hassan's team of spycatchers. Both stood up when they saw their new boss.

"No need for any of that," said Merhi, "now or in the future. We are a team, sit, sit."

They sat. Merhi perched on the edge of the unoccupied desk. "Where is…?" He gestured at the desk.

"Claude," said the stocky, bearded Khalef. "Claude Gerges, sir."

"Claude, where is he?"

"Out on a recce over in Bourj Hammoud," the balding, clean-shaven Haddad had a cigarette between his lips.

"It's on his calendar." Khalef nodded at the laptop on his desk, one of the standard-issue models not an ATS.

"Which I have access to," Merhi nodded and smiled. "Thanks

for the oblique reminder, Tamer. You'll have to bear with me, this is all new to me. Not only your good selves but also my promotion to God-like status. I'm told I have to have special garments whose hems you can kiss. Alternatively there is my arse."

Haddad and Khalef gave rueful laughs. The ice was broken.

"Obviously I want to get up to speed on matters, on how you operate." Merhi saw Khalef glance at his laptop. "I know, I know, it's all in your reports, which I have access to. But I wanted to talk to you all, both as individuals and as a team. I want to get to know you. I want you to know me. I want to know how you operate and I want you to know how I operate, what I expect, what I accept. And what I won't accept. I don't know how the late Brigadier operated and frankly I don't care. With his murder things have changed." He looked from one to the other, holding each gaze, making a point. He spoke while his eyes were still on Khalef. "For example, I will expect daily face to face briefings from each of you. I know it will be in your report in the system, but I want to hear it from you. I must be kept up to speed on everything. As well as that we will have team meetings at least once a week and more frequently as necessary. Do you understand?"

Haddad and Khalef exchanged glances. Both said, "Yes, sir."

For a moment, Merhi did not speak. He knew he had not only broken the ice but had pushed them through it. Then he said, "This room. You are happy here? It is secure?"

"As far as we know," said Haddad.

It was Merhi's turn to give a rueful chuckle. "Indeed."

Haddad stubbed out the butt of his cigarette on the side of a waste bin and picked up the packet on his desk, flipping the top and offering it to Merhi. They were not Camel King Size. Merhi shook his head, *"Merci."*

As Haddad lit up, Merhi said "What you and the late Brigadier did in eradicating the Jewish spies will go down in the history of the ISF. It was remarkable. But we all know the battle with the Jews is ongoing. A new wave of spies is probably being recruited as we speak."

"But that gives us time," said Haddad. "They'll all be new."

"No more twenty year espionage veterans," said Khalef.

"Yes," said Merhi. "Good. New shoots are tender, they are easy to rub out, not like gnarled old branches which require severe chopping."

Haddad and Khalef looked puzzled at the gardening simile, but their nods confirmed they had got his drift.

"So if you need additional support I have other men downstairs. Just let me know. Eventually I intend to get all of you together, as one team. But one step at a time, eh?"

"Sir."

"Sir."

"The first step I want to take – and this is not on the system," he looked at Khalef, " – is to introduce myself to our other interested party." He pushed himself up off the desk. "How do I go about meeting Hizbullah?"

## Bourj Hammoud, Beirut, 16:00

Bourj Hammoud is the Armenian district of Beirut in the north-east of the city, on the right bank of the Beirut River. Most of Lebanon's two hundred thousand Armenians live here in distinct neighbourhoods, each affiliated to a different region of Armenia. It is one of the most densely populated areas in the whole of the Middle East, save only for the refugee camps. The streets are narrow and claustrophobic but the colourful ethnic community ensures a lively, noisy atmosphere. The area is famous for its jewellery, low-priced clothing and craft shops – and that was why Sergeant Claude Gerges was there that afternoon. Next week was his twentieth wedding anniversary and he wanted to get his wife Michelle something special. Something special but not too dear.

Really he should be shopping in his own time not the firm's, but if anybody asked he would explain that he was monitoring his local informants *(Christian Armenians despised the Jews, Armenians or not, whom they blamed for the Armenian Genocide of 1915 when the Ottoman government systematically exterminated its minority Armenian subjects and drove them from their historic homeland in what is now Turkey).*

In his pocket Gerges had an amber necklace and matching earrings which he had bought in Dikran Jewellers in the Blanco Centre in Master Mall Street. Michelle would like them... he hoped. With women you could never tell, not even after twenty years.

Michelle was away at her mother's in Bhamdoun for a couple of days, due back tomorrow, so he would not have to sneak the jewellery back into the apartment, which was good – she could always tell when he was up to something.

Now he walked south down Arax Street. The roads in Bourj Hammoud were too narrow for comfortable driving so he had parked just off Bechara el Khoury Street, over near the river.

Being only about five metres wide, Arax Street, like most of the streets in the district, has become pedestrianised by default over the years. Every building has a shop on the ground floor, their wares spilling out of their shop fronts and onto the sidewalk. Cars could come down here but it would be a trek and a feat of supreme driving dexterity to avoid the pedestrians.

Difficult for cars, but someone on a motorbike could negotiate the street with little problem...

At the Karasoum Manoug, the Church of the 40 Martyrs, Gerges doglegged right then left into Marache Street, the busiest street of the neighbourhood. His nose was assailed by the heady smells of spices, meats, cheese and roasted coffee beans from Café Garo on his left and Nerses al-Halabi on his right. He half thought about stopping for a coffee and perhaps buying some *loukoum*, Turkish delight, for Michelle, but he had to get back. A text message from Tamer Khalef had tipped him the wink that the new boss was on the prowl.

He did another dogleg, past the *soujouk* (Armenian sausage) shop. Only as the streets became quieter did he become aware of a low rumbling behind him, but he dismissed it as residual noise from the bazaar-like shopping area.

He walked on, the streets still narrow but now more residential than commercial. At this time of day there were very few people about. If it wasn't for that rumbling, the place would be silent.

As he crossed the road he looked behind him. A little way back was a motorbike, coming his way. It was a big, powerful machine, hence the rumbling. The person on it was dressed all in black. Gerges' police instinct noticed that the rider was wearing a crash helmet. It was unusual to see a motorbike rider in Beirut obeying the law!

After the shadows of the narrow residential streets, Gerges emerged into sunlight by the river. Here it was more industrial. Across the river he could see the top of the electricity ministry building. He reached his car, a white Dodge Durango. The car bipped and flashed its lights as he unlocked it. Gerges turned as the motorbike pulled up nearby. Probably someone needing directions for somewhere.

The rider pushed down the kickstand and swiveled off the bike. Gerges opened the driver's door of the Dodge but did not get in. He nodded as the rider came towards him. "*Bonjour. Salaam.*"

The rider said nothing.

## Rafic Hariri International Airport, Beirut, 18:05

Flight EK953 from Dubai touched down at Rafic Hariri International Airport Beirut precisely on time. With only hand baggage and using Lebanese passports, the Ibrahim family were soon through the controls.

At the Information desk out on the main concourse, The

Damascene produced his passport and picked up an envelope that had been left for him under the name of Joseph Ibrahim. Kanaan and the twins watched as he ripped the top off the envelope and tipped a set of car keys and a car park ticket into his hand. The Damascene looked at the tag attached to the keys, nodded and said "Our transport awaits. Not a chariot, oh King of Lebanon, but you ladies will like it. Come."

"You have trustworthy suppliers," said Kanaan as they moved off. "What would you have done if the envelope had not been there?"

"There was never any danger of that," said The Damascene. "But, to answer your question hypothetically, I would have killed someone."

Kanaan stopped, turning back to the women. "Here," he thrust the handle of his case towards them. "I am tired of wheeling this."

A set of green eyes and a set of brown eyes looked at The Damascene. He gave a subtle nod and Paradise reached forward and took the case.

"Shall I take yours?" Love asked stretching out her hand towards The Damascene's case.

"No."

They started walking again, towards the three-level car park, the men in front, the women behind. Outside, darkness was falling. As they walked, The Damascene said quietly "It is 2012 Kanaan, remember that."

"What do you mean?"

"You might have been King here once but you are no longer. The women work for me, not you. They are your protectors, not your servants."

"Pah, there are only two good places for women: either behind or underneath a man. They should know their place."

"As should a dead man."

Kanaan continued walking. After a moment's reflection he asked, "Are you threatening me?"

"Yes. We are assigned to get you here for your meetings and then into Syria. Then our contract is finished, and I for one will be pleased to see the back of you after seven years. We have been paid to transport you and keep you safe. But be aware that payments can be returned."

"What are you saying?"

"I am saying that when we get to our destination you will take your own fucking bag." Louder he said, "The car is on the third level. Are you sure you can make it up the stairs, old man?" He turned round. "Ladies, *yalla*." He reached out and took Kanaan's case from Paradise.

Two green eyes smiled at him.

## Mount Lebanon 20:30

There were only two security checks on their way from the airport, one by the army and one by Hizbullah. On both occasions the armed guards were boyish and flirtatious when they saw the two identical women in the front of the new Jeep Wrangler Ultimate, and on both occasions the mood changed when they became aware of the two men in the back. For the army, a few words of greeting in Arabic by The Damascene was all it took. For Hizbullah, The Damascene handed over their passports, explaining that his sisters and father had been to the airport to meet him on his return home from working in Dubai. He gambled, correctly, that the guards would not notice that all the passports had UAE exit stamps.

Now the Jeep turned off the main Damascus road and crunched down the cinder track, its beams illuminating the entrance to the three-storey apartment block. In the back seat Kanaan gave an ironic humph. "Well, well, my apartment. It is still active."

"*Your* apartment?" said The Damascene.

"I paid for it."

"I inherited it when you died."

"Oh did you now?"

"Do you have the deeds?"

"Of course not."

"You don't have the deeds, I have the keys."

The car pulled up and they got out. Lights were on in all the apartments except the one on the top right. Kanaan began to walk towards the entrance.

"Your case," called The Damascene.

Kanaan stopped and turned, glaring at the man he knew as Captain Mebarak, the man with the long hair and one ear. In the name of Allah, thought Kanaan, was Mebarak deliberately humiliating him? He should have killed him twelve years ago when he was his prisoner in The Onion Factory in Aanjar.

The beautiful, deadly twins were standing either side of Mebarak expressionlessly staring at Kanaan, waiting. Waiting like bitches ready to attack at their master's instruction.

With a raised eyebrow of disdain, Kanaan walked to the open back of the Jeep and tugged out his case, knocking one of the other cases out and onto the cinder ground. He stepped over it as he came back round.

"Keys?" He held out his hand.

"Love, would you escort Abu Yo'roub up the stairs?" The Damascene handed the keys to the twin with the brown eyes. "Do not use the lift, a power cut is imminent at this hour. Top floor on the right. Paradise and I will bring the bags."

Love unlocked the entrance door and gestured for Kanaan to precede her. A few moments later, The Damascene and Paradise carried in the four cases. They could hear Kanaan mumbling on the stairs above them.

Love stopped outside the door on the top floor. She had overtaken Kanaan on the way up, knowing that her tightly-clad ass might give the old man incentive to manage the six flights, and she now watched him as he puffed his way up the last staircase, holding on to the handrail. So, she thought, this out of breath, wheezing, long-haired, bearded grey old man was to be the next President of Syria? Even if he succeeded, he would not last long, Allah would see to that (and if he did not, maybe she and her sister would).

The Damascene and Paradise caught up with Kanaan as he came up the last step.

"You're out of shape, old man," taunted The Damascene.

"Should have used the bloody lift," snarled Kanaan. "Look, the electricity has not gone out."

"But it will," said The Damascene, "it will. This is Beirut. Where the power cuts have their own timetable."

Love opened the front door to the apartment and stood back. The Damascene went in, turning on the light. He took enough paces so that the others could enter and then he put down the cases, looking at the place. He was not spiritual but there were memories here. Good memories. Bad memories. Haunting memories...

But he pushed the fingers of history away. He had a job to do.

The apartment was a duplex, spacious and well furnished. Tiled flooring, minimal but tasteful decoration, good quality appliances – even a flat screen smart television on the wall, a Sony. Opposite were full-length sliding windows, which led out onto the balcony. The views out over the city were enviable even in the dark, the lights of Beirut twinkling like a fairyland beyond the woodland below (subconsciously he wondered if that was the first time Beirut had ever been compared to a fairyland!). Here and there were small dark patches in the vista where the power was out. Far in the distance there were lights gliding on the blackness of the Mediterranean.

The apartment looked unused, but he knew differently. For two reasons. Firstly there was no dust on the surfaces – but his companions would not notice that, for at that moment the power went out!

Behind him there was movement from the twins and complaining grunts from Kanaan. Then two soft beams caressed the darkness – the twins had their cell phones out.

"It will be back in half an hour," said The Damascene over his shoulder. "I suggest we unpack and then go to eat somewhere."

"Somewhere where the bloody power is," mumbled Kanaan.

"My bedroom is the first upstairs," The Damascene pointed upwards with his finger. "Abu Yo'roub yours is in the middle, ladies you are at the other end. If you wish to wash, there will only be cold water for now. I will turn the hot on for when the power returns."

He turned and tried to hide the momentary jolt as he looked at the twins. Their beautiful faces were harshly illuminated from below by their phones – and they had both taken out their contact lenses. Four white eyes stared at him unblinking.

Quickly he recovered. "Please. Make yourselves at home."

"It *is* my home," said Kanaan as he picked up his case.

"Was," corrected The Damascene. "Your next home is the Presidential Palace in Damascus." Or, he thought, a coffin.

As Kanaan and the women went upstairs, The Damascene walked over to the window and looked out into the darkness. Down below, power went back on in one area of Beirut and out in another.

He thought of her. How was she progressing? Was she somewhere down there at this moment? Or was she with them up in Jounieh? He looked to his right, to the north. Wherever she was, he knew she was near. And she had been here. It was the second reason he knew the apartment had been used.

He could smell jasmine.

## Sodeco, Beirut 21:30

Gisele Merhi dabbed at her mouth, leaving an impression of her MAC Relentlessly Red lips on the napkin. Opposite her, Carla Chedid rolled the final drip of ice cream back over her bottom lip, sucking her finger. At ninety degrees to both women, Gisele on his left, Carla on his right, Jihad Merhi tried not to stare at Carla. The ice cream had to be white, didn't it?

They were in *La Piazza* restaurant, by the main Damascus road down in Sodeco. It was one of Jihad's favourite eateries and he had introduced Carla to it the last time she was in Beirut. It was an amazing setting. They were inside but were sitting in an Italian town square; on the walls around them were murals of houses, some even with laundry hanging out to dry. It was quaint, charming and, unusually for a restaurant with such a strong theme, the food was excellent. Gisele and Carla had had pasta dishes, Jihad a pizza. For dessert both women had had strawberries with ice cream, Jihad chocolate cake (and ice cream).

The restaurant was busy but not full. Jihad had chosen it because, with its discreet table geography, it was an ideal situation for the unmonitored discussion of clandestine affairs (certainly more free from eavesdroppers than the ISF offices). But, as it happened, most of the discussion had been about the women's shopping evening ('discussion' being the women talking about what they had and had not bought, which they already knew, and Jihad trying to look remotely interested). The only nod to work had been a quick "Any progress?" from Carla answered by a pursed-lip shrug from Jihad.

Now Jihad finished his coffee. His eyes drifted to Carla as she and Gisele discussed the merits, the sheer orgasmic pleasure, of a pair of Louboutin booties they had both lusted after in the Beirut Souks in Fakhry Bey Street. Carla Chedid, or Suzi Saad as she was calling herself this time, with her thick long black hair, so black eyes, olive skin, elegant but nailless fingers – the most dangerous woman he had ever met. And the most attractive. Save for Gisele. And married to the most dangerous man he had ever met. An unusual, potentially volatile combination.

His mind wandered, thinking thoughts he shouldn't. He was married. *She* was married. Clandestine affairs...

"Jihad? Jihad!" Gisele was tapping him on the arm.

"Mm? Sorry, I was away somewhere."

"Away with the fairies?" asked Carla.

"Away with the Israeli spies."

Gisele put her napkin on the table. "Let us go. Get *l'addition*."

As Jihad signaled to a waitress using the universal sign, he asked, "Where are you parked, Carla?"

"Down behind your building. I left the bike there when I came to see you this morning."

Jihad's arm was still in the air. Slowly he turned his head. "Your bike?"

"Can you drop me back?"

"You have a bike? I thought you had a car."

"A motorbike. My husband turned me on to them. Much, much easier in the traffic, especially in Beirut. Something wrong, Major?"

"No, no, I'm just surprised, that's all."

"Can you drop me back? I'll follow you to Jounieh."

When Jihad did not respond, Gisele said "Of course we can. Jihad, what is wrong with you? And put your arm down."

Jihad obeyed. "Sorry, sorry."

"Too much thinking of Israeli spies," scolded Gisele, but warmly. "Leave work at work." Her eyes met Carla's. "Both of you."

Fifteen minutes later, and after Jihad had been left with his own thoughts for ten minutes while the women went to the toilet together upstairs, they left the restaurant.

As the Toyota Land Cruiser V8 pulled away onto Damascus Street heading north-west, a Jeep Wrangler Ultimate turned in to the restaurant's parking area from the south-east. Four people got out, two men, two women. As they walked into the restaurant, one of the men, the old one, was grumpily mumbling something about "Fucking power cuts…"

# 27 October 2012
# 11 Dhu al-Hijja 1433

## Jounieh, Lebanon 02:30

Tonight it was cloudy, no star pinpricks in the ceiling of the sky to amaze her while she waited. But the cloud cover also meant that it was warmer.

Carla was naked on the balcony of the Merhis' apartment. Her hosts were asleep and she knew them well enough to know they would stay that way for several hours yet, helped in the Major's case by the copious amounts of whisky he had drunk over dinner. Gisele had been self-generous with the white wine also. Carla had not even finished half a glass.

The journey back up the Coastal Highway had been interesting. Major Merhi had driven with the exaggeration of an intoxicated driver, speeding then slowing down, speeding then slowing down. After five kilometres, Carla had overtaken the Toyota and had reached the apartment fifteen minutes ahead of them, parking up in front of the building like she had last night.

Now she performed some stretching exercises out on the dark balcony while she waited. She was touching her toes when her left hand glowed.

She straightened. *"Habibi."*

"All is well?"

"Yes. You are here?"

"You have been in the apartment."

"Yes."

"I could smell you."

"You want to smell me?"

There was a pause. Then, "You know I do."

"I left something for you. In our bedroom. In my underwear drawer. I have not had time to do any washing."

Another pause. "You are…"

"I am what, *habibi*?"

"You are a witch."

"I am a djinn. You are under my spell. As I am under yours. When will I see you?"

"You are a djinn, you can see me whenever you want."

"That is true. Are things progressing?"

"A meeting has been arranged. It will be over soon, one way or the other. How about you?"

"Things are… interesting. I need to be certain. Hands are being played very close to chests." As she spoke the simile, she looked down at the nailless fingers of her right hand. Then she asked, "My present is with you? They are here?"

"Yes."

"Good."

The Djinn smiled into the darkness of the night.

Inside the apartment, standing well back in the deepest shadows so that he could not be seen from outside, Major Jihad Merhi watched the naked woman standing on his balcony.

## Mount Lebanon 02:40

On the balcony looking out over Beirut, The Damascene also smiled. His eyes were closed, imagining his wife was next to him.

"When?" said Carla into his ear.

"Soon. We will get this matter sorted and then they are yours."

"It is the best present you have ever given me. How can I

thank you?"

"We will... think of something." He opened his eyes. The woodland below the block was pitch black but Beirut twinkled beyond. "I have to go."

"I am missing you, my husband."

"And me you." He took the Nokia away from his only ear and pressed the red icon.

He stood looking out over Beirut, the city that held so many memories. The city of so many deaths. He was still wearing his jeans but he was shoeless and naked from the waist up. The light breeze of the late evening caressed his hairless skin.

He became aware of a presence and turned.

Behind the glass balcony door, a pair of white eyes stared at him unblinkingly. She wore only a white thong. Her hair was down, falling over her chest, caressing but not covering her breasts. Without the contact lenses, he could not tell which twin it was. The sisters were identical, their skin porcelain, literally statuesque. This one was so still she resembled one of the living statue street performers down in Nejmeh.

The only hint of colour was the pink bullet scar on her left shoulder. But had she been shot or had it been her sister? The Damascene had been there when it had happened, over in Aanjar two years ago, but he did not know which one of them had been wounded. They had both bled.

He held the stare as the balcony door slid open. She stepped out, parts of her body reacting to the night air. Even though she was barefooted, she matched The Damascene in height.

She said, "She is here?"

"Yes."

"Good."

"When will we have our present?"

"Soon. We will get this this matter sorted and then she is yours."

She nodded. Then she said, "I wanted to thank you for today. For being so... *gallant*. For taking the suitcase." So it was

Paradise.

The Damascene shrugged. "I know you are more than capable of looking after yourself – yourselves. But, even in this day and age, I cannot abide rudeness to a woman from a man. Especially *that* man."

"You were kind."

"It is a bad trait of mine."

She reached out, touching the hair on the left side of his head. "He did this to you?"

"Yes."

"And you let him live?"

"It suits my purpose. For now."

She smoothed away the hair from the scarred hole where his left ear used to be, pushing it back between her fingers, her hand grasping the back of his head, gently pulling him towards her. He could feel the heat rising from her body against his naked chest. She brushed his groin as she reached for his right hand.

Their left cheeks touched, her warm breath soothing against his sensitive scars as she whispered, "Come with me."


Twice before the twins had used him to sate their lust but this was the first time he had been taken by just one of them. On her own, Paradise was doubly energetic, as if making up for her sister's absence. Riding him, bucking, reaching her first satisfaction within three minutes, falling breathless down onto his chest.

The Damascene gave her thirty seconds and then flipped her over onto her back. As he began to take pleasure, he looked at her face below him. At the jet black hair, the black eyes, the olive skin…

He stopped and she snapped open her eyes. Her white eyes.

He was suspended inside her, hard but unmoving. He saw the scar reappear on her shoulder and her hair turn back to blonde. He pulled out of her.

"Master?"

"On your knees."

"Yes Master." She obeyed. As he slid himself back into her, she said "Master, give me more than you've ever given anybody."

As the scar disappeared and her hair turned back to black, he did.

In the third bedroom at the end of the landing, Love was on her knees on the bed, her hips bucking, lunging with every thrust that was made into her sister. She was wet. She was open. She felt Paradise begin to climax for the second time and her nostrils flared with pleasure. The women were silent lovers but they both threw their heads back, their mouths opening wide.

In their minds they both bayed liked wolves.

In the middle bedroom, the old man with the long grey hair and beard slept fitfully, sometimes snoring, sometimes grunting, sometimes snorting. He dreamt he was in a *barjeel*, a wind tower, hiding, looking down into an *hammam* that was Syria. In the *hammam* a thousand women were bathing, naked and oblivious to him and what he was doing to himself. Each woman was tall with blonde hair. They were having fun, some were washing each other, some were doing more than that.

And then suddenly they changed. The women were dressed, all in black. Their heads and faces were covered by black *niqabs* so that only their eyes were visible. They were wailing. The death ululation.

Then the women froze, their heads turning upwards. Two thousand white eyes stared at him. Two thousand white eyes of Syria.

And they shook their heads in unison.

No.

## Jonblat, Beirut 08:45

A preoccupied Jihad Merhi pushed through the doors on the second floor of the State Security Building and walked down the corridor towards his office. He had not slept well and he had exchanged grumpy words with Gisele before she left for an early class down at the General Security Building in Ras en Nabaa (he would phone her at her break time and apologise).

He had been so engrossed in his thoughts on the way in he had not really been aware of the hour's drive (the traffic had been moving, the car, himself and his packet of Camel King Size had been on autopilot). Random thoughts, disparate recollections and images had flashed into and out of his mind like feral daydreams.

Drinking whisky with Captain Manar al-Jayouchi in the Bourj al-Shimali refugee camp in Tyre. The attack on the coastal road. The assassin on a motorbike. Blood shooting out from the body of Abdul Abdulrahman. Fadi Lattouf farting. His new team. The reappearance of Carla Chedid. A spy in the ISF. The list of names. The need to contact Hizbullah. Dinner with two women. Carla riding a motorbike (a coincidence, surely?).

And, above all, Carla naked on his balcony in the middle of the night, bending over, stretching. Talking to somebody on the phone…

"Sir? Sir!" Sergeant Deeb el-Gharib's voice intruded into Merhi's ponderings as he passed the General Office door. "Major!"

Merhi stopped. "What is it, Deeb?"

"Good morning, sir."

"Good morning."

"We've had an urgent phone call. From the local police up on Armenia Street in Bourj Hammoud. They've found a car in the Beirut River."

"So? Nothing unusual in that. Is the coffee on?"

"Yes. The river is low so it was visible this morning."

"Get to the point, Deeb. Jad," he called to one of the corporals, "pour me some sludge, if you would be so kind. Any biscuits?"

"The point is, sir," continued el-Gharib, "they ran number plate recognition and called us straight away."

"Why?"

"It is registered to Claude Gerges, one of your new team."

"What?"

"Sergeant Claude Gerges. His car is in the Beirut River. Over in Bourj Hammoud."

## Bourj Hammoud, Beirut, 09:40

Merhi could see the car on the river bed as he drove over Yarevane Bridge and took the slip-road on the immediate left. Although the Beirut River had been turned into a canal in 1968, the water retained its natural ebb and flow. Currently it was low, the water itself metres from the crumpled once-white Dodge Durango which was lying on its side.

The graffiti-daubed canal walls were high, but here and there slip-roads led down to what would be the water's edge at high tide or the river bed at low tide.

Merhi parked at the top of the slope. As soon as he opened the Toyota's door, he was hit by the stench. This was one of the most polluted parts of the city, the river being defiled by industrial waste, sewage and refuse from the perfect storm of the factories along the bank, the nearby waste disposal and treatment centre and the city slaughterhouse just to the south in Karentina. This was the end of October. He could not begin to imagine what the stench would be like in high summer. Quickly he lit up a Camel King Size.

There were just a few people about, no crowds. The denizens of Beirut were inured to whatever the river might throw up. Cars, bodies – recently even a live crocodile. Earlier this year the river had mysteriously turned an eerie deep red for a few days.

Subsequent investigations had pointed the finger at dye illegally dumped from a nearby factory – but many Beirutis suggested it was the blood of the hundreds of thousands of Lebanese murdered by internecine strife since 1985. Who was to say they were wrong?

There were two uniformed policemen standing well to one side as a civilian tow truck edged slowly backwards towards the Durango. At the back of the tow truck a man in overalls was stretching out the tow hook ready to capture the crumpled vehicle.

Merhi did not want to walk on the riverbed of silt, shingle, sand and shit but he had no choice.

"Major Merhi, ISF," he said as he crunched across, being careful to maintain his balance. He did not show any identification but his building ID was still around his neck.

"Ah, Sergeant Kanj, sir," said the plump, older man on the right wearing the sergeant's uniform (which could have been a clue). They shook hands. "You're just in time."

"Details?"

"It was called in by a local on his way to work at oh seven hundred. Saw it in the river. Didn't give a name, the usual. We ran number plate recognition. Came up as belonging to one of you ISF guys."

"How did it get there?"

Sergeant Kanj pointed up and behind to where the canal-side railing had been smashed apart. "Doesn't take much, they're nearly fifty years old, not maintained, rusted, rotted, dangerous."

Merhi thought that description could be applied to himself – except for the 'nearly'! He asked, "Anyone inside?"

Kanj shrugged.

"Was it submerged?"

The younger policeman spoke. "Partly. You can see the stains on the roof. Where the water reached. Corporal Skaff, sir." They shook hands.

As Merhi watched, the man on the back of the tow truck managed to hook the chain inside the shattered back side window. He scurried back to the base of the boom and gave it a pulse of power. The chain went taut and held. The man looked back, waiting for his command.

"Okay sir?" asked Sergeant Kanj.

Merhi nodded. "Do it."

Kanj raised his hand and the boom whirled into motion.

The Durango began to complain as slowly, slowly it was pulled upwards. Then gravitational force took over and it fell down onto its wheels with a bang, bouncing, water trickling from the bottom of its door frames.

The mechanic went to unhook the chain to place elsewhere for towing.

"Hold on," said Merhi. "Let's just take a look."

The two policemen accompanied him over. Merhi kept his cigarette in his mouth, deliberately letting the smoke go up his nostrils to cover the ambient stench of the river. All the Durango's windows were cracked and broken, but the car looked empty.

"No one," said Sergeant Kanj.

Corporal Skaff breathed a sigh of relief. "*Alhamdulillah.*"

Merhi tried the driver's door but it was stuck. "Here give me a hand, Skaff. But be careful of the glass."

Bracing himself as best he could on the damp stony river bed, Merhi put both hands on the door handle as Skaff stood behind him and reached forward, gingerly grasping the bent door frame. Through his cigarette Merhi said, "One, two... three!"

With a sharp metallic wail, the door opened about twenty centimetres – and stagnant river water flowed out over Merhi's feet like a flushed lavatory. "Oh for fuck's sake." He looked down. Just his feet, not the Corporal's. "Pull, pull, pull."

They got the screaming door open and stood back, Merhi squelching.

"Oh dear," said Sergeant Kanj.

Corporal Skaff stared. Merhi just sighed.

There, lying in the foot well, was Claude Gerges.

With a bullet hole in the middle of his forehead.

## Jonblat, Beirut 13:00

Lieutenant-Colonel Ghanem never worked Saturday afternoons and Merhi had been lucky to catch him as he was preparing to leave. The deaths of members of Lebanon's security forces was an all-too-common occurrence – it came with the job description, especially in these times – but, as the Commanding Officer of the victim, Ghanem had to show willing.

"Did you take charge?"

"The local police have been relieved of any involvement," said Merhi. "I've kept it within my team. I've got Chadidi, Mostafa and Yammine making local enquiries, see if anyone saw anything. There's no street CCTV in the area, but the factories might have something. Harrak is on to that. We've taken the body to USJ. Doctor Patel will retrieve the bullet for us. It'll be with forensics shortly. And he'll give us an approximate time of death."

'USJ' was the in-house term for the *Hôtel Dieu de France* hospital on Naccache Boulevard, a few streets away from the General Security Building down in Ras en Nabaa (the hospital being an affiliate of the *Université Saint-Joseph*, the research university, one of the top academic institutions in the Middle East, who had three campuses nearby).

Doctor Patel was, in fact, as Lebanese as Jihad Merhi. He always performed the death examinations on any murdered member of the security forces (not autopsies - the cause of death rarely needed to be established).

"Good," said Ghanem. He sniffed. "It was a professional hit?"

"One bullet," Merhi poked his index finger into the centre of his own forehead. "A professional single-tap assassination."

"What was, er, Gerges working on?"

"He was one of the Brigadier's – my – spycatchers."

"I know, I know. What specifically?" Ghanem sniffed again.

Merhi shrugged. He was about to say sarcastically "Catching spies?" but Ghanem had screwed up his face.

"Major, what *is* that smell?"

"Smell? I can't... Ah, sorry, it is me. My feet got a little wet when we were retrieving the body."

"From the Beirut River?"

"Yes."

"Hell."

"Exactly. I haven't had time to change and I have no other shoes here anyway."

"Good grief."

"Indeed. My men work autonomously, Colonel, it is how the Brigadier organised it. The other two – Haddad and Khalef – don't know specifically what Gerges was doing. They don't discuss things in the office because of the..." He made a circular motion around his ear and pointed upwards.

Ghanem raised his eyebrows. It was well known that he thought The Listeners and The Watchers were at the very least harmless, at the most urban myths.

"Their reports are in in the system, though," continued Merhi. "And they have access to each others' diaries, calendars et cetera. But when one of them decides to go out, the other two don't ask why or where."

"You need to change that."

"Maybe. It's only been four days, I've yet to decide how I'm going to take things forward with this new delegated structure."

"Perhaps you should get down to it."

"I said I would report in a week and I will. I am aware you want results not problems, you have made that clear. Now I have the new problem of Gerges' death. I will have a look at his case files when I get downstairs and I'll ask Khalef to look also and give me his analysis. It can be left with me."

Ghanem nodded and sniffed again as he looked at his watch.

"There is one thing," said Merhi. "Something that has not been delegated, it falls to the CO."

"What is that?"

"The death notification."

Ghanem's eyes shot up, his face draining.

"It's down to you... sir. His wife needs to be told. Haddad was closest to him, he is waiting to go with you. His wife has been away, she was expected back home - " it was Merhi's turn to look at his watch " – about now."

Ghanem sat back in his chair, sighing deeply. But, to his credit, he nodded. "Of course... of course. Do they have children?"

"No. They live up in Hazmieh, so it shouldn't take too long. Haddad has the address."

"I will go now." Ghanem stood up. "See, Major, we both have responsibilities in our new ranks which we have to face. This will be my first notification. It would be nice if it was the last."

And camels might fly, thought Merhi.

"I need to get some air." Ghanem went over and opened his window.

Merhi said, "One thing, sir," he put his hand into his pocket as he stood up. "Claude had these on him. Perhaps you could pass them on to his wife."

Onto Ghanem's desk he placed an amber necklace and matching earrings.


## Ras en Nabaa 14:00


At the same time as Doctor Patel was removing the bullet from deep in the brain of Claude Gerges (with an unfortunate liquid suction noise), a few streets away Gisele Merhi was sitting in her car outside the General Security Building. Classes always finished early on a Saturday.

Her phone was on the passenger seat next to her. Silent, no display. She thought Jihad might have called her. He had been in a bad mood this morning and they had exchanged words before she left for her morning class. The usual procedure when this happened was for him to make a contrite call at her break time. Perhaps she should call him?

She thought also of Carla. Carla was an enigma. Was she really here just to deliver a message to Jihad about a spy in the ISF? If so, job done, she could go now, thank you very much, bye-bye. But the agent known as The Djinn never revealed her full agenda. Last time that had led to her nearly dying at the hands of those female assassins, the Abu Joade twins.

Was Carla up to something else? She needed to be careful. As she had acknowledged, there were people in Lebanon who still wanted to talk to her about the Hariri killing, people who did not have Carla's wellbeing as their priority. And, closer to home, the longer she stayed, the more doe-eyed Jihad would become. Gisele knew her husband at least had the luke-warms for Carla, if not the hots (men will always be men), but she also knew Carla was no threat. She was a flirt, a tease (and not only with men) but access to her body was reserved solely for her own husband, she had made that clear to Gisele in one of their girl-on-girl talks. Jihad was quite safe from her.

Perhaps another girl-on-girl talk was called for, in the guise of a Saturday afternoon shopping trip. Maybe Gisele could find out how long she would be staying. And what she was really up to.

She picked up her phone.

## Jonblat, Beirut 14:15

Jihad Merhi's telephone rang as he sat down behind his desk back in his own office. He picked it up, at the same time noticing that the screen of the ATS laptop was now blank. It had locked after five minutes of no use.

"Merhi."

"*Salaam* Major, it is Mohammed Patel."

"Doctor! What have you got for me?"

"I have one bullet. A fine specimen, no fragmentation or expansion, very much Hague Convention. It was a very smooth extraction. Which means that it was a very smooth entry also. It would have been quick."

"Instantaneous?"

"You know I do not believe there is such a thing as instantaneous death. Almost instantaneous. He would have been aware of a thump, a light, pain and then nothing. He would have been brain dead while he was still standing."

"Fired from close range?"

"Not too close, the bullet did not exit. One shot, from a few metres maybe."

"Any idea on size?"

"I am not an expert. Less than 9mm."

"I'll send someone over to collect it. Time of death?"

"Less than twenty-four hours, more than eighteen hours."

"Doctor, *merci ktir*. The Lieutenant-Colonel is making the notification right now, so we'll get back to you about release of the body."

"I will keep it nicely chilled until then. Now I'm off to watch some football. Chelsea are playing Man United tomorrow but the Man City – Swansea match should be good today."

Merhi smiled, said "*Ma`a as-salāma,*" and hung up.

He liberated the last Camel King Size from the packet on his desk, lit up and then shouted, "Deeb!"

Momentarily the old Sergeant popped his head round the door. "Sir?" Then he frowned, sniffing, but he said nothing.

"Anyone about?" asked Merhi.

"Just Hmedeh. The others are still over at Bourj Hammoud."

"Get him over to Doctor Patel's office. There's a bullet waiting. Forensics are expecting it. Top priority."

"Is it...?"

"Yes."

Sergeant Deeb el-Gharib nodded, not needing to say anything. He and Merhi had worked together a long time, they were of the old school. And they both knew that the ISF would not rest until they had got the bastard that had killed one of their own. And had returned the compliment.

He turned to go but Merhi called him back.

"Oh, Deeb."

"Sir?"

"Any news on my door being fixed...?"

## Somewhere in Beirut 14:30

"Any news on my door being fixed...?"

The Confession smiled. Major Merhi you were nothing if not human. In amongst all the spies, all the death, all the problems, you were still concerned about domestic comforts. The glass in your door had been cracked and dangerous for only seven years. Facilities would get round to it!

Maybe in your lifetime.

The Confession watched the screen of the MacBook as Merhi began accessing the open case files of the late Claude Gerges. It was interesting stuff, but nothing The Confession did not already know – except for the fact that the ISF knew it too. They were good, this team. Good enough to eliminate all the Israeli spies in Beirut. Nearly all.

And that was the reason for The Confession.

## Nejmeh, Beirut 15:00

"Hi Carla, it's Gisele. I've been trying to call you but there's been no reply. I'm in Downtown, so if you're about and fancy some shopping, maybe a bite to eat, give me a call. Just us girls. Speak soon. Bye, bye, bye."

Gisele had found a space for her Toyota in the parking area in Weygand Street, opposite the Patchi department store. Saturday afternoons were always busy in Downtown so she had been lucky. Now she crossed the street through the slow-moving traffic and entered the pedestrianised area known as the Beirut Souks. The Grand Café was on her left, the Beirut Municipality block on her right.

She was dressed in denim jeans, black ankle boots, and a white T-shirt beneath a short black waxed jacket, her black DKNY bag worn across her body. She held her phone in her hand.

From further down the street, someone who had just emerged from the other parking area up by Martyrs' Square saw her and began to pick up pace.

Gisele's phone rang as she was crossing Hassan el-Kadi Street.

"Gisele. Hi. You want to meet?" said the deep voice.

Gisele liked that about Carla. Direct, to the point. No lame excuses about why she hadn't returned the earlier calls or not picked up her messages. Carla would see no necessity to explain herself.

"Hi sweetheart, you in the area?"

"I can be."

"Fancy a little retail therapy?"

"Always."

"I'm just going to have a look in Gucci. Shall I meet you there?"

Carla laughed. "I am not on a Major's salary, *habibi*! But I am hungry. I'm a little way out. I can be downtown in, say, twenty minutes."

"How about if we meet on the corner outside the Grand Café?"

"I'll see you there. Twenty minutes. Kisses."

Gisele smiled as she pressed the *End* icon.

The person further down the street turned right by the Grand

Café, heading north, two minutes behind Gisele.

## Jonblat, Beirut 15:15

The short, plump, bearded Tamer Khalef was the only person in the small office on the fifth floor when Jihad Merhi entered. Well he would be, Merhi reasoned to himself, Nabil Haddad was out on the death notification with Lieutenant-Colonel Ghanem and Claude Gerges was… dead.

All the drawers in Gerges's desk were open and empty, like gaping toothless mouths. A cardboard box of personal belongings sat on the desk top, pathetic items like his leave chit, his mug, a photo of his wife. Already he was being removed. The team was nothing if not efficient.

Khalef accepted a proffered Camel King Size, not least to cover the strange smell that had come in with the Major.

"Grim times, Tamer." Merhi sat in Haddad's seat, deliberately leaving Gerges's alone.

"Indeed, sir," sniffed Khalef. "First the Brigadier, now Claude."

"You think they are connected?"

"We thought we knew who did the Brigadier. Maybe we were wrong. But this is a different MO. The Party usually don't use firearms for their jobs."

"You think The Party killed the Brigadier?"

"Word is, the Brigadier was marginalising them, not keeping them in the loop. They did not like that."

"They would kill him for that?"

Khalef shrugged.

"If that is so, then it is a strange logic," reasoned Merhi. "All the spying activities were directed at them, so your eradication of the Israeli infiltration was for their benefit."

"Yes, but - "

"I know – this is Lebanon. If a plant offends you, chop it down, no matter how much it has pleased you in the past.

Death is the first, not the last, resort in this damned country."

"Indeed."

"And if the murders are linked then does that mean Claude upset them in some way also?" pondered Merhi.

"I doubt it, he had no direct contact with them."

"Quite. And they usually don't kill the foot soldiers. I think we are dealing with two different things here..."

Khalef heard the unspoken conjunction. "Or...?"

"Or, if they are connected, it is nothing to do with The Party at all."

There was a contemplative silence for a moment, then Khalef said, "I've fixed up a meeting for you, as requested."

Merhi sighed, smoke flowing down his nostrils as if there was a bonfire in his brain. Hell's teeth, he did not need this now.

Khalef tore a piece of paper from a pad on his desk. "Tomorrow at 17:00. At this address. The name's on there."

Merhi took the paper. "A Sunday evening in southern Beirut. How nice. Can it be put back, considering what's happened?"

Khalef shook his head. "I wouldn't, sir."

Merhi nodded. "Sure, *je comprends*."

As he leant forward to stub out his cigarette in Khalef's ashtray, the telephone on the desk rang.

Khalef picked it up, answering with his name. "Who? Oh yes, hello. Yes, he's here... Right, I'll tell him." He put the phone down. "That was Peter Harrak, from your team - "

"Our team."

"He's on his way back. He's got something on one of the factories' CCTV."

## Nejmeh, Beirut 15:20

The person following Gisele watched as she came out of the Gucci shop in Motrane Street and then followed her at a safe distance. Shopping crowds were both a help and a hindrance to a tail. They kept the tail invisible but they also meant that the subject could disappear from view easily and quickly. But this time the tail knew where the subject was going.

As Gisele arrived at the Grand Café corner, Carla was coming along Weygand Street from the right. Carla was dressed in her short leather biker's jacket, jeans and boots.

"Like them?" she asked, showing her right foot. The small ankle boot had double zips and a buckled strap closure going around the heel. "Giuseppe Zanotti. Sorry I did not have time to change, *habibi*, I did not bring any other clothes, I didn't think I would be going out out!" She laughed as they kissed three times on the cheeks.

"Darling, you look stunning in whatever you wear," smiled Gisele. "Or don't wear."

Carla put on an admonitory face. "You have been a naughty girl, Gigi."

Gisele frowned. "Me? What do you mean?"

Carla nodded at the Gucci bag in Gisele's hand.

"Ah, just a little something. To celebrate Jihad's promotion. Look." She took out a belt, black patent with a metal double-G as the buckle.

"Oh yes, very nice. Gucci. Gisele. Gigi. Jihad will like it."

Gisele returned the belt to the bag. "Where would you like to eat?"

"How about here?"

"Good, why not?"

"I fancy a shisha," said The Djinn. "Do you indulge in bad habits, *habibi*?"

## Jonblat, Beirut 15:45

"It's not good," said small, wiry Peter Harrak. "It's distant and of course high definition it ain't. But it's something."

Harrak, Merhi, Khalef and Sergeant Deeb el-Gharib were seated around a computer in the General Office on the second floor. Harrak had just fed a disc into its side.

"Which factory did it come from?" asked Merhi, taking a mouthful of sludge while his cigarette was still in the side of his mouth with the dexterity of a true hardened smoker.

"The same one that was suspected in the red dye business earlier in the year. They were only too keen to help the authorities. As it happened, they were the only place that had anything." Khalef gave a puzzled grimace. "Sorry, sir – what's that smell?"

"It's me," confessed Merhi. "From the fucking river this morning. All over my shoes. Short of going around in my bare feet, there is nothing I can do right now."

"You could go home, sir, have a nice early Saturday," smiled el-Gharib.

"There is that, Deeb, yes. I could use your health and safety as a reason!"

The men laughed.

The computer had decided it liked the disc and agreed to play it. After a few jumps, a grainy scene appeared on the screen.

It was a black and white northward view with the river on the left, shot from a height of about ten metres, the camera probably half way up the factory wall. In the top left of the screen the date read --/--/--. In the top right the time read 00:00:00.

"No time, no date," said Merhi. "Not very security conscious then?"

"I don't think they ever look at it," said Harrak. "Only if they ever had any break-in. And that place is so rank nobody would ever willingly go near it."

"Sure we're looking at the right time?"

"Wait, sir."

In the foreground were the factory's outside warehouses, obviously the original subjects of the CCTV, but beyond them at the top of the screen the riverside road headed northwards.

Faraway a light-coloured car was parked on the road. Indistinct but it was big enough to be a Dodge Durango.

Nothing was happening. If it had not been for a bird flying past they could have been looking at a still photograph.

Then a figure walked casually into the top corner of the screen. As it did so, a motorbike pulled up on the far side of the road. The rider pushed down the kickstand and got off. The rider was wearing what were probably motorbike leathers; the head was covered by a dark helmet with the visor down.

The first figure reached the car and opened the door, turning to look back at the motorbike rider. Walking towards the car, the rider's left arm came up.

And the first figure fell backwards into the Dodge.

"Wahw!" It was Khalef who gasped but all four men sat backwards, a subconscious reaction of shock and avoidance. Deeb el-Gharib blew out his cheeks, shaking his head. Merhi frowned.

Harrak was nodding. "There's more."

On the screen the motorbike rider went round to the other side of the car, out of sight of the camera. Moments later the legs of the victim slid backwards and upwards, into the car. The rider came back round and climbed into the driver's seat, closing the door. Moments later, the car reverse-turned, backing out of the screen.

"Is that it?" asked Merhi. Harrak raised his hand.

Suddenly the Durango came back into view, moving forward, heading directly towards the river. It did not decrease speed but in one fluid motion crashed through the riverside railings and fell down into the river, out of sight of the camera.

"Holy shit!" said Khalef. "You bastard."

The rider ran into the screen from the top right and stopped by the smashed railing, looking over into the river. Five seconds later, the rider calmly walked back across the road to the bike, got on, pushed forward off the kickstand and drove away.

Harrak clicked the mouse. "That's it."

The four men were quiet, contemplative, reflecting on the murder of their colleague.

After a full minute, Khalef said "Well, we know how but we don't know who. Can't identify anything from that."

"At least it's something," said Harrak defensively.

"Yes," said Merhi. "Well done Peter. It might have told us more than we realise, Tamer. Upload that onto the system and send me the link. I need to think." Merhi stood up. The other three men also stood.

"I'll make some more sludge," said Deeb el-Gharib.

"Good idea," nodded Merhi. "You men take what you want and then bring the pot into me, Deeb. I'll be in my office. I will not be disturbed."

Merhi watched the murder of Claude Gerges, over and over. His office door (with the cracked glass) was closed and, as he had instructed, nobody disturbed him.

After the seventeenth viewing he froze the picture at the point where the rider was walking towards the still-living Gerges. Then he advanced the video frame by frame, watching as the rider's left arm rose. Even frame by frame it was quick and efficient. There was no hesitation about the killing, no last second doubt – one of the frames, just one, even had a flash coming out of the end of the rider's arm.

Merhi sat back in his chair. There was something about the rider... The biker's leathers hid a lot, and the helmet and visor certainly obscured the face, but the rider was slim and quite small. The Lebanese were not a tall race, the average male height was 176.2 centimetres, 5 feet 8 inches. Lebanese women were a good 12 centimetres, 5 inches, smaller. Merhi did not have any cross-reference on the screen to judge accurately but, even allowing for a possible boost by the riding boots, the rider looked below average height.

For a man.

Merhi's face was stone. Oh shit.

An assassin on a motorbike. He thought back to the attempt on Abdul Abdulrahman on the way back from Bourj al-Shimali. An assassin on a motorbike...

The incident played again in his head. The bike drawing level with the car. Lattouf trying to take evasive action. The rider firing... and he remembered the things that had registered with him at the time but which had then been lost in the brainfreeze of age: the gun had been in the rider's left hand... the left hand was ungloved revealing a thin wrist... delicate enough to be a woman's wrist...

Like a four-reel slot machine in the Casino du Liban, the recollections clunked home. One, two, three...

A female assassin on a motorbike shooting at Abdulrahman. The very same evening Carla Chedid turns up at his apartment – using, as he discovered only subsequently, a motorbike. A coincidence surely? She was a conundrum, The Djinn, a Lebanese agent exiled from Lebanon, married to a man who was one of the most lethal, cold-blooded mercenaries currently operating, a man she had once been hunting... But she had come back for a reason and Merhi knew it was not simply to warn him there was an Israeli spy in the ISF. Was it to hunt the spy herself? Was Claude Gerges the spy? Merhi rubbed his chin. Now, that would make sense. Shooting at Abdulrahman, the Israeli spy. Assassinating Claude Gerges, an Israeli spy...

Without warning, the fourth reel of the slot machine clunked into place. Carla again. Going up the stairs in this building... She had arrived two days ago (seemed like two weeks) and had gone to the Merhis', with no place to stay. Conceivably she could have hired a motorbike at the airport (did they do that?). But she had no suitcase, so anything she had would have to fit in the sidebox on the bike. It was a small sidebox. When she had appeared outside his apartment two days ago, she had been wearing a T-shirt, leggings and baseball shoes. They would fit in the sidebox, together with her large shoulder bag. If she had brought biker leathers with her, they would interchange in the sidebox with the other clothes. But what would not fit in the sidebox was another pair of boots. When she had walked up the stairs in this building yesterday in the elysian pool of Merhi's admiring gaze, something had niggled him. He now knew what it was. The boots. She said she had been shopping that morning so her clothes were new – but the boots were used, the heels worn and scuffed. Unless she had been to a charity sale (and The Djinn would never do that), where did the boots come from? Did she have another base in Beirut? Was she lying to the Merhis? And if so, why?

The fourth reel on the slots had fallen into place. But did he have a line of golden bells or even a line of cherries? Or was he, in fact, a loser?

What the hell was going on?

He picked up his telephone.

## Nejmeh, Beirut 16:40

"What's going on, Carla?"

The two women were sitting outside the Grand Café at a table for two. Carla's leather biker's jacket was draped over the back of her seat and her thin white T-shirt showed once again that she wore nothing underneath it. Most of the other tables around them were taken but nobody was paying them any attention. Beautiful Lebanese women were plentiful in downtown Beirut on a warm Saturday afternoon, many exposing much more than The Djinn.

They had eaten a mezzé of *tabouleh, labneh, kebbeh* and *falafel* with flatbread, and Carla had had some *knefeh* to satisfy her sweet tooth (Gisele had declined). Now they relaxed with coffee and Carla smoked a mint-flavoured shisha.

Carla smiled. It was a question she had been expecting. She put it back. "What do you think is going on, *habibi?*"

"You have come to tell us there is a spy in the ISF."

"Yes."

"And... much as I love your company, my darling..." Gisele let it hang.

"Why am I still here?"

Gisele agreed with a shrug.

Carla took a final draw on the shisha pipe, wound the hose round the body of the *argileh* and carefully placed the pipe across the plate. "Yes, you deserve an explanation. No Sajida moments this time." She smiled briefly. "I think there is something more going on. The report I received was in Hebrew – which did not help, I can't exactly Google a translation service for a stolen secret document. I have a knowledge of the language but not the nuances. The spy situation might - *might* – have resolved itself. We will see very shortly. Then the other matter will come to a head."

"What is the other matter?"

Carla looked Gisele in the eyes, deciding how much to say. "It would be wrong to speculate. I might be completely wrong."

"That I very much doubt."

"I was wrong in the Hariri killing."

At that moment Gisele's phone rang. She picked it up from the table, looked at the screen and pressed the green icon. "*Habibi.*"

From across the table, Carla could hear a voice on the other end but the words were indistinct. It was a deep voice, male, and presumably Jihad (unless there was something Gisele wanted to confess). The caller spoke at length, Gisele unusually not saying a word. At one point, although she did not want to, Gisele's eyes looked towards Carla. It was just for a nanosecond, but The Djinn caught it. And at that instant she knew what the phone call was about.

"Yes," said Gisele. "Yes, yes *d'accord*. Okay *habibi*. I'll see you later." She pressed the red icon.

Across the table, Carla appeared uninterested, sitting back in her seat, relaxing.

"That was Jihad," said Gisele. "He's going home. He got wet

earlier in the Beirut River and he's stinking the building out."
She smiled but not with her eyes.

"*Merde alors!*" laughed Carla. "No threesome for us then.
Here, I mean."

"No. I have to pee." Gisele stood up. "Do you want to?"

"No. I'm fine."

Carla watched Gisele go into the restaurant, then she
signalled a waiter for *l'addition.*

As she went upstairs, following the stick-figure signs for the
lavatories, Gisele felt the *wasm,* the scar, on her neck throb. A
sure sign of stress. Jihad had been brief to the point of curt but
basically he had said – heaven help us – that Carla was a killer
on a motorbike? And that she was killing Jewish spies? *What?*
That was not correct, simply not correct. How many whiskies
had her husband had?

Jihad had told her not to say anything if she was with Carla,
and by her silence he had known she was there. He had asked
her to 'be normal' (yeah, right), stay with Carla, there was
nothing to worry about (the Merhis weren't Jewish!) and that, at
the end of the day, she might be doing the ISF a favour. He had
to work it out. She was not, of course, to say anything to Carla
directly.

The women's lavatory was empty and she went into the first
cubicle (checking there was paper) and sat down.

She did what she had to do and stood up, wiping herself.
Outside, the door to the lavatory opened.

And the lights went out.

"Shit!" she said, her curse in keeping with the location.
"Hello? Hello? Is anyone in here?" Perhaps the person had gone
out again as soon as the power went off. She finished wiping,
hopefully threw the paper into the bowl and fumbled for the
flush button, finding it after a couple of slaps against the wall.

There is nothing darker than a windowless indoor lavatory
when the lights are out. It was black, totally pitch black, as if she

had suddenly been struck blind.

Or was dead.

What a time for a bloody power cut! Lebanon you would try the patience of the apostles.

She flapped her way out of the cubicle, her arms in front of her. She found the sinks, wondered what the hell she was doing (hygiene and cleanliness were not the first priority when you had just lost your sight) and flapped her way to the left, along the wall, over pipes, over the light switch and to the door.

She slapped her hands down the door and found the handle, turned it, pulled – and was nearly blinded by the light from outside as the door opened.

"Shit!" she shouted again, bending over, screwing up her eyes. "What the fuck!" With a growl she straightened up, slowly, slowly opening her eyes, getting used to the light again. Her hand was on the doorframe, her fingers still against the light switch. She felt the switch. It was up. She pushed it down – and the lights came on in the lavatory.

It wasn't a powercut, somebody had turned the lights off. Some stupid fucking idiot. Hadn't they realised someone was in there?

Still shaking her head and breathing heavily, her scar pulsing, she went back down the stairs. No point in complaining to the management, if it was a member of staff they would not admit to it.

Outside, the table where they had been sitting was being reset.

Carla was nowhere to be seen.

## Coastal Highway, Lebanon 17:00

On a Saturday evening, traffic was going *into* Beirut so the journey northwards was relatively light. Jihad laughed through the cigarette smoke and mentally gave two fingers to the lanes of crawling vehicles on his left. They might reach the capital in time for midnight at the Sky Bar.

He drove with the air conditioning full on and all the windows open. Not until he had been in the Toyota for ten minutes in the crawl of Beirut had he realised just how much his feet and lower legs stank of the shit of the river. The stench was so thick you could almost taste it. No wonder his staff had encouraged him to go home early! As it was, he had had things to do – but five in the evening was still an early departure compared to other times of manhunt. Or womanhunt.

He had come to his own conclusion about the motorbike killer, and he was happy with his reasoning. But, for the next part of this affair, he needed his friend again. There were some things he could not do on his own.

He glanced down at the lightly clinking carrier bag in the passenger's foot well which held four hundred Camel King Size and three one-litre bottles of Johnnie Walker. You were a good friend, Johnnie, and he would be seeing you soon (and tending to the welfare of the Camels).

But this time it was another friend he needed.

## Bourj el-Barajneh, Beirut 17:15

With a bang that could be heard as far away as Cyprus, the front door of *chez Lattouf* in Annan Street crashed open into the ever-suffering wall and stood trembling like a guard caught sleeping on sentry duty. "Family, I am home!" boomed the voice of Captain Fadi Lattouf of the Palestinian Civil Police. "Baba is here!"

As always, he was ignored. The sounds of gunfire and explosions came from the iMac computer in the far corner (Lattouf had inherited the machine from his cousin Chadi). Four of his children were gathered around it. In another corner his youngest, five year old Little Wissam (or Fadi Mk II), was sitting in front of an old black and white portable television (yes it still worked) watching loud and horrific violence – a *Tom and Jerry* cartoon. That left one unaccounted for.

"Wife!" shouted Lattouf as he threw down yesterday's *Al-Mustaqbal* newspaper which was left for him each night on the solitary table outside the café down the road.

"Your dinner will be ready in ten minutes!" called Nada Lattouf from the kitchen.

"Where is Lana?"

"Upstairs. On the iPad."

Lana was their eldest daughter, thirteen now and growing up fast. And, like all fathers, Lattouf was not and would never be equipped to deal with a teenage female. He had given her the iPad two years ago to thank her for the way she had helped him solve the al-Mahdi case (it would be best not to dwell on the dubious provenance of the iPad – in fact, it was their second one: Lattouf had put his finger through the first one on the night he brought it home).

Lattouf sniffed the air. Chicken livers! Sniff. Beans... flageolet! Sniff. Rice!

Nada popped her head round the kitchen door, smiling. "You go and have your shower, get changed into your comfortable clothes, relax."

"I will." It never occurred to Fadi that each night his dinner was always *almost* ready, just giving him enough time to shower away the sweat and smells of the Bourj el-Barajneh refugee camp. He thought it was always perfect timing on *his* part.

Upstairs in the family bathroom, he sang his own versions of selections from *The Sound of Music* ("Ford every mountain, climb every stream-ah!") as he stood under the less than enthusiastic shower spray and soaped himself with X-Men shower gel (*The Pirates of The Caribbean* had run out yesterday. Didn't last long this stuff, three palms-full and the bottle was empty).

He was walking naked back along the corridor, still damp in the parts of his body that neither he nor the towel could reach, humming "High on a hill stood a pile of goat's turd, lay odelay

odelay he hoo!", when he heard music coming from his bedroom. It was the universal theme tune to Sky News.

He stopped. Was Lana in there on the iPad? If so, he was busted. Nada had told him not to walk around naked anymore, now that the children were getting older. Frantically he looked around for something to cover himself, grabbing a small teddy bear from the floor and ramming it over his private parts.

Then he realised. Lattouf, you are an imbecile! It was his cell phone ring tone! He had been mighty pleased with himself to get the Sky music as an illegal download recently (the police office in the camp was now equipped with a broadband connection).

Still defiling the teddy bear, he walked into the bedroom. His phone was in his jacket which he had thrown onto the bed. He fumbled with one hand, realised he didn't need the bear's protection anymore and slung it, then retrieved his phone. He did not have his reading glasses to hand so he could not see who was calling.

He answered in time-honoured fashion, shouting "Yes?"

"Fadi, it's Jihad Merhi."

"Cap – Major! Evening of pure unadulterated joy, my dear friend! How are you?"

"Good, good."

"And your good lady?"

"Fine, fine. Fadi, I need you to repay a compliment."

"You are the most handsome man I have ever seen."

"No, no, no. Are you fay oom aft...?"

"Hold on, my friend, this is a bad connection."

"I undring fee cud..."

"Hold." Lattouf took his phone away from his ear and slapped it up and down in his palm. "Is that better?" He listened and then frowned. Did Jihad just say "Bollocks"?

"Wait, I will take you downstairs. I am just out of my shower. I will just slip my comfortable clothes on. Can you hear me?" Without waiting for an answer, Lattouf threw the phone on the bed and put on his comfortable clothes: a sleeveless vest and baggy Y-front underpants, both of which might have been white at one time.

He walked down the stairs, trusting in Allah because his gut completely blocked the staircase from his view. He was shouting down the phone but Jihad was still saying strange things. There was only one thing for it.

He opened the front door and walked out into Annan Street. Immediately the reception improved.

"Can you hear me now?" asked Merhi.

"Indeed, my friend, indeed. That is better."

"Fadi, are you free tomorrow afternoon?"

"For you always."

"Like I accompanied you to Tyre, I would like you to accompany me somewhere."

"Anywhere, my friend, anywhere."

"It's nearby to you. I have a meeting and I don't think it's good that I go alone."

"Who with?"

"Hizbullah."

Lattouf was quiet. Then he said lowly, "You have some interesting bedfellows, my friend."

"Don't I just? Will you come?"

"Of course, for you."

"*Merci ktir*, Fadi. I'll pick you up just after three."

"I will get Nada to cook us a feast for afterwards. I saw some magnificent sheep's testicles in the butcher's today."

"You are... too kind."

"Tomorrow then, my friend."

"Tomorrow."

"Allah's blessings upon you."

Wondering why passers-by were giving him strange looks and a wide berth, Lattouf scratched his bottom, turned and walked regally back into his house, his underpants wedged firmly up his butt crack.

# Jounieh, Lebanon 18:45

"So you think she is doing your job for you, killing the remaining Israeli spies?" Gisele was standing in the doorway of the Merhis' steamy en-suite bathroom. Her husband had just stepped out of the shower, the hairs on his body flat against his skin and dripping. He was still relatively slim at fifty-three, almost lithe, and he was greying gracefully. Even 'down there'. At one time of playful lust, Gisele had likened his greying pudenda to Mount Lebanon with snow on the peaks (or his *falafel* and *kibbeh* with a dusting of icing sugar).

"It fits," Jihad rubbed the towel over his head, under his arms, down his chest. "You know what she's like. I'll do a complete, in-depth analysis of Gerges and his work tomorrow, see if anything comes up. I'll go in early then go to meet Lattouf. I won't say a word to Ghanem until I'm sure."

"But she'll never eradicate all the Israeli spies in Lebanon. The Jewish espionage machine is like the Lernaean Hydra. Cut one head off, another two appear."

"So says the trainer." Jihad had reached his *falafel* and *kibbeh*. "You're right, of course. It will be an ongoing battle. But getting rid of the old school is a triumph."

Gisele came over, took the towel from him and began to rub it down his back. "And what if you are wrong?"

Jihad closed his eyes and tilted his head back, enjoying the all-too-rare sensation of having someone else dry him. "I will face that if I come to it. Perhaps I should ask her." He turned. Gisele kept the towel on his back so that her husband was now in her arms. Captured. His *falafel* had turned into a *makanek* (a Lebanese sausage).

"You think she will turn up?" she asked.

"You know how she appears and disappears at will, causing mischief and leaving mayhem in her wake. Truly a djinn."

"If you say so." Gisele could smell whisky on his breath. "But it is unlike her to disappear quite so suddenly, and just after your phone call to me."

"You think she has been taken? Again?"

"Who would take her? If your theory is correct all the spies have been eradicated. Or maybe she is on the run."

"From what?"

"A good question, my husband. You can ask her if you find her."

"You never find a djinn, the djinn finds you. But there is one thing I know," he felt the towel on his bottom and grinned wickedly. "You won't find her up there!"

Gisele pushed him away in mock disgust, thwacking him with the towel. Jihad laughed and turned his back to her in offerance. "But look by all means!"

## Ashrafieh, Beirut 20:00

She had been in two minds whether to return, but it was central and it was convenient. Her husband had taken over the apartment so she couldn't go there. There were hundreds of other hotels in Beirut but she knew the Hotel Albergo on Abdel el Wahab el Inglizi Street well – she had nearly died the last time she had been here. She was on the fourth floor, same as before, but her room this time was at the other end of the corridor, facing out back.

Carla stood at the window, wearing just her T-shirt, thinking back two years to the attack by the *houri*. A *houri* who, it had turned out, was one of an identical pair. Even now she could feel the rope around her throat, feel her life force leaving, her soul screaming for release…

Breathless, she snapped herself back to the present. She held her hands up against the window, looking at her fingertips. Her nailless fingertips. And, as she did often, she went back again, back to Byblos, feeling the pain as her nails were prised off one by one…

A tear formed in the corner of her left eye but it did not fall.

She would not allow it to. She had shed enough tears over the murdering antics of those bitches. But she would have her revenge. Soon now. They were here, in Beirut. Her husband had brought them for her. It had been a masterful tactic by Marwan, employing the bitches. The twins had seen him only briefly at the climax of the al-Mahdi affair, and they thought he had come for al-Mahdi not to rescue his wife. Subsequently he had found them again, mercenary to mercenary, employing them to bodyguard the next President of Syria – at the end of which he was giving them to his wife.

Their missions were running parallel. When they were both finished, the bitches would be hers. She looked forward to what she was going to do to them.

But first she had the matter of the Israeli spies to finalise.

## Mount Lebanon 20:10

Two statues stood on the balcony, their eyes fixed on the horizon, watching darkness fall over Beirut. Statues with long blonde hair, porcelain skin and white, white eyes. They were barefooted and both wore denim-look jeggings. One wore a green shirt, the other a brown shirt. This had been at the insistence of the older man who was inside discussing things with the younger man.

Nothing moved except their shirts which flapped lightly in the warm breeze slithering up from the city below.

Then the statue on the left, the one in the green shirt, spoke, only her lips moving. "She is here."

There was a five second pause

"I can feel it," said the other statue.

Another pause.

"Can you smell her?"

Pause.

"I can smell her blood."

Pause.

"The blood from her rancid, evil womb."

Pause.

"We will make her watch as we convert her."

Pause.

"I will kiss her as you eat her entrails."

Pause.

"The whore will become one of us, we will consume her."

Both statues began to breath heavily. Slowly, their eyes closed. "We are becoming excited," said the statue in the green shirt. "We will need The Master again tonight. Do you think he will drink us?"

"He will not resist."

They were silent, both sharing the one thought of what would happen. Erotic waterboarding.

Two minutes later, four white eyes snapped open. Their heads turned. The rigor of the statues left them.

"Let's go inside," said Love. "It looks like they've finished their discussion. Tomorrow they will have their meeting with The Party and then we will get the old fool to Damascus."

"Then after that..." said Paradise.

"Then after that..." agreed Love.

# 28 October 2012
# 12 Dhu al-Hijja 1433

## Jonblat, Beirut 08:45

Although the Internal Security Force of Lebanon was not a five-days-a-week nine-to-five job, the building was always quieter on a Sunday morning. Same with the roads, Merhi had done the journey from Jounieh in almost record time.

A check of the rosters had revealed that Corporals Jad Chadidi and Omar Mostafa were on duty, the rest of his team (his *old* team) were off. Of the two remaining superheroes (his *new* team), Tamer Khalef was due in, Nabil Haddad was off - this was a pity as he had wanted to ask Haddad how things went with Ghanem and the death notification yesterday.

Merhi was first in so he had brewed a pot of sludge while his computer did what computers do when you turned them on. Now he sat at his desk, a full mug of sludge to hand, the computer waiting in anticipation like a whore on hourly rates (obedient, compliant, willing, open to suggestions, but always in command).

Merhi was content with his conclusion that Gerges had been the Israeli spy. His assassination fitted perfectly with the attempt on Abdul Abdulrahman. So was the biker killer Carla? Had to be, it was too much of a coincidence to think otherwise. She arrives back in Lebanon, the killings start. But why hadn't she told him? If she had said she was here to eliminate the Israeli spies, he would have helped her, given her access to their system, even gone with her on the hunt. Whatever she wanted.

But that was the nature of The Djinn. She played things her

way, to her own rules. Sometimes reticent, often dangerous, usually mysterious, and always, always so damned attractive.

His thoughts wandered, but not to the appeal of The Djinn, that had been just a window. He thought about his wife Gisele and how she had taken him up on his offer to search for Carla last night. He laughed. Then they had played their 'Kiss and Tell' game (where they talked about their past lovers) and things had got steamy. For once, the smoke in the Merhis' apartment had not been caused by Camel King Size!

The screensaver on the laptop kicked in and brought him back to the present. Right, time to access all case reports, staff appraisals, security vetting reports and other HR files, anything and everything in the system which contained the word 'Gerges'. He would find something, anything that he could take to Ghanem. "Results not problems."

After which he might have to find The Djinn. Ghanem would not like it but she deserved a medal. Because of her questionable status and the fact that certain parties still wished to talk to her about the Hariri killing, he could not identify her to the Lieutenant-Colonel by her real name (which was what? Carla Chedid? Zahia Zalloum?). He would use her current *nom de guerre* Suzi Saad…

## Somewhere in Beirut 09:00

The Confession watched the MacBook as the reports that Jihad Merhi was accessing came up on the screen, tab after tab. The Confession sat back, watching. All very interesting, Major, and probably of no use to you whatsoever.

Next to the MacBook were two sheets of paper. The Confession leant forward and picked them up. The Israeli report in Hebrew and the list of names. After a brief glance, the report was flipped back down onto the vanity unit. The list of names was retained.

The list of twelve names with two crossed through.

## Mansourieh, Lebanon 11:30

The village of Mansourieh, ten kilometres east of Beirut, sits on top of a ridge and is bordered to the south and southwest by the Beirut River. The river here is a real river, wider with steep natural banks of shrubs and trees, not the artificial, heavily polluted canal it becomes in Beirut.

During the French mandate, the river was dammed at Mansourieh to divert water for the irrigation of the Hadath and Kfarshima coastal plains to the south of the capital. On top of the dam is a narrow, picturesque bridge known locally as 'Jisr es-Sid', quite simply the Bridge of the Dam.

It was a place Sergeant Nabil Haddad always liked to go, even more so since his wife had left him twelve months ago (she had blamed the pressures of his job, he had blamed the local baker with whom she was a mite too friendly). He still lived in their house in the village (his wife and two children (and the baker) had moved north to Broummana) and on Sundays he liked to attend the Maronite church of Saint Thérèse just down the road in Mkalles.

That Sunday was pleasant and sunny. He enjoyed the walk down to Mkalles but a persistent neighbour (coincidentally a female and coincidentally a widow) had insisted on giving him a lift back up after Mass. Obligingly she had dropped him at the top of the small road, hardly more than a pedestrian pathway, that led down to the dam.

Nobody was about, the dam was off the tourist trail and the locals didn't care about it. Birds twittered and chirped. He felt like the only human around, a complete contrast to the maelstrom of Beirut.

As it neared the bridge, the road dropped steeply and the birdsong was drowned out by the roar of the water flowing over the dam.

Haddad walked to the centre of the bridge. Leaning against the rail, he lit up a cigarette and closed his eyes, enjoying the hit, enjoying the sun. Because of the booming of the water he did not hear the motorbike approaching from the main road, the way he had come. And even if he had heard it, it would have meant nothing to him – he had not seen the CCTV of the motorbike killer yesterday, he had been out on the death notification with the Lieutenant-Colonel and had then gone straight home.

Aware of a rumbling in the air, Haddad opened his eyes as the bike touched the bridge and drove to within eight metres of him. The rider was dressed in classic biking gear, all leather (including some rather snazzy boots), black helmet and black visor. Incongruous for the weather and the tranquil location but necessary for the highways of Lebanon. Haddad's natural police instinct mused that it must be the only biker in the country to obey the law and wear a crash helmet…

The rider dismounted and flipped open the lid of the hardshell side box.

Haddad was a little irked that his solitude was to be interrupted but he accepted this was a public place and he couldn't always have it all to himself, so he nodded his head in acknowledgement and greeting as the rider turned. It was the last voluntary movement he ever made.

The bullet went through his right eye, this time not stopping but taking out the back of his head in an explosion of white bone and pink brain matter. Nabil Haddad knew nothing about it. One moment he was alive, smoking, enjoying the sun and the sounds of the water, next he had ceased to exist. Blackness, oblivion.

The force of the bullet bent the body backwards against the rail, swaying. The rider ran forward, placed the gun on the ground and with both hands grabbed Haddad by the knees. Using the body's own momentum, the rider lifted the knees upwards and pushed.

The body tipped back and over the edge of the bridge, coins and keys flying from its pockets, arms outwards as if it was attempting flight. It hit the top edge of the dam with a thud and then span the last twenty metres into the cascading river.

The rider looked over the edge as the body was swept downstream, face down, arms out. Turning to go, the rider noticed something on the ground and bent down. It was Haddad's cigarette. A casual flick of the fingers and the cigarette flew through the air, falling, over and over. It was grabbed greedily by the water and pushed on its way, chasing the body. Another piece of unwanted garbage in the Beirut River.

The rider put the gun back into the side box, started the engine, pushed off the kickstand and drove away off the Bridge of the Dam.

Or the Bridge of the Damned.

## Jonblat, Beirut 12:00

Jihad Merhi sat back in his chair, took off his reading glasses and rubbed his eyes. Three hours. Three hours of nothing. He lit up his twelfth cigarette of the morning.

Well, not nothing. He had come right up to speed on all Gerges's cases, both current and historic, and he had read the encrypted files on Gerges's informants and what he had on each of them. And he had gotten to know Gerges intimately, both professionally and privately, through his staff appraisals and annual security vetting reports. He had even accessed his finance and credit records. Married, no children, with leanings towards Maronite Christianity, the wife more than Claude. But what Merhi did not have was anything, anywhere which gave even the slightest indication that Gerges was anything other than a loyal Lebanese. He had been responsible for the arrest or elimination of around thirty of the hundred-plus spies dealt with over the last two years.

But of course, as Merhi had reasoned before, if Gerges was a deep-cover for the Israelis his cover would be... deep. It was bizarre that the more nothing showed the more possible it was that he was an agent. Damned if you do, damned if you don't, Claude.

Merhi thought of requisitioning his cell phone records but he knew that would tell him nothing. Any phone Gerges used to contact his controllers would be a one-use disposable, his own phone would be pure.

So he had nothing to take to Lieutenant-Colonel 'Bring me results not problems' Ghanem.

He couldn't be wrong about Claude Gerges. Could he? He needed to talk to Carla. Where was she?

Merhi pulled open the bottom drawer of his desk and looked at his friend Johnnie. He moved to shake hands but then pulled his arm back. Best not. Not today. Not with whom he had to meet this afternoon.

And he was not thinking of Fadi Lattouf.

## Mount Lebanon 12:30

"Ladies, I will not need you. There are some places you cannot go."

Paradise and Love turned towards The Damascene as he came down the stairs. They were dressed in combat cargo pants tucked in to heavy black boots, white sleeveless vests with *keffiyeh* scarves tied around their necks. Their contact lenses were in.

They inclined their heads, one to the left, one to the right. "Master?" said Paradise.

"This is a very delicate time. They will not take kindly to you. They will not want women there." The Damascene explained, out of courtesy not out of necessity.

"We are not women," said Love simply.

"You know what I mean. To them, you are."

The twins looked at each other, turned back to The Damascene, then looked at each other again.

"As you wish," said Paradise turning back once more. They knew better than to argue. While he was subservient in the bedroom last night (he had survived the waterboarding), he was their controller for this mission, their master, their *pay*master. And they knew from experience he was a dangerous man.

"Right, ready?" came a gruff voice from above.

Two brown and two green eyes moved upwards as Ghazi Kanaan came down the stairs. He was dressed in a plain grey suit and a white shirt done up to the neck, no tie. His hair was still long and his beard remained, on The Damascene's instructions. The twins bowed their heads as he reached the bottom step.

Kanaan raised a sardonic eyebrow. "What is this, humility at last?"

"They will not accompany us today," said The Damascene.

"Really? Why not?"

"Because I said so."

Kanaan opened his mouth to argue but then jumped as the women's heads came back up. They had removed their contact lenses. "In the name of Allah!" he growled. "I have told you not to do that."

"Come," said The Damascene. "You do not want to be late for your... sponsors."

With one more withering look at the twins, Kanaan followed The Damascene out of the apartment. Four white eyes watched him go.

Downstairs, the local man and his English wife from the apartment opposite were entering the building. The Damascene held the door open for them, but Kanaan swept regally through. The couple acknowledged The Damascene's nod of greeting and head-shake of apology.

Kanaan went over to the Jeep, tugging at the passenger door. "Well, open it."

"Not that," said The Damascene. "We're not taking it."

"What do you mean?"

The Damascene walked over to a Suzuki 1500 VL Intruder motorbike parked on the gravel a little way away.

"You have got to be joking!" said Ghazi Kanaan.

The Damascene climbed aboard the bike, starting it with one turn of the ignition. Kicking off the stand, he rolled over to Kanaan. "Get on."

"I'm not getting on that!"

"You are."

"Fuck off."

The Damascene sighed – and grabbed Kanaan by the balls with his left hand. Kanaan stiffened, instinctively going up on his tiptoe. "Get on," repeated The Damascene.

"I – I am paying you," gasped Kanaan. "Show me respect – ah!"

"You paid me to protect you and to get you to Damascus, old man." The Damascene spoke softly. "All the money in the world could not buy my respect for you."

"I - " A tug on the balls shut Kanaan up.

"I have gotten you this far, haven't I? And I will get you to Damascus. Where we are going today, this is a better mode of transport. We will take the back ways, avoiding the roadblocks. A car is a very big target. A bike is not. It is faster in the city. And if things go date-shaped it will provide us with a very quick means of escape. Now get on." He unclenched his left hand.

Kanaan was pale and sweating. Meekly he said, "Helmet?"

"Man-up, Abu Yo'roub, this is Beirut."

Without another word, Kanaan climbed onto the bike.

"Hold me," instructed The Damascene. "Lean in."

Reluctantly Kanaan did so.

"You've been on my back for seven years," said The Damascene. "Another hour on this bike will do you no harm... Mr President."

The Suzuki crunched up the gravel to the main road, turned

right and zoomed off. On the back, Ghazi Kanaan prayed to Allah that his balls were the only things that would go date-shaped today.

As the Suzuki zoomed off north-west on Damascus Street, another motorbike, sitting discreetly at the side of a parade of shops on the other side of the wide road, started up. It was difficult performing a straight traverse across the busy highway, but the rider managed it. As soon as the bike was off the road, the engine was turned off again and it was allowed to roll down the cinder track. It stopped at the beginning of the parking area in front of the apartment block.

Ten metres away, three cars were parked. Kicking down the stand, the rider dismounted and went over to the car on the left. The black Jeep Wrangler Ultimate.

A black leather glove was pulled off and four nailless fingers were stroked down the side of the Jeep, caressing, sensual, almost tender.

Lifting the visor, the helmeted head looked up at the apartment on the top right. There was no movement, no one looking out.

Her instinct was screaming at her to do it now, use the element of surprise. Kill the bitches, kill, kill. But it was not yet time. There were other things to do yet. She would wait. As would the pair of professional gardening secateurs she had in her pocket.

Pushing the visor down, she climbed back onto the bike, kicked off the stand, started the engine, scrunched up the gravel track and turned right onto the main road.

## Bourj el-Barajneh, Beirut 15:30

Jihad Merhi knocked on the rotting wooden door of the small house in Annan Street. Really, he thought, the Chief of the Civil Police of the Palestinian Security Force in the Bourj el-Barajneh refugee camp, who was also the senior officer of all the Palestinian camps in Lebanon, deserved better accommodation than this. But, of course, this small, ramshackle 'villa' in amongst the terrace of equally small and ramshackle shops was like a palace compared to the conditions in the camps. And the official line would be that he was Palestinian and Lebanon was doing him and his countrymen a favour anyway.

Before Merhi could think any more seditious thoughts, the door was flung open, a thick-screwed hinge flopping out of the doorframe and back in again. Fadi Lattouf stood there in his vest and underpants.

Merhi frowned and looked at his watch. "Fadi, we mustn't be late."

"Afternoon of cautious optimism, my dear Major! What should I wear? I forgot to ask."

"Not your uniform. Something respectful."

Lattouf looked Merhi up and down. The Major was wearing dark slacks, a grey jacket and a blue open-necked shirt. He nodded. "I'll take your lead. Come in, my friend, come in."

"I'll wait in the car." If he went into the house he might not get out this side of the Prophet's birthday (peace be upon him).

"Nada has made some cakes with leftover rice, filled with jam – and just a trace of chicken livers. I think there might be one left. That woman is the Delia Lawson of Palestine, the Gianna Garten of the kitchen!"

"Later, Fadi, later. You have the cake, top up your energy for the journey. I'll be in the car."

Fifteen minutes later, the front door reopened and Lattouf stepped out. He was wearing scruffy trainers, his rough blue denim jeans and the pink and blue checked shirt which was older than most of his children and which he always wore when not in uniform. Above it was a well-lived-in black leather bomber jacket which almost fit him. And wrap-around dark glasses.

"Lose the glasses," advised Merhi as the Palestinian pulled

open the Toyota door.

Without argument, Lattouf pulled off the glasses and threw them over his shoulder. "In matters of fashion, I bow to you my friend."

"I like the jacket," Merhi was raised twenty centimetres into the air as Lattouf climbed into the car. "Haven't seen that before."

"It is new," which it palpably wasn't. "At least, for me. I was given it."

"A very generous gift, second-hand leather sells for a good price up in Hamra."

"The previous owner... will not be needing it anymore."

Deciding it was better not to pursue the matter, Merhi started the engine. Before he could pull out, Lattouf touched him on the arm. "My friend, can we go indirectly?"

"What do you mean?"

Lattouf looked uncomfortable. "I cannot be seen to go where we're going. You know, the groups," he nodded in the direction of the camp.

Merhi understood. Fatah and Hamas might not take kindly to the camp police chief meeting with Hizbullah. And, after all, Fadi was doing him a favour. "*Je comprends.* Tell you what," he looked at his watch. "We have time, traffic won't be too bad on a Sunday. I'll head back into town, then we'll loop over and come down the back streets."

"Thank you, my friend. Allah has caressed your brain with wisdom."

Merhi doubted that, but he didn't argue. Going to meet Hizbullah was one of the most foolhardy things he had ever done. But he had no choice, it came with the new job.

Annan Street was light of traffic so he pulled out and did an immediate U-turn, then took a left, heading west towards the coast.

## South Beirut 16:45

Jihad Merhi never liked coming into southern Beirut. Driving *through* it was tolerable, you kept to Camille Chamoun Avenue, but driving *into* it was like entering a different world. Which, in fact, it was.

Haret Hreik, their destination in the Dahieh suburbs, was to the north of Bourj el-Barajneh, so they had driven west to the coast, north along Rafic Hariri Avenue, east along Saeb Salam Avenue and then south again.

It was the heartland of Hizbullah. Restoration after 'the events' (the civil war) had not proceeded at the same pace as the rest of the city, and, over twenty years later, many buildings here still carried the reminder of war, pockmarked with shell scars and myriad bullet holes. Some buildings still remained simply destroyed shells. There was even a rusted old car still on its side as if it had taken root, in the same place as it was thirty years ago when people hid behind it from the sniper-fire. And died behind it. A *de facto* monument to futility.

And, of course, there was evidence of more recent conflict. Dahieh ('the southern suburb') had been carpet-bombed to rubble by the Israelis in July 2006. Eight years of rebuilding had not eradicated the visual scars. And there was newer bomb damage caused by the current and continuing Sunni and Shi'a internecine strife, the Syrian civil war being played out in the theatre of Lebanon.

The yellow and green Hizbullah flag was everywhere, in windows, draped between buildings, even painted onto walls, sometimes just abbreviated to the raised straight arm holding the Kalashnikov. It was matched in quantity and locations by images of the Hizbullah leader, Sayyed Hassan Nasrallah.

Merhi had got used to the political decoration on his visits to Lattouf in Bourj el-Barajneh but here, in streets unknown to him, he could feel the intimidation, not helped by the roadblock as they entered the area. Merhi told the serious, unsmiling paramilitaries who he was, where he was going, who he was going to see, and the Toyota was allowed on its way.

"So I am Sergeant Deeb el-Gharib?" grinned Lattouf as they drove not too fast not too slow.

"For these purposes, yes," nodded Merhi. He was scanning the buildings.

"I am your deputy. Like in a cowboy movie!"

"If you like."

"I ride shotgun."

Merhi was preoccupied. "I think it's this way."

They turned a corner. The streets seemed busier because they were narrower. A motorbike with two men on board came from the opposite direction, weaving in and out of the traffic.

"See that!" Lattouf turned in his seat, looking out the back window.

"No, what?"

"Two gay boys on a Suzuki! The old one on the back looks terrified! Look at the way he's holding on to his boyfriend!" He laughed. "Probably going over to Sin el Fil for an evening of ass-splitting!" He turned back and then frowned. One of the gay boys looked familiar. He looked into the wing mirror but the motorbike had already disappeared. He shook his head. No, Lattouf did not know any gays.

"Ah, here it is, of course," said Merhi. Up ahead was a walled and gated compound, heavily guarded by armed militia, no pretence of discretion. He pulled over in front of a recently rebuilt shisha café. "Ready, Fadi?"

Major Jihad Merhi and Sergeant Deeb el-Gharib stepped out of the car and headed across the road for their meeting with the Commander of the Hizbullah Intelligence Division.

## Mount Lebanon 17:30

Love and Paradise were sipping sparkling mineral water on the balcony when they heard the key in the apartment door. By the time the door had opened they were inside, one on one side of the room, one on the other, hands in the claw position. They stood down when The Damascene and Ghazi Kanaan entered.

The Damascene's hair was in its usual neat ponytail, Kanaan was windswept and grumpy.

The twins did not ask the question but they inclined their heads.

"It is a go," said The Damascene. "They have agreed. In three days we will take Abu Yo'roub into Syria where we will be met by the Syrian Army. We will accompany them on to Damascus where Abu Yo'roub will be kept safe until Assad is removed."

"How will that happen?" asked Love.

"They have asked me to do it. I have said no. At this time…" He looked at Kanaan. "I might change my mind when I'm there."

"It is dangerous."

"So am I."

Paradise asked, "And the opposition?"

"They are intrigued by the proposal. Replace Assad, open the gates of the city to all parties, call a ceasefire. The Free Syrian Army, the Al-Nusra Front and the Islamic Front have all said they will not stand in the way."

"And the others?"

"They will be handled. So, ladies, Abu Yo'roub, let us mark this occasion. Let us eat."

"First I need a shower," Kanaan growled as he went up the stairs. "I still don't see why we couldn't have taken the car."

"Cheer up, Abu Yo'roub, your destiny is about to be fulfilled," called The Damascene as Kanaan walked into the bathroom and slammed the door. He turned to the *houri*. "Maybe more than he knows. Right, we should prepare too. We will go to Antelias, to the Bourj al-Hamam restaurant. We will celebrate. Then when we return…" He watched as the twins walked up the stairs.

Paradise said over her shoulder, "Perhaps we can celebrate

some more."

## Ashrafieh, Beirut 17:40

In her room in the Hotel Albergo, Carla pulled the headphones out of her ears and thought about what she had just heard.

Three days… Three days and the end of the Syrian war might begin. Or the beginning might end. With the irony of history, it might be that Ghazi Kanaan, The Butcher, the erstwhile King of Lebanon, was the catalyst for peace in the country. Or would they be just changing one dictatorship for another? The problem with the Middle Eastern culture was that fighting was ingrained, like a drug. If they had nothing to fight over, they would find something. Witness her own Lebanon.

But that was not her problem. Her problem was a list of names and a report in Hebrew which she had at last managed to understand.

Gently she laid her iPhone down on the vanity unit. Her other problem was the murdering twins, the *houri*. Again her husband would be with them tonight. But was it infidelity when you screwed creatures that were not human?

She looked at herself in the mirror, at her luxuriant long black hair, at her dark skin, at her black eyes. She undid the black and gold hairclip holding her scrunch and shook her head, her hair falling over her face. She stared into her one visible eye.

Was it time for her to confess…?

## Bourj el-Barajneh, Beirut 18:30

"Well, I think that went better than you expected, my friend." As they drove over a pothole in the road, Lattouf raised a hand too late to stifle a dislodged, sour, bi-directional burp that shot out either side of the cigarette in his mouth. Bekaa Valley olives were the best in the world – must be their proximity to the cannabis and opium crops. The nuts had been good too, and the fruit juice.

"Indeed." Merhi was relieved but he was under no illusion. The meeting with the Commander and two Lieutenants had retained a formality and a pleasantness. They had welcomed Merhi as the ISF's new spycatcher-in-chief and had expressed polite remorse over the assassination of Brigadier al-Hassan. But they were still in denial over the extent of the Israeli penetration into their activities, inferring that the hundred-plus arrests over the last two years had been massive overkill by the security services (in some instances literally). But it was a face-saving denial. They knew, Merhi knew, and they each knew the other knew that the spycatchers had done Hizbullah a huge favour. When Merhi told them that there was one suspected deep-cover agent left, operating from inside the Internal Security Force, they had expressed confidence that Merhi would find the man. Quickly. Merhi had resisted the urge to tell them he might already have been found, and by a rogue outside agency.

Now they were out. The direct journey back to Bourj el-Barajneh had taken only ten minutes. "It is done," said Merhi through his cigarette. "Formal introductions made. My man Khalef can talk to them in the future, he's their usual link."

Suddenly Lattouf sat bolt upright, slamming his hand on the door, pressing buttons. The passenger window went down, up, down, up and then all the way down. As they turned into Annan Street he threw his cigarette out into the road, waving a hand, attempting to expel the smoke.

"Tell her it was me," said Merhi sympathetically. "Tell her it was me."

At that moment, Merhi's phone rang. It was in the well between the front seats, next to the packet of Camel King Size and bottle of Sohat water.

Merhi was pulling into a space near Lattouf's house, so he said "Get that for me, would you Fadi?"

Leaving the window open, Lattouf leant to his left and picked up the iPhone. "I cannot see who it is, I haven't got my glasses."

"Just answer it then."

Lattouf proded in the general direction of the green icon. "Hello?" he shouted. "What? Yes, this is Sergeant Deeb el-Gharib. What? Oh, *you* are Sergeant Deeb el-Gharib." He took the phone from his ear and said, "It is Sergeant Deeb el-Gharib."

Merhi put on the parking brake. "Give it to me... Deeb? Yes, *bon soir*... Oh good, what do they say?... Right, fine. You in tomorrow?... Right, I'll see you then." He pressed the red icon with his thumb. Turning the engine off, he said "Ballistics have got back on the bullet that killed Claude Gerges."

"The spy?"

Merhi nodded. "A small bullet. 5.7mm. They've run it through the system but there's no match on file."

Lattouf nodded, pressing the button to close the window. He said casually, "A Herstal FN Five-seveN as I thought. That supports your theory, Abu Samer."

"I'm sorry?"

"The 5.7mm bullet, designed and made specifically by Herstal of Belgium to fit their FN Five-seveN pistol and F90 personal defence weapon. You were right."

Merhi tried not to look gob-smacked. "Right?"

"It's the same person who shot at – what was his name? The Palestinian child?"

"Abdul Abdulrahman."

"Abdul Rahman, yes. That was an FN Five-seveN. Did you not notice?"

"I had other things on my mind, Fadi."

"Lattouf does not miss these things. It was an FN Five-seveN. Same gun. So, same perpetrator. So, you are right. Somebody has killed the spies for you. Your case is over. You could have told Hizbullah."

Merhi's eyebrows were raised.

Lattouf opened the car door. "How do you like your testicles, Major? Well done, medium, rare or blue?"

## Jounieh, Lebanon 22:00

"How was it?" asked Gisele after they had embraced.

Jihad took off his jacket. "I feel ill. No man should be forced to eat testicles, it is against nature."

Gisele grinned as she went over to the cabinet. "I meant your meeting." She began to pour him a whisky.

"Successful. Nerve-wracking but successful." He patted his right hip. "I felt naked without my gun. It's surprising the reassurance it gives you." He took the full tumbler.

"But with them it was the wisest move."

"Yes, we were thoroughly searched. Even Fadi's arse did not escape scrutiny."

"Please!"

"Talking of reassurance, I think Lattouf has done it again. Did you know he was an expert on firearms?" He flopped down on the couch, being careful not to spill a drop of his nectar.

"Er, no?"

"Well he is, apparently."

"What happened?" Gisele sat down next to him.

"The Party were not too happy that we still have a spy left but they were content to leave it with me to get results."

"Like a football manager."

"Sure."

"And we know what happens to unsuccessful football managers."

Jihad breathed out heavily, his eyebrows acknowledging the point. Then he said, "Lattouf has scored a last-minute winner. The lab phoned. The bullet removed from Claude Gerges was a 5.7. Lattouf tells me it is made specifically for the Herstal F90 and FN Five-seveN. He says that it was a Five-seveN that Carla used to try to kill the Palestinian boy on the way back from Tyre. He saw it."

"So that confirms it?"

"As far as I am concerned, yes. She has killed Gerges the spy.

She has done it for me."

"That is typical of her. But why has she disappeared?"

"Well, she has killed a member of the ISF. There are those that would have her arrested even though the victim was an Israeli spy. Ghanem, for example."

"Will you tell him?"

"I will have to. But I need to speak to Carla. Has she been in touch?"

"No."

"If she's still in the country I will give her time to leave. I don't have her number, can you give it to me?"

## Antelias, north of Beirut 22:15

She sat on the motorbike outside the Bourj al-Hamam restaurant knowing they could not see her. Out here it was dark and moonless, inside the place was bright. They were sitting towards the front of the restaurant over on the side beneath one of the impressive back-lit faux-stained-glass windows of drawn scenes of old Lebanon. Her husband's back was against the wall so that he had a view of everyone in the place and anyone who entered. The bitches were either side of him, Kanaan opposite.

Should she do it now? She could just walk in, pop the bitches in the head, kiss her husband and leave without breaking stride. But no, that would be too easy, that would be too quick. They were not Israeli spies. She wanted the bitches to feel it, to know they were dying, to know who was killing them, to know they were dead. She wanted to witness their souls screaming for life as they were dragged down to hell.

And she wanted to cut their fingers off one by one. The human body has nine orifices. She wanted to insert a finger into each one and keep one for herself as a souvenir.

She watched as her husband settled the bill and they all stood up. Her husband said something and the older man nodded and went off, probably to the toilet.

Silently she wheeled the motorbike further into the shadows. Her husband and the bitches came out. They were talking but they were not touching, not arm in arm, not holding hands. Which was reassuring. The bitches laughed at something her husband said.

Momentarily, Kanaan appeared and they walked over to the Jeep Wrangler, the men getting in the front, the bitches in the back. Then the bitch on this side stopped by the open car door. Slowly she turned, staring into the shadows.

Carla knew she could not be seen, and yet the bitch seemed to sense something.

Then the Jeep started up and the bitch turned back, rubbed her eyes and slid into the car, closing the door. As the Jeep pulled away, a face with two white eyes stared out of the back-side window.

Looking straight at The Djinn.


As she threw her leg over the motorbike, her right breast tingled. Of all the times! She pushed off the stand, started the bike and drove off, her headlight piercing the darkness like a tracking laser. Touching the Bluetooth button on the outside of her helmet, she said "Yes?"

"Carla, Jihad Merhi."

"I cannot talk right now, Major."

"Where are you? I need to see you." When she did not respond he continued, "I want to thank you."

"What for?"

"You know." Again no response. "Can we meet?"

"We will, but not yet."

"When?"

"Soon now Major, soon. Things will be resolved."

"You need to leave Lebanon." Nothing.

Then she said: "Things are not finished."

"What do you mean?"

"I will be in touch."

She pressed the side of her helmet as she reached the Coastal Highway and turned south for Beirut. The Jeep Wrangler was about five hundred metres ahead.

## Jounieh, Lebanon 22:20

Merhi frowned, the phone in one hand, his whisky in the other.

"What did she say?" Gisele had her hand on his thigh.

"She seemed preoccupied. Said... said things are not finished."

"There are more spies?"

Jihad shrugged as he put the phone down on a side table. "I don't see how there could be. She was the one who told me about 'a spy' in the first place. I don't know what she's up to. But..." he lit up a cigarette. "She said she'd be in touch."

"When?"

He shrugged again as he blew out smoke.

Patting his thigh, Gisele stood up. "I'm going to bed. You could do with a good night's sleep too, my husband. Things might seem clearer in the morning." She stretched and yawned. "You coming?"

Jihad smiled. Even after all these years of marriage, he got a thrill looking at his wife's body, especially when she wore those shorts and vest. It aroused and calmed him at the same time. "Always the trainer, always the good advice," he nodded. "I'll be along in a minute, I'll just finish my chat with Johnnie and bed the Camels down for the night."

"Don't be too long," she said from the doorway. "I might need help getting to sleep."

# 29 October 2012
# 13 Dhu al-Hijja 1433

## Jounieh, Lebanon 06:15

Well, the trainer was not always right. Things seemed no clearer in the morning.

Jihad leant against the kitchen counter drinking espresso and eating a jam-filled donut. He was dressed for work: dark blue suit trousers, open-necked white shirt, gun on his hip. The traffic on the Coastal Highway was always heaviest on a Monday morning so he was leaving early to arrive at his normal time. Gisele would not be too far behind him, she had a new course (Interrogation Techniques Level 2 Part 1) starting at 10:00 down in Ras en Nabaa.

She came in, dressed in her first-day-of-new-course outfit of knee-length black skirt and blue shirt. "Will you ever stop eating those things?" she scolded, taking an orange from the fruit bowl and loading a capsule into the Nespresso machine.

"Your course started already?" smiled Jihad. "Spousal Interrogation Basic?" He was tempted to dab a speck of jam on her nose but he didn't want the course to change into Spousal Abuse Post Graduate (F to M).

"You smoke too much, you drink too much and you eat those things. You must look after yourself more. Think of what you are putting into your body." She ignored his lecherous leer. "They will be the death of you."

He tapped her bottom as she walked past, her coffee in one hand, orange in the other. "No, *you* will be the death of me, after what you did to me last night." He rinsed his cup in the sink.

"Two nights running! And me an old clapped-out incapable fifty-three year old!"

"You are not incapable, I'll give you that. About the rest, you are right." She squealed as splashes of water flew in her direction. Then she asked, "You going in now?"

"*Oui.*"

"I'll leave round about seven. Is your head any clearer this morning?"

"Frankly, no. I don't know what Carla is up to, but it seems she'll tell me in her own good time. Need to know, as always. I'm going to go through the files of Haddad and Khalef today, to get myself up to speed and also to see if there is anything else. But we can't have more than one spy, surely? The spycatchers can't be the spies!"

"You know what the Israelis are like. What better cover?"

"But that cannot work, eliminating your own spies defeats your own objectives."

"Maybe. But remember Security Induction Course Day 1 Module 1: suspect everyone, trust no one, question everything, check everything. Then do it all over again."

"I remember when there were enough hours in the day to do that. Right, I've got to go." He pecked Gisele on the cheek (he knew better than to mess up her lipstick on a work day) and went out into the hallway, pulling on his jacket. "I'll see you tonight."

"Shall I cook?"

"No, I'll get something out. Don't know what time I'll be back."

She would cook anyway, they both knew it. "Take care, husband."

"Another day, another dollar."

Jihad closed the front door behind him, unaware that to that maxim could be added 'another death'.

## Mount Lebanon 06:30

Paradise and Love awoke simultaneously, as they always did. They were lying in the wide double bed like inverted bookends, their bodies mirror-imaging. White eyes looked at each other and they smiled and kissed.

*"Sabah el-khair, habibi,"* said Love. "We slept well."

"As we always do when satisfied."

They touched the space in between them. The Master never stayed the night. He was always there when the sisters went to sleep but never when they woke up. He would be back in his own bedroom.

Paradise got up, slipped on her pants and a vest, and went out (it was her turn to prepare breakfast while Love showered). Behind the closed door of the next bedroom, Abu Yo'roub was snoring as if he was in the finals of a lumberjack competition. Further along, The Master's bedroom door was open. Paradise looked in, wondering if it was signal that The Master required more pleasure. But the room was empty. His bed was made but she knew that when he was alone he always slept on the floor. He was not on the floor.

He was not downstairs either, not even out on the balcony performing his daily stretching exercises. He was gone, up and out early.

Paradise knew it was not her place to concern herself with The Master's activities. If his absence impacted on her and Love's duties, they would be informed as necessary.

She began to prepare *ftoor*.

## South Beirut 06:35

The Suzuki 1500 VL Intruder weaved through the back streets. Beirut was a late-to-bed early-to-rise city and already the streets were busy but at this hour the daily gridlock had not yet taken hold. The Damascene drove fast but kept within the speed limit.

Half an hour ago he had received a call.

He was needed urgently.

## Somewhere in Beirut 07:30

The Confession looked at the list of twelve names. Twelve names with three crossed through. Three was good but this was taking too long, the rate of reckoning needed to be increased.

The open MacBook showed the calendar entries for today for all the sinners. Like there were mass weddings and, sometimes in this country of death, mass funerals too, perhaps there should be mass penance? Communal retribution.

The Confession put down the coffee cup and looked out of the window. It was a bright, sunny day. Nine names left out of twelve.

Or was it ten out of thirteen?

## Ashrafieh, Beirut 09:00

Carla left the Hotel Albergo and turned right on Abdel el Wahab el Inglizi Street. She was wearing a short green cotton dress and a white jacket, her Barbour messenger bag over her shoulder, her Prada sunglasses hiding her eyes from the low sun of the autumn morning. As always, her black hair cascaded down her back, bouncing as she walked, with a scrunch held by the black and gold hairclip.

Her biker's leathers were in the panniers on her Honda VFR1200FD which had overnighted in the secure indoor Parking next to the ABC shopping mall eight hundred metres down the road (one did not turn up at the exclusive Hotel Albergo on a motorbike!).

Bikes were becoming fashionable in Beirut. As she crossed over to the north side of the narrow, busy street, she saw more than one motorbike manoeuvring in between the slow-moving vehicles. One of the bikers even wore a helmet!

She reached the Parking and made her way down to the lower level. It was quiet down here, some cars, just two bikes in the motorcycle area, no people. But she knew there were cameras. There were always cameras. She could hear echoing brake squeals from higher levels as drivers negotiated the always-too-tight turns of this typical parking area. As with any indoor car park in the world, the place smelled of petrol and piss.

Retrieving her leathers from the panniers, she walked up into the mall, found the nearest rest room and changed.

Back at the bike, she took her helmet from the top box (there would be at least two bikers wearing helmets on the streets of Beirut today, something of a record!), started the bike and set off up the slope to the exit.

She was at the barrier when she noticed something and held back. Over the other side of the street a bike was waiting by the kerb, a big bike, possibly a Ducati. The rider, like her, was clad in leather, with a helmet and black visor. Was it the one she had noticed coming down the street on her way in? If not, make that *three* bikers wearing helmets on the streets of Beirut today.

An SUV came up the exit slope, a GMC Yukon, and she waved it ahead of her, patting her pockets as if looking for her ticket. The driver of the Yukon fed his ticket into the slot, there was a momentary pause while the machine thought about it, and then the barrier raised.

As the Yukon drove out, Carla side piggy-backed it, keeping level with the vehicle, hidden from the view of the biker opposite. She resisted the urge to gun her engine and speed away, that would only draw attention, so she kept level with the Yukon for a few metres and then whipped the bike left into the narrow Madrassat es Salam Street. Quickly she pulled over by the road leading to the back of the Empire cinema, looking round, waiting for the other bike to appear at the top of the road.

Nothing happened, no bike appeared. Beneath the visor she

smiled. She set off again, taking an immediate left into Mariam Jahchan Street. At the end of the street she stopped, looking left across the road. The Ducati was still there, opposite the parking exit.

Carla settled back in her seat. She had a good idea who it was. Someone who had recognised her in the street, someone who knew she favoured the Hotel Albergo. Someone who had come looking for her and had found her. Someone who wanted her dead?

Well, two people could play the waiting game...

## Bourj el-Barajneh, Beirut 09:30

It was a fine day but the sun's rays did not find their way down into the Bourj el-Barajneh Palestinian refugee camp. The one square kilometre of basic brick constructions which pass as dwellings are packed so tight together that the sun stops at the top of the buildings, not daring to venture down. Most paths between the buildings are less than half a metre wide, some alleyways even tighter.

Normally Captain Fadi Lattouf would not attend a call-out in the camp, that was the responsibility of Sergeant Alarab who himself would delegate it to one of the Corporals. But this crime, if true, was different. It was the most heinous crime of all, and it demanded the presence of the police chief. It was a crime greater even than rape (of which there was very little), murder (some), violence (plenty) and robbery (hardly any – what did these poor souls have that was worth stealing?). The crime needed to be dealt with expeditiously and the results erased before the groups found out: someone had daubed a Star of David on one of the walls in the north of the camp. What was worse (if anything could be worse), it was over a wall-stencil of the smiling face of Abu Ammar (Mohammed Abdel Rahman Abdel Raouf Arafat al-Qudwa al-Husseini, popularly known as Yasser Arafat).

Lattouf stepped gingerly over broken water pipes and around liquid puddles (which might not be water), ducking as necessary beneath overhanging electricity cables. Next to him Sergeant Alarab was equally cautious, even more so because he carried a tin of paint.

The crime would not be solved, of course. In a camp of thirty-thousand inhabitants pressed into one square kilometre of hell, very few crimes were solved, very few miscreants brought to justice – at least by the police. The groups had their own justice system and meted out their own punishments.

Even with their knowledge of the camp, it took Lattouf and Alarab half an hour to find the defiled wall and another twenty minutes for Alarab to paint over the abomination. Unfortunately it meant that the face of Yasser Arafat was obliterated as well, but that could not be helped. And now there was a nice blank piece of black brick that would be daubed upon by nightfall, hopefully this time with something patriotic.

As Lattouf ambled back to the police offices out near Annan Street, he saw a group of five boys playing football in a small, rubble-strewn open area. When the loose ball rolled over towards him, he kicked it back with glee, smiling and nodding as he walked on. He was past the boys when, with a dinging thud, the ball hit him on the back of the head.

Suddenly, all was quiet. Even the ball had not bounced away, it had fallen at his feet in shame. Lattouf turned. Five pale faces looked at him. None of them could have been older than ten. Lattouf looked down at the ball then back to the boys.

A snot-nosed urchin put his right arm across his heart. "S-sorry, *ustaz*." *Ustaz!* Cheeky little sod. "I – I was aiming at him." He pointed at one of his pals.

Lattouf bent down and picked up the ball in one hand, the plastic distorting in the agonising grip. His eyes went from the ball to the boys. Then he said, "No harm done. But be careful. Don't go breaking any windows." A daft thing to say, he realised. Were there any windows in the camp that were not broken? He threw the ball back and, without so much as a thank you, the boys continued playing as if the incident had never happened.

Lattouf walked on, wondering if it was lunchtime yet (Nada had given him a package of finely sliced leftover testicle with a white sauce and couscous). Then he stopped. Slowly he turned back to the boys who were once again oblivious to his presence. He watched them, passing the ball, trying to tackle each other, kicking the ball towards the one goal marked out with stones. Sometimes scoring, sometimes shooting and missing.

Lattouf frowned in thought.

Shooting and missing…

## Snoubra, Beirut 10:00

Sergeant Tamer Khalef, short, plump, bearded, spycatcher, sat at a table outside *Pain d'Or* beneath the Itani Building. Snoubra means pine tree in Arabic, and local legend says that a pine tree covering over forty square metres once stood at this spot. Imported Egyptian watermelons were sold under the canopy of the tree. Khalef did not have watermelon, he had a sweet flaky pastry and his second espresso.

On the table was a folded copy of that morning's *L'Orient-Le Jour* newspaper. The paper was folded because inside it was an envelope. And inside the envelope was five hundred US dollars.

Khalef looked at his watch. 10:00. He finished his coffee, stood up, brushed pastry flakes from his jacket, tucked the paper under his arm and began walking in the direction of the Hotel Bristol. He stopped outside a boys' toys shop, admiring the televisions, cameras and computers in the window.

"Can I help you, sir?" A small, wiry, not-too-clean man had come out of the shop. "You are interested in something? I give you good price."

"No, no," said Khalef. "Just looking. How much is that?" He tapped the newspaper on the window in the general direction of a Canon SLR camera.

"For you? Five hundred dollars." The small man smiled, showing a gap either side of his two brown front teeth.

"Too much," said Khalef and walked away.

"Thank you, sir!" called the small man who somehow now had the newspaper under his arm. "May Allah's blessings be upon you!"

"Whatever," mumbled Khalef. Five hundred dollars was steep but the small man's information had proved useful. A similar shop down in Dahieh – who just happened to be the small man's business rival – was suspected of including malware in the computers, smart TVs and even cameras it was supplying to certain local residents. Malware which enabled a third party not only to listen to but also to see everything that was going on in the vicinity of the device. That third party may or may not be Mossad.

Khalef had blocked off the entire morning in his calendar for this visit, it was a nice sunny day, so he decided to walk back to the office. He headed north-east up Dunant Street. He would cut through to the Sanayeh Public Garden, enjoy a smoke, maybe watch some old men playing cards, backgammon or chess...

## Sanayeh, Beirut 10:15 – 11:00

The Sanayeh Public Garden has never actually been called that. When it was created in 1907 it was called the Hamidi Public Garden, then over eighty years later it was renamed the René Moawad Public Garden in honour of the 13th President of Lebanon who was assassinated nearby by a 250 kilogram car bomb on 22 November 1989 after just seventeen days in office. But to locals the place has always been simply the Sanayeh Public Garden.

It was early yet, a few old men were shuffling about or sitting down with groans but no games had started. Further out near

Sanayeh Street, two artists were setting up their work for exhibit.

Tamer Khalef found a bench near the centre of the park and lit up a Cedars cigarette. The sound of Beirut was a constant three-sixty degree hum but the further you went into the gardens the more muted it became, so here it was just a background purr. No sound could be distinguished separately.

So he was not aware of the sound of the motorbike engine as it circled the perimeter of the gardens...

With a sigh and an exhaled lungful of smoke, Tamer Khalef stood up, stretching his back. Time to return. He had just received a phone call from Sergeant Deeb el-Gharib asking him if he knew where Nabil Haddad was, his colleague's calendar was blank which meant he should be in. Khalef had a good idea where Haddad might be but he didn't say so – the good Christian Haddad went to church on a Sunday, where there was a widow that was always pestering him. Maybe this week he had succumbed to her charms and was having a lie-in after a day of ravagement! He looked forward to hearing a blow by blow account.

As he walked nearer to the edge of the gardens, the sound of Beirut increased. By the time he was at the Rue Spears exit, the city had engulfed him again. Now there was too much noise for him to distinguish one noise from another. So he was not aware of the Ducati motorbike approaching.

He crossed the road, turning left at the Faculty of Law Administration and Political Science Building into Halwani Street. It was a straight five minutes' walk north to the State Security Building. Cars passed by, people walked on the sidewalk.

The motorbike drove at a reduced speed a little way back, the rider leaning forward, steering with the right hand, something metallic and black in the left. Gradually the bike drew level with Khalef. The left hand raised.

Suddenly there was a thunder of acceleration and another bike roared into the street, heading fast for the Ducati. The second bike clipped the Ducati's back wheel and then roared on, not stopping. The Ducati wobbled and tipped. Instinctively, the Ducati rider jumped out and away, like a pilot ejecting from a crashing warplane, avoiding the bike as it fell, expertly rolling on impact with the ground to minimise injury.

Lithely the rider stood back up, avoiding a hooting car and quickly hiding the gun in the half-open leather blouson. One or two people were looking but most seemed not to care. Not removing the helmet or raising the visor, the rider ran back over to the Ducati. The machine had cut out and was half under a parked Mitsubishi Outlander. The rider dragged it out. With a superhuman effort, and after four attempts, the rider managed to pull the bike back upright. It was scraped but there seemed to be no serious damage, no fluid leakage. It started after the second turn of the key.

By now, Tamer Khalef had reached the intersection with Bank of Lebanon Street. He had heard the sound of a mild impact, which was an every day every minute occurrence in Beirut. He looked back to see a motorbike rider walking across the road to an overturned bike. He shrugged. At least the rider was wearing a helmet!

He crossed Bank of Lebanon Street and entered the State Security Building.

The Ducati reached Bank of Lebanon Street, turned right and drove away.

## Somewhere in Beirut 11:00

The Confession slammed a gloved hand down onto the fuel tank of the bike as it wove in and out of the traffic as Bank of Lebanon Street became Michel Chiha Street, heading into central Beirut. By the British Embassy, the bike nearly took out two tourists heading for the nearby Grand Serail, the Prime

Minister's offices. Fists were shaken. Choice words were shouted in return but they were confined within the reflective visor.

As it entered downtown, the bike was forced to slow by the narrowness of the streets and the amount of traffic. In Martyr's Square, in between The Tomb of the Martyr Rafic Hariri and the Virgin Megastore, The Confession pulled over.

The visor was raised. The chin strap was unclipped and the helmet was pulled off. Hair was shaken out. Two leather gloves were pulled off and slapped against the fuel tank. The Confession sat back in the saddle in contemplation, breathing heavily, bringing emotions under control.

That should have been another name crossed off the list. It would have been had it not been for that meddling bitch. How had she managed to turn the tables so that the hunter became the hunted? But the interference had been inevitable. The Confession had been too kind, too understanding. Too friendly.

The Confession had failed. The Confession did not like failure. It was not, as they say, an option.

And it was only temporary.

It was time to end it.

## Jonblat, Beirut 11:00

"Have you found him?"

"Nothing yet, sir," said Sergeant Deeb el-Gharib from the doorway. "He's not answering his mobile and I've tried his home. I've phoned Khalef but he doesn't know where he is."

"Okay, keep trying, will you?"

"Sir. Oh by the way, Facilities have been on. The door will be done this week."

"Thank you, Deeb."

Merhi did not like the management side of the work, rankers (somebody who had come up through the ranks) never did, unlike the college-educated twats that came straight in at senior level and were good for nothing else. But it would be his pleasure to tear Nabil Haddad's bollocks off when he turned up.

First thing this morning, Merhi had gone up to what he had taken to calling The Spycatchers' Office on the fifth floor, only to find it empty. A check of calendars revealed that Khalef was out with a source in Snoubra but Haddad's calendar was blank, which meant he was due in. He had not turned up, no phone call, no text message, not even an e-mail. From a reading of the HR files, he had found out that Haddad lived alone so maybe, giving him every benefit of the doubt, he was lying in bed too ill to even reach his phone. Merhi would have to send somebody up to Mansourieh later if needs be.

Haddad's non-appearance had prompted him to call a team meeting for this afternoon. The spycatchers were too remote up there, too autonomous in their little eyrie on the fifth floor. He would announce at the meeting that both his teams would be situated together here on the second floor, that would enable cross-working also, thereby enhancing the resources of both his teams without any actual increase in staff. That would please Lieutenant-Colonel Ghanem. Results not problems. Deeb el-Gharib had sent out the e-mail moments ago. Team Meeting, General Office, 16:00 today, Monday 29 October.

"So you think – what was his name? - *Gerges* was the spy?" said Lieutenant-Colonel Pierre Ghanem in a tone that said he didn't believe a word of it.

"I am satisfied," said Jihad Merhi. "You said to bring you results not problems. I am bringing you the result."

"What about his wife? I felt nothing untoward when I made the death notification."

"You wouldn't. She probably knows nothing about it. But I'll have her brought in for interrogation."

"Go easy. She took it badly."

"Of course, but what better time? I doubt she knew a thing,

but we'll find out." Merhi reached into his pocket for his cigarettes and then remembered where he was. Ghanem's office was a smoke-free zone.

"And he was killed by a member of the GSU?"

"Yes."

"After receiving intelligence from abroad?"

"Yes."

"Fortuitous. It's a pity we didn't expose him ourselves."

"In the war with the Jews we must utilise all resources whether they are at our direct disposal or not."

Ghanem nodded. Then he said, "I am not happy that a member of the GSU takes it upon himself to kill a member of the ISF though." He raised his hand as Merhi was about to interject. "But I can understand in this instance. Needs must. But it should not happen again. So it's a 'Well done', Major."

"I would like to honour the GSU operative."

"No."

"As you wish. On other matters, I have done a brief report for you on the future of the team, as requested. It should be in your in-tray," he nodded at Ghanem's laptop. "I'm bringing them all together, I have room on the second floor. They will cross-work as one unit. So saving resources and, indeed, freeing a room up here."

"Good, Major, good. We'll make a manager of you yet."

Please don't. "I'm having a team meeting this afternoon at sixteen hundred. Will you come to it?" He knew Ghanem was usually on his way home by that hour.

But the Lieutenant-Colonel surprised him. "Actually, yes, I think I will. We can show them what a good management command you and I make. Send me the agenda, will you?"

Sergeant Deeb el-Gharib intercepted Merhi as he passed by the General Office door. "Boss – sir. Two things. Khalef is back. And Captain Lattouf has been trying to get hold of you."

Merhi wondered if his groan was out loud or just in his head.

"Why the hell didn't Lattouf ring my mobile?" He pulled the iPhone from his pocket. It was dead. "Shit. Battery. Okay Deeb, thanks. Did he say what it was about?"

"Not as far as I could make out, sir. You know how he shouts."

"I'll call him later. Any sludge on?"

"Just brewed a fresh pot."

Back in his office with his coffee, Merhi took his lightning charger from a drawer, plugged it into a wall socket, plugged his phone into the charger, inserted the systems access card into the ATS laptop then stuck his right index finger on the laptop's biometric pad. The screens on the laptop and the phone illuminated simultaneously. He lit up a cigarette as he waited for the Desktop screen to appear on the computer.

Suddenly his floor started buzzing. His iPhone was glowing. The charging wire was not long enough to stretch up to the desk so he had to bend over in his chair, stretching the wire as he quickly raised the phone to his ear. He had seen who it was, he needed this call.

"Ms Saad."

"Major, we need to meet."

"Are you all right?"

"Yes but there is something you need to know. I cannot tell you over the phone."

"Of course not. When and where?"

"The Palestinian Code, tomorrow at 16:00."

"The what?"

"Think, Major, we have used it before. Your friend."

"My...? Oh! Yes, yes. I'll be there. Thank you for sorting out our little problem. With the... interloper."

"That *is* the problem. I have sorted nothing."

"You are being modest - "

"You are in great danger. *Tomorrow. Sixteen hundred.* You understand what I am saying?"

"Yes - "

She was gone.

Merhi looked at the screen showing just his wallpaper of the Jeita Grotto and placed his phone back down on the floor.

Now what was that all about? He stayed bent over, cigarette in his mouth, looking like he was hiding behind the desk. Carla had used The Palestinian Code before – it was named after Fadi Lattouf. Originally it was the code he and Merhi used when they met for clandestine liaison between the ISF and the Palestinian Civil Police in the dark days (as if the days were any brighter now!). The named time less twenty-six hours. So tomorrow at sixteen hundred would be today at fourteen hundred. He looked at his watch. Under two hours' time. The location would always be the same: the Food Court on the second floor of The Dunes Shopping Mall over in Verdun.

Fourteen hundred was cutting it fine. If she wanted to see him straightaway why didn't she just come here to the office? And what did she mean, he was in great danger? And she had sorted nothing? Killing Gerges the spy had sorted everything. Unless she was going to confirm his speculation that there was more than one spy...?

Slowly, slowly he straightened up, his back stiff and on the verge of a spasm, coming up from behind his desk like a dragon rising from its rest, exhaling smoke. Then he jumped and the cigarette almost fell from his mouth, ash cascading onto his lap. A giant creature was standing in his office doorway.

"Lunchtime of bounteous ideas, my friend," smiled Fadi Lattouf. "*Al-salaam 'aalaykum.*"

## Somewhere in Beirut 12:15

"You are in great danger. *Tomorrow. Sixteen hundred.* You understand what I am saying?"

"Yes - "

The Confession pulled out the ear buds and placed the iPhone down on the table. *Tomorrow, sixteen hundred* meant

*Today, fourteen hundred.* And the location, always the Food Court in the Dunes Shopping Mall. Hopefully Merhi remembered The Palestinian Code.

The MacBook was on the table with the Team Meeting notification and small Agenda on the screen. There was now an additional e-mail above it. The Confession filled in the time, so that the e-mail read:

> Subject: Team Meeting Notification amendment
>
> The Meeting will now start at 14:00 in the General Office. Attendance is mandatory.
>
> JM

The Confession pressed the Send button and the e-mail went on its way, forwarded to all.

Finishing the black Americano coffee, The Confession nodded thanks at the barista behind the counter and left the café.

The bike was parked two streets away, but that was no problem. The Confession no longer needed to rush.

## Jonblat, Beirut 12:15

"Shaitan's bollocks, Fadi, how did you get in?"

Lattouf was in his uniform trousers and open-necked blue shirt under the black leather bomber jacket. The 'Visitor' ID was around his neck. "My twin brother signed me in. Your Sergeant, Deeb el-Gharib, my fellow shotgun." He laughed. "Fadi and Deeb, the el-Gharib brothers!"

"I'm busy right now, Fadi, I have an urgent appointment in Ver - " Oh shit.

"Verdun? Are you going to Verdun? The Dunes?"

"No, I - "

"Perfect. I've hardly eaten all day, I am starving." It must have been a full half hour since he had finished yesterday's leftover testicles and couscous together with a side helping of scrapings from the children's plates. "I'll give you a lift."

On cue, car horns started blaring from the street below. Merhi refused to go over to the window, knowing what he would see. "Your car or your official van?"

"My car, of course. It is less conspicuous."

## Verdun, Beirut 12:30

Fifteen minutes later (after pausing at the lavatory to let Lattouf open his bladder and send alarm bells ringing in the flood defences of Beirut) they were in the less conspicuous bright orange Datsun Bluebird coughing and growling down Dunant Street. In between making derogatory remarks about the local drivers, Lattouf was waxing lyrical about the plethora of masticatory delights that awaited them in the Food Court of the Dunes Shopping Mall: *McDonald's*, *DipnCrunch*, *Doodle Doo*, *Haagen Dazs* and their mutual favourite *Cup Cake*. Such was his enthusiasm that Merhi was unable to ask him the reason for his appearance in the ISF offices until they were driving into the mall's parking area.

"What did you want, Fadi?"

"Thank you, my friend. A supersized Big Mac Meal with Coke, two apple pies, a Smarties McFlurry and a cup cake and coffee for dessert."

"No, why did you call? Why did you come to see me?"

Lattouf found a free bay and pulled up sharply, glaring at a Ford Mustang coming towards him with equal intentions for the space. "No way, flash boy!" He gave dismissive flicks of his hand out of the window and then crunched the Bluebird's manual gear shift into reverse. Merhi closed his eyes and trusted in God.

Actually Lattouf parked with the dexterity of an expert. As he switched off the engine and Merhi opened his eyes, Lattouf said "Football statistics."

"I'm sorry?"

"I will explain upstairs. It is something for you to consider. Let us go before I expire from starvation. *Yalla.*"

As they got off the escalator at the second floor, Lattouf's face fell. *Cup Cake* was no longer there! And *Doodle Doo* was just history. But his face rose again when he saw that there was now a *Zaatar w Zeit* selling *manousheh* (filled flat bread) and an *Urbanista* ('Food, coffee and people'). And thank Allah for *McDonald's!*

Merhi instructed Lattouf to find a table, and he went over to order, thanking God that he had been to an ATM this morning.

It took him ten minutes, by which time Lattouf had not only found a table but, by a combination of unfortunate bodily sounds and his sheer physical presence, had cleared all the tables around also, as if that corner of the Food Court was a crime scene – which it would become as soon as Lattouf started murdering his food.

The tray held the pre-requested items from *McDonald's* plus three grease-wrapped *manousheh* and two double espresso.

Merhi sat down opposite, taking one of the coffees and a *manousheh.* "I got you one *zaatar* and one *jibneh.*"

"Bless your hands, my friend, you are too kind. But you are a bad influence, you know. Nada has me on a diet."

Merhi reached out to take the other two *manousheh* but Lattouf snatched them faster than a hand-grabbing money box. "But I am not ill mannered. As always, you are generous." Lattouf opened a *manousheh* wrapper, tore the twenty centimetre long folded over flatbread in half, put both halves together on top of each other, bent them over into a semi-tube shape and slid the entire construction into his mouth.

Merhi had known the Palestinian giant for too long to be even remotely fazed. He looked at his watch, then glanced around the Food Court and over to the escalator. It was 13:00. One hour to his meeting with Carla. One hour to feed and get rid of Lattouf. "So," he said, "what is it about football statistics that brings you all the way into town to see me?"

"You were not answering your phone." Had the *manousheh* been chewed at all or simply swallowed whole?

"It was dead."

"Ah." Lattouf flipped open the lid of the Big Mac box with the gleaming eyes of an explorer opening a chest of treasure. "It is just something that occurred to me in the camp today. Something to consider. Regarding your internal spy."

"That is done with."

"It probably is, as we said. Have you told The Party yet?"

"About the conclusion? No."

"Good. Just in case." Half the Big Mac disappeared.

"What in the name of Christ are you trying to say, Fadi?"

"Isa and all the prophets. I might be just crossing my eyes and dotting my tees here. You know how when you watch football on TV, especially those English matches, they have statistics coming up, number of fouls, number of corners, number of shots, number of shots on target, number of shots off target."

"And?"

"The gun, the FN Five-seveN. Same gun, same perpetrator, we know, right? The attempt on – what was his name, the Palestinian child?"

"Abdul Abdulrahman."

"Him. Yes. A shot but off target."

"Yes, *I* was the one that shot him."

Lattouf finished off the Big Mac. "So how can we be certain that Abdul Rahman was the target?"

Merhi sat back in his chair, frowning. What was Lattouf going on about? "Because he was spying for the Israelis."

"And your man – what was his name?" A handful of fries followed the Big Mac.

"Gerges. Claude Gerges."

"How do you know he was a spy? Do you have proof?"

"Because Ca – because he was shot too. Two Israeli spies. Eliminated. Perfect goals, to use your analogy."

"What if the goals were disallowed for offside?"

Merhi said nothing.

"What if the gun was not aimed at Abdul Rahman at all?"

The incident was playing in Merhi's mind. Lattouf driving along the coastal road, their windows open. The motorbike behind drawing level. The gun. *The bullet missing him by five centimetres...* And Carla's recent phone call. *"You are in great danger..."*

No, it could not be. That would mean everything he had thought, everything he had assumed, was wrong. It would mean that Claude Gerges was not a spy.

"What if the gun was aimed at you?"

## Jonblat, Beirut 13:15

The Confession walked into the State Security Building and nodded at the Corporal on security duty, taking the MacBook out of the shoulder bag and laying it on top of the bag on the inspection table. The Corporal picked up the MacBook and gave it a cursory visual check, then he checked the empty bag and nodded. The Confession walked through the metal detector. No alarm went off.

Gathering up the MacBook and the bag, The Confession walked over to the Reception desk, greeted the Corporal on duty there, and signed in.

## Verdun, Beirut 13:20

"It is just a theory," said Fadi Lattouf, Smartie McFlurry caught in his beard like fairy lights on a Christmas tree. "An alternative scenario."

It had taken Merhi several minutes of contemplation to even entertain what had been suggested but reason and cold logic told him that Lattouf had a point. Nothing about this matter had sat easily with him. Carla had said there was a spy in the ISF – she had not said anything else. He had formulated his own hypothesis and had run with it, but Lattouf had now turned that on its head. That was not to say Lattouf was right but it was worth considering (suspect everyone, trust no one, question everything, check everything: Security Induction Course Day 1 Module 1).

"So in your alternative scenario, I was the target."

"Yes."

"Why?"

Lattouf finished his ice cream (the apple pies were but a memory) and frowned at the tray. "That I do not know," he said distractedly. He lifted several wrappers and the Big Mac box, looking underneath.

Merhi sighed. He was in desperate need of his psychoactive chemical but the Food Court was non-smoking. "*Cup Cake* has gone, Fadi, remember? But I'll get you a coffee."

"I couldn't eat any more anyway, I am full." Lattouf couldn't keep the disappointment from his voice as he patted his rotund gut. "I think Nada's diet is shrinking my insides. But I'll enjoy a coffee, thank you. A triple espresso and an Americano please."

Merhi stood and walked towards *Urbanista*.

"Oh Abu Samer," called Lattouf. "Maybe I can squeeze in a New York cheesecake?"

Merhi nodded, "Two triple espressos, one Americano and one slice of cheesecake," and continued on.

"No," shouted Lattouf. "One cheesecake."

## Jonblat, Beirut 13:20

The Confession walked up the stairs, the visitor's ID tag bouncing, the lanyard with the continuous pattern of twee Lebanese flags outside of the hair at the back.

As The Confession reached the landing of the second floor,

the door swung open and Sergeant Deeb el-Gharib came through with a folder in his hand. He smiled when he saw The Confession and reached back to hold the door open. *"Ah, bonjour,* nice to see you again."

*"Bonjour* Deeb, is he in?"

"No, he's out at the moment but he'll be back soon. Have you come for the meeting?"

"Yes. I am a surprise Agenda item. Any other business."

el-Gharib smiled. "There's some sludge, if you want it."

"Thank you."

"You know where it is. Make yourself at home." He looked at the computer in The Confession's hand. "Use his office if you want some peace and quiet."

"Thank you, I'll just prepare for this afternoon."

The Confession went through the doors, Sergeant Deeb el-Gharib went up the stairs.

## Verdun, Beirut 13:35

Merhi watched as the last of the whole cheesecake (and his US $40) said goodbye to the world. Lattouf burped out of politeness (and necessity) and picked up his Americano.

Merhi had had a quick Camel in the lavatory while Lattouf was snuffling his cheesecake, and he now felt calmer. "So, what does it mean if the assassin was aiming at me?" It was a half-question half-rumination.

"Have you upset anybody?"

"In this job? Well now, let me see…"

"You have been a good boy? No upset husbands?"

"Fadi!"

"I joke, my friend." Lattouf wiped his beard clean with his hands. "There is a problem you Lebanese have, I have noticed it before."

"Just the one?"

"The Lebanese have many problems. One day we might

discuss them. Right now I am thinking of one problem in particular."

Merhi didn't really want to hear it. Problems? Lebanese?

Lattouf continued. "You always take things personally."

"I what?"

"As a race. You Lebanese always think it's all about you. On a personal level. You think you are the wasp's ankles whereas in reality you are ostriches."

"What are you saying?" Merhi could not keep the pique from his voice. He did not need to be lectured on the Lebanese psyche by a bloody Palestinian!

Lattouf swilled Americano. "Perhaps the assassin was not aiming at Jihad Merhi."

"But just a few minutes ago you said I was the bloody target!"

"The Major of the ISF was the target. Not Jihad Merhi. It was not personal."

The empty Americano cup was put upside down on the other detritus on the tray. Merhi was staring at Lattouf. Lattouf gave a sympathetic, almost regretful, smile. "It is worth considering."

"But Gerges was shot…"

"Yes. And if he was not your Israeli spy, why was he? What would he have been?"

"What?"

"If they had managed to shoot you and then shoot him, what would he have been?"

"The second victim?"

"No."

"No?"

"The third victim."

"The third…?"

Lattouf held up four massive fingers, like a butcher holding up four meaty sausages. "Your Brigadier was the first." He bent one finger down. "Then it would have been you." Another finger. "Then Gerges." Third finger down.

Merhi knew his mouth was open slightly but he made no effort to close it.

Lattouf still had one finger in the air, unfortunately the middle finger. "Are the ISF spycatchers being killed off one by one?"

Merhi moved his mouth but nothing came out.

"And if so," Lattouf wiggled his finger. "Who is the next one?"

## Jonblat, Beirut 13:40

Jacket and bag left in Major Merhi's office, sludge finished (it wasn't too bad, it had the same consistency as Turkish coffee only with grit), The Confession walked up the stairs to the fifth floor carrying the MacBook. People passed on the stairs, one or two nodded.

Lieutenant-Colonel Ghanem's PA, Violette, was behind her desk. She looked up and smiled in recognition. "Hello! How are you? It's been a while since *you've* been up to the rarified atmosphere of the fifth floor!"

"I like to confine myself to the troops," said The Confession. "Keep my feet on the ground. But I have to discuss something with the Chief, is he in?"

"He might be having his nap. Wait there."

Violette went over to Ghanem's door, tapped lightly, gently opened it and peeked in. Then she straightened up and announced the visitor. There was a deep response and then Violette turned, deftly pushing the door open behind her. "He'll see you."

"*Merci ktir*, Violette." The MacBook was placed on the corner of Violette's desk. "Could you look after this for me?"

"*Bien sûr.*"

The Confession went in, lifting the ID tag and pulling off the lanyard over the dark hair. Violette closed the door.

Ghanem stood up, hand outstretched. "How are you? Nice to

see you again, I hear you have been having great success."

"Oh, one tries, sir." The Confession shook the outstretched hand.

Ghanem was expecting the light Arabic handshake (in the Middle East a firm handshake indicates aggression) but instead his fingers were grabbed and he was pulled forward, as if the visitor wished to embrace. He jolted, knocking over a mug of tea on his desk, and his first instinctive reaction was to smile at the stupid accident.

But then the lanyard was whipped around his neck. "Wha - "

Two steps and The Confession was behind Ghanem, expertly pulling the lanyard across Ghanem's windpipe, using the plasticised ID tag as a garrote, twisting it sharply.

Ghanem's hands went to his throat but the lanyard was already too tight. The Confession kicked him behind the knees and he went down, the movement tightening the lanyard even more. He was gasping.

The Confession pulled backwards, hearing Ghanem's ageing knees cracking, his gasps turning into gruff wheezes. The Confession twisted the garrote even more, using forearm strength, shaking Ghanem's head from side to side, seeing thick spittle flying from his mouth as his swollen tongue tried to move to let air in.

Ghanem's nails were clawing at his own neck, drawing blood, his white shirt collar becoming light red. His mouth was moving but no air could go in or out. His body was jerking as he tried to breathe. The Confession pushed his head backwards and forwards, side to side, the lanyard with the twee little Lebanese flags cutting, choking, strangling…

Ghanem tried to reach backwards to grab The Confession but his weak hands just flapped in the air. The Confession banged Ghanem's head on the desk. Once, twice… The lanyard was merciless. Strength left Ghanem, his hands dropped. Eternal darkness descended. Spilt tea dripped onto the floor…

The Confession maintained the garrote for five minutes after

Ghanem died to ensure his spirit had left his body. It was five minutes shorter than the time given to Mahmoud Abdel Rauf al-Mabhouh in Dubai in January 2010 because al-Mabhouh was suffocated not strangled.

Gently The Confession lowered Ghanem's body to the floor behind his desk. The lanyard with the Lebanese flags was embedded deep into the bloody neck, like a patriotic necklace. Or a choker. It would be too messy to remove it, so The Confession left it where it was, unclipping the Visitor ID tag from the back.

Opening the office door by just fifteen centimetres, The Confession said "Violette, I left my laptop on your desk, could you bring it in please...?"

## Verdun, Beirut 13:55

Merhi looked at his watch. Five minutes to go, and Lattouf was still there, eating an éclair to help his fourth mug of coffee go down. The cream on Lattouf's beard made him look like he was foaming at the mouth. Which was what Merhi should be doing after the insulting comments Lattouf had made about the Lebanese. Comments which made Merhi all the more angry because they were true.

And Lattouf's postulation about the spycatchers being killed off became more and more plausible with each second, with each thought. He had forgotten about the very public slaying of Brigadier Wissam al-Hassan. Had that only been ten days ago? It was the Brigadier's assassination that had brought Merhi into the realm of spycatching.

And Lattouf's theory cast a sinister shadow over the absence of Sergeant Nabil Haddad this morning. Had the fourth victim already been claimed?

He needed to talk to Carla. Maybe that's what she wanted to tell him, that the spycatchers were being killed, confirming Lattouf's premise. On reflection it was good that Lattouf was still here, he should hear what Carla had to say.

He looked at his watch again. Two minutes.

Opposite, Lattouf sighed contentedly, licking cream from his fingers and mouth in such a lascivious manner that Merhi felt personally violated. Lattouf leant sideways and, with a gratified smile, farted like a bull elephant on heat.

## Jonblat, Beirut 13:59

Violette didn't know she had died. One moment she was bringing in the laptop as requested, the next nothing. It was all over, blackness, as if her life had never happened in the first place. Her neck broke easily with one expert jerk of The Confession's arms.

The Confession caught the MacBook with one hand and lowered Violette to the floor with the other, flopping her body face down on top of Lieutenant-Colonel Ghanem behind the desk, Violette's arms either side of the dead man, her legs apart. Violette's skirt had raised making the scene look like a necrophilial sexual defilement. Considerately, The Confession pulled the dead woman's skirt down and kicked her legs together.

Crouching, The Confession flipped open Ghanem's jacket and removed his gun from his waistband holster, the standard-issue Browning 9mm. Drool rolled from Violette's half-open mouth onto Ghanem's swollen purple lips.

The Confession stood up and took one look around the room. Fingerprints did not matter, a false gossamer skin was being worn on the hands. Any residual DNA traces did not matter, they would match up with the fingerprints which would lead to the data of a person who had died years ago.

The Confession left the office and closed the door, taking a small, metallic object, like a matchbox, from a pocket. It was cutely named a 'Treble Clef' by its inventors in the south. Putting it by the lock, The Confession wiggled the box in place, pressed the On button, pushed it, turned it – and heard the lock click. Then a similar maneouvre slid the internal security bolt across. The door was now locked and bolted from the inside, just like the room in the Al Bustan Hotel in Dubai two years ago.

Putting the Treble Clef back in a pocket, The Confession took out a phone and looked at the time.

14:00.

## Verdun, Beirut 14:01

Jihad Merhi looked at his watch for the thousandth time. Across the table, Fadi Lattouf sat back like a satisfied Buddha, hands resting on the plateau of his stomach.

Merhi's phone rang. He took it from his inside jacket pocket, looked at the screen and then banged his finger against the green icon.

"Where are you?" as he said it he looked around the Food Court and then out into the shopping area.

"I am here."

"I cannot see you."

Watching Merhi's eyes dashing from one side of the Food Court to the other, Lattouf joined in even though he did not know what he was expected to see.

"Of course not. The Palestinian is with you."

"Yes, we had… other business."

"I cannot appear if he is there."

"Well, he is," Merhi looked across the table. "And he has an interesting theory."

"That the spycatchers are in trouble? Your team is being killed?"

"How did you know?"

There was silence.

"Carla…?"

"Because it is true."

"What?"

"I finally figured out the cryptic report. It is simple. The list of names is a hit list. You put paid to the total Israeli espionage operation in Beirut. Now they are putting paid to you."

"Revenge?"

"The Israelis are good at that. And with your team removed they can initiate new operations, new people, get their activities back up to speed. They cannot be in a position of disadvantage, especially with what is happening in Syria. We have said before, Major, that battles might be won but the war is never over."

"But you said there was a spy in the ISF."

"There is."

Merhi frowned. "What are you saying? They are getting help from the inside?"

"Perhaps more than that."

"I cannot believe that one of my men would be responsible for – Just a minute, we have the CCTV. It shows you killing Claude Gerges."

Lattouf was staring at Merhi, fascinated at the one side of the conversation he could hear, eyebrows raised.

The voice on the phone said, "Shut up you idiot."

"Don't you fucking tell me to - "

"It was not me!"

Merhi span around in his seat again. "Show yourself."

"And have you and your fat friend arrest me? Believe me when I say I have only Lebanon's interests at heart. Only your interests."

"Are you sure they're not Israel's interests?"

Silence again. Then, softly, she said "You do not understand, do you?"

"What?"

"For the majority to live, some have to die."

Merhi shook his head. "No, they do not. That is a myth. Show yourself now, come in and we will sort this out together."

"No. It is better that I stay outside."

"Then consider yourself wanted."

"I have been wanted for seven years."

"Our business is not finished. I will find you."

"*I* will find *you*. In the meantime, Major…"

"What?"

"Get back to your office as quick as you can. Your team is in danger."

"Carla, what have you done?"

"I will find you, Major."

"You little bitch, I'll… Hello?...Hello?" Merhi threw the phone down onto the table. It landed on the tray, its fall broken by the empty Big Mac box. Greasy papers flew onto the floor. "Fucking bollocking arseholes!"

People from the non-evacuated tables were beginning to look. Merhi eyes searched the area again. He was fuming, face red with anger. Then he pulled his Camel King Size from his pocket, lit one up and swallowed the burning smoke like a dehydrated man in the desert gulps water. He glared at Lattouf as if it was all his fault.

While Merhi still breathed heavily, Lattouf's fingers walked daintily across the table and took a cigarette from the packet. "My friend," he said as he leant further forward and picked up the lighter. "Can you smell jasmine?"

## Jonblat, Beirut 14:05

"Hi, sorry I'm late." The Confession walked into the General Office, jacket over forearm, bag on shoulder.

"Don't worry," said Sergeant Deeb el-Gharib, pouring himself some sludge. "The boss isn't here yet."

A makeshift conference table had been set up by pushing three desks together. "Where's he gone?" The Confession found an empty place at the end nearest the door and put the bag on the seat.

"Don't know. His calendar is blank."

"He'd have our bollocks if it was one of us," grunted Sergeant Tamer Khalef who was smoking over by the window.

The rest of the team laughed ruefully. The five Corporals were already seated around the makeshift table: Jad Chadidi, Omar Mostafa, Michel Yammine, Peter Harrak and Emad Hmedeh.

The Confession threw the jacket over the back of the chair, opening the bag and taking out the MacBook.

"Where's your...?" asked Khalef, making motions at his own ID tag around his neck. "We all have to wear them nowadays. If you haven't got one on we must 'confront' you. Mwah-ha-haah!"

The Confession held up the ID tag. "The neck-thing broke, fell off and got wedged somewhere."

"Cheap crap," Khalef blew smoke out of the half-open window.

"I'll have a word with Facilities," said el-Gharib. "They're coming up sometime this week to fix the boss's door. Right, I'm just going for a leak. If the Major turns up, don't start without me."

Jad Chadidi looked at his watch. "Don't know why he had to change it to two o'clock anyway if he's going to be late."

"Ours not to reason why, Corporal, ours not to reason why." el-Gharib went out.

"So, to what do we owe this honour?" Michel Yammine asked The Confession. "Or is it a secret?"

"New procedures," explained The Confession. "New ways of working. I've been asked to talk about them. I'll tell you more later."

"No handouts, I hope," said Peter Harrak. "There's nothing worse than fucking handouts at a meeting."

The Confession smiled at the faux-complaint. "Actually I do have something you can have now." The Confession flipped open the top of the bag, rummaged inside with a screwing action of the right hand – and brought out Ghanem's Browning

9mm, now with an AAC Spider 2 suppressor on the end.

It was over in five seconds, less than one second for each of the six men in the room.

Peter Harrak went first, on the left next to The Confession, the right side of his head taken off. Then the gun swung over to the right, a bullet into the forehead of Emad Hmedeh. Still on the right, the left eye of Michel Yammine. Left, the top of the head of Omar Mostafa. Left, the entire face of Jad Chadidi.

Sergeant Tamer Khalef had actually begun to move away from the window, but he had been distracted by Yammine's blood splashing into his face. His right hand was at his waistband when a bullet slammed into his heart, sending him sprawling backwards on top of the sludge table, mugs and pot flying, breaking, dark coffee splattering over an area disproportionate to the amount spilled.

It was done.

The Confession looked around, satisfied, then put the jacket back on, put the MacBook into the bag, the bag over a shoulder and walked out into the corridor, closing the door. Once again, the Treble Clef was used and the door was locked from the inside. The Confession walked off, gun in hand.

On the coffee table back in the General Office, blood oozed out of the chest of Tamer Khalef, mingling and mixing with the spilt coffee.

Adding body to the sludge.


The lavatories were out on the stairwell, male and female on alternate floors. On this floor it was the *Femmes*. The Confession did not have time to wait, an informed guess needed to be made. It is easier to carry a full bladder downwards than upwards, so The Confession went down.

The *Hommes* lavatories on the first floor smelled, as *Hommes* lavatories do everywhere (tomcats will be tomcats). The three urinals were empty, one out of the three cubicles was in use. The Confession entered the cubicle next to the occupied one.

Standing on the bowl, The Confession looked carefully over the wooden partition into the next cubicle.

Deeb el-Gharib was squatting, trousers around his ankles. He was reaching for paper when The Confession shot him in the top of the head from above. Because of the downward trajectory, there was no blood spatter, no outwards shards of bone, a maroon hole just appeared in the top of his head and the body slumped but remained in the sitting position. The bullet would later be found amongst the excreta in the bowl, having passed straight through what was once Deeb el-Gharib.

The Confession gingerly unscrewed the hot suppressor, placed it and the gun in the shoulder bag, and left the cubicle, giving a little shove on the occupied cubicle's door. No need for the Treble Clef this time, the subject had locked the door himself.

Over by the outside door, The Confession turned. Of all the deaths that had been ordered, that of the long-serving Sergeant Deeb el-Gharib was the saddest. He had been like a permanent fixture of the Internal Security Force, the wise, experienced *maître d'* of the second floor. If only the spycatchers had not come his way…

With respect, The Confession said "Ours but to do and die, Deeb, ours but to do and die," and left the lavatory.

## Jonblat, Beirut 14:50

Traffic had been busy on Rachid Karame Street down in Verdun and by the time the same street became Dunant Street in Snoubra it was crawling at less than walking pace. The occupants of the bright orange Datsun Bluebird did not know that the cause of the inordinate delay (rather than the usual ordinate delay that was expected) was the butterfly-wing effect of an altercation between two motorbikes in next door Sanayeh earlier that day.

The traffic started moving freer again as they turned into

Spears Street by the Sanayeh Public Garden. Lattouf crunched the Datsun into third gear and sped up, squealing left into Halwani Street. Immediately they could see the flashing lights up ahead. Tape was festooned across Justinien Street which ran down the side of the State Security Building. It looked like a carnival was in progress, but there weren't any cheering crowds. Army vehicles intermingled with police vehicles and fire service vehicles. Traffic was being moved on on the crossways Bank of Lebanon Street, uniformed policemen banging on the hoods of any gawking ghouls, shouting at them to keep moving.

Lattouf kept his hand on the horn and Merhi held his shield up to the window as Lattouf forced, forced, forced his way across the traffic. A policeman frowned at them, gesticulating wildly and shouting, then saw the shield and waved them on. With a final stab of acceleration, the Datsun broke through one of the tapes across Justinien Street as if it was the winner of a marathon. It screamed to a stop by the Aresco Palace Theatre.

Merhi leapt out, Lattouf following after two failed attempts to lift himself out of the driver's side.

"What happened?" Merhi was shouting. "What happened?"

There was chaos all around. The quantity of flashing lights was blinding. Nobody seemed to know what they were doing, nobody seemed to be in charge. There was too much tape, the default position of law enforcement when they felt helpless: tape it off. It was similar to the headless chicken pandemonium when one of the city's daily car bombs went off, except here there was no explosion damage.

Merhi ran closer to the building, grabbing a young Lieutenant he recognized. "What happened?"

The Lieutenant looked confused, desolate. Afraid. "They – they've killed them."

"Who? Who's killed who?"

"The second floor. All of them."

"What are you saying?" Merhi shook the Lieutenant by the

shoulders. "Speak to me."

"They're dead. The spycatchers."

"All of them?"

The Lieutenant nodded.

"How?"

"Shot."

Lattouf ran up, puffing.

"How could they all have been shot?" snarled Merhi. "*All* of them?"

The Lieutenant nodded again.

"I don't understand – Will somebody please turn those fucking sirens off!"

The chaos continued, one or two sirens were muted but not all of them.

"Where is *Muqaddam* Ghanem?"

"Don't know, sir."

Merhi looked up at the building. He could see his offices on the second floor, one of the windows was half-open. Lights were flashing inside, people taking pictures. His eyes travelled up to the fifth floor. Behind one of the windows, lights flashed there too. Ghanem's suite.

In the name of God.

He patted the Lieutenant's shoulder in thanks then said, "Fadi, I'm going in. Come."

"Me?"

"Yes, come. I'm going to need you." Merhi looked around once more, frowning at the noise and chaos.

Lattouf snarled and took a deep breath. "TURN THE FUCKING SIRENS OFF!" His shout swept over the street louder than bomb percussion. Windows rattled as far away as Beirut Port. An earth tremor was felt in Jordan. But it had the desired effect. The place went suddenly and eerily silent. All eyes looked towards Merhi and the giant.

Then a sweet little tune played from somewhere. It might have been playing for some time, but they could not have heard it above the din. Merhi frowned at Lattouf. Lattouf frowned at Merhi. "It's not mine," said the Palestinian.

"Shit, it's me," Merhi reached into his jacket and pulled out his iPhone. He tapped the screen, read what was on it and froze. Did his face go a little greyer?

"What is it, Abu Samer?" asked Lattouf.

Merhi still stared at the screen. Then he passed the phone to Lattouf. The Palestinian frowned and pulled a face, trying to focus. Holding the phone at the longest arms-length he could manage, he finally made it out. It was a message from Carla. Only four words.

RUN FOR YOUR LIFE

# PART FOUR
# الجزء الرابع

# THE CONFESSION
# اعتراف

## Mount Lebanon 15:30

There was no music playing when The Damascene entered the apartment, but Paradise and Love were in the living area dancing. One was wearing ear buds connected to an iPod on her waist, the other was not and yet she danced in time with her sister, as if she could hear the music also. They were wearing pink vests and white denim shorts. Their contact lenses were in, in deference to their guest. When they saw The Damascene they stopped dancing, Love (with the green eyes) turning off the iPod and removing the ear buds.

"Where is he?" asked The Damascene, walking into the kitchen area.

"Upstairs, at prayer," said Paradise.

The Damascene nodded, taking a flatbread from a packet, tearing it and scooping up some hummus from a bowl left over from lunch.

"May I get you something?" Love came into the kitchen area.

"You look tired," said Paradise.

"This will be fine. Thank you." He poured himself some orange juice. He looked into the green eyes then into the brown eyes. "It has been a busy morning. Our friends asked me to come back. They were all there today even those that weren't yesterday."

"And they have all agreed?" asked Paradise as her sister poured fresh coffee.

"Eventually, yes. It was fraught. At one point I thought they would come to blows, which of course would be nothing new. They were so fractious, it was like a meeting of the Lebanese parliament."

"Perhaps it was, some would say they are the true parliament of this country not the powerless ineffectual puppets in Nejmeh Square."

"There is that. *Merci.*" He took the tiny cup of Turkish coffee from Love. He leant on the breakfast bar, the sisters in front of him. "There has been a change of plan…"

## Jonblat, Beirut 15:35 – 17:00

Merhi and Lattouf stood behind the tape looking into the General Office. This was one of the few tapes Merhi had not ripped away in anger as he walked through the building. *This* was the crime scene – at least, one of the three crime scenes. The door was ripped off having been kicked in, locked from the inside the Scene of Crime Officers said.

At the insistence of the SOCOs they had put on white forensic suits and overshoes, hoods up. Merhi's fitted perfectly and was done up at the front. Lattouf's suit stopped halfway up his limbs and would only do up at the front if another three metres of fabric had been added. His hood reached to the back of his head only, his overshoes surprisingly fitted perfectly until he realised they had split across the soles.

Silently they looked in at the scene. They did not have facemasks and the smell of hour-old death touched their noses. The smell of blood, the rank internal smell of human beings, the dry-sour smell of piss, the rich smell of shit. And coffee.

Six bodies. Cadavers that just an hour or so ago had been living, breathing beings. Merhi's team. Each had died quickly, of that there was no doubt, but Merhi was of the school of thought that humans do not die instantly. Each of them probably had at least ten seconds of sentience after they had been shot to realise they were dead. Tamer Khalef possibly had more because he was shot in the heart not the head.

Then he thought of Deeb el-Gharib whom he had already seen downstairs. The most undignified death, trousers and pants down, arse unwiped. He hoped it had been quick.

Next to Merhi, Lattouf was still, saying nothing.

Merhi sighed a deep, deep sigh. A sigh of emptiness. "Fadi, let us go upstairs, we should see it all. Will you be okay with the stairs?"

Lattouf nodded. "Better that than get stuck in the lift in this place of death."

On the fifth floor, secretary Violette's room looked normal although there were SOCO minions dusting, measuring, photographing. The door to Lieutenant-Colonel Ghanem's room had also been kicked in, but it seemed to have been done more carefully, the door was still on its hinges only the frame broken, unlike the door to the General Office which had been shattered. Perhaps rank was respected even in death – or maybe the door was simply newer.

This locking the door from the inside was becoming an Israeli calling-card. They probably had some new toy that did it.

Inside, behind the desk, Violette was on top of Ghanem, her lips resting on his poking tongue. They were staring into each others' eyes. Merhi wanted to feel sick but he couldn't. He did not feel anything.

Behind him, Lattouf said lowly "Whoever has done all this will die, my friend."

"That is for certain, Fadi. I only hope it is soon and it is at my hands."

"Allah will be merciless. Trust in him."

Merhi turned away from the bodies. "I do, by whatever name he is known. But I am sure, sometimes, he would not mind a little help." There was a sincerity in his eyes as he said, "Thank you for coming in with me, Fadi."

"My friend, we are a team. Lattouf and Merhi, remember?"

Merhi placed a tender hand on the huge round shoulder of the Palestinian. With a small, deep, sad laugh he countered, "Merhi and Lattouf. Need a smoke?"

"More than I ever have."

"*Yalla*, there is nothing we can do here."

As they were walking down the stairs, Merhi's mobile rang, a phone call not a text. It was a number he did not recognise. Surely this was not that murdering bitch Carla ringing to taunt him?

"Merhi."

"Ah, hello, Major Merhi? Sorry to ring you on your mobile, switchboard gave it to me as you were not answering your phone and this is urgent. It's Facilities here over in Ras en Nabaa. When would be a convenient time for us to come and fix your door?"

Outside even the weather had turned sombre. The sky had clouded over as if showing a mark of respect to the deceased – or maybe just as a prelude to the Beirut winter which would arrive soon, two months of cold and rain before the sun returned in February.

Merhi and Lattouf sat on the metre-high wall at the side of the steps leading to the entrance to the building. Official vehicles were still parked everywhere, some lights still flashed, but there were no sirens (and possibly there never would be again after Lattouf's admonishment) and no more headless chickens. Order had descended. As had something else: news crews, TV vans and reporters.

Merhi and Lattouf had kept their forensic suits on, hoods still up (well, in Merhi's case), so that they looked like two tired SOCOs having a break, a good camouflage against any media intrusion. If they knew a Major was out here, and the sole surviving person of the murdered team at that, they would be swarming like hornets.

Down at the end of the street, the road had been re-taped, a policeman lifting it as necessary to let people and vehicles in and out. The traffic was still heavy on Bank of Lebanon Street but it was moving. Any incident in Beirut was old to the public after two hours, done, dusted, how many dead? Whatever, move on.

Merhi drew hard on his cigarette and swallowed smoke. Lattouf sat with his cigarette between his lips, smoking without hands. They watched the comings and goings, people in uniforms, people in forensic suits like theirs, people in civilian clothes. The media kept on the other side of the road. Down near the Aresco Palace Theatre, TV crews had set up so their on-the-spot reporters could broadcast with the State Security Building in the background.

Lattouf took the cigarette from his mouth. "You think it was this djinn, this Carla?" he said contemplatively.

Merhi was quiet for a while before he replied. "I don't want it to be but it must be. The problem is she never says what's going on. Always cryptic. A hint here, a piece of information there. Always need to know. Well, I'll tell you what, Fadi, I fucking well need to know now."

"I always thought you and her... You know, when she stays with you..."

"No chance. Not for the want of thinking. But do you really think I would risk losing Gigi? For a... a..."

"For a djinn?"

"And anyway you have seen her husband. Not somebody I would want to cross."

"And you think she has now turned assassin?"

"The Israelis are wiping out the spycatchers. You said it. She said it. Maybe she has turned, maybe she is freelancing like her husband."

"Maybe," Lattouf shrugged, his eyes fixing on a pretty female TV reporter who was eating a sandwich. "She said there was a spy in the ISF."

"Disinformation, distraction."

"Maybe." The TV reporter finished her sandwich and Lattouf lost interest. "Have you written up your reports on this case?"

"Well, not today obviously. But up until yesterday. Ghanem is... *was*... very strict about it."

"So your report states that there is a suspected Israeli spy in the ISF?"

"Yes."

"And you suspected that spy to be – what was his name?"

"Claude Gerges."

"Yes."

"And he was killed by an agent of your sister GSU."

"Yes. Where is this going?"

"But now all your team is dead. Killed *after* Gerges."

"Yes."

"So it could not have been him."

"No, I will be amending my report."

"But you have not amended it yet. Your report still says there is a spy in the ISF. All your team is dead."

"Yes."

"Except one."

Merhi was about to flick his cigarette butt into nearby bushes but he stopped with his hand in the air, his head turning to Lattouf.

Lattouf gave a shrug with a downturn of his mouth. "Just thinking of it from the point of view of an investigator coming in cold. To me, the one survivor would be a great person of interest."

Merhi let the cigarette butt take flight.

"Even if he was the leader of the team," said Lattouf.


Down on Bank of Lebanon street, a motorbike pulled up to the Police Do Not Cross tape. The leather-clad rider wore a helmet, unusual for Beirut. Lifting the visor, the rider looked up Justinien Street. In amongst all the media, all the official vehicles, all the people, the rider noticed two men in white forensic suits sitting on the wall outside the State Security Building. The smaller man could have been anybody, from this distance it was hard to tell. But the larger man, who seemed to be bursting out of the forensic suit like an over-inflated balloon, could only be one person. And that meant the rider knew who the smaller man was too.

The final target.


Still in the forensic suit with the hood up, Merhi pushed past other people dressed in a similar manner and went into his office. He needed his laptop, he needed to amend and augment his report. He couldn't do it here but neither could he remove the machine from the crime scene – at least, not openly.

Lattouf had made a good point. The sole survivor of the murdered team would come under great suspicion, the prime suspect – especially as his own report said there was an Israeli spy in his squad. He did not want to sit in a room for hours, maybe even days, while some high-flying twat from the GSU grilled him as to what was going on - because he couldn't tell them, he did not know himself. Not yet. If he made himself scarce and updated his report, that might keep them at bay for a while. Give him time to figure out what was really happening. And, if necessary and as advised, run for his life.

Turning his back to the cracked, frosted glass of his office door, he slipped the laptop inside his forensic suit and zipped it back up to the neck. It looked like he had a hard, square groin (a cyber hard-on!) but he might get away with it, people outside were too busy to even notice one more person in a white suit.

He went out into the corridor, closing the office door behind him. Cameras still flashed, white suits still went here and there. Incongruously, as he walked away he wondered if Facilities would fix the General Office door as well as his own. Or would that take another seven years?

Downstairs, Lattouf was standing over the other side of the road by his Datsun. Merhi knew he would not be able to retrieve his Toyota from the building's car park, the place would be in lockdown, so Lattouf was going to get them out of there. He and Lattouf had decided to keep their forensic suits on. Should anyone query why the Datsun was being removed they could say they were taking it away for analysis.

As it turned out, no one stopped them. They had to crawl away slowly so as not to take out several esteemed members of the Lebanese media (the *Al Jazeera* bimbo came within one centimetre of having her ass poked by a Datsun Bluebird wing mirror) and down at Bank of Lebanon Street the policeman proudly and conscientiously in charge of the tape took one look at their forensic suits and held the tape high for them to slip under, Merhi giving a thumbs-up of thanks.

As they turned left, the street becoming Michel Chiha Street, Merhi's phone rang. He looked at the caller ID and answered. "Hi *habibi*."

"Jihad," said Gisele. "I am hearing things. What is going on? Are you all right?"

## Coastal Highway, Lebanon 17:10

It took ten minutes to explain, not helped by Gisele's constant interruptions as to his health and well-being. His team were dead – yes, every one of them. Shot. He could be a prime suspect. Ridiculous yes but that was the way these things worked, she was the trainer she would know that. Guilty until proven innocent. He would sort the matter out but he couldn't do it at the office, too much uproar. He was on his way home. What? Fadi Lattouf was driving him, in his car yes – it was a long story. His Toyota was in lockdown. If she was asked, she did not know where he was. Was she on her way home? One hour to prepare for tomorrow's Interrogation Techniques Level 2 Part 1 Day 2 and then she would be leaving. Yes, he would take care. By the time she arrived home he might have got it all sorted. Love you too. Bye, bye, bye.

He had not told her about Carla's text message.

As he hung up he noticed the little red dot with a 1 in it by the phone icon. He had a voicemail. He accessed it on the third attempt.

"Ah, Major Merhi, this is Lieutenant Sebastien, GSU. I have been assigned today's assassinations. I wonder if you could contact me please, as a matter of urgency. My number is…"

# Mount Lebanon 17:20

On his prayer mat in the bedroom, Ghazi Kanaan sat back on his haunches, wincing at the pain in his old bones. *Maghrib salat* was completed. Normally he would not observe all five prayers of the day (often he would not observe any) but these were different times, he needed all the help and blessings of the Almighty that he could get.

In two days he would enter Syria. By the end of the week, his country could have a new President. The al-Assad dynasty would be over. He knew his sponsors regarded him as a temporary dressing on the open wound that Syria had become, an interim catalyst to draw the many factions around the conference table, but he had different ideas. Arabs could not be governed by egalitarian means, history had shown that. Democracy was not within their cultural psyche – witness Iraq and Libya and what was happening in Egypt, and the constant pathetic violent stalemate that was Lebanon. Arabs needed to be told how they were to be governed, not be allowed to choose – witness Saudi and even Oman, the UAE and the other Gulf States. Syria did not need democracy, it needed a new dynasty. And he would supply it.

He stood up. Through his half-open bedroom door he could hear the sounds of cooking coming from downstairs. And the sounds of a male and female voice coming from the bathroom along the landing.

The Damascene leant forward as Love rinsed his hair. Gently but effectively her fingers massaged his scalp. It was weird, even for this mistress of the eerie, to feel an ear in one of her hands and nothing in the other.

"Stand please." Although she used the adverb, it was not a request.

The Damascene rose, water rolling down his tanned body.

Love stayed on her knees by the side of the bath. She could

see by his reaction that her washing had pleased him. "You will need us again tonight?" she asked.

"Our mission reaches its climax," he said, without a hint of innuendo. "Our minds must be clear, not preoccupied with stress or corporal needs. The best way to deal with these things is to confront them. So yes, you will be required."

She smiled, the green contact lenses illuminated from behind.

"Tell your sister," he instructed.

"She knows. She has heard you. So, soon now we will have our bonus?"

"The bonus will be yours."

She leant forward and kissed his reaction. Then she stood up, undoing the cord from around her waist and letting the thin cotton robe fall to the floor. "I must wash for dinner also," she said as she stepped into the bath next to him. "Will you help me?"

## Coastal Highway, Lebanon 17:20

"I think we may have company," said Fadi Lattouf as they drove over Nahr el Kalb (Dog River). His eyes were switching between the road ahead, the rear view mirror and the wing mirrors.

Jihad Merhi had been preoccupied, his dual core train of thought composing the amendments and augmentations he would make to his report and wondering whether or not he should phone this Lieutenant Sebastien, whoever he was. "Mm, what?"

"Way back, there is a motorbike."

"Fadi, there are loads of motorbikes, all around us. This is evening on the Coastal Highway."

Lattouf squinted in the rear view mirror. "In black leathers, helmet, visor down."

Merhi leant forward to look into the right wing mirror and then turned around to look out of the back window. About six vehicles back was the motorbike, as Lattouf had said. It was gaining on them. "Shit."

"Is it him?" asked Lattouf.

"Her," corrected Merhi. "It is a her. It's Carla." He took his Browning from his waistband. "Okay, if this is what she wants."

"You want me to lose her?"

Merhi laughed mirthlessly. "You'll never outrun her in this rust bucket!"

Lattouf took his hands off the wheel, shaking them in supplication, then quickly putting them back on again as the Datsun veered. "My friend, I have not had Donna for two years without making some little, er, modifications to her!"

*Donna? He called his car Donna?*

"What is it to be?" asked Donna the Datsun's Dad. "Fight or flight?"

Merhi looked back once more. Carla knew where he lived but he might have a better chance in a gunfight in the mountains and there would be less chance of collateral damage. A shootout here on the Highway could cause utter carnage. He said, "Flight."

Lattouf wrenched the gear stick down and hard to the right.

Suddenly Merhi was pressed back in his seat, like an astronaut at the point of take-off. He expected his face to gurn with centrifugal force at any moment. With a beep, beep, beeeep on the horn, Lattouf swerved out into the left lane, 60 to 200 in 15 seconds.

Briefly, the bike disappeared way back. Then the rider realised what was going on and the bike began to move forward again, but it was not approaching at even half the rate it was before. At this pace they could race all the way up the Highway and still be well in front at Byblos.

Merhi remained turned in his seat, gun in hand, not only because he wanted to keep an eye on the bike but also because he would rather not see what was happening in front of the vehicle. The noise of the horn was deafening. He would put his trust in God – and Fadi Lattouf.

"Bravo, Fadi," he said. "Bravo. *Yalla, yalla, yalla.* We'll get her in the mountains."

"That is the problem with taking in waifs and strays," Lattouf had taken his hand off the horn but he still had to shout over the screeching of the engine. "They always then know where you live."

Merhi turned to him, frowning. "But how did she know I was in this car?"

"Might have seen us, might have been following since your offices."

"And we didn't spot her?"

"They can appear and disappear at will."

"Who can?"

"Djinn."

Merhi looked back. "That apply to their motorbikes as well?"

They were coming up to the Kaslik turn off. The bike was still four cars back, at a level distance, not gaining.

"We turn off here, Fadi."

"Yes, my friend."

"Don't you think you better slow dow - "

Merhi banged his head on the window as Lattouf wrenched the car to the right. "No need, Donna can handle bends at speed."

But the Datsun did now have to slow. The road was narrower, climbing, bending its way up the mountain, but Lattouf still took it like a man who had complete trust in Allah. Merhi remained on point, but the road was so twisted that he could not see further than half a kilometre back.

"Sometimes I read your Bible," said Lattouf, one hand on the wheel, one hand on the gear stick, feet moving up and down as if he was playing a pipe organ.

Merhi didn't really think it was the time to have a theological argument. If you want to call God Allah, Fadi, then Allah He is – at least until we get out of this alive. "Really?"

"As I am sure you read the Koran."

"Of course." What was a lie when you were facing imminent eternity?

"Your Saint Matthew said it."

Merhi seriously thought of turning the gun on the Palestinian. "Said what?"

"The first will be last and the last first."

"Well good for him."

"Saving for the Brigadier, you were supposed to be the first of your team to be killed, down in Tyre. But now you are the last. Funny, eh?"

"My sides are splitting."

"The first will be last..."

Merhi banged against the door again, this time with his back, as the Datsun skidded to the right at ninety degrees and shuddered to a stop, gravel dust rising like a smokescreen. He looked out of the window. Somehow they were at his apartment block.

"Right, out!" He unclipped his seatbelt, pushing open the car door. He was used to the height of his Toyota and he jarred his knee painfully when the ground met him half a metre earlier than it usually did.

Lattouf emerged through the gravel dust from around the front of the Datsun like a genie appearing out of smoke. "Do you have another gun?"

"No."

"I will pretend."

They leant against the shield of the car, Merhi resting his arms on the roof, pointing the Browning down the mountain road, Lattouf resting his arms on the roof, his hand shaped like a gun, his barrel fingers pointing down the mountain road.

# Jounieh, Lebanon 18:30

It was getting dark, getting cooler, and the mist on the mountains above was becoming lower by the minute. Soon they might literally have their heads in the clouds.

It had been fifteen minutes and Merhi and Lattouf had not moved from their positions. Lattouf in particular held his arm rigid in readiness, ready to go "Peew, peew, peew" at any bad guy who came up the mountain road. But nobody had, nobody did.

"Don't understand it," Merhi pushed himself up off the Datsun. "She hasn't come. Where is she?"

Lattouf took the signal and relaxed. The Datsun groaned as he pushed himself up off of it. "Maybe she does not fancy taking on two strong men on her own."

Merhi looked around, wondering where the two strong men were, but the gesture was lost on Lattouf. "If she can take on the might of the Lebanese Internal Security Force I don't think we would be any problem for her." He stared down the mountain road which was now covered in mist. "Is she playing with us? What is her game?"

"A game that only one side can win. There can be no stalemate now. Your pieces have been taken and it is just you and your Queen. And your loyal pawn." Lattouf shivered. "It is coming, you know. Winter. I hate Lebanese winters."

"I suppose Palestinian winters are better?"

"We are further south, we have a meteorological superiority."

"Of course you do, by all of eighty kilometres. Come, let us go upstairs." Merhi stopped. "Gisele. She will be here in maybe half an hour. I must warn her." He reached for his phone.

"I don't think this djinn is interested in your wife, Abu Samer. It is you she wants. When your Queen arrives perhaps you should take the advice you have been given."

"Shit, no signal." Merhi held the iPhone in the air, doing the universal little circular dance of a human being without a cell phone connection. "Dammit. Must be the clouds. I'll use the landline. What are you saying, Fadi? That I should run?"

"Tactically retreat and regroup."

"Let's discuss it upstairs."

"I will just move Donna."

Merhi looked over at the outside parking area. Most other residents were home. "You can squeeze in there, that's where I would normally go, but leave room for Gisele. Or there is an actual sheltered car park down under the building if you would prefer."

"Here will be fine," said Lattouf. "Donna is used to spending her nights out under the... clouds."

He parked expertly, man and machine as one, leaving plenty of room for Gisele's Toyota. Merhi was no longer surprised at his dexterity.

"Gisele will be fine," said Lattouf as he ambled towards the building's entrance.

"Aren't you going to lock it?" Merhi nodded at the Datsun.

"Doesn't lock. If Carla was coming she would have been here by now. Perhaps she is retreating and regrouping also."

"True." Merhi held the door open for the Palestinian to squeeze through.

"But we must be on our guard now, until this is finished," counselled Lattouf.

"We?"

"We. You ate my testicles. We have the bond of salt. I am in this with you. We will triumph. But we must be careful, the djinn, like God, moves in mysterious ways."

"The Bible again," said Merhi as he watched Lattouf ascend the stairs with remarkable lightness considering his massive frame.

"Not at all," said Lattouf over his shoulder, his voice echoing in the stairwell. "That is a common misconception by you Christians. And no, it is not the Koran either. Nor is it Winston

Shakespeare. It is the first line of a hymn by Englishman William Cowper, 1731 to 1800. *'God moves in a mysterious way, His wonders to perform, He plants His footsteps in the sea and rides upon the storm.'* Marvelous what you can learn on the game show channel." He reached the landing and stood outside Merhi's front door. "Do you have any food, Abu Samer? A morsel of cheese perhaps? A piece of bread? A whole cooked chicken? All this exercise is making me hungry. I think I have shed ten kilos since we left Beirut."

## Mount Lebanon 19:00

Ghazi Kanaan finished the last spoonful of *ashta* (clotted cream with rose water with a fresh strawberry decoration) and put down his spoon. He picked up his coffee, leaning back in the chair. They were seated around the dining table, Kanaan at one end, The Damascene at the other, Love and Paradise on either side. Their main course, a spiced lamb and apricot tagine prepared by Paradise, was long gone, lingering only in the air and their memory. Kanaan would never admit it openly but these bitches could cook.

"Of course Syria has chemical weapons," said Kanaan in response to a question from The Damascene. "We first obtained them from Egypt back in 1973 as a deterrent against the Jews. Later we developed our own capability, with the help of... certain friends."

"But it has never been admitted."

Kanaan sighed, shaking his head like a parent tolerating the ignorance of a child. "They know we have them. We know they know we have them. What is there to admit? It is, if you like, an open secret."

"Does Syria have them or does the regime have them?"

"The regime is Syria. Syria is the regime. And always will be."

The Damascene finished his coffee. "I need to get some air.

Abu Yo'roub, will you join me?"

"No, it is too cold out there."

"There is something we must discuss." The Damascene's eyes quickly looked from Paradise to Love then back to Kanaan.

The old man received the message. "If we must."

They went out on to the balcony, The Damascene sliding the door closed behind them. Inside, the twins began to clear away the table.

It was dark outside. The sky was occluded by cloud, the lights of Beirut twinkling like stars way down beyond the wooded mountainside, giving the unnerving impression of the world being upside down. The earth above, the stars below.

"What is it, Mebarak? I am freezing," grumbled Kanaan. "Why don't you just tell those bitches to fuck off? We should not have to come out here."

"What happened in Aleppo in August?"

The question surprised Kanaan. "What? What are you talking about? Aleppo? How should I know? I haven't been to Syria for seven years, as well you know."

"But you have contacts, you must have heard something."

Kanaan looked out over Beirut, over Lebanon, over the country where he had been King for twenty years. He thought about it for a long time before answering. "I have heard that there have been tests – only tests mind – of certain chemical weapons."

"But it has always been the stated position of the Syrian leadership that these weapons – which anyway they don't have – have been made to be used only in the event of external aggression against Syria. They have said they would never be used against the Syrian people."

"And they have not been!" snapped Kanaan. " It *is* external aggression. Those bastards who are against the regime are not true Syrians."

"You are condoning it?"

"No, I am explaining it."

For a minute neither of them said anything else. Then The Damascene asked, "What will the next regime do?"

Kanaan thought before answering. "There will be no 'next regime', you know that is not what's going to happen. Assad will be removed, I will take over. The regime will stay the same. It is for the good of Syria."

Looking out over Beirut, Kanaan had not heard the balcony door slide back open because it had done so silently. He was not aware of the twins stepping out onto the balcony, no longer wearing their contacts lenses. He saw the man next to him turn and give a short nod, but he thought he was agreeing with his last comment.

Literally his last comment.

Paradise and Love took three steps across the balcony, grabbed one of Kanaan's legs each and threw him over the side of the building.

People do not shout and scream when they are falling to their death, that is only in television and movies. People are too busy wondering what is happening to them or, if they have their wits about them, trying to grab hold of something, to worry about screaming. All Kanaan was aware of was that suddenly he was flying. A not unpleasant sensation but not one that was expected. As he fell he tasted strawberry-flavoured spiced lamb tagine. And just before his head was impaled on a vertical branch of one of the pine trees in the wood below he realised that the last word he ever said was 'Syria'.

The Damascene looked over the edge of the balcony, the *houri* standing next to him. He could see nothing in the darkness below but he knew nobody could survive that fall. He was sad. Not because Kanaan was dead but because he had not had the pleasure of actually physically killing him himself.

The meeting in southern Beirut that morning had been extraordinary, not only for the fact that most known and relevant factions involved in the Syrian civil war had been present by representation (Hizbullah, the al-Abbas Brigade, the PFLP (Popular Front for the Liberation of Palestine), the FSA (Free Syrian Army), the Islamic Front, the al-Nusra Front, the Ahfad al-Rasul Brigade, the Syria Revolutionaries Front, the Army of Mujahedeen, and the Kurdish units) but that they had all agreed on one thing: chemical weapons must not be deployed in the war. The news had come through overnight about the chemical weapons 'testing' by the Syrian regime in Aleppo two months ago. Something that the Opposition factions had thought would never happen, would never be allowed to happen, had happened. This instantly changed the dynamics, the course and the intentions of the war. Anyone who supported Bashar al-Assad or the Alawite regime must, by default, be considered an apologist for the use of chemical weapons. And as such could no longer feature in the Opposition's plans.

The *houri* moved so that they were standing either side of The Damascene. Their arms came up, one left arm, one right arm, hands resting on his shoulders.

"So do we now get our reward?" asked Love.

Slowly, The Damascene turned. He looked at the glinting white eyes, the flared nostrils, the cheeks just flicked with a hint of pink after the satisfaction of the kill.

"Yes," he said. "The reward is yours. You have earned it."

"And you have earned us," said Paradise as the three of them went back into the apartment, the balcony door sliding closed behind them.

*[In November 2013, skeletal remains were found in the wood underneath the apartment building on the Damascus road on the slopes of Mount Lebanon. The body had not been discovered before because it had been wedged high up in the mass of pine trees, invisible from above and invisible from below. It was discovered after a human tibia bone fell out of the trees and nearly hit a local hunter on his way home.*

*The skeleton has never been identified. There is absolutely no reason to connect it to Major General Ghazi Kanaan, Syrian Interior Minister and erstwhile 'King of Lebanon', who of course was found dead in his office in the Interior Ministry in Damascus on 12 October 2005 having been shot through the mouth by a .38 Smith & Wesson.]*

## Jounieh, Lebanon 19:05

Gisele Merhi opened the front door of the apartment and froze. A gun was pointing straight into her face. For the briefest of seconds she thought that her life was over, but then she relaxed when she saw that it was her husband who was holding it.

"Gigi, thank God." Jihad embraced his wife. Behind him Fadi Lattouf put down the chef's knife which he had been holding in the air as if he was re-enacting the shower scene from *Psycho*.

"Jihad, what the hell is going on?" Gisele looped her bag over one of the hooks on the wall and pulled off her black jacket. "Your team is dead?"

"Every one of them. And she's after me."

"Who is?"

"Carla."

"*What?* I don't understand."

Jihad explained as he followed his wife into the kitchen, Lattouf ambling along behind. "It's simple really. She is working for the Israelis. They are annihilating all the ISF spycatchers, not only in revenge for our success but also to leave the way clear for a new wave of spies to emerge in Beirut."

"But Carla? She was here with us, she said there was a spy in the ISF."

"Disinformation. And she has told me to run for my life."

"She has told you to run for your life and yet she wants to kill you?" She opened the fridge door.

"I think she's playing a game, enjoying the hunt. You know what she's like. The mysterious Djinn!"

"Where's the chicken gone?" Gisele frowned into the fridge.

Both men looked guilty. Lattouf smiled wanly like a fox caught with feathers in his mouth.

"I see. You have fed our guest."

"Just an *hors d'oeuvre*," said Lattouf. "We had a stressful journey."

Jihad explained about the motorbike on the Coastal Highway, their evasion and then their attempt at confrontation. "But she didn't follow us up here."

"But she knows where we live."

"Yes, Fadi made that point too."

"There is another point I would like to make," said Lattouf. The Merhis looked at him. "That is a mighty fine sea bass you have there," he nodded at the fridge. "Your cooking is divine, Umm Samer. Will you be...?"

She sighed. "Gisele, please. Or Gigi. Not Umm Samer. I can make it stretch to three."

"Yes, particularly if you add vegetables and rice. Often I advise Nada on her cooking."

"And I am sure she appreciates that. I'm going to get out of these work clothes, have a shower and then I will prepare it."

"I'm going to access the system," said Jihad. "Update my report. See if I can get an ATL out on Carla. We've got to get her."

"Is it too much to hope that she has changed her mind?" wondered Lattouf. "She has got everyone else, maybe she will leave you alone. Because of your friendship. The two of you. You two, I mean." He flapped his hand between Jihad and Gisele.

"Then what was all that down on the Highway?"

"A good point, my friend. I am just talking out loud."

"Come Fadi, my woman needs her space."

In the lounge, Lattouf said softly "Not Umm Samer?"

"The boys are mine, not hers."

"I did not know that."

"Rita, my first wife, died many, many years ago. Gigi

adopted the boys, but she is not their biological mother."

"If I have caused offence I must apologise to her."

"No, no, don't worry."

"How are the boys? I have not asked."

"Fine, fine. Samer is a pharmacist in Rome, Sary plays for Inter Milan Under 21s. They say he has a good future."

Lattouf nodded. "We must socialise more often, Abu Samer. After we've got this little matter out of the way."

Jihad said, "She is stressed, you know. Gisele."

"As I hope Nada would be if I had been threatened."

"She has been touching her *wasm*."

"I beg your pardon?"

Merhi touched his neck. "The scar. She calls it her *wasm*, her camel's brand. She always touches it when she is stressed or nervous."

"I like camels, supreme creatures."

"Talking of which," Merhi offered his cigarette pack.

Lattouf helped himself. "Purely for medicinal purposes. To relieve the stress of the day."

Merhi went over to the drinks cabinet. "Would you like a Coke?"

"You are the most genial host."

"I'm having a little whisky in mine." He held up a bottle of Chivas Regal. "But you Muslims don't drink, do you?"

"Alcohol, no. So I will just have a small one," Lattouf held up three fingers as Merhi poured the Chivas into two glasses. "Purely for medicinal purposes."

"To relieve the stress of the day?"

"What a good idea."

## Ashrafieh, Beirut 19:20

Carla sat on the easy chair in her room in the Hotel Albergo, her legs in the lotus position. She was in her T-shirt and pants, her biker's leathers over the chair in front of the vanity unit. Her eyes were closed, the headphones still in her ears, her iPhone on the chair in the warm canyon created by her legs.

She had not only heard them at dinner, she had watched them as well. She could see the entire lounge area via the camera in the Sony smart TV on the wall of the apartment, even when the television was not on. She had seen and heard her husband and Ghazi Kanaan discussing the chemical weapons capability of the Syrian regime. Then they had, literally, taken it outside and she had lost access to them. But she had seen the bitch *houri* tidy up the table then walk calmly back into the room and, seemingly, bow their heads to each other. She knew what that meant. They were taking out their contact lenses. And she knew what that meant also. They did not like to kill with their lenses in.

She saw them glide across the lounge. It was probably an optical illusion, a deception of the camera angle, but it looked like the balcony door slid open without either of them touching it. They went outside.

Five minutes later they were back. With Marwan, her husband. But without Ghazi Kanaan.

What had happened? Well, it didn't take a genius (or a djinnius) to work it out. The lenses had been removed for a purpose. Kanaan had been, in *houri* parlance, converted. But why? After seven years? Something must have gone terribly wrong. Someone must have changed their mind big time.

As her husband and the bitches had re-entered the lounge, one of the bitches was speaking. " – earned us." The three of them walked across to the stairs on the right of the television, out of view.

"She is ours." (It might have been the other bitch talking, Carla couldn't tell, their voices were identical.) "I will suck her essence from her putrid carcass."

Marwan did not respond, but Carla heard his footsteps on the stairs (the *houri* would be soundless) and she knew where they were going. She had microphones in the bedrooms but no cameras, but she did not change the phone App to follow them. She did not need aural confirmation of what was about to happen.

She took out the earphones, wondering what her husband would do when she made her confession. What would they *all* do? For she had the matter of Major Jihad Merhi to finalise also. Nobody would like what was going to happen, but things needed to be finished.

Once and for all.

## Jounieh, Lebanon 19:30

"First things first," said Jihad Merhi, exhaling smoke. "I'll amend my report and then put the ATL out on Carla – pity we don't have any pictures of her." He was sitting at the table in the lounge, the ATS laptop open and humming in front of him.

Lattouf was lounging on one of the leather couches, enjoying his second Chivas and Coke. Purely for medicinal purposes. "Is there not one in her staff records?"

"She is GSU, not ISF. I doubt I'll be able to access them, even on this. But I'll try – oh fuck."

"My friend? What is it?"

"Fadi, look at this."

With a crackle of leather, Lattouf arose from the couch. He frowned over Merhi's shoulder. "I don't have my glasses."

Merhi ripped the ones from his own face and passed them over.

Lattouf frowned at the screen. "Ah."

Merhi's report was on the screen in the background but a banner had flashed up over it. It was an ATL, an Attempt To Locate. Priority: Immediate. On the screen was a picture of Major Jihad Merhi of the Internal Security Force. Wanted for questioning in connection with the shootings in Jonblat this afternoon. Immediate apprehension required but approach with caution, considered dangerous.

"Shit and fuck!" Merhi grabbed his phone from the table, his thumb moving like someone in the final stages of Parkinson's, tapping and scrolling to his Missed Calls log. He pressed more icons then put the phone to his ear.

After a few moments, he said "Lieutenant Sebastien, Major Jihad Merhi... No, I have been busy. Avoiding the assassin. Just got your message. What's this fucking ATL?... I told you, I just got your message... No, I'm not at home. Somebody is trying to kill me... My team was not safe in our own fucking building, what good would protective custody do me?... I don't know, maybe tomorrow. I've got to sort this out... No, I told you, I'm not at home... Right, okay." He tapped the red icon. "*Con.*"

"What did he say?" asked Lattouf.

"Wants to speak to me immediately. Suggests *if what I am saying is true* that I should come into protective custody. Jesus -"

"Isa and all the saints."

" – that's straight out of Securing Custody Techniques Basic Day 1. But he said he'll take the ATL down."

"That is good. And Carla?"

"This has got to end, Fadi, this has got to end. Let's put the ATL out on her." Merhi paused, fingers hovering over the keyboard like a concert pianist awaiting the fall of the baton. Then he said, "What the hell do I say?"

"Just describe her and why she is wanted."

"What? Name: Zahia Zalloum, Carla Chedid, Suzi Saad? Known as The Djinn? Member of the General Security Unit, at least was. Sent into exile. Wanted for questioning over the assassination of Rafic Hariri. Known involvement in the al-Mahdi incident. Now thought responsible for the extermination of the entire ISF spycatcher division – except me?"

"Just name, description and current reason for interest." Lattouf was pouring more whisky into Merhi's glass, and taking a top-up for himself also. "It is a pity we do not have a photograph but that is the position in which we find ourselves."

"I'm going to look like a fool."

"A fool who is under arrest for multiple counts of murder if we don't sort this out."

"You're right." Merhi's fingers began to move over the keyboard.

Lattouf went over to the patio doors, looking out into the darkness. He couldn't see much outside, mostly the reflection of the room behind him, but it looked like the mist had cleared although the sky was still black. The winter's rain would not be too far away.

"How about this?" said Merhi after a few minutes. Lattouf turned around, staying by the glass door.

"Carla Chedid also known as Zahia Zalloum. Maybe using the name Suzi Saad. AKA: The Djinn. Female. Age: 30+. Nationality: Lebanese – I assume. Height 1.4 metres approx. Build: Petite."

"What about her...?" Lattouf nodded to his own chest and made an 'arthritis' gesture with the hand that was not holding the glass.

"Stop it. Hair: Black, long, thick. Eyes: Black. Skin: Type 4. Wanted for questioning in connection with the murder of ISF officers. Known to use a motorbike as method of transportation. Last known location: Beirut. Immediate apprehension required. OIC: Me... What do you think?"

"Better than nothing, but without a photograph..."

"I know, I know. I'll try it and see." Merhi's fingers moved over the keyboard again, accessing programs, copying, pasting, confirming his Authority To Issue, Are you sure you wish to proceed? Yes. "There, it's gone."

"So all we do now is wait?"

From the kitchen there came the sound of sizzling. "And eat," said Merhi, turning in his chair.

"I am famished," said Lattouf. "And talking of eating, we should consider a tethered goat."

"A what?"

"A tethered goat. To supplement your ATL. You. If Carla

wants to kill you, if she is coming for you, we should stake you out in plain sight. Lure her. And when she comes, pounce!"

Merhi was not going to let on that he had though the same thing, but he needed more than Fadi Lattouf to do the pouncing. "Thank you, Fadi, we 'll cross that *jisr* when we come to it."

From the kitchen, Gisele called "Dinner in two minutes!"

"That's our cue to wash and freshen up," Merhi turned back to the laptop. "I'll close this down for now - " He paused. "Hold on…" He moved his finger over the track pad, clicking and refreshing. He gazed intently at the screen and then said, "You fucker."

"What is it?"

"Sebastien. He has not removed the ATL on me."

"Not only that," said Lattouf. "Look." He pointed out into the darkness.

Merhi came over. He tried to see but the internal reflection was too strong. "What?"

"Down there."

Merhi strained to see. "Turn the lights out, Fadi."

Lattouf waddled over to the light switch on the wall. The room was plunged into darkness save for the rectangular beam from the screen of the laptop.

Now Merhi could make it out. The immediate mountainside could not be seen from the apartment because of the wide balcony, but beyond the edge there was a good view of the Coastal Highway way down below and the first half kilometre or so of the mountain road.

And on that mountain road was a convoy of vehicles with flashing lights.

"But I told him I wasn't here! The bastard. How did he - ?"

Lattouf took two steps over to the table, picked up Merhi's iPhone and slammed it onto the floor, stamping on it once, twice, three times. Merhi looked on aghast.

"Your GPS," explained Lattouf.

Merhi's mouth moved then his voice came out afterwards,

almost out of sync. "What the fuck? Couldn't you have just removed the battery and the SIM?"

"No time to worry about that now. Anyway it was a 4, you need an upgrade to the 5. I have done you a favour."

"What is going on?" Gisele was standing in the doorway, illuminated from behind. "What was that banging?"

"Gigi, we need to go. They're coming for me." Jihad nodded backwards to the balcony.

"How far?"

"Ten minutes."

Gisele left the doorway, moving fast, first to the kitchen to turn off the food then to the bedroom.

"But how can we get past them?" Lattouf quickly finished his drink.

Jihad was busy closing down programs on the laptop, signing out, pressing buttons. "Upwards. There is a back way, over the top, around Harissa. We'll take my – er, we'll take Gisele's car."

"But what about Donna?"

"Don - ?"

"If we are running, she is quicker than any Toyota."

"Ready?" Gisele was back in the doorway, bag over her shoulder.

Merhi pulled out the systems access card from the side of the laptop. "We're taking Donna."

"What?"

"Fadi's car."

"We are?"

"It is faster," said Lattouf.

Gisele gave her husband the raised eyebrows.

"It is, believe me," confirmed Jihad as he slipped his Browning into the holster on his waistband and pulled on his jacket. "You are in for... an experience - "

"I will drive," announced Lattouf.

" - in more ways than one." He kissed Gisele on the forehead.

"*Yalla*, let's go."

They dashed down the stairs, the Merhis in front, Lattouf a little way behind balancing a platter of pan-fried sea bass in his right hand.

## Jounieh, Lebanon 20:45

The three cars pulled up outside the apartment block, their flashing red, white and blue lights illuminating the area, looking like a mobile disco had come to town. Already other residents of the building were looking out of their windows.

Lieutenant Jacques Sebastien, young, wet behind the ears, out to make a name for himself, got out of the first car, followed by his Sergeant Christof Howdra. From the other cars, assorted crime scene and anti-terrorist officers appeared, the latter carrying a frightening array of weapons.

Sebastien looked up at the building. "Which one is it?"

"Top floor, sir. All of it," said Howdra.

"Someone's there, the lights are on."

"Shall I clear the building?"

"No time." Sebastien nodded at the assembled men behind him. "We're going in now."

## The Lebanese Mountains 21:00

Donna the Datsun Bluebird complained like a newborn baby as it headed up into the mountains but it kept it's speed, putting the Merhis' apartment building out of sight way behind them. Inside, Donna smelt of petrol, sweat, old leather, perfume, farts and pan-fried sea bass.

They reached the top, up by the village of Ghosta, and there were three sighs of relief as they joined the road which would take them round to Harissa and onwards.

"Right," said Lattouf relaxing, his sweat betraying the effort of the drive up the mountain. "Where exactly are we going?"

"Friends are out of the question," said Merhi, watching the beams bounce in the darkness on the marginally better road. "I could simply go and face Sebastien and co, but in the office, on my terms. But would that be a good idea right now? I didn't manage to amend my report, so officially I'm still saying there is a spy in the ISF. And I'm the only one left."

"What does our trainer say?" Lattouf glanced in the rear view mirror. Gisele was in the back seat with a platter of cooling pan-fried sea bass on her lap.

"I don't think going in to confront them at this time is the best idea." The fish bounced as the marginally better road became marginally worse again. "We need to take stock, regroup, plan. Somewhere safe where we will not be found – by anybody."

"My place it is then," nodded Lattouf. "Good choice, that's what I would have done."

Jihad protested. "But Fadi, we can't endanger you and your family."

"My friend, I am in this now almost as much as you. I am glad I'm not the target but I am involved. It is my duty to protect you. The bond of salt. Nada will not mind, in fact she will insist, and the children would love to see you. And, let's face it, who would think of looking for a fugitive Major of the Lebanese Internal Security Force in the Bourj el-Barajneh Palestinian refugee camp!" He was the only one in the car to laugh. "That is a brilliant idea, Umm – Gisele."

Gisele frowned at the back of Lattouf's head. "But what about the roadblocks? The ATL on Jihad is an Immediate App-rehension, they will be checking vehicles."

"I know where they will be," said Jihad. "We'll drive around them."

"And I know the streets of south Beirut," said Lattouf. "We'll drive around them too!"

They had rounded Harissa and were now descending again, the road no less treacherous because of the downward inclination. They would hit the Coastal Highway at Nahr el Kalb. Literally, thought Jihad Merhi, if the brakes on this rust bucket failed.

They were the only ones on the winding, twisting road at this hour. Outside it was dark, lonely and sinister. Inside, Fadi Lattouf sniffed and once again looked in his rearview mirror. He asked, "I don't suppose anybody thought of bringing a fork or a spoon, did they? Or a piece of bread?"

## Mount Lebanon 21:30

Love and Paradise lay naked, face down on the wide bed in The Damascene's room, heads turned towards each other, smiling. They did not sweat, never had never would, despite the exertions. But their activities had left them with pink scratches on their bottoms and thighs, the whiteness of their skin emphasising the scars of the sexual battle, making the marks look worse than they were. By the morning they would have disappeared.

The Damascene stood by the side of the bed, looking at the women, the creatures that it had taken him two hours to subdue and even then only temporarily. His dark hairless body was glistening, his face and groin wet. They always paid particular attention to the hole in the left side of his head and their bodily fluid was still oozing out of it, like syrup. The teeth marks on his shoulders and upper arms would still be there in the morning and for some days to come.

One of the twins purred. The other one leant over and licked her back, like a cat washing a kitten.

The Damascene pulled open a drawer. Two items were inside. One was a cell phone. The other was a Holding Cross, a ten centimetre long piece of solid olive wood carved into the shape of a cross with the cross beam uneven to fit comfortably between a person's fingers, made exclusively in Beit Sahour, near Bethlehem in Palestine. It was his weapon of preference, he had killed many with it.

He touched the phone and the cross. Suddenly he was aware that the air had changed behind him. He turned. The twins were standing a metre away, their white eyes glistening. He could feel the heat emanating from their bodies.

"You are superb," said the one on the left. "Truly you give us more than anybody ever has."

"You are Shaitan's acolyte," said the other one.

"I am simply human," said The Damascene. "Unlike you."

"There is one thing more that you have to give us."

He stared into the white eyes on the right. "She is yours."

"Now?"

"Now."

The two faces smiled, eyes half closing in ecstasy. The one on the left said, "Then we will clean ourselves and prepare." She noticed something on her sister's left breast, touched it with her finger and put the finger in her mouth.

"We shall make a clean conversion," said the one on the right as they walked out of the bedroom.

The Damascene stared at the doorway for a few moments, the image of their identical bodies imprinted on his mind. Then he turned back to the drawer and picked up one of the objects.

## Ashrafieh, Beirut 21:45

In her room in the Hotel Albergo, Carla looked at the item on her iPhone, spreading her fingers, zooming in, shaking her head in sadness. Oh Jihad, you stupid, stupid man. Why had you put out the ATL on her? You had no picture but it was a good description, especially the bit about the motorbike. Now she would have to be careful. But at least you were running. Running for your life, that was good. But if only you knew. Now she really would have to find you. Your GPS had stopped two hours ago, last location Jounieh. Very good, you had realised they were tracking you. You might be able to avoid your law enforcement colleagues but you could never outrun a djinn.

Especially a djinn that had not only cloned your phone but your wife's as well.

She looked at the ATL again. Would they be stopping all bikers in Beirut? She would be covered by her leathers and the helmet and visor – but what if they asked her to take the helmet off? Female. Age: 30+. Nationality: Lebanese. Height 1.4 metres approx. Build: Petite. Hair: Black, long, thick. Eyes: Black. Skin: Type 4. They would have her.

So, it was time for the confession. For something no one knew, not even her husband. She had no choice.

She stood up and removed the black and gold hairclip from the scrunch at the back of her head. She leant forward, shaking her hair, letting it cascade down around her face. Then she reached up, massaging her head where the scrunch had been. Rubbing, maneuvering, shaking, pulling, gently, carefully, painfully, ripping...

Her hair came off in one piece. She straightened up, looking at herself in the mirror, at the close-cropped white stubble on her head. She peeled off her dark eyebrows. Then she leant forward, rubbing her eyes. And straightened up again, the black contact lenses in her hands, her white eyes staring back at her from the mirror.

The mirror of her true soul.

## Jounieh, Lebanon 21:45

Lieutenant Jacques Sebastien was not happy as he pushed through the main door of the apartment building and went back outside into the night. In fact his young, wet behind the ears face looked like it might burst into tears at any moment, his pout making him look like a duck.

Merhi was not there. And neither was his wife. But the smell of cooking and the warmth of the hob told Sebastien he had missed them only by minutes. They must have seen them coming. Their apartment was like a watchtower up there, they had a good view down the mountainside. He should have thought of that.

His men had searched the other apartments in the block, just in case some kindly misguided neighbour was giving the Jewish spy sanctuary, but they had come away empty-handed. Neighbours said how nice the Merhis were and hadn't the Captain recently been celebrating a promotion?

To make his presence felt, and out of sheer spite, Sebastien had ordered that the Merhis' apartment be ransacked. His men had been reluctant but they had complied, no drawer unturned, no cupboard unemptied, no mattress or chair unripped, no skirting board unprised, no power source unscrewed. And all they had at the end of the carnage was what they had found on first entering the apartment: a smashed iPhone and an official ATS laptop, which was useless without the machine- and person-specific systems access card, which was nowhere to be found.

Sebastien stood with his hands on his hips looking up at the dark sky. So where had Merhi gone? No vehicle had passed the convoy on the road so he must have gone up the mountain. There must be a way out up and over. But what had they used? Merhi's official Toyota was in lockdown at the State Security Building, Madame Merhi's ex-official Toyota was here, right in front of him. Surely they weren't fleeing on foot across the mountains, like a Levantine version of *The Sound of Music*?

Sebastien stared at Madame Merhi's car. They would take that away. He did not expect to find anything but they would examine it until it was a write-off, just for the sake of it. He turned and then turned back again. There was an empty space next to the Toyota... Had they had help? Was someone else with them? Perhaps he should have ordered his team to dust the apartment for fingerprints, but it was too late now, they had been all over it. It had not been that type of search.

"Sir?" Sergeant Howdra walked out of the darkness by the side of the building.

"Yes Christof, what is it?"

"There's another parking area under the building, sir. It's a bit of a slope to get down there, it's hardly ever used, so the neighbours tell me. It's empty now."

"So?"

"Empty except for one thing." Howdra nodded over his shoulder as one of the Corporals came round the corner wheeling something up the slope.

## Beirut 22:30

There are many ATLs on the security systems of Lebanon, some going back as far as the events (the civil war) and one even to the French mandate. ATLs are usually read by law enforcement officers on the day they are issued and are then left on file in the system until the subject is later apprehended for some other reason. There is one exception: ATLs flagged 'Immediate Apprehension'. They appear on the system in red and demand a proactive response for 48 hours: enquiries, searches, road blocks (after 48 hours their colour is changed to black and white and they join the thousands of other ATLs waiting like *yatama* for the attention that will never be paid to them).

The Djinn had seen that the ATL on Carla Chedid was for Immediate Apprehension. The Last Known Location was Beirut. Therefore there would be checks on various main arteries going out of the city and some in town also. But she would be allowed to proceed – she looked nothing like the description given.

She left the Hotel Albergo dressed in her leathers, nodding at the Concierge desk as she crossed the foyer. Nobody knew who the woman with the cropped white hair and white eyes was but she walked purposefully as if she was a guest, as if she belonged. She must have been checked in on the previous shift.

The roads of Ashrafieh were busy and she attracted no

attention other than the occasional stud smile (a woman in leather, wow!) as she walked the eight hundred metres to the indoor Parking next to the ABC shopping mall. She picked up her Honda VFR1200FD. This time there was no one waiting for her as she left. She drove down Ashrafieh Street, touched Elias Sarkis Avenue and crossed Damascus Street.

Damascus Street. The Green Line of Beirut during the events of 1975 to 1990, the division between the Muslims to the west and the Christians to the east. Called the Green Line because of the foliage that grew in the uninhabited space. Nowadays there was no trace of the foliage, no evidence of the Green Line – except in people's memories.

And further down that long, long street, in the apartment on the slopes of Mount Lebanon, were the *houri*, the bitches that two years ago had taken her, tortured her, raped her, killed her and brought her back to life – but never, not even during the most debased moments when they had done things to her that only a female would know how to do to another female, had the *houri* discovered the true djinn. They had said that they thought she was like them, but they had not known how right they were.

Well, tonight they would find out.

And they would die.

The Djinn drove down Bechara el Khoury Avenue then took a right into the backstreets of southern Beirut.

## Mount Lebanon 22:30

The *houri* were dressed in denim-look jeggings, baseball boots, black T-shirts and black cotton jackets which gave a sharp monochromatic contrast to their blonde/white hair and white eyes.

The Damascene handed over the phone he had taken from the drawer in the bedroom. "The tracker app is open. The blip is her."

Love took the phone, checked the battery (full) and studied the screen. A small red dot was moving over a map of Beirut.

"What if she ditches her phone?" asked Paradise looking over her sister's shoulder. "Or has ditched it already? How can we be certain this is her?"

"She can ditch as many phones as she likes," said The Damascene. "The signal is not coming from her phone."

"The bug is on her bike?" asked Love.

"Her clothes?" Paradise.

"No."

The *houri* smiled. "She is the bug," said Love.

"It is inside her," said Paradise.

The Damascene said nothing.

"Has it been there long?" asked Love. "We didn't find it when we were inside her."

"We didn't have eyes on our fingers," said Paradise.

Love smiled at the memories.

"It was a wedding present," said The Damascene. "I always like to know where my property is. She knows nothing about it."

"You are a bad, bad man." Paradise kissed him on the mouth, her tongue – barbed like a cat's – licking the inside of his upper lip.

"Very bad." Love's rough tongue scratched the hole of his left ear.

"The money has been transferred," said The Damascene. "When you are finished, you may return here to collect your things and leave that phone."

"We will leave pictures on it for you - "

" – of her empty shell."

"The door will be open. Latch it when you leave. I will not see you again."

"Until the next assignment?" wondered Paradise.

The Damascene did not respond to the suggestion. As the *houri* went out the door, he said "May ad-Dajjal go with you."

"Our father always does," said Love as they went down the stairs.

## Bourj el-Barajneh, Beirut 23:00

"Wife, you have saved my life," said Fadi Lattouf in earnest gratitude, putting the spoon down after his third bowl of *shorbat adas* (lentil soup). "And it went particularly well with the cold sea bass. Abu Samer, you are not hungry?"

Jihad and Gisele Merhi sat awkwardly at the table in the room which served as the sole living area in the small two-storey abode that was *Villa Lattouf*.

Jihad said. "Fadi, you are too kind. And Nada, I mean no disrespect, but two bowls is enough, *merci*."

"Nada, this bread is wonderful," said Gisele. "Did you make it yourself?"

"Nothing more than any wife would do," smiled Nada Lattouf modestly. If she had minded her husband turning up late at night with unexpected guests, and these two unexpected guests at that, she had not shown it. When Fadi had slammed through the front door with a bang loud enough to awaken the dead as far away as Tripoli (but not the six Lattouf children who were all asleep in their bedroom upstairs), shouting "Woman, we need sanctuary!", she had greeted the Merhis warmly, her only concession to their arrival being to retire momentarily to put an *hijab* over her head. Now she stood up. "I shall make coffee. Or is it too late?"

"It is never too late for *qahwa*!" Fadi spoke for them all. After the journey they had had, after the day they had had, after the life they had had, they needed coffee. Now.

After Nada had gone into the kitchen, carrying an armful of plates, Fadi asked, "So, what are we going to do?"

"*I* am going to rip the tiny bollocks off Lieutenant Sebastien and feed them to him like grapes, that's what I'm going to do," growled Jihad.

"After you've cleared your name," said Gisele with the calm and reason of a trainer. "Priorities, Jihad."

Jihad sighed. He was desperate for a cigarette but he knew smoking was banned by the woman of the house. "I shall go in tomorrow. Confront them on *my* terms. There was no way I was going to be led off in handcuffs in the middle of the night from my own home. Sebastien will have some explaining to do, I can tell you."

Gisele nodded. "Pity you didn't bring the laptop with you."

"Yes, I could have amended my report here and now. Do you have Wifi, Fadi?"

"In the office, in the camp. It sometimes stretches this far."

"But you know what? At the end of the day - "

"Which this is," agreed Fadi logically.

" – I'm the innocent party here. I'm not the fucking Israeli spy!" He looked towards the kitchen and then gave a silent mouth-shrug of apology for the swearing. "Is it my fault I'm still alive and all the others are dead?" Gisele touched his right hand with hers, subconsciously raising her left hand to touch the scar on her neck. Jihad noticed the movement and gave her hand a squeeze. Then he asked, "Can we go outside, Fadi? I'm dying for a Camel. Angel, do you want one?"

Gisele shook her head.

"We will go out the back," Fadi got up, remembering not to lean on the table for support (what had happened last time did not bear thinking about). "It is not good to be out in the street at this hour."

While the women washed up, the men were in the little two square metre walled yard at the back of the house. Fadi had received special dispensation to have one cigarette, just the one mind, Nada was not having him slip back into old habits.

For half a cigarette (which was just two drags in Fadi's case) they said nothing. Then a sigh by Jihad broke the silence, so Fadi said "You will sleep in our room tonight, you and your good lady."

"Not at all, Fadi, not at all. We will sleep downstairs on the chairs. That is your room."

"You are our guests."

"And you..." Jihad looked at the Palestinian giant, the mountain of a man with the scruffy salt and pepper beard, the ridiculous comb over, the concerned face, and the explosive stomach which would have western doctors prescribing him statins like M&Ms. The man who had put himself and his family at risk. "You are a true friend." Jihad extended his hand. "Thank you. I will not forget this."

"What are friends for?" Fadi took the hand and then pulled Jihad towards him, crushing him in a bear hug.

When the hug was released (which was entirely at Fadi's caprice, Jihad did not have the ability to move while in hold), was there a wetness in the corner of a Lattouf eye?

"I have never had friends, you know. Not real friends." Fadi looked everywhere but at Jihad. "In my job and..." he gestured at himself. "How could I? I am so pleased that I can help you."

Jihad did not know what to say.

Fadi's hands were clasped together, his head bowed. "When you told me about your first wife I was, you know, proud. Proud that you would entrust me with such knowledge. Only a true friend would do that. You do not judge me, Abu Samer. You accept me for what I am."

Jihad felt the guilt of the world descend on his shoulders. He had not judged him? Like shit. Only not to his face. Coward. Now he felt like pulling out his gun and blowing his own brains out. He reached up and kissed the Palestinian three times on the cheeks. "I *am* your friend, Fadi." He tried his own hug but all he succeeded in doing was to put his head on the giant's chest as if he was a medic listening for a heartbeat. "But that doesn't mean I'm sleeping in your room tonight! We'll stay down here."

Fadi laughed as the sadness evaporated from his eyes. "If you can convince Nada, I will agree!"

"I'll put Gisele onto that!" He clapped Fadi on the shoulder.

"Any more of this open emotion and we'll be comparing willie size!"

"That would put you at an unfair disadvantage. And I will not be giving you a head start!"

"Come, it's going to rain at any minute. You'll probably feel it up there before I do, you big lump."

Laughing, the two men went back inside.

In the kitchen, the plates had been washed up and were draining on the side. The smell of coffee came from the living area.

Fadi and Jihad walked in. And stopped dead, the smiles falling from their faces.

Nada was sitting on one of the battered old couches, pale, her eyes desperate.

Gisele was standing against the far wall.

Pointing a Herstal FN Five-SeveN at the men, the new BFFs.

## Jonblat, Beirut 23:15

There were plenty of empty spaces around Major Merhi's decuma grey Toyota Land Cruiser V8 in the car park of the State Security building. Most other vehicles had been allowed to leave once the Toyota had been checked by the bomb unit and found to be clear. The fact that nothing suspicious had been found would not stop the Toyota being stripped down to its chassis, thought Lieutenant Jacques Sebastien as he parked Gisele's blue Land Cruiser LC5 two spaces away. He left the dipped beams on for illumination and stepped out, beckoning Sergeant Howdra who had been following him in one of the official vehicles.

"Chris, give me a hand, would you?"

Howdra came over as Sebastien raised the back of the LC5.

"It'll be easier getting it out," assured Sebastien.

They leant in, grunting, groaning, pulling.

"It's spilt some oil," said Howdra.

"Who cares? This car will never see the Coastal Highway again, not after I've finished with it."

Howdra humphed and braced his arms, steadying himself. With a few scrapes and a final bounce, they managed to get the item from the back of the car, both of them frantically steadying it as it hit the floor. It was the item Sergeant Howdra had found in the never-used parking area underneath the Merhis' building.

The Ducati Multistrada 1200 motorbike.

## Bourj el-Barajneh, Beirut 23:30

The Confession looked at the three people in front of her: the idiot Lattouf, his stupid fat wife and… her own husband.

"Gigi?" Jihad gave the puzzled half laugh of disbelieving bewilderment that humans give when they are confused. He made to come towards her but she stopped him with a flick of the gun.

"Draw your gun, Jihad."

"What?"

"Draw your gun and pass it to me. Don't try any heroics because I will shoot you."

"What's going on?" He asked the question as he pulled his Browning from the holster by his fingertips, holding it out.

She took it with her right hand. "Sit down." She motioned to the couch.

Jihad shook his head, still not comprehending.

"Now."

Staring at his wife, he went over and sat next to Nada Lattouf.

"And you." She moved the gun towards Fadi.

Knowing he would not fit on the couch with Nada and Jihad, Fadi went to sit down on the opposite couch, also knowing that by doing so he would be widening the range over which Gisele would have to aim.

"Not there!" snapped The Confession. "Do you think I am

stupid?"

"Anyone who uses a SWR Spectre 2 suppressor on a Five-SeveN is not stupid," said Lattouf. "You must have an EFK threaded barrel as well then."

"Well now, you're not as thick as you look, are you?"

"No."

"Sit on the floor. At your wife's feet. Where you belong."

Fadi did as he was told, dropping arse-first onto the floor like a hundred and seventy kilo sack of potatoes falling off a lorry in the Beirut Vegetable Market in El Chiah.

"Gigi?" said Jihad. "What the hell - ?"

"Shut up, Jihad."

"Please," said Nada. "I do not know what this is about but please - my children."

"Your children will be safe." Just for a moment there was a flicker of woman-to-woman compassion in The Confession's eyes. Then she said, "Unless they come down stairs."

Nada sniffed.

"Start that bloody wailing and I will shoot you," said The Confession. "And your damn children."

Nada looked up with red-rimmed eyes but she did not wail.

"What is going on, Gigi?" Jihad's face was stone. "Is there something I do not know?"

The Confession laughed mirthlessly. "Something you do not know? You know nothing, you pathetic man. For fourteen years you have known nothing. Fourteen years of your smoking, your drinking, your fucking, your damned family with whom I had to pretend to get along, even to *like*, when all I wanted to do was scream, to put a gun to their heads."

"*You* married me."

"On orders."

There was silence. On the floor, Fadi popped out a sharp little fart but he was ignored. "Excuse me, the fish."

"On orders?" said Jihad.

"Sorry *husband*, this isn't a movie. No expatiation, no

explanation."

Jihad rubbed his hands down his face. *"'There is a spy in the ISF.'* Carla was right, wasn't she? And it *was* me..."

"Only you didn't know it."

"The one remaining Israeli deep-cover operative in Beirut. My wife."

The Confession touched the *wasm* on her neck. "But now the spy has to go."

"You are leaving?"

"No, you are. As far as everyone is concerned you are the spy, remember?"

"Why did you miss me at Tyre?"

"The speed, the angle..."

"No. I know you. If that was you then you deliberately missed. Couldn't you bring yourself to kill me? And why haven't you popped me off in the last four days? It would have been so easy. When we were sleeping, even when we were fucking - "

"Shut up. And you shut up too!" A whimper had come from Nada causing Fadi to put a comforting hand on her foot.

"You were saved by the God you do not believe in," continued The Confession. "At the very moment I was aiming into your window, word came through that I was to hold off. My controllers had just read my report that the new head of the spycatchers was my own husband, they needed time to consider, to see if that changed things."

"And did it?"

"It would have done if it had not been for that interfering bitch Carla. I could have slipped back into my cover, played the dutiful wife for fourteen more years, feeding them information from the head of the spycatchers. But she had to tell you there was a spy, didn't she? You had to start investigating. So I was ordered to continue with my mission."

"Who are your controllers?"

"Well now, who do you think?"

"Mossad," said Fadi Lattouf.

"Give the fat guy a cigar. Oh no, that would mean you would have to go outside and smoke it behind your wife's back, wouldn't it?"

"You abuse me, you abuse my family's hospitality - "

The Herstal spat.

Nada gave a stifled scream, she couldn't help herself. Fadi looked at the hole in the linoleum between his legs. Two more centimetres and Abu Samer would have won the willie contest.

Jihad had jumped as the gun went off. Now he was shaking his head. "This isn't you, Gigi - "

"This *is* me. The clues have been there, you have just been too blind to see them."

"Or too trusting - of my own wife. A fourteen year secret, a fourteen year lie..." Jihad sighed deeply and then looked up. "You bitch." His whole body, his demeanour, his very aura, was suddenly different. He had changed. Each of the people in the room could feel it. As if the sigh had expelled his *qarin*, the *djinni* who is the constant companion of each human being, always whispering negative, bad, evil or disobedient thoughts. "Right, let's do this. But leave Fadi and Nada alone. You will have to run now anyway."

"Oh, he's laying down terms, is he? And who says I will have to run? Only you three know my secret." She held the Herstal in her left hand, the Browning in her right. She nodded at the room. "The problem with these old cardboard boxes they put you Palestinians in. They're like tinderboxes. They can go up with just the smallest spark - "

"You fucking - " Jihad leapt to his feet.

The guns twitched in his direction.

There was a thumping on the front door.

"Who is that?" asked The Confession.

"I am the Chief of Police of the camp," said Fadi from the floor. "It could be anybody. Maybe one of the tinderboxes has gone up."

"Get up. Answer it." She moved around the edge of the room, Jihad's eyes following her, his body shifting, always keeping her in front. She stopped by the far wall, outside the kitchen, so that she now had a view back into the room, the door to the small hallway at one o'clock. "Try anything and I will put a bullet in your fat wife's brain. Jihad, why don't you sit down?"

"I will stand." His eyes were cold.

"As you wish, whatever."

With some huffing, puffing and one more little accidental fart, Fadi rolled up onto his knees then stood up. He walked across the room, opened the door to the hallway and went out.

"Remember," warned The Confession. Fadi said nothing.

The three people in the room heard the front door grinding open. But there was silence, no voices, no muffled unintelligible conversation like the sound on a prime time television programme, not even any grunts. Nothing. Except the door being closed again.

Fadi came back in, shaking his head. "There was no one there."

The Confession raised the Browning in her right hand pointing it at the giant. "A bit late for the children to be playing Knock Down Yasser, isn't it?"

"But never too late for Djinns and Ladders," said a deep voice from the kitchen doorway as a gun was pressed hard against The Confession's head.

Everyone in the room froze. Nada on the couch, Fadi over by the hall doorway, Jihad in the centre, The Confession where she was, looking straight ahead at her husband but staring right through him.

Fadi's mouth dropped. Jihad frowned. Who on earth was this. *What* on earth was this? It was probably female, there were curves even though the body was hidden in biker's leathers.

The hair was close-cropped and white. The eyes... the irises were white almost translucent, nearly blending with the sclera, the pupils also white but with the thinnest black ring.

Nada gasped and her hands began to shake as her lips moved, whispering softly *"'A'oothu billaahi minash-Shaytaanir-rajeem. Allaahu laa 'ilaaha 'illaa..."* I seek refuge in Allah from Satan the outcast - Allah! There is none worthy of worship but He... A *dua'a*, a prayer of supplication to protect against evil.

"I am sorry you had to see me like this," said the deep voice. "But it was your fault, Major, you put the ATL out on me."

"*Carla?*"

Fadi had not managed to close his mouth up. "W-... w-...?"

"Captain Lattouf, please tell your wife she has nothing to fear from me. Unlike you." She bumped the gun, a small Beretta 82, against The Confession's head. She reached with her right hand to take the Browning. "Let it go, let it go. There's a good little Jew."

"I am not - "

"Give the other one to your husband. Jihad take it." She nodded at the Herstal in The Confession's left hand.

But before Jihad could move, two things happened.

A voice from behind Fadi Lattouf said, "Daddy what is happening, who is that strange lady?"

And the lights went out.

Power cut.


In the darkness, there was a gunshot, a smash, a child screamed, an adult gasped.

For a moment there was the absence of sound which always happens after something monumental has happened, as if the world is coming to terms with the unexpected. Then: "Wait, wait!" said the voice of The Djinn. "Nobody move. Wait."

A bright beam pierced the room like a light-sabre. It was the torch on The Djinn's iPhone. It moved from person to person. Nada was still sitting in the chair, her eyes staring, possibly in total catatonia. Jihad was standing where he had been; he looked down at his body to ensure he had not been shot. Fadi was on his knees on the floor, arms outstretched, protecting the person behind him. Thirteen year old Lana Lattouf was standing shocked in the hall doorway, a quarter of her iPad in her hand, the rest of it scattered into glass and plastic crumbs on the lino. A bullet was embedded in the wall just inches from her chest.

The Confession was nowhere.

"She's gone," said Jihad.

"Not past me," said Fadi.

"Past me," said The Djinn. "I smelled her. She's gone the same way I came in. Over the back wall. I'm going after her." The beam whipped round into the kitchen and then disappeared with The Djinn.

In the renewed darkness, Fadi groaned to his feet. "Quickly, we can get her. She has to come out into Annan Street at some time. We call it Rome."

"What?" said Merhi.

"All roads lead here." Lattouf turned and bumped straight into his daughter. "Lana look after your mother. Abu Samer! *Yalla!*" The front door slammed open.

Jihad Merhi turned his head to the kitchen then turned towards the front door. "Lana," he murmured. "Do what your father says. We won't be long." He followed in Fadi's wake, realising he had no weapon, he had not had the chance to take the Herstal of off Gisele, and Carla had kept the Browning.

But he had his hands. "Fadi, wait!" he called in a loud whisper. "Where are you?"

Back in the house, Lana Lattouf walked carefully over to her mother. Her feet had been scratched by the exploding iPad but she felt no pain.

"Mama? Mama?" she shook Nada Lattouf and felt for her face in the dark. "It will be all right, Mama, it will be all right. Baba will sort it out. Allah is with him."

Even at thirteen, she did not know if she believed the words she was saying. But what she did believe in was the God of her age: the power that was social media. As she had walked silently down the stairs she had been recording all the sounds and talking that had been going on. She had come into the room and had recorded two seconds of the strange leather-clad creature that was over by the kitchen. If only her iPad had not been smashed, think of the sensation that would have caused on YouTube.

She would have gone viral.

# 30 October 2012
# 14 Dhu al-Hijja 1433

## Bourj el-Barajneh, Beirut 00:05

The Djinn jumped over the back wall as if it did not exist, landing in a crouched position on the other side. She had never been to the Bourj el-Barajneh refugee camp so she had no way of orientating herself save for her internal body compass. North was straight ahead. It was dark but she turned the beam off on her iPhone, letting her eyes adjust naturally. Still in the crouching position, she raised her head and sniffed. Gisele had turned right. She would be looking for the quickest way out of the camp.

Tucking the small Beretta 82 into her leathers and keeping the Browning in her hand, The Djinn set off after The Confession.

"Fadi? Fadi!"

As Jihad Merhi walked cautiously down Annan Street, he noticed a massive oval shape at the side of the road. In the darkness everything was shadow, but this shade was panting for breath, leaning against a car.

"Do not worry, my friend," came Lattouf's voice from the shape. "I am always like this, it's the same when I go to the gym. Good cardio-vascular exercise."

The gym? "Where are we?"

Lattouf got his breath back. "The entrance to the camp is just down here on the left. This is my commute to work every day."

"Three minutes?"

"I know. I am a martyr. I am always exhausted by the time I get in."

"So we just wait?"

"She will come out this way."

"There *is* only one way in and out of the camp?"

"There is only one *road* in and out of the camp."

"So she could get out other ways?"

"Of course. This is not a prison. There are no high walls with barbed wire, no sentry towers. We are displaced Palestinians."

"Maybe we should go in. You can be my eyes, you'll know her likely route if she doesn't come out this way."

"If you think we should. But this exit needs to be guarded, her passage needs to be blocked."

As only a man can, Merhi thought that he would never again be doing that to Gisele. Whether or not he got out of this alive.

Lattouf pushed himself up off the car. As they walked warily towards the entrance to the camp, Merhi held out his hand. "It is starting to rain."

"Yes, it has been raining up here for a few minutes."

Merhi looked up at his friend and smiled.

Even if they had realised it, the knowledge would not have helped them as they were unaware of the significance, but they did not know and never would: the car Lattouf had been leaning on was a Jeep Wrangler Ultimate…

The Confession could not run as fast as she would have liked. Too much rubble on the ground, too many dangerously low cables hanging between the buildings (which she saw only at the last second as they bobbed down out of the darkness), too many broken half-open windows which could never be closed. It was like being on a Ghost Train at a fairground.

It was not meant to end like this. Her cover had been deep, her cover had been good. She could have stayed where she was, playing the bereft widow (with a sizeable Major's widow's pension), retaining her position as one of Lebanese State

Security's top trainers, while all the while spying for Tel Aviv. Maybe she would have married again, in-house, to somebody in the security services (of a rank no lower than Captain, of course, the information quality would not be sufficient lower down).

Had it not been for one person. Damn you, Carla Chedid, damn you. She should have killed you at the ABC centre. She had intended to, because she had realised you were getting close, but somehow you had evaded her.

The Confession splashed into something wet on the floor, nearly turning her ankle. She ran on, feeling the rain starting.

She reached the road colloquially known as the Champs Elysée because it was the widest road in the camp: just over one metre across. She stopped. If she turned right, it must lead out of the camp. But if she turned left...?

Was it too late? Could she still salvage this? The only people who knew about her were here in this camp tonight. If they were all gone she could still save this operation...

The Djinn ran through the darkness, overhanging cables trying to capture her neck, the shadows of the permanently open windows grinning at her, the silhouettes of doorways gaping at her like the shocked, toothless open mouths of harridans.

She stopped at a corner, an intersection of three alleys. Once again she raised her head and sniffed. The camp was notorious for its smells but, like a tracker dog, once she was tuned in to a scent it stuck with her (well, she had been called a bitch enough times). Gisele was ahead and to the left.

Something dripped on her head from a cracked pipe above. She did not have the protection of her Carla-hair now and she could feel the wetness on her scalp instantly. She also felt it beginning to rain.

In the darkness to her left she could see four tiny pinpricks of light. Were there some residents out with torches? At this hour she would expect everybody to be inside. Who would be out in a power cut in the rain?

But they were not torches, they were not throwing any beams. They were just tiny lights, like LEDs. They were moving very subtly, like stringed fairy lights in a gentle breeze.

The rain became heavier, soaking the rubble and mud at her feet. There was a far-off rumble of thunder.

The Djinn remained completely still, not even breathing...

"Do you have any guns?"

Lattouf and Merhi were standing across the entrance to the camp in a not very enthusiastic they-shall-not-pass formation. Merhi spoke softly, almost whispering, not only in respect to the hour but also not to betray their presence in the darkness should Gisele come this way.

"The Palestinian police are strictly forbidden to carry arms," Lattouf's whisper was like a shout from a normal man. "It is one of the Conditions of Tolerance laid down by your government."

"You have not answered my question."

"Of course I do! I have two in my office. A Lee-Enfield No. 5 carbine and a Heckler & Koch HK 416."

"How far is your office?"

"One minute down there. Don't you remember? Near the old butcher's shop."

Merhi had been inside the camp once before but he had tried to blot it out of his mind. "Oh yes. Let's get them."

"But what if she goes past?"

"What can we seriously do if we're unarmed? She has the Herstal."

"But if we lose her...?"

"Okay, look, you go. I'll hide in the shadows, I might be able to break her neck."

Lattouf did a double-take but realised Merhi was not joking. "I will be right back."

The big oval shadow disappeared into the dark as Merhi stepped into a doorway out of the rain.

***

The Djinn pressed herself into the lee of the wall, feeling the crumbling, uneven breezeblocks on her back. The lights were still bobbing in the air, but were they coming towards her? They were so tiny it was hard to tell.

The rain became harder, turning from a shower into a substantial downpour. This would be in for the night. She sniffed the air again but the force of the rain was now masking any scent.

The lights were definitely coming her way. Somehow she had found herself against a black piece of wall which seemed recently painted. This would serve as a good camouflage for her leathers but it would enhance her white hair, her head would stand out. And so would her eyes...

She straightened up, holding the Browning out in front of her with both hands. Her eyes...

The four pinpricks of light stopped about five metres away. Then two of them moved forward to the left, the other two to the right.

"Hello sister," said a familiar voice, the voice of her nightmares.

"We have waited for this moment for so long," said the other voice, identical to the first.

"We have been patient."

"Now we have our reward."

There was a flash of lightning and Love and Paradise were illuminated in front of her.


Fadi Lattouf raced like an Olympic Champion towards the portakabin that served as the Bourj el-Barajneh police office. At least, he did in his mind. In reality he wobbled little faster than walking pace, gasping like a drowning man just pulled from the sea, a simile given extra credence because his hair and face were now soaking wet from the rain. As he reached the door, fumbling for his keys, finding the right one for the padlock, the electricity came back on in the camp. Not that it made much difference, there were no suddenly-blinding streetlights, no swathes of light to disorientate him, just a few diffused reflections coming from some of the windows in the dwellings. A radio began to play again, somewhere a dog barked.

He fumbled with the padlock then wrenched it off, the lock plate ripping out of the wood. Pulling open the door, he stumbled inside.

One light in one of the windows above showed that the electricity had come back on. The *houri* were still in shadow but The Djinn could now see them clearly.

"I am not your sister."

"Oh yes, truly you are," said Love.

"You became as one with us when we converted you," agreed Paradise.

"You never converted me, you bitches. You defiled me, you killed me, but you never, ever, converted me."

"Really? Look into your mirror."

"What mirror?" The Djinn still held the Browning in both hands.

"Look at us. We are your mirror. You are one of us. You are our sister."

The Djinn raised the gun and fired at the *houri* on the right, Paradise. The striker came down on the spring of the gun but nothing happened. The Djinn pulled the trigger again, pointing the gun at Love, then again, back to Paradise.

The twins giggled. *"Really?"* said Love. "Come, come, don't be silly."

The Djinn pushed her left hand into a pocket, pulling out the small Beretta 82 and slipping off the safety, firing towards Love. The hammer came down and hit the primer but nothing happened.

"Put them down," instructed Paradise tolerantly. "Put them down."

"I would like to say we don't want to hurt you," said Love.

"But we do." Both *houri* put their hands up to their left shoulders where they had been shot two years ago.

The Djinn relaxed, bending her knees, dropping the guns the last twenty centimetres to the ground. Slowly she straightened back up, raising her hands in the air.

"Tonight we complete your total conversion," said Paradise. "You will reach ecstasy, like you did before."

"With us inside you," said Love. "You will die in rapture."

"Right here?" said The Djinn, clasping her fingers behind her head.

"No, on an altar of sacrifice." Love placed her hand on The Djinn's left shoulder, Paradise did the same on her right shoulder. The Djinn could feel the burning even through the leather.

"We have the perfect place," said Paradise. "*Yalla.*"


The Confession held the Herstal FN Five-SeveN in front of her as she walked down the Champs Elysée. Here and there a few lights were back on which helped her to see but it was still, basically and literally, as dark as night. Somewhere a baby cried. The rain was easing but her hair was plastered to her head, water dripping off her nose.

As much as she would have liked to continue in post, playing the widow, she realised she could not. Killing the head of the spycatchers was one thing – she would still do that if she was able – and killing the idiot Lattouf and his fat wife would be a relief for the world. Carla could be a problem but not an insurmountable one. But one thing she would have to do, and one thing she could not do, was to eliminate the Lattouf children. All six of them. She was not some sort of weird bitch machine like Carla, she was a woman – a Lebanese Israeli Intelligence Agent maybe, but a woman still. She might have shot the Lattouf girl, that was a collateral of war, but she could not cold-bloodedly kill the other five. So she would have to go. Get away. Live to fight another day?

She could see a few more lights on in Annan Street, about fifty metres away. Lattouf's car would be out on the street, she would hot wire it (Pursuit Evasion Techniques Level 4 Day 5) and be on her way. There were safe houses all over the country. She would head south.

Then a voice from behind her said, "Hello Gigi."

The alleys were so narrow they could not walk three abreast, so while Paradise held The Djinn's hands at the back of her head Love walked on, sufficiently in front to be out of kicking distance. At one point The Djinn stumbled, going down on one knee in a puddle that might have been water, but she was instantly dragged back up again by Paradise. They seemed to be heading towards the front of the camp.

They squeezed down an alley so tight that The Djinn's raised elbows almost touched both walls. It led to a small courtyard area. Three sides were blank walls with windows above. In the fourth wall there was an old door, broken and open. The Djinn could smell blood. Ancient blood and lots of it.

"The camp morgue," explained Love as if she was a tour guide. "Used to be a butcher's shop. A fittingly good use, don't you think?" She brushed rain off of her brow.

"The altar is inside," said Paradise.

"There is also a disposal gulley. You will meet al-Mahdi in pure, hollow form. No blood, no entrails. You will be a virgin again. See, are we not considerate?" Love's eyes shone just a little brighter in anticipation. "We will keep you alive as long as possible. You will enjoy this. Your rapture. Come."

As Love pushed the door open, Paradise shoved The Djinn forward. And that was the mistake.

The shove meant that Paradise let go of The Djinn's hands. Instantly The Djinn jumped forward, kicking Love in the back, sending her tumbling through the doorway. The Djinn turned to Paradise – and held up her left hand.

Paradise had her hands in the raised claw position, but what she saw stopped her from moving. In The Djinn's left palm was a tattoo of *ayn al hasud*, the evil eye. And it was glowing, the eye white, the sclera a deep blue.

Paradise's distraction was only momentary, but it was enough. The Djinn put her right hand back up behind her head and from inside the neckline of her leather jacket pulled out her husband's gift: a Holding Cross. As she leapt through the air, she twisted the cross in her palm so that the down beam poked out between her first and middle finger, the cross beam held within her fist.

The solid olive wood landed with a horrible cracking thud above Paradise's left eye. A scream came from inside beyond the doorway. Paradise gasped, her claws trying to raise to her head. The second strike split her skin. The third cracked her skull and she fell.

The Djinn was on top of her like a feral demon, banging the Holding Cross into the same place on her head, hearing the skull crack more, feeling it open. Something splashed up into her face but she kept thumping the cross against the skull, feeling hot, soft substance on her fingers.

Only when there was a seven centimetre hole in Paradise's head and the light had gone out of the open white eyes did The Djinn stop. Paradise was staring up into the rain. Her face was smiling.

The door behind banged and The Djinn whipped around. Love staggered out into the yard, holding her head above the left eye, blood and light pink matter oozing between her fingers. She looked at The Djinn, opened her mouth, and fell to her knees.

The Djinn stepped over, raised her fist with the Holding Cross – and then watched as the light switched off in Love's eyes and she fell sideways onto the wet, muddy ground. Her left leg twitched violently as the soul left her body, following her sister from the earth. Then she was still for eternity.

Slowly, The Djinn lowered her arm. She looked from one

body to the other.

"*Ila jaheem ma'ik*," she said.

Go to hell.

"What is happening?" Jihad Merhi stepped out of the doorway into the rain. "Is this a nightmare? Am I asleep?"

The Confession raised the Herstal Five-seveN. "You have been asleep for fourteen years."

"When...? How...?"

"Before I met you. Paris 1997, when that mad bitch shot me." Her left hand went up to her neck. "I was saved by the Israelis. Not by my own country but the Israelis. Without them I would have been dead. A woman called Melanie Nathanson recruited me. She remains my controller to this day."

"So everything has been a lie?"

"You were my target, I was to seduce you, marry you, even adopt your sons. And wait."

"Did you kill Rita?"

"We are not that callous. It was a genuine car accident. That was when we chose you, when she died. You were a rising *Molazim*, a Lieutenant with a good future. And a widower. You had a vacancy, we filled it."

"When were you activated?"

"Five years ago."

"Five years? When you started going back to work?"

"Having brought up your sons."

"Our sons."

"Your sons."

Jihad brushed water from his hair. He was grateful that the rain was falling onto his face. She wouldn't be able to see his tears.

"How did you become a killer?"

"I always have been. Even in Paris. That stupid bitch shot me but I killed her. And recently I have done things that you cannot even imagine. The nights I have been away – do you really think I have been giving classes somewhere else, in Tripoli, in Jbeil, up in Baalbeck for an overnight stay?"

"I had no idea."

"Husbands never do. They take everything for granted and they always become complacent. That is why I was ordered to marry you. To be the picture of domestic bliss."

Jihad sighed. Water dripped off of his chin, only some of it was rain. "So what now?"

"Now I have to complete my mission."

"You are going to shoot me?"

"Then the confession will be over. Job done. Thank you, Jihad, it has been fun."

She pulled the trigger and the Herstal spat flame.

The force of the bullet sent Jihad Merhi flying backwards, feet off the ground, slamming into the doorway he had stepped out of, his head banging against the door like a fugitive seeking sanctuary. A sanctuary that would be too late. Wordlessly his body sank to the ground.

And was still.


The Confession heard the bullet zip past her ear like a giant hornet before she heard the gun blast. She leant to her left, firing five rapid shots into the darkness. There was a thump, then a blinding pain in her right wrist as the Herstal exploded out of her hand.

As she saw the idiot Lattouf emerge from the night, a gun in his hand, firing, she turned and ran, zig-zagging over the rubble, crouching, not stopping, not looking back (Pursuit Evasion Techniques Level 2 Day 1). Bullets thudded into the ground near her feet, flew over her head, hit the walls, shards of breezeblock scratching her head, cutting her face.

Then the bullets stopped, but she kept running, down the wet, stinking path, out into Annan Street, putting the camp of death behind her.

\*\*\*

"Abu Samer? Jihad? JIHAD!" Fadi Lattouf dropped the empty Heckler & Koch HK 416, dashing over to the body in the doorway. "In the name of Allah the most merciful, no, no!"

The giant fell to his knees, reaching out, touching a foot, shaking the leg. "Jihad... Jihad... No."

Gently, tenderly, he put an arm under the flopping head and pulled the body up into his arms, like a father cradles a child. He began to rock back and forth. With a sob, he began to recite *"Inna lillahi wa inna ilayhi raji'un..."* Surely we belong to Allah and to Him shall we return...

"Can I help?"

Lattouf's head snapped round. The woman in leather with the short cropped white hair and spooky white eyes was standing out on the path, the woman who used to be Zahia Zalloum then Carla Chedid then Suzi Saad. Something dark had been splashed across her face, giving her a strange freckled look. She did not have a gun, just an old carrier bag in her hand containing what looked like small sausages. Freshly made sausages because blood was dripping from the bag.

"What are you?" said Lattouf.

"I am what you see."

"You can do things, can't you?"

The Djinn shrugged.

With watery eyes, Lattouf asked "Can you raise people from the dead?"

The Confession ran out into Annan Street. It was quiet as befitted the hour. Very few lights were on in windows but as the street was of normal width, not tight and intimidating like the camp, it was easier to see out here. She was holding her right hand. Her wrist felt broken, but she could drive one-handed, at least to get away out of this area. She wondered if her Ducati had been discovered underneath the apartment block in Jounieh. She could sorely do with it now. She flipped her wet hair away from her face. The Lattouf house was only a minute or two up the road, the car was outside.

She maintained her run. There was nobody about but the Palestinian might be stupid enough to follow her. Mind you, she would hear him from kilometres away, like you hear a freight train in the distance long before it reaches you.

She saw the Datsun Bluebird up ahead. Outside the house. Just for a second her *qarin* whispered in her ear that she still had the opportunity to go inside and rid the world of Lattoufs forever. She could stay in Lebanon, play the grieving widow...

She dismissed the thought. Only because it was impractical, for no other reason.

She was grateful that the car did not lock. She had the door open when she became aware of a presence behind her. Keeping her injured right hand against her body, she turned.

A tall man was standing there. A man she knew. A man she liked. They had a history, especially in her fantasies. He was dressed in a leather jacket above a collarless white shirt. His hair was long, tied back into a simple ponytail, the left side pulled down to ensure it covered the hole where his left ear used to be.

"H- hello," she smiled. "I didn't expect to see you here." Was this her rescuer? Her knight in shining armour? Across the street she saw a motorbike, probably a Suzuki, she remembered he liked them.

"My mission is completed," he said.

"Really? So is mine. What say we get out of here?"

He shook his head. "That will not be possible. I have spent a long time on this mission. It started in 2010."

"Before we met?"

"Yes, when we met I did not know."

"Know what?"

"That you were one of them. Now you are the only one left, the last of the confession."

"What confession?"

"The group of Jews that killed Mahmoud al-Mabhouh in Dubai. You were in the room, weren't you? You were the one that injected him."

She stared at him in shock. How the hell did he know that?

"Hamas send their regards," said The Damascene. His hand came up, the Holding Cross protruding between his index and middle fingers. It rammed into the head of The Confession. She fell back into the car, The Damascene on top of her.

He did not stop punching until her head was unrecognisable, by which time she had been dead for three minutes.

He folded her feet into the car, then pushed the body over onto the passenger seat. There was blood and gore on the driver's seat but it could not be helped. It would wipe off his leather jacket and he could buy new jeans. He got in the car, closed the door and fiddled beneath the dashboard for a few moments. The Datsun roared into life.

The Damascene drove off, taking the last of The Confession with him.


Fadi Lattouf carried the body of Jihad Merhi in his arms. He was solemn, sad, still mumbling the verse from the Qur'an, the verse for the dead and those who had experienced tragedy in their life. His trousers were wet but he was oblivious to the rain.

The Djinn walked next to him. Despite the grief, one part of Lattouf wondered about the sausages the woman was carrying. He had never seen sausages with nails before…

He saw a car drive off up ahead, but he thought nothing of it. At his house he kicked the front door open, being careful not to bang the body as he carried it in.

Nada was inside, pale but back in the world. Lana was with her. Lattouf could hear his other children awake upstairs. Nada gasped when she saw her husband carrying his friend, and she flinched away just a little when she saw The Djinn, especially with her bloodied hands and gore-splattered face.

Lattouf laid the body down on the couch. "Bring water, woman, he must be washed."

As Nada and Lana went into the kitchen, The Djinn knelt on

the floor beside the couch, stroking the still, pale face of Jihad Merhi.

Lattouf still mumbled his prayers, his eyes dull with sorrow and pain.

Pain…?

Nada and Lana carried in a brimming basin, but Nada stopped as she saw her husband, now no longer shielded by the body of his friend. "Fadi? The blood!"

"I know, it is Jihad's."

Why was the pain getting worse?

"No, Baba, look, look!" Lana pointed at her father's stomach.

Lattouf looked down. There were three bullet holes in his shirt, holes that were pumping blood. His trousers were already saturated, but not with the rain as he had thought

Fire shot through his belly like the skewers of Shaitan.

"Well, in the name of Allah…" said Fadi Lattouf. His eyes rolled into his head and he crashed onto the floor with the force and finality of a giant sequoia tree falling to earth.

# EPILOGUE
# خاتمة

# FIVE MONTHS LATER
# أشهر خمسة وبعد

# 23 March 2013
# 12 Jamada 1 1434

## Jbeil, Lebanon 10:30

He sat at one of the tables outside the Bab el-Mina (Harbour's Gate) Restaurant looking out over the ancient Old Port of the Byblos of history. A few small boats were moored at the harbour side, bobbing contentedly, awaiting their masters on this warm, sunny Saturday. Over by the surviving but crumbling fortified Crusader tower at the harbour's entrance, a boat full of tourists set off for a short – and very expensive – trip along the coast.

The restaurant was not yet open so he had bought himself a coffee and a hummus wrap at the Citadelle Café up near the souk. It was his local, they knew him there. In fact he had bought two coffees and two wraps because he was expecting a guest.

He had asked his guest to come to his offices in the souk but his guest had asked to meet here first of all. There was nowhere more private than out in public.

It took him five minutes to eat the wrap (his appetite was not what it was) and he was casting lustful eyes at the second one when he saw his guest walking along the harbour side. He stood up, a grin creasing his face, huge hand raised into the air. "My friend, my friend!"

The guest stopped about three metres away, looking at the giant and shaking his head, smiling. There was a wetness in his eyes. He said simply, "Fadi."

Fadi Lattouf said simply, "Jihad."

They embraced with three cheek-kisses. Jihad went to step away but Lattouf pulled him back for three more kisses. "It is good to see you, Abu Samer."

"And it is good to see you, you great lump."

"Lump! Look at me! I am half the man I used to be!"

It was true he had lost a quarter of his bodyweight. In a normal person that would have been dangerous. In Fadi Lattouf it made no visual difference whatsoever. "Nada is trying to build me up, she says I am too skinny. She likes her men more… rotund."

Jihad laughed. They both knew that had it not been for Lattouf's rotundity, his massive gut, he would have died from his wounds in Bourj el-Barajneh five months ago.

"Sit, sit, my friend," urged Lattouf. "I have bought you breakfast."

They sat. Jihad took the lid off the coffee and reached for the wrap. Then he stopped, looking at Lattouf's doe-eyes, and pushed the wrap over. "You have it. I'm not hungry."

"It would be a shame to waste it," agreed Lattouf, and the wrap began its final journey.

Jihad Merhi let the warm sun caress his face as the Palestinian ate. After a moment he said, "Who would have thought, eh Fadi?"

Lattouf looked at his friend, his much-changed friend, unrecognisable from the man who used to be a Major in the Internal Security Force. His hair was now completely grey but he had let it grow and it was now a tight, if thinning, mop of curls. His five-day-old stubble still held reluctant flecks of brown. He had never been fat, but he had lost the layer of middle age, he was trim, fit.

"No regrets?" asked Lattouf.

"Total regret," said Merhi.

"About us?"

"No, no, we had always talked about it. It makes sense. But about everything else? Well, you know how I feel."

Lattouf shook his head. Allah had looked after Jihad, He had bestowed His blessings. Five months ago the bullet had past clean through Jihad's body, in the chest out the back, just nicking his spinal cord. He had spent weeks in hospital and, thanks to Allah, the cord damage was non-consequential and he had made a complete physical recovery. He had been thoroughly investigated by his erstwhile colleagues in the ISF and GSU (the one called Lieutenant Sebastien had been a particular little *ilishael*, he was a turd, he would go far), the eventual findings being that while Major Jihad Merhi had not known what was going on and had committed no crime, he *should* have known what was going on and should have stopped the crimes that *were* committed. Ignorance and trust were crimes in themselves. He was requested to fall on his sword. Jihad Merhi had been retired on a Major's pension, no lump sum.

What had happened to Merhi's wife might never be known. Was it her that had driven off in Lattouf's Datsun Bluebird on that fateful night? Who knew? Neither she nor the Bluebird had ever been seen again (although in early February the burnt-out shell of a vehicle had been found in a ravine near Birket el Bouhairi, on the border with Syria, the closest point of the border to Damascus. It was thought the vehicle had been obliterated by insurgent or regime rockets. Rumour had it that one, just one, flake of orange paint was found on the metallic skeleton).

Merhi finished his coffee and looked at his friend. His true friend. God had looked after Fadi, He had bestowed His blessings. Fadi had spent a month in hospital, undergoing three operations to remove the bullets from his gut and repair the internal damage (anaesthetising the giant had been difficult and additional supplies of desflurane had had to be flown in from Saudi Arabia). The doctors had agreed that the bullets would have killed a normal person but the sheer size of the Lattouf gut had prevented any mortal damage (which nevertheless did not stop the doctors advising him to lose weight 'for the sake of his health').

The groups had asked Lattouf and his family to leave Bourj el-Barajneh (outside agencies could not be permitted to wreak havoc in a Palestinian refugee camp, that was the preserve of the groups). A new police chief had been sought and Captain Manar al-Jayouchi from down in Bourj el-Shimali had moved up two months ago. Fadi Lattouf had retired – with nothing.

Nothing, that is, except the property he had inherited from his cousin Chadi two years ago. The property in the Jbeil souk, up near the Roman road and backing onto the cemetery, a two-storey building with enough room upstairs to house a family of seven and with spacious (by souk standards) offices downstairs.

"I have something for you." Lattouf picked up a carrier bag from the seat next to him and took out a large rectangular object wrapped in tissue paper. "Now it is for real." He smiled as he handed the object to Merhi.

It was heavy, making a scraping sound like there were two items inside. Merhi laid it down on the table and opened the tissue paper to reveal a golden metallic rectangle about twenty-five centimetres by fifty, with pre-drilled holes in the corners. A business wall-plate.

### Lattouf & Merhi

Muhaqqiq Khass
Détectives Privé
Private Enquiry Agents

"Lattouf and Merhi?"

"Look at the other one."

Merhi raised the plate and removed another piece of tissue paper to reveal an almost identical plate underneath – except this one read 'Merhi & Lattouf'.

"Why worry?" said Lattouf. "We put one one side of the door the other the other! Palestine and Lebanon, working side by side as always!"

Merhi smiled, nodding. "I don't know how you do it, Fadi, but you always come up with the solution."

Lattouf spread out his hands in self-deprecation. "Allah guides me."

"You know, my friend, I believe he does." Merhi looked out over the harbour. "A new beginning, eh? Do you know what today is Fadi?"

"Saturday?"

"In the Christian calendar, tomorrow is Palm Sunday." (Lattouf looked at his hands.) "In the Eastern Orthodox and Byzantine churches, the day before Palm Sunday is known as Lazarus Saturday. He was the friend who Jesus – Isa – raised from the dead. Fitting, eh?"

"We rise like the *anka'oo*, the phoenix. No one can keep Lattouf and Merhi down!"

"Merhi and Lattouf."

"Now, *yalla*," Lattouf stood up. "Nada is expecting us. We are having a little celebration, to mark the start of our new career, our new life. She is cooking camel tongue and pigeon livers, with garlic couscous."

"And a little salad?"

"Of course! We must have our five a day!"

The men laughed. As they walked away along the harbour's edge, Fadi reached round and pulled his pants from his backside, releasing a loud, rumbling fart. "Excuse me, the hummus." The water of Byblos Harbour trembled and Jihad Merhi wondered if Cyprus should be warned to expect a tsunami later that day.

## Midtown, New York City, USA 09:30 (local time)

The woman in the black leathers lay on the roof of the New York Public Library and looked down the telescopic sight of the Accuracy International AWSM Sniper Rifle. It was a fine, windless day – always preferable. Down below, Manhattan's commuters were crossing Bryant Park, some picking up their morning coffee, some stopping for a quick breakfast at the Southwest Porch eatery. She could have picked off any of them should she have wished but she was a professional. She had just one target.

She thought back. Was it only six months ago when she had met Benjamin David down there? The civilian support at the Israeli Consulate who had given her the information that led to those events in Lebanon? Seemed like a lifetime ago.

She no longer worked for the Lebanese Department of General Security, she had quit after the carnage in Bourj el-Barajneh (quite frankly, her masters had been pleased to see her go, too much of a liability being exiled from Lebanon but still working for the country at the United Nations). She was now freelance. Like her husband. She had decided it was time for a new life. Literally.

She moved onto her right hip to ease the pressure on her belly. She was just beginning to show. Yesterday she had felt the first flutter. The doctors had said it might be twins – but they always said that, didn't they?

Twins… No way, she had had enough of twins, she was not going to be the catalyst for them to be born again. Her baby was going to be singular and normal. Well, as normal as the child of a djinn could be.

She threw back her jet black hair, her black left eye focusing down the scope. It was 09:30 and, like all good freelance mercenaries, she had done her research, she knew her target well. He would be on time.

Over the far side of the park she could see a man sitting on a bench. A dark haired bearded man from the Syrian Consulate over on Second Avenue. She saw him look at his watch and then he noticed somebody coming towards him from the south eastern side of the park, underneath her. She made a final adjustment to the recticle, the crosshairs, in her scope and waited.

Her target walked into her view. She would have one shot only and she would be merciful. He would not even know he was dead. She followed his back across the park and waited until he stopped in front of the Syrian

She focused on the head of her target. The man in the denim jeans, leather jacket and collarless white shirt, long hair pushed back in a ponytail but pulled down the side of his face to cover his missing left ear.

Her nailless finger tightened on the trigger…

You have made The Confession.

You are absolved.

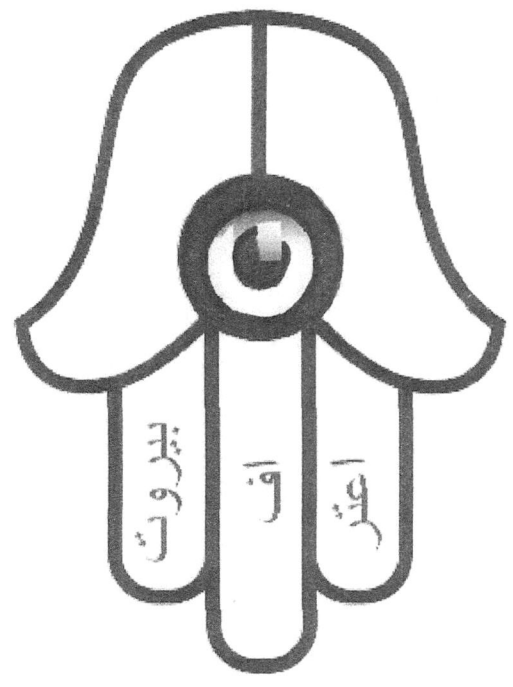

# GLOSSARY OF ARABIC AND HEBREW WORDS AND PHRASES
## معجم للغة العربية والعبرية والكلمات والعبارات

## Arabic

| | | |
|---|---|---|
| *'aalaykum al-salaam* | - | [and] upon you peace |
| *Abbaya* | - | voluminous black overdress worn by local women in Arabia |
| *Abu* | - | a *kunya,* a name honourably given to the father of an Arabic child, Abu (father) plus the name of the first son, as in Abu Yo'roub |
| *ad-Dajjal* | - | in Islam: the Great Deceiver, the devil |
| *Agal* | - | rope (usually two circles) worn on the head, holding a *keffiyeh* in place |
| *Ahbal* | - | idiot |
| *Alhamdulillah* | - | praise be to God/Thank God |
| *al-Janna* | - | paradise/heaven |
| *Al-salaam 'aalaykum* | - | peace upon you |
| *Anka'oo* | - | phoenix |
| *Arak* | - | aniseed-based drink, a relative of absinthe, ouzo and similar |
| *Argileh* | - | Lebanese word for shisha pipe or *nargileh* |
| *Ashta* | - | clotted cream with rose water |
| *Asr salat* | - | afternoon prayer |
| *Ayn al hasud* | - | The Evil Eye |
| *Azan* | - | call to prayer |
| *Baklava* | - | layers of filo pastry filled with chopped nuts and sweetened with syrup or honey |
| *Barjeel* | - | windtower |
| *Chou esmak* | - | what is your name? [to a man] |
| *Dishdasha* | - | the standard Arabic male outer garment, ankle length long sleeves, like a robe; also called a *thawb* and a *kandura* |
| *Djinn* | - | origin of the English word 'genie'. In Arabic folklore and Islamic teachings, djinn, humans and angels make up the three sentient creations of God. Djinn can be good, evil, or neutrally benevolent. in modern usage it can also mean a seductive, beguiling female |
| *Dua'a* | - | a prayer of supplication |
| *Eid* | - | a festival or holiday, notably *Eid al-Fitr* (the Festival of the Breaking of the Fast) at the end of Ramadan, and *Eid al-Adha* (the Festival of the Sacrifice) which always falls on 10 Dhu al-Hijja in the Islamic calendar |
| *Eid Mubarak* | - | 'Blessed *Eid*', a greeting used at *Eid* |
| *Falafel* | - | deep fried ball or patty made from ground chickpeas and/or fava beans |
| *Falaj* | - | irrigation system of underground channels supplying water from mother wells dug into the water table |
| *Ftoor* | - | breakfast |
| *Ghadae* | - | lunch |
| *Ghouleh* | - | a female *ghūl* (ghoul), a demon |
| *Habibi* | - | darling (said to a male but now often used for females also) |

| | | |
|---|---|---|
| *Habibti* | - | darling (said to a female but *habibi* usually used) |
| *Hammam* | - | bath/bath house |
| *Hamsa* | - | a palm-shaped amulet with an eye in the centre |
| *Hijab* | - | scarf or veil covering the female head and chest, with the face exposed (sartorial) |
| *Hojari* | - | silver frankincense, the best quality |
| *Houri* | - | in Islam, houri are the companions of humans and djinn who enter paradise. They have great beauty and are noted for their white eyeballs and black pupils. They can be male and female. In European usage, houri are voluptuous, beautiful, alluring women |
| *Ibneh* | - | a soft, white cheese similar to feta |
| *Ila jaheem ma'ik* | - | go to hell |
| *Ilishael* | - | shit |
| *Insh'allah* | - | God willing |
| *Izaar* | - | a male garment like a sarong which can be worn under a *dishdasha* or as a lower outer garment. |
| *Jisr* | - | bridge |
| *Kakhbar* | - | swear word: equivalent to 'son of a bitch' |
| *Kebbeh* | - | meatballs stuffed with pine nuts and minced meat |
| *Keffiyeh* | - | Middle Eastern headdress |
| *Khaetrak* | - | goodbye (to a man)[Levantine Arabic] |
| *Khodi balik* | - | be careful (said to a woman) |
| *Kifak* | - | how are you? [To a man] |
| *Knefeh* | - | a baked dessert of semolina pastry and cheese served with a sweet syrup |
| *Labneh* | - | strained yoghurt |
| *Loukoum* | - | Turkish delight (confectionary) |
| *Luban* | - | frankincense |
| *Ma'amoul* | - | small, decorated shortbread pastries with nut filling |
| *Ma`a as-salāma* | - | goodbye ('Go in peace') |
| *Mabruk* | - | Congratulations; good luck |
| *Maghrib salat* | - | sunset prayer |
| *Majlis* | - | meeting room, sitting room, lounge |
| *Makanek* | - | a spicy Lebanese sausage |
| *Manousheh* | - | filled flat bread (with cheese, zaatar and similar) |
| *Maqluba* | - | meat, rice and fried vegetables placed in a pot, which is then flipped upside down when served, hence the name, which translates literally as "upside-down" |
| *Marid* | - | a large and powerful wish-granting djinni, a giant |
| *Mekhallel* | - | pickled vegetables |
| *Moghrabieh* | - | semolina cooked with meat and spices |
| *Molazim* | - | Lieutenant |
| *Mukhabarat* | - | the Intelligence/Security Service |
| *Muqaddam* | - | Lieutenant-Colonel (military rank) |
| *Nazar* | - | eye-shaped amulet to ward of the Evil Eye |
| *Niqab* | - | veil or mask covering the female face (sartorial) |
| *Qahwa* | - | coffee |
| *Qarin* | - | a *djinni* who is the constant companion of each human being, always whispering negative, bad, evil or disobedient thoughts |
| *Ra'id* | - | Major (military rank) |
| *Rakwe* | - | long-handled coffee pot used for serving Turkish coffee |
| *Sabah el-khair* | - | Good morning |

| | | |
|---|---|---|
| *Sahir* | - | a wizard |
| *Salaam* | - | peace (greeting) |
| *Salat al-Janazah* | - | funeral prayer |
| *Sayadieh* | - | fish with rice |
| *Seejaere* | - | cigarette |
| *Shayla* | - | headscarf |
| *Shorbat adas* | - | lentil soup |
| *Shukran* | - | thank you |
| *Tabouleh* | - | a salad traditionally made of bulgur, tomatoes, cucumbers, parsley, mint, onion and garlic, and seasoned with olive oil, lemon juice, and salt |
| *Umm* | - | a *kunya,* a name honourably given to the mother of an Arabic child, Umm (mother) plus the name of the first son, as in Umm Samer |
| *Ustaz* | - | 'Uncle', a term of respect for elderly males |
| *Wa'l-aks* | - | vice-versa |
| *Wasm* | - | the owner's brand on a camel |
| *Yadreb asfoorayn behajar-* | | 'Kill two birds with one stone' |
| *Ya khorg* | - | asshole |
| *Yalla* | - | come/let's go |
| *Yatama* | - | orphans |
| *Za'atar* | - | a popular Middle eastern herb mixture (ground dried thyme, oregano, marjoram, mixed with toasted sesame seed, and salt) |

## Hebrew

| | | |
|---|---|---|
| *Benzona* | - | son of a bitch |
| *Bodel* | - | a young person, usually Jewish, running errands and performing chores for Mossad agents |
| *B'seder* | - | okay |
| *Harah* | - | shit |
| *Mah Ha'Inyanim?* | - | how are things? |
| *Mamash Tov* | - | really good |
| *Ma shimkha* | - | what is your name? |
| *Sayan* | - | an 'assistant', an operative recruited locally to help with Mossad operations in their own country |
| *Shalom* | - | hello/peace |

# DAVID CULLEN

# THE BAALBECK DECISION

## MURDER IS NEVER WHAT IT SEEMS

The first adventure of Jihad Merhi and Fadi Lattouf

# THE BAALBECK DECISION

## David Cullen

**2004. A dangerous time in Lebanese politics**

Prime Minister Rafic Hariri is forced to resign
– but it looks like he will sweep back into power in 2005
bringing in a wave of change for Lebanon.
There are those that want that
and there are those that do not.

The Damascene comes to Beirut to protect Hariri.
Al-Rajul comes to Beirut to kill Hariri.
But who sent them? And why?

And what links a serial killer in the Palestinian
refugee camp of *Bourj el-Barajneh* with the tumultuous
events which are about to engulf the region?

Lebanon will be changed forever by

## THE BAALBECK DECISION

ISBN: 978-0-9559911-4-1

# THE BYBLOS
# DISCOVERY
## SOME THINGS SHOULD REMAIN HIDDEN

The second adventure of Jihad Merhi and Fadi Lattouf

# THE BYBLOS DISCOVERY

## David Cullen

**2010. Is there something the world does not know?**

In New York City a diplomat dies mysteriously after revealing a cryptic message, which makes an exile return to Lebanon after five years.

In Beirut, a body turns up on the doorstep of Captain Fadi Lattouf of the Palestinian Civil Police in the *Bourj el-Barajneh* refugee camp. It's not long before Lattouf is calling on his old friend Captain Jihad Merhi of the Lebanese Internal Security Force. But in the dog-eat-dog world of Lebanese security, Merhi is having his own problems.

And in Tripoli, Lebanon, the *houris* await. They are the protectors of a secret that could blow the Middle Eastern order apart. But is the world ready for The Second Coming...? Death will visit those who make

## THE BYBLOS DISCOVERY

ISBN: 978-0-9559911-5-8

**1974. A world in turmoil. Terrorism is rife.**
**In the Middle East,** *El Fateh* plan their first nuclear strike. The Irishman, their hardware supplier, wants a very special item in payment.
**In the Mediterranean,** Cyprus is an island about to be divided. Resistance leader Grivas is dying. He wants to hit his enemy from beyond the grave.
**In Israel,** the security services want to finish off their enemies once and for all.
**In Europe,** Sally wants to find her missing lover.
In a world about to implode, they all have one common link:

**THE EYE OF MAKARIOS**
ISBN: 978-0-9559911-0-3

**1978. Only two people still alive know the explosive dark secret of the British Royal House of Windsor.**
One lies in her dotage in France, the other continues to rule the royal household in Britain as she has done for 40 years.
A robbery in Paris. The secret is stolen.
It must be found at all costs. Police enquiries draw a blank. They need help. There is only one man with the skills to locate the secret – Jacques Mesrine, France's Public Enemy Number One.
But there are those that want the secret for themselves and others who will stop at nothing to ensure the secret remains hidden.
Can Mesrine find the secret before the hunters find him? Death, treachery and double-cross all lead to

**THE MESRINE CONCLUSION**
ISBN: 978-0-9559911-1-0

**1997. Three women are out for revenge.**
In Greece, a lover discovers that justice has not been done.
In England, a princess seeks to humiliate her ex-husband.
In France, a daughter vows retribution after eighteen
years.
A secret which they thought was buried forever
comes back to haunt the British Royal House of Windsor.
And the deaths must start again.
And this time to preserve the secret they will even kill the
mother of the future King of England...
Exactly what happened in Paris on August 30 1997?
Who really killed Princess Diana?
And what is

**THE WINDSOR SECRET**
ISBN: 978-0-9559911-2-7

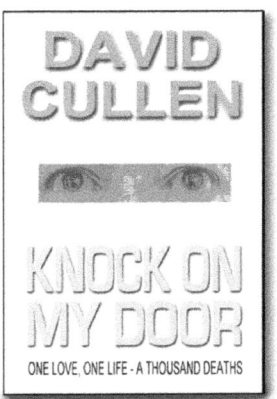

*"They say a lady should always have some secrets, layers which
she allows to be peeled away only by the intimate few, a striptease that
goes beyond the physical... The hard part is when the layers of your
mind are stripped away also, level by level, until the very core of your
being is exposed. And if that is attacked too, if the very essence of who
you are is taken away, what are you left with? Nothing. So how far
shall I strip for you? How far should I go? All the way?"*

Based on true events, David Cullen tells the story
of Carly, a woman who thought she had met The One to
take her to heaven – and found herself in the depravity
of hell itself.

**She thought he was the love of her life. He thought he
was the end of it.**

**KNOCK ON MY DOOR**
ISBN 978-0-9559911-3-4

All David Cullen books are available from amazon, Lulu, barnesandnoble.com and all other online booksellers and thru all good bookshops. They are also available on amazon Kindle and as ebooks from Apple iBookstore, Barnes and Noble nook etc.

www.ingramcontent.com/pod-product-compliance
Lightning Source LLC
Chambersburg PA
CBHW072058020726
47501CB00003B/632